Born in Peru and raised in Chile, **Isabel Allende** is the author of numerous bestselling and critically acclaimed books, including *The House of the Spirits*, *Daughter of Fortune*, *Paula*, *My Invented Country* and *The Japanese Lover*. Her books have been translated into more than 35 languages and have sold more than 65 million copies worldwide. *The Japanese Lover* was an international and *New York Times* bestseller. Isabel Allende lives in California.

Praise for *Of Love and Shadows*

'Allende skilfully evokes both the terrors of daily life under military rule and the subtler forms of resistance in the hidden corners … She can just as deftly depict loving tenderness as convey the high fire of eroticism. And when you've successfully mingled sex and politics with a noble cause, how can you go wrong?'

New York Times Book Review

'Allende is a born storyteller'

Chicago Tribune

'Isabel Allende is a writer of deep conviction, but she knows that in the end it is people, not issues, who matter most. The people in *Of Love and Shadows* are real, their triumphs and defeats are so faithful to the truth of human existence that we see the world in miniature. This is precisely what fiction should do'

Washington Post

'We are by turns enchanted and ~~Allende has married the world of~~ ibly'

Review

'Constan ... lling'

ronicle

ALSO BY ISABEL ALLENDE

Eva Luna
In the Midst of Winter
The Japanese Lover
The Stories of Eva Luna

ISABEL ALLENDE

Of Love and Shadows

Translated from Spanish by Margaret Sayers Peden

SCRIBNER

LONDON NEW YORK TORONTO SYDNEY NEW DELHI

Originally published in Spain as *De Amor y de Sombra*
Published in the United States by Atria Books, an imprint of
Simon and Schuster Inc., 2016
This edition published in Great Britain by Scribner, an imprint of
Simon & Schuster UK Ltd, 2018
A CBS COMPANY

SCRIBNER and design are registered trademarks of The Gale Group, Inc.,
used under licence by Simon & Schuster Inc.

1 3 5 7 9 10 8 6 4 2

Simon & Schuster UK Ltd
1st Floor
222 Gray's Inn Road
London WC1X 8HB

Simon & Schuster Australia, Sydney
Simon & Schuster India, New Delhi

www.simonandschuster.co.uk
www.simonandschuster.com.au
www.simonandschuster.co.in

A CIP catalogue record for this book is available from the British Library

Paperback ISBN: 978-1-4711-7345-5
eBook ISBN: 978-1-4711-7346-2

Printed and bound by CPI Group (UK) Ltd, Croydon, CR0 4YY

MIX
Paper from
responsible sources
FSC® C020471

Simon & Schuster UK Ltd are committed to sourcing paper that is made from wood
grown in sustainable forests and support the Forest Stewardship Council, the leading
international forest certification organisation. Our books displaying the FSC logo are
printed on FSC certified paper.

Of Love and Shadows

PART ONE

Another Spring

Only love with its science makes us so innocent.

—Violeta Parra

*T*he first sunny day of spring evaporated the dampness that had accumulated in the soil through the winter months, and warmed the fragile bones of the old people who now could stroll the gentle orthopedic paths of the garden. Only the old depressive remained in his bed, because it was futile to take him out into the fresh air when his eyes saw nothing but his own nightmares and his ears were deaf to the clamor of the birds. Josefina Bianchi, the actress, dressed in the long silk dress she had worn to declaim Chekhov a half century earlier and carrying a parasol to protect her veined-porcelain skin, walked slowly among the flower beds that soon would be crowded with flowers and bumblebees.

"Poor lads," smiled the octogenarian when she saw a slight trembling in the forget-me-nots and divined there the presence of her admirers, the ones who loved her in anonymity and hid in the vegetation to spy on her as she passed by.

The Colonel inched forward, braced on the aluminum walker that helped support his cotton-wool legs. To celebrate the birth of spring and salute the colors, as was his duty each morning, he had pinned on his chest the cardboard and tin-foil medals Irene had made for him. Whenever his agitated breathing permitted, he shouted instructions to his troops and ordered the tottering great-grandfathers off the Parade Grounds where they were in danger of being flattened by infantry troops displaying their most spirited parade step and their spit-and-polish leather boots. Near the telephone wire, the flag flapped on the breeze like an invisible turkey buzzard, and his soldiers stood rigidly at attention, eyes front, drum-roll reverberating, manly voices raised in the sacred hymn that only his ears could hear. He was interrupted by a nurse in bat-tle uniform, silent and sly as those women usually are, armed with a napkin to wipe away the saliva that dribbled from the corners of his lips and collected on his shirt. He wanted to offer her a decoration, or a promotion, but she spun away, leaving him standing there with his good intentions unful-filled, after warning him that if he dirtied his pants she was going to paddle his behind, because she was sick and tired of cleaning up after other people. Who can this madwoman be speaking to? the Colonel wondered, deducing that she was ob-viously referring to the wealthiest widow in the land. She was the only one in the encampment who wore diapers, owing to the cannon shot that had blown her digestive system to bits and consigned her forever to a wheelchair, although not even that had earned her the slightest respect. If she dropped her guard for an instant, they stole her hairpins and her ribbons. The world is filled with ruffians and scoundrels.

"Thieves! They've stolen my house slippers!" screeched the widow.

"Be quiet, dear, the neighbors can hear you," her nurse commanded, pushing the chair into the sun.

The invalid kept firing accusations until she ran out of breath and had to stop or else die, but she had sufficient strength left to point an arthritic finger at the satyr who was furtively opening his fly to expose his doleful penis to the la-dies. No one paid the least attention, except for a tiny old lady dressed in mourning, who regarded the poor dried fig with a certain tenderness. She was in love with its owner, and every night left the door to her room encouragingly ajar.

"Whore!" muttered the wealthy widow, but had to smile as she suddenly remembered times long gone by, before her husband died, when he had paid with coins of gold for the privilege of being clasped between her heavy thighs, a not infrequent event. She had ended up with a bag so heavy that no sailor alive could have slung it over his shoulder.

"Where are my gold coins?"

"What are you talking about, dear?" replied the absent-minded woman who was pushing her wheelchair.

"You stole them! I'm going to call the police."

"Don't be a pest, dearie," the other replied, unperturbed.

The hemiplegic had been propped up on a bench in his elegantly British, leather-elbow-patched jacket, legs wrapped in a shawl, serene and dignified in spite of the deformity of one side of his face, his useless hand tucked into a pocket and an empty pipe in the other. He was waiting for the mail; that was why he demanded to be seated facing the main door, to watch for Irene and know at first glance whether she was bringing him a letter. Beside him, taking the sun, was a melancholy old man with whom he never spoke because they were enemies, although neither remembered the cause of their disagreement. Occasionally, by mistake, one of them would speak but receive no answer, more out of deafness than hostility.

On the second-floor balcony where the wild pansies were still without leaf or bloom appeared Beatriz Alcántara de Beltrán. She was wearing grass-green suède pants and a French blouse of the same shade, matching her eye shadow and malachite ring. Fresh and tranquil after her session of Eastern exercises for relaxing tensions and forgetting the night's dreams, she held a glass of fruit juice good for improving the digestion and toning the skin. She breathed deeply, noting the new warmth in the air, and counted the days left before her vacation trip. It had been a hard winter and she had lost her tan. Frowning, she inspected the garden below, beautiful in the budding spring, but she was oblivious to the light on the stone walls and the fragrance of moist earth. The perennial ivy had survived the last freezes, the red roof tiles still shone with night dew, but the coffered and shuttered pavilion of her guests seemed faded and drab. She decided she would have the house painted. Her eyes counted the old people and reviewed every minor detail to assure herself that her instructions were being carried out. Everyone was there except the poor depressive, who lay in his bed more dead than alive. She also inspected the nurses, noting the clean starched aprons, the hair pulled back in a bun, the rubber-soled shoes. She smiled, satisfied; everything was functioning smoothly, and the danger of the rains with their attendant epidemics had passed without snatching away a single one of her clients. With any kind of luck, the rent would be paid for a few more months, since even the bedridden old man might last the summer.

From her observatory Beatriz spied her daughter Irene entering the garden of The Will of God Manor. Annoyed, she could tell that she had not used the side door with access to their private patio and the stairway to the secondfloor rooms where they had installed their living quarters. Beatriz had had the separate entrance constructed specifically so she could avoid walking through the geriatric home when she left or entered the house; infirmity depressed her and was something she preferred to observe from a distance. Her daughter, in contrast, never missed an opportunity to visit the guests, as if she actually enjoyed their company. She seemed to have discovered a language that overcame their deafness and faulty memories. Now she was wandering among them, handing out soft candies in consideration for their false teeth. Beatriz watched her walk over to the hemiplegic, show him a letter, help him open it—since he could not with his one good hand—and stand by his side whispering. Then she went for a brief stroll with the other old gentleman, and although her mother could not hear the words from the balcony, she supposed they were talking about his son, his daughter-in-law, and his grandson, the only subjects that interested him. Irene gave each one a smile, a pat, a few minutes of her time, while on her balcony Beatriz stood thinking that she would never understand that bizarre young woman with whom she had so little in common. Suddenly the old satyr stepped up to Irene and placed his hands over her breasts, squeezing them with more curiosity than lust. She stood motionless for a few moments that to her mother seemed interminable, until one of the nurses noticed what was happening and ran to intervene. Irene stopped her with a gesture.

"Leave him alone. He's not hurting anyone," she smiled.

Beatriz abandoned her observation post, biting her lips. She went to the kitchen where Rosa, her servant, was chopping the vegetables for lunch, lulled by a soap opera on the radio. She had a round, dark, ageless face, an enormous midriff, voluminous belly, gargantuan thighs. She was so fat that she could not cross her legs or scratch her back. "How do you wipe your bottom, Rosa?" Irene had asked when she was a little girl, marveling before the inviting bulk that every year increased a few pounds. "Where do you get such strange ideas, little one! Pleasingly stout is what beauty's about," Rosa replied without changing expression, faithful to her custom of speaking in proverbs.

"I'm worried about Irene," Beatriz said, sitting on a kitchen stool and slowly sipping her fruit juice.

Rosa said nothing, but turned off the radio, inviting the

confidences of her *patrona*, who sighed deeply. I have to speak with my daughter; I don't know what in the world she's up to, or who any of that riffraff she runs around with are. Why doesn't she go to the Club to play tennis, where she can meet some young men of her own class? She uses the excuse of her work to do whatever she pleases. Journalism has always seemed a little questionable to me, more suitable for someone of a lower class. If her fiancé knew some of the ideas that Irene gets in her head, he wouldn't put up with it. The future wife of an Army officer can't allow herself such luxuries—how many times have I told her that? And don't tell me that worrying about a girl's reputation is out of style; times change, but not that much. Besides, Rosa, now the military move in the best society, it's not the way it used to be. I'm tired of Irene's outrageous behavior. I have my own worries, my life isn't easy—you know that better than anyone. Ever since Eusebio ran off and left me with a frozen bank account and a trainload of expenses that would run an embassy, I've had to work miracles to keep my head above water; but it's all so difficult, the old people are a burden, and after all's said and done I think they cost me more expense and energy than I earn from them. Getting them to pay their rent is like pulling teeth, especially that damned old widow, she's always behind on her monthly payment. This business hasn't turned out to be a bed of roses. I don't have the strength to go trailing around after my daughter to see that she creams her face at night and dresses properly, and doesn't scare off her fiancé. She's old enough to take care of herself, isn't she? Look at me; if I didn't keep at it, what shape would I be in? I'd look like most of my friends, with a face lined with wrinkles and crow's-feet, and rolls and bulges everywhere. I've kept the figure of a twenty-year-old, though, and look how smooth my skin is. No, no one can say that I have an easy life—just the opposite, all these surprises are killing me.

"You can see the gates of glory, *señora*, but the Devil's got you by the tail."

"Why don't *you* talk to my daughter, Rosa? I think she pays more attention to you than she does to me."

Rosa set her knife on the table and looked at her mistress without sympathy. On principle, she never agreed with her, especially in anything concerning Irene. She did not like to hear her little girl criticized; still, she had to admit that in this case the mother was right. As much as Beatriz, Rosa longed to see Irene in a filmy veil and virginal flowers, leaving the church on the arm of Captain Gustavo Morante, walking between two rows of raised sabers; but her knowledge of the world—acquired through soap operas on radio and television—had taught her that it was everyone's lot to suffer in this life and to bear many trials and tribulations before reaching the happy ending.

"It's best to leave her alone. A cicada born will sing to its last morn. Irene won't live a long life, anyway—you can see that in her eyes."

"Rosa, my God! What kind of foolishness is that?"

Irene entered the kitchen amid a whirlwind of full cotton skirts and flying hair. She kissed both women on the cheeks and opened the refrigerator door and poked around inside. Her mother was on the verge of delivering an impromptu lecture, but in a flash of lucidity realized that any word from her would be useless, because that young woman with the finger smudges on her left breast was as remote from her as someone from another planet.

"Spring's here, Rosa. The forget-me-nots will be blooming soon," Irene said with a wink of complicity Rosa had no difficulty interpreting; both of them had been thinking of the baby-that-fell-through-the-skylight.

"What are you up to?" Beatriz asked.

"I have to go out on a story, Mama. I'm going to interview a kind of saint. They say she works miracles."

"What kind of miracles?"

"She removes warts, cures insomnia and hiccups, comforts the forlorn, and makes it rain," Irene laughed.

Beatriz sighed, with no sign of appreciating her daughter's humor. Rosa returned to her task of chopping carrots and suffering along with the radio soap opera, muttering that when live saints are at work, dead saints will shirk. Irene left to change her clothes and look for her tape recorder as she waited for Francisco Leal, the photographer who always went along with her on assignments.

Digna Ranquileo looked at the fields and noticed the signs that announced the change of seasons.

"Soon the animals will be in heat and Hipólito will be off with the circus," she muttered between prayers.

She had the habit of talking with God. That day, as she performed her breakfast chores, she lost herself in long prayers and confessions. Her children often told her that people laughed at her for that evangelical fixation. Couldn't she do it silently, and without moving her lips? She paid no attention to them. She felt the Saviour as a physical presence in her life, nearer and more helpful than her husband, whom she saw only during the winter. She tried not to ask too many favors of the Lord, because she had learned that celestial beings are bored by too many requests. She limited herself to seeking counsel in her endless doubts and pardon for her own and others' sins, giving thanks in passing for any small benefactions: the rain stopped, Jacinto's fever is gone, the tomatoes are ripe. Nevertheless, for several weeks now, she had been regularly and insistently importuning the Redeemer with prayers for Evangelina.

"Heal her," she prayed that morning as she poked the kitchen fire and arranged four bricks to hold the grill above the burning wood. "Heal her, God, before they carry her off to the asylum."

Never, not even in the face of the parade of supplicants praying for miracles, did she believe that her daughter's attacks were symptoms of saintliness. She believed even less in possession, which was what her garrulous women friends were convinced of after seeing a movie in town about exorcism, in which foaming at the mouth and rolled-back eyes were signs of Satan. Her common sense, her contact with nature, and her long experience as the mother of many children led her to deduce that all this stemmed from either a physical or a mental illness, and had nothing to do with evil or divine intervention. She attributed it to childhood vaccinations or to the onslaught of menstruation. She had always been opposed to the Public Health Service, which went from house to house rounding up the children crouching in the garden or hiding under the bed. Even though they struggled and she swore they had already had their shots, the aides still chased the children down and mercilessly injected them. She was sure that those liquids collected in the blood and caused changes in the body. In addition, although menstruation was a natural event in every woman's life, for some it stirred the humors and put perverse ideas in their heads. Either of the two things could be the source of the terrible illness, but of one thing she was sure: her daughter would grow weaker, as happens in a really bad illness, and if she did not get better within a reasonable time, she would end up completely out of her head or in the grave. Others of her children had died young, felled by epidemics or surprised by accidents that were beyond treatment. That happened in every family. If the child was an infant, they did not cry over it, for it went straight to heaven to be with the angels, where it interceded for those on earth whose time had not come. Losing Evangelina would be more painful, since she would have to answer to her real mother. She did not want to give the impression of not having looked after the girl, because people would talk behind her back.

Digna was the first in her house to get up and the last to go to bed. With the rooster's first crow she was already in the kitchen placing twigs on the still-warm coals from the night before. From the moment she began to boil the water for breakfast, she never sat down but was always busy with the children, the washing, the meals, the garden, the animals. Her days were all the same, like a rosary of identical beads shaping her existence. She did not know what rest was, and the only time she found relief was when she had a new baby. Her life was a chain of routines that varied only with the seasons. For her, there was nothing but work and weariness. The most peaceful moment of the day came at dusk, when she sat down with her sewing and a portable radio and was transported to a distant universe of which she understood very little. Her destiny seemed neither better nor worse than any other's. At times she concluded that she was a lucky woman, because at least Hipólito did not behave like a field hand; he worked in the circus, he was an artist, he traveled, he saw the world, and when he came back he told of the wonderful things he'd seen. He likes his wine, I don't deny it, but at heart he's a good man, Digna thought. He was never there to help her when it was time to plow, to sow, to harvest, but her wandering husband had qualities that compensated for all that. He never dared hit her unless he was drunk, and then only if Pradelio, the oldest son, was nowhere nearby, because Hipólito Ranquileo never raised his hand in front of the boy. She enjoyed more freedom than other women; she visited her friends without asking permission; she could attend the religious services of the True Evangelical Church, and she had reared her children according to its gospel. She was accustomed to making decisions, and only in the wintertime, when her husband returned home, did she bow her head, lower her voice, and, out of respect, consult him before acting. But that time, too, had its advantages, even though often rain and poverty seemed to last an eternity. It was a time of calm; the fields rested, the days seemed shorter, dawn came later. They went to bed at five to save candles, and in the warmth of the blankets she could appreciate the worth of a good man.

Because he was an artist, Hipólito had not participated in the agricultural unionization or any of the new plans of the previous government, so when things returned to the ways of their grandfathers, he was left in peace and his family suffered no misfortune. Daughter and granddaughter of countryfolk, Digna was prudent and suspicious. She had never believed the words of the advisers, and knew from the beginning that the Agrarian Reform would never succeed. She had always said so, but no one paid any attention to her. Her family was luckier than the Floreses, Evangelina's real parents, luckier than many others who worked the land and had lost their hopes and their skins in that adventure of promise and confusion.

Hipólito Ranquileo had the virtues that make a good husband; he was calm, not at all wild or violent, and Digna knew nothing of other women, or other vices. Every year, he brought home some money and also some little gift that was often useless but always welcome, because it's the thought that counts. He had a gallant nature. He never lost that virtue, like other men who almost as soon as they're married treat their wife like a dog, said Digna; that's why she bore him children happily, and even with a certain pleasure. Thinking about his caresses, she blushed. Her husband had never seen her naked; modesty above all, she maintained, but that did not make their intimate moments any less magical. She had fallen in love with his beautiful words, and decided to be his wife before God and the Civil Registry, and that is why she never let him touch her but came virgin to her wedding, just as she wanted her girls to do, that way they would be respected and no one could call them loose; but times were different then, and now it's not so easy to look after your girls, you turn your head and they're down by the river, you send them to the village to buy sugar and they're gone several hours, I try to dress them decently but they hike up their skirts, unbutton their blouses, and paint their faces. Oh, dear Lord, help me to look after them till they're married, and then I can rest; don't let the disgrace of the oldest one happen again, forgive her, she was very young and hardly knew what she was doing, it happened so quick, poor girl, he didn't even take time to lie down like human beings, he did it standing up against the willow tree down back, like dogs; look after the other girls, and don't let some fresh young fellow come along and go too far with them, because this time Pradelio would kill him and shame would fall on this house; with little Jacinto I've had my share of shame and suffering, poor baby, he's not to blame for his stain.

Jacinto, the youngest, was really her grandson, the bastard fruit of her oldest daughter and a stranger who arrived one autumn evening and asked to spend the night in their kitchen.

The baby had had the good sense to be born when Hipólito was on the road with the circus and Pradelio was fulfilling his military service. So there was no man to take revenge, as would normally be the case. Digna knew what she had to do: she bundled up the newborn child, fed him with mare's milk, and sent the mother off to the city to work as a servant. When the men came back, the deed was done and they had to accept it. Soon they got used to his presence, and ended up treating him like just another child. He was not the first fatherless child to be brought up in the Ranquileo household; others had been taken in before Jacinto, lost orphans who knocked at their door. With the passage of the years the true parents were forgotten, and all that remained was habit and affection.

As she did every morning when the dawn was peeping from behind the mountains, Digna filled the gourd with *maté* for her husband and placed his chair in the corner near the door where the air was freshest. She melted a few lumps of sugar, placing two in each large tin cup as she prepared the mint tea for the older children. She moistened yesterday's bread and set it over the coals; she strained the milk for the younger children, and in an iron skillet, blackened with use, stirred some scrambled eggs and onion.

Fifteen years had passed since the day Evangelina was born in Los Riscos Hospital, but Digna could remember it as if it were yesterday. She had given birth many times, her children were born easily and, as she always did, she raised herself on her elbows to watch the baby emerge, confirming the resemblance with her other children: their father's coarse black hair and the white skin of which she was so proud. That was why when they brought her a swaddled infant and she saw the blond fuzz covering an almost bald skull, she knew without any doubt that the child was not hers. Her first impulse was to reject it, to protest, but the nurse was in a hurry and refused to listen to her story; she deposited the bundle in Digna's arms and left the room. The baby girl began to cry, and Digna, with a gesture as old as time, opened her gown and gave the baby her breast as she commented to her neighbors in the maternity ward that there had been a mistake, this wasn't her baby. After she had nursed the infant, she got out of bed with some difficulty and went to explain the problem to the head nurse, but the nurse replied that Digna was mistaken, nothing like that had ever happened in this hospital, it was strictly against regulations to go around exchanging babies. She added that Digna must be overwrought and, with no further ado, gave her an injection. Then she sent her back to bed. Hours later, Digna Ranquileo awakened to the racket being raised by another new mother at the far end of the ward.

"They've given me somebody else's baby!" she was screaming.

Alarmed by the uproar, nurses, doctors, even the hospital director, came running. Digna seized the opportunity to state her own problem, in the most delicate way possible to avoid offending anyone. She explained that she had given birth to a dark-haired baby girl but they had brought her one with blond hair who didn't bear the slightest resemblance to her own children. What would her husband think when he saw the baby?

The hospital director was indignant: Stupid, thoughtless women! Instead of being grateful for the care we're giving you, you're creating a disturbance. The two women decided that for the moment they would be silent and wait for a better time. Digna deeply regretted ever having gone to the hospital, and blamed herself for what had happened. Until then all her children had been born at home with the aid of Mamita Encarnación, who supervised the pregnancy from the first months and appeared on the eve of the birth, remaining until the mother was able to take over again. She came with her herbs for hastening the delivery, her scissors blessed by the Bishop, her clean, boiled rags, her healing compresses, her balms for nipples, stretch marks, and birth tears, her thread for stitching, and her unquestionable wisdom. While she was making ready for the baby on the way, she chatted incessantly, entertaining her patient with local gossip and stories of her own invention whose aim was to ease suffering and make time pass more quickly. For more than twenty years that tiny, nimble woman, enveloped in an immutable aroma of lavender and smoke, had helped almost every baby in the district into the world. She asked nothing for her services, but she made her living from her craft because grateful people passed by her little house to leave eggs, fruit, firewood, fowl, or a recently bagged rabbit or partridge. Even in the hardest times, when the harvest failed or the animals failed to drop any young, Mamita Encarnación lacked for nothing. She knew all of nature's secrets about giving birth, as well as some infallible formulas for aborting, using herbs or candle stubs, that she used only in cases everyone knew were justified. If her knowledge failed, she used her intuition. When the infant finally made its way into the world, she cut the umbilical cord with her miraculous scissors, to assure strength and good health, and quickly inspected the child from head to toe, to be sure there was nothing untoward in its formation. If she discovered a defect, anticipated a life of suffering or a burden for others, she abandoned the newborn to its fate; but if everything was as God intended, she gave thanks to heaven and with a couple of spanks proceeded to initiate the babe into the hustle and bustle of life. She gave borage to the mother to expel black blood and foul humors, castor oil to cleanse the intestines, and beer with raw egg yolks to insure abundant milk. For three or four days, she took charge of the house, cooking, cleaning, serving meals to the family, and overseeing the brood of children. So it had been with each of Digna Ranquileo's babies, but when Evangelina was born, the midwife was in jail for illegally practicing medicine, and could not attend her. For that reason and no other, Digna had gone to the Los Riscos Hospital, where she felt she was treated worse than a criminal. When she entered, they taped a number around her wrist, they shaved her private parts, bathed her with cold water and antiseptic, with no thought of possibly drying up her milk for all time, and placed her beside a woman in the same condition on a bed without sheets. After poking around, without her permission, in all her bodily orifices, they made her give birth beneath a bright lamp in full view of anyone who might happen by. She bore it all without a sigh, but when she left that place carrying a baby that was not hers in her arms and with her unmentionable places painted as red as a flag, she swore that for the rest of her life she would never again set foot in a hospital.

Digna finished scrambling the eggs and onion and called the family to the kitchen. Each one appeared with his or her chair. As soon as the babies began to walk, she assigned them their own chair, personal and inviolate, the only possession in the communal poverty of the Ranquileo family. Even the beds were shared, and clothing kept in great wicker baskets from which every morning the members of the family pulled out what they needed. No one owned anything.

Hipólito Ranquileo sipped his *maté* noisily and chewed his bread slowly, owing to his missing teeth and others that were dancing in his gums. He looked healthy, though he had never been robust, but he was growing old; suddenly the years had piled up on him. His wife attributed it to the roving life of the circus, the endless wandering with no fixed course, not eating well, smearing his face with the unholy paint God tolerated for the poor women walking the streets but never intended for decent folks. In a few years the gallant youth she had taken for her sweetheart had turned into that shrunken little old man with the nose like a clay pot and face like papier-mâché that came from too many years of facial contortions, who coughed too much and sometimes fell asleep in the middle of a conversation. During the months of cold and forced inactivity, he liked to entertain the children by dressing in his clown's costume. But beneath the white mask and enormous red mouth opened in an eternal guffaw, his wife saw the furrows of exhaustion. As he grew more decrepit, it was increasingly difficult to get work, and she nurtured the hope of seeing him settle down on their farm to help her with the chores. Now progress was being forced upon them, and the new laws weighed heavily on Digna's shoulders. Farm people, like everyone else, had to adjust to the market economy. The land and its produce were now a part of the free-enterprise system; each person prospered according to his performance, his initiative, and his entrepreneurial efficiency; even illiterate Indians suffered the same fate, to the great advantage of those who had money, because for a few cents they could buy, or rent for ninety-nine years, the lands of poor farmers like the Ranquileos. But Digna did not want to abandon the place where her children had been born and raised to go live in one of the new agricultural villages, where every morning the *patrones* chose the number of laborers they needed, saving themselves the problem of tenant farmers. That was poverty within poverty. She wanted her family to go on working the plot of land that was their heritage, but every day it became more difficult to defend it from the big enterprises, especially without the backing of a man to help her in the hard times.

Digna Ranquileo had a soft spot in her heart for her husband. For him, she set aside the best portions from the stewpot, the largest eggs, the softest wool to knit his sweaters and socks. She brewed herbs for his kidneys, to clear his thoughts, to purify his blood, and to help him sleep, but it was evident that in spite of her care Hipólito was growing old. At that moment, two of the children were fighting over the last of the scrambled eggs and onion and he sat watching, indifferent. In normal times he would have cuffed their ears and separated them, but now he had eyes only for Evangelina; he followed her with his gaze as if he were afraid he would see her transformed into a monster like those in the circus. At that hour the girl was merely one more in a jumble of shivering and uncombed children. Nothing in her appearance gave any indication of what would happen in a few hours, precisely at noon.

"Heal her, Lord," Digna repeated, covering her face with her apron so they would not see her talking to herself.

The day dawned so mild that Hilda Leal suggested they eat breakfast wrapped only in the warmth from the kitchen stove, but her husband reminded her that she had to be careful and not catch cold because as a girl she had had weak lungs. According to the calendar, it was still winter, but the color of the early mornings and the song of the larks heralded the arrival of spring. They should save fuel. It was a time of shortages, but in consideration of his wife's frail health Professor Leal insisted on lighting the kerosene stove. Day and night, this ancient contrivance circulated from room to room, accompanying the movement of the occupants of the house.

While Hilda was setting out the crockery, Professor Leal, in overcoat, muffler, and slippers, stepped out to the patio to put grain in the bird-feeders and fresh water in the bowls. He noted the minuscule buds on the tree and calculated that soon branches would be covered with leaves, like a green citadel to shelter the migratory birds. He liked seeing them flying free as much as he hated cages, and he considered it unforgivable to imprison them simply for the luxury of always keeping them in sight. Even in small details, he was consistent with his anarchistic principles: if freedom is the first right of man, with even greater reason it should be the right of creatures born with wings on their backs.

His son Francisco called from the kitchen, announcing that the tea was ready and that José had arrived for a visit. The Professor hurried in, because it was unusual to see his son the priest so early on a Saturday, as he was in such demand in his never-ending task of giving succor to his neighbors. He saw José sitting at the table, and noticed for that first time that his hair was getting thin at the nape of the neck.

"What is it, son? Is anything wrong?" he asked, clapping him on the shoulder.

"Nothing, Father. I wanted to eat a decent breakfast, one prepared by Mama."

José was the sturdiest and least polished of the family, the only one without the long bones and aquiline nose of the Leals. He looked like a Mediterranean fisherman, and nothing in his appearance betrayed the delicacy of his soul. He had entered the Seminary as soon as he graduated from high school, and—except for his father—that decision surprised no one, because from the time he was a boy he had had a Jesuit's outlook on life and had spent his childhood dressing up in bath towels, pretending to be a bishop and saying mass. There was no explanation for his inclinations; in their house no one openly practiced religion, and his mother, although she considered herself a Catholic, had not gone to mass since she was married. Professor Leal's consolation in the face of his son's decision was that his son wore a workman's clothes instead of a cassock, lived in a proletarian barrio instead of a monastery, and was closer to the tragic alarms of this world than to the mysteries of the Eucharist. José was wearing a pair of pants passed down from his older brother, a faded shirt, and a sweater of thick wool knitted by his mother. His hands were calloused from the plumber's tools with which he defrayed the expenses of his existence.

"I'm organizing some little courses on Christianity," he said in a sly voice.

"So I've heard," replied Francisco, who had every reason to know, since they worked together at a free clinic in the parish and he was well informed about his brother's activities.

"Oh, José, don't go getting mixed up in politics," Hilda pleaded. "Do you want to go to jail again, son?"

The last worry in José Leal's mind was for his own safety. He hardly had enough energy to keep count of the misfortunes of others. He carried on his back an inexhaustible burden of sorrow and injustice and he often reproached the Creator for so severely putting his faith to the test: if divine love existed, so much human suffering seemed a mockery. In the arduous labor of feeding the poor and sheltering the homeless, he had lost the ecclesiastical polish acquired in the Seminary, and had been irreversibly transformed into a rugged man divided between impatience and piety. His father favored him above all his sons, for he could see the similarity between his own philosophical ideals and what he qualified as his son's barbaric Christian superstition. That assuaged his sorrow; he had come to forgive José's religious vocation, ceasing to grieve at night with his head buried in the pillow, so as not to worry his wife as he vented his shame at having a priest in the family.

"In fact, brother, I came looking for you," said José, turning to Francisco. "I want you to come over to see a young girl. She was raped a week ago, and since then hasn't spoken a word. Use your knowledge of psychology because God can't cope with such problems."

"I can't come today. I have to go with Irene to take some photographs, but I'll come see the girl tomorrow. How old is she?"

"Ten."

"My God!" Hilda exclaimed. "What monster could do that to a poor innocent child?"

"Her father."

"That's enough, please!" commanded Professor Leal. "Do you want to make your mother ill?"

Francisco poured tea for everyone, and for a while they were all silent, searching for a topic of conversation to ease Hilda's anguish. The only woman in a family of men, she had succeeded in imposing her sweetness and discretion. They could not remember ever having seen her irritated. In her presence there were no boyish wrangles, no off-color jokes, no vulgarity. When he was a child, Francisco had suffered from the fear that his mother, worn down by their harsh life, might be imperceptibly disappearing, and would one day dissipate like the mist. Then he would run to her side, hug her, cling to her clothing in a desperate attempt to retain her presence, her warmth, the smell of her apron, the sound of her voice. Much time had passed since then, but his tenderness for her was still his most unswerving emotion.

After Javier married and José left for the Seminary, only

Francisco remained in his parents' home. He lived in the same room he had as a boy, with pine furniture and bookshelves crammed with books. Once he had thought of renting his own place but, deep down, he enjoyed his family's company and, besides, did not want to cause his parents any unnecessary sorrow. For them, there were only three reasons why a son would leave home: war, marriage, or the priesthood. Later they would add a fourth: flight from the police.

The Leals' house was small, old, modest, greatly in need of paint and repair. At night it creaked softly, like a weary, rheumatic old woman. Professor Leal had designed it many years before, convinced that the only indispensable features were a large kitchen where they could live their lives and where he could set up a clandestine printing press, a patio where Hilda could hang the clothes and he could sit and watch the birds, and enough rooms to hold beds for their children. Everything else depended on largeness of spirit and liveliness of the intellect, he said when anyone complained of the cramped quarters or unpretentiousness. They were comfortable there, and there was space and the good will for welcoming friends in trouble and relatives from Europe escaping the war. Theirs was an affectionate family. Far into adolescence, even after they grew a mustache, the boys still crept into bed with the parents to read the morning newspaper and to ask Hilda to scratch their backs. When the older boys moved away, the Leals felt as if the house were too big; they saw shadows in the corners and heard echoes in the hallways, but then the grandchildren were born and the habitual hubbub returned.

"We need to repair the roof tiles and replace the pipes," Hilda said every time it rained or a new leak appeared.

"Why? We still have our house in Teruel, and when Franco dies we'll be going back to Spain," her husband replied.

Professor Leal had dreamed of returning to his homeland from the day the ship steamed away from the coast of Europe. Outraged by the Caudillo, he vowed never to put on a pair of socks until he knew Franco was dead and buried, never imagining how many decades would pass before his wish was fulfilled. His vow produced scales on his feet and created difficulties in his professional dealings. On occasion he had to meet with important figures, or was commissioned to administer examinations in various schools, and his bare feet in the large rubber-soled shoes stirred a certain amount of prejudice. He was extremely proud, however, and rather than offer an explanation, he preferred to be considered an eccentric foreigner or a penniless wretch whose salary did not allow him to buy stockings. The only time he was able to take his family to the mountains to enjoy the snow, he had to remain inside the hotel with his feet as blue and frozen as herrings.

"Put on some socks, dear. After all, Franco doesn't know about your vow," Hilda implored.

He shot her a withering glance overflowing with dignity and sat in solitary splendor beside the fire. Once his mortal enemy had died, he put on a pair of brilliant red socks that embraced all his existential philosophy, but within half an hour was forced to remove them. He had gone sockless far too long, and now could not tolerate them. Dissembling, he swore to continue to go without socks until the fall of the General who ruled his adopted country with a fist of iron.

"Dammit, you can put them on me when I'm dead," he said. "I want to go to hell in red socks!"

He did not believe in life after death, but any precaution in that direction was no strain on his generous temperament. Democracy in Spain had not persuaded him to wear socks, or caused him to return, because his children, his grandchildren, and his roots in America held him there. The house, however, went without the needed repairs. Following the military coup, more urgent matters occupied the family. Because of his political ideas, Professor Leal was placed on the list of undesirables, and forced to retire. He lost none of his optimism when he found himself without work and on a minimal pension, but printed leaflets in his kitchen offering literature courses, and distributed them wherever he could. His few students helped stabilize the family budget, and allowed them to live simply and still help Javier. Their eldest son encountered serious difficulties in providing for his wife and three children. The Leals' standard of living declined, as it did for so many in their situation. They gave up season tickets to the concerts and theater, books, records, and other refinements that had cheered their days. Later, when it was evident that Javier could not find a job, his father decided to build a couple of rooms and a bath in the patio and take in the whole family. The three brothers worked on weekends laying bricks under the direction of Professor Leal, who derived his knowledge from a manual bought in a secondhand book sale. As none of them had experience in masonry, and as several pages were missing from the manual, the predictable result, upon completion of the work, was a building with tortuous walls that they attempted to disguise by covering them with ivy. Javier opposed to the end the idea of living at his parents' expense. He came by his pride naturally.

"What feeds three will feed eight," said Hilda, imperturbable as always. Once she made up her mind, there was seldom room for argument.

"Times are bad, son. We have to help each other," added Professor Leal.

In spite of the problems, he felt satisfied with his life and would have been totally happy had he not been tormented from his earliest years by the devastating revolutionary passion that shaped his character and his life. He dedicated a good portion of his energy, time, and income to spreading his ideological principles. He educated his three sons in his doctrine, he taught them from the time they were small to operate the clandestine printing press in the kitchen, and he took them with him to hand out pamphlets at factory doors behind the backs of the police. Hilda was always at his side in union meetings, with her tireless knitting needles in hand and her knitting wool in a bag in her lap. While her husband harangued his comrades, she drifted off into a secret world, savoring her memories, embroidering affections, reliving her happiest recollections, totally divorced from the clamor of the political discussions. Through a long and gentle process of purification, she had succeeded in erasing most of the privation of the past, and guarded only the happy moments. She never spoke of the war, the dead she had buried, her accident, or that long march toward exile. Those who knew her attributed her selective memory to the blow that had split open her skull when she was young, but Professor Leal could interpret the small signs and suspected that she had forgotten nothing. She simply did not want to burden herself with ancient woes, and for that reason she never mentioned them, nullifying them through silence. His wife had accompanied him down life's road for so long that Professor Leal could not remember his life without her. She marched steadfastly beside him in street demonstrations. In intimate collaboration, they raised their sons. She helped others more needy than she, camped outdoors on nights during strikes, and rose at dawn to take in sewing when his salary would not stretch far enough to support the family. With the same enthusiasm with which she had followed him to war and into exile, she carried him warm meals when he was arrested and put in jail; she had not lost her equanimity the day their furniture was attached, or her good humor as they slept trembling with cold on the third-class deck of a refugee ship. Hilda accepted all her husband's eccentricities—and they were not few—in uninterrupted peace, because throughout their long life together her love for him had only grown.

A long time before, in a small village in Spain, amid steep, grapevine-covered hills, he had asked her hand in marriage. She replied that she was a Catholic, and intended to continue to be so, that she had nothing personal against Marx, but that she would not tolerate his portrait above the head of her bed, and that her children would be baptized in order to avoid the risk of dying outside the Church and ending up in Limbo. The Professor of Logic and Literature was a fervent Communist and an atheist, but he was not lacking in intuition, and he realized that nothing would change the opinion of that blushing and frail young girl with the visionary eyes, with whom he had fallen irrevocably in love, and therefore found it preferable to negotiate a pact. Their compromise was that they would be married in the Church, the only legal form of marriage in those days, that their children would receive the sacraments but would go to secular schools, that his accent would be heard in the choice of the boys' names and hers in the girls', and that they would be buried in a tomb without a cross but with a pragmatic epitaph of his composition. Hilda accepted, because that lean man with a pianist's hands and fire in his veins was the man she had always wanted to share her life. He fulfilled his part of the bargain with characteristically scrupulous honesty, but Hilda did not have the same rectitude. The day their first son was born, her husband was immersed in the war, and by the time he was able to come for a visit, the boy had been baptized Javier, like his grandfather. The mother was in a very delicate condition and it was not the moment to begin a quarrel, so Leal decided to give him the nickname of Vladimir, Lenin's first name. He was never successful; when he called the boy Vladimir, his wife asked him who the devil he was referring to and, besides, the child gazed at him with astonishment and never replied. Shortly before the next birth, Hilda awakened one morning recounting a dream: she would give birth to a boy and he was to be called José. They argued wildly for several weeks, until they reached a reasonable solution: José Ilyich. Then they tossed a coin to decide what name they would use and Hilda won; that was not her fault, but the fault of a fate that did not like the second name of the revolutionary leader. Years later when the last son was born, Professor Leal had lost some of his enthusiasm for the Soviets, so the child was spared being named Ulyanov. Hilda named him Francisco in honor of the Saint of Assisi, the poet of the poor and the animals. For this reason, and because he was the youngest and so like his father, she favored him with a special tenderness. The boy repaid his mother's absolute love with a perfect oedipal complex that lasted until his adolescence, when the tickling of his hormones led him to realize there were other women in this world.

That Saturday morning Francisco finished his tea, slung the bag containing his photographic equipment over his shoulder, and told his family goodbye.

"Button up tight, the wind on that motorcycle is deadly," his mother said.

"Leave him alone, woman, he's not a boy anymore," her husband protested, and all their sons smiled.

For the first months after Evangelina's birth, Digna lamented her misadventure and wondered if it was punishment from heaven for having gone to the hospital instead of staying in her own home. In sorrow thou shalt bring forth children, the Bible clearly said, and so the Reverend had reminded her. But she came to understand how unfathomable are the designs of the Lord. That little blond infant with the pale eyes might have some part to play in her destiny. With the spiritual aid of the True Evangelical Church, she accepted her trial and prepared herself to love the baby girl, in spite of the fact that she was a difficult child. She often thought of the other baby, the one her child's spiritual godmother, her *comadre* Flores, had taken with her but by all rights belonged to Digna. Her husband consoled her, saying that the other baby seemed healthier and stronger and certainly would grow up better with the Flores family.

"The Floreses own some good land. I've even heard that they're going to buy a tractor. They're higher up in the world. They belong to the Farmers Union," Hipólito had reasoned years ago, before adversity crushed the house of Flores.

After the births, the two women had attempted to claim their own babies, swearing that they had seen the infants born and from the color of the hair realized there had been an error; but the hospital director would hear nothing on the subject, and threatened to send them to jail for slandering his institution. The fathers suggested that the families simply trade babies and everyone would be happy, but the women did not want to do something illegal. They decided temporarily to keep the one each had in her arms, until the muddle could be cleared up by the authorities, but after a strike in the Office of Public Health and a fire in the Civil Registry, where the personnel was replaced and all the archives were destroyed, they lost any hope of obtaining justice. They decided to bring up one another's babies as if they were their own. Although they lived only a short distance apart, they had few occasions to meet, for they lived isolated lives. From the beginning they agreed to call each other *comadre* and to baptize the baby girls with the same name, so that if one day they reclaimed their legal surnames they would not have to get used to a new given name. They also told the girls the truth as soon as they were old enough to understand, because sooner or later they would find out anyway. Everyone in the region knew the story of the switched Evangelinas, and there would always be someone eager to repeat the gossip.

Evangelina Flores was a typical dark-haired, solidly built country girl, with bright eyes, broad hips, opulent breasts, and heavy, well-turned legs. She was strong and happy by temperament. To the Ranquileos fell a weepy, moonstruck, frail, and difficult child. She received special treatment from Hipólito, out of respect and admiration for the rosy skin and light hair so rare in his family. When he was in the house, he kept an eagle eye on the boys; he wanted no liberties taken with that girl who was not of their own blood. Once or twice, he surprised Pradelio by tickling her, fondling her under cover of play, nuzzling and kissing her, and to rid him once and for all of any desire to paw her, Hipólito gave him a couple of licks that knocked him halfway to the next life, because before God and man, Evangelina was the same as his own sister. Hipólito was home only a few months, however, and the rest of the year his orders could not be enforced.

From the day he had run off with a circus at the age of thirteen, Hipólito Ranquileo had followed that life and had never been interested in any other. His wife and his children bade him goodbye as the good weather began and the patched tents flowered. He went from town to town, traversing the land, showing off his artistry in the bone-crushing circuits of the carnivals of the poor. He had performed many different jobs beneath the big top. First, he was a trapeze artist and juggler, but over the years lost his equilibrium and dexterity. Then, during a brief incursion, he cracked the whip over a few miserable wild animals that stirred his pity and ruined his nerves. Finally he resigned himself to playing the clown. His life, just like that of any farmer, was ruled by the state of the rains and the light of the sun. Fortune did not smile on second-rate circuses in the cold, damp months, and he hibernated by his hearth, but with the awakening of spring he waved goodbye to his loved ones and set off without a qualm, leaving his wife in charge of the children and the work in the fields. She directed those activities better than he, since several generations of experience flowed in her veins. The only time that he had gone to town with the money from the harvest to buy clothing and provisions for the year, he got drunk and was robbed of it all. For months there was no sugar on the Ranquileo table, and no one had new shoes; this was the source of his confidence in relegating the business affairs to his wife. She also preferred it that way. From the beginning of her married life, the responsibility for the family and farm chores had fallen on her shoulders. It was normal to see her bent over the trough or following the plow in the furrow, surrounded by a swarm of children of various ages clinging to her skirts. When Pradelio grew up, she had thought he might help her with the hard work, but at fifteen her son was the tallest and most strapping youth ever seen in those parts, and it had seemed natural to everyone that after serving his time in the military he would join the police.

When the first rains began to fall, Digna Ranquileo moved her chair to the little gallery and settled herself there to keep an eye on the bend of the road. Her hands never rested, occupied with weaving a basket of wicker or altering the children's clothes, but her watchful eyes wandered from time to time to glance down the lane. Soon, any day now, the tiny figure of Hipólito would appear carrying his cardboard suitcase. There he was, the same as in her longing, finally materializing, nearer and nearer, with steps that had grown slower with the years, but always tender and joking. Digna's heart gave a leap, as it had the first time she saw him in the ticket window of a traveling circus many years ago, wearing a threadbare green-and-gold uniform and with a zealot's expression in his dark eyes, hustling the crowd to step right this way, don't miss the show. In those days he had a pleasant face, before it had been plastered over with the mask of a clown. His wife was never able to welcome him naturally. An adolescent passion squeezed her chest and she wanted to run to him and throw her arms around his neck to hide her tears, but months of separation had aggravated her shyness and she greeted him with restraint, eyes lowered, blushing. Her man was there, he had returned, everything would be different for a time, because he took great pains to make up for his absence. In the following months, she would invoke the charitable spirits in her Bible to prolong the rain and immobilize the calendar in a winter without end.

In contrast, the return of their father was a minor event for the children. One day when they came home from school or from work in the fields, they would find him sitting in a wicker chair beside the door, his *maté* in hand, blending into the drab autumn landscape as if he had never been away from those fields, from that house, from those vines with their clusters of grapes drying on the pruned vines, from the dogs stretched out on the patio. The children would note their mother's worried and impatient eyes, her briskness as she waited on her husband, her apprehension as she watched over those meetings to fend off any impertinence. Honor your father, the Old Testament said; the father is the pillar of the family. And that was why they were forbidden to call him Bosco the Clown, or to talk about his work; don't ask questions, wait till he feels like telling you. When they were little—when Hipólito was shot from a cannon from one end of the tent to the other, landing in a net amid the reverberation of gunpowder and flashing an uneasy smile— and once they had survived their fright, the children could feel proud of him, because there he soared like a hawk. Later, though, Digna did not allow them to go to the circus to see their father declining in pitiful pirouettes. She preferred them to hold that airy image in their memories and not to be embarrassed by the grotesque trappings of an old clown, beaten and humbled, exaggeratedly breaking wind, piping in a falsetto voice, guffawing without any reason. Whenever a circus passed through Los Riscos trailing a moth-eaten bear and summoning residents over loudspeakers to witness the grandiose international spectacle acclaimed by audiences everywhere, she refused to take the children because of the clowns—all alike, and all like Hipólito. Nevertheless, in the privacy of their home, he put on his costume and painted his face, not to caper about in an undignified manner or tell vulgar jokes, but to delight them with his stories of the weird and the shocking: the bearded woman; the gorilla man, so strong he could pull a truck by a wire held in his teeth; the fire-eater who could swallow a blazing torch but not snuff a candle with his fingers; the albino lady dwarf who rode on the hindquarters of a galloping she-goat; the trapeze artist who fell headlong from the highest tent pole and splattered the respectable public with his brains.

"A man's brain looks just like calves' brains," Hipólito explained as he ended the tragic anecdote.

Sitting in a circle around their father, his children never tired of hearing the same tales over and over again. Before the wondering eyes of his family, who listened to his words suspended in time, Hipólito Ranquileo recovered all the dignity lost in the tawdry shows in which he was the target of ridicule.

Some winter nights, when the children were asleep, Digna pulled out the cardboard suitcase hidden beneath the bed, and by candlelight mended her husband's professional costume; she reinforced the gigantic red buttons, darned rips and tears here and sewed on strategic patches there; with beeswax she shined the enormous yellow shoes, and in secret knit the striped stockings of his clown's garb. In these actions she displayed the same absorbed tenderness as in their brief amorous comings together. The silence of the night magnified every sound, the rain drummed on the roof tiles, and the breathing of the children in the neighboring beds was so clear that the mother could divine their dreams. Wife and husband embraced beneath the blankets, subduing sighs, enveloped in the warmth of their discreet and loving conspiracy. Unlike other country people, they had married for love, and in love engendered their children. That is why even in the hardest of times, in drought, earthquake, flood, or when the kettle was empty, they never lamented the arrival of another child. Children are like flowers and bread, they said, a blessing from God.

Hipólito Ranquileo took advantage of his days at home to put up fences, gather firewood, repair tools, and patch the roof when the rain slackened. With the savings from his circus tours, the sale of honey and pigs, and their strict economies, the family survived. In the good years they never lacked for food, but even in the best of times money was scarce. Nothing was thrown away or wasted. The youngest wore clothing handed down from the oldest, and continued to wear it until the fatigued threads would tolerate no further mending and the patches themselves sloughed off like dried scabs. Sweaters were raveled to the last thread, the wool washed and reknit. The father fashioned espadrilles for the family, and the mother's knitting needles and sewing machine rarely lay idle. They did not feel poor, like other farmers, because they owned the land they had inherited from a grandfather; they had animals and farm tools. Once, in the past, they had received the credits awarded to all farmers, and for a while believed in prosperity, but then things returned to the old rhythm. They lived on the periphery of the mirage of progress that affected the rest of the country.

"Look, Hipólito. Don't keep watching Evangelina," Digna whispered to her husband.

"Maybe she won't have her attack today," he said.

"It always comes. There's nothing we can do."

The family finished eating breakfast and went their various ways, each carrying a chair. From Monday to Friday the children walked to school, a half hour's rapid walk. When it was cold, the mother gave each child a stone heated in the fire to put in a pocket to keep their hands warm. She also gave them a piece of bread and two sugar lumps. Earlier, when milk was still being served at school, they used the sugar to sweeten it, but for several years now they had sucked the lumps like caramels during recess. That half-hour walk had turned out to be a blessing, because by the time they got home, their sister's crisis was over and the pilgrims had left. But today was Saturday, therefore they would be present, and that night Jacinto would wet his bed in the anguish of his nightmares. Evangelina had not gone to school since the first signs of her disturbance appeared. Her mother remembered the precise moment their misfortune began. It was the day of the convention of frogs, although she was sure that that episode was not related to her daughter's sickness.

They had been discovered very early one morning, two fat and majestic frogs observing the landscape near the railroad crossing. Soon many more arrived, coming from every direction, little pond frogs, larger well frogs, white ones from irrigation ditches, gray ones from the river. Someone sounded the alarm and everyone came to see them. Meanwhile the amphibians had formed compact rows and begun an orderly march. Along the road others joined in, and soon there was a green multitude advancing toward the highway. The word spread, and the curious came on foot, on horseback, and in buses, commenting on this never-before-seen marvel. The enormous living mosaic occupied the asphalt of the principal road to Los Riscos, halting any vehicles traveling at that hour. One imprudent truck attempted to drive forward, but skidded on squashed corpses and overturned amid the enthusiasm of the children, who avidly appropriated the merchandise scattered in the underbrush. The police flew over the area in a helicopter, ascertaining that two hundred and seventy meters of road were covered with frogs so closely packed that they resembled a glistening carpet of moss. The news was broadcast by radio, and in a short time newspapermen arrived from the capital, accompanied by a Chinese expert from the United Nations who reported that he had witnessed a similar phenomenon during his childhood in Peking. This stranger descended from a dark automobile with official license plates, bowed to the right and to the left, and the crowd applauded, very naturally confusing him with the director of the Choral Society. After observing that gelatinous mass for a few moments, the Oriental concluded that there was no cause for alarm, this was merely a convention of frogs. That was what the press called it, and as it occurred during a time of poverty and shortages, they joked about it, saying that instead of manna, God was raining down frogs from the sky so that the chosen people could cook them with garlic and coriander.

When Evangelina had her attack, the participants in the convention had dispersed and the television crews were removing their equipment from the trees. It was twelve o'clock noon; the air sparkled, washed by the rain. Evangelina was alone inside the house, and on the patio Digna and her grandson Jacinto were slopping the pigs with the kitchen garbage. After going to take a look at the spectacle, they had realized that there was nothing to be seen but a revolting mass of slimy creatures, and had returned to their chores. A sharp cry and the sound of breaking crockery alerted them that something was happening inside the house. They found Evangelina on her back on the floor, weight on her heels and neck, arched backward like a bow, frothing at the mouth and surrounded by broken cups and plates.

The terrified mother resorted to the first remedy that came to her mind: she emptied a bucket of cold water over the girl, but far from calming her, the alarming signs grew worse. The froth turned into a rosy slobber when the girl bit her tongue; her eyes rolled backward in her head, lost in infinity; she shook in shuddering convulsions, and the room was impregnated with anguish and the smell of excrement. The tension was so high that the thick adobe walls seemed to vibrate as if a secret trembling were coursing through their entrails. Digna Ranquileo hugged Jacinto close, covering his eyes to spare him that dreadful sight.

The attack lasted several minutes and left Evangelina drained, the mother and the brother terrorized, and the house turned upside down. When Hipólito and the other children returned from watching the convention of frogs, it was all over; the girl was resting in her chair and the mother was picking up the broken pottery.

"She was stung by a black widow spider" was the father's diagnosis when they told him about it.

"I've gone over her from head to foot. It wasn't a bite."

"Then she must have had a fit."

But Digna knew the symptoms of epilepsy, and she knew that it did not wreak havoc with the furniture. That very afternoon she made the decision to take Evangelina to *don* Simón, the healer.

"Better take her to a doctor," Hipólito counseled.

"You know what I think of hospitals and doctors," his wife replied, sure that if there was a cure for the girl, *don* Simón would know it.

This Saturday it would be five weeks since the first attack, and up till now nothing had helped her. There stood Evangelina helping her mother wash the earthenware dishes while the morning sped by and the dreaded hour approached.

"Get out the mugs for the flour water, daughter," Digna directed.

Evangelina began to sing as she lined up aluminum and enameled-tin receptacles on the table. Into each she measured a couple of tablespoons of toasted flour and a little honey. Later they would add fresh water to offer to the visitors who arrived at the hour of the trance in hopes of being benefited by some minor miracle.

"After tomorrow I'm not going to give them a thing," grumbled Digna. "They're going to ruin us."

"Don't talk like that, woman," Hipólito replied. "After all, people are coming out of affection. A little flour isn't going to make us any poorer," and she bowed her head because he was the man and was always right.

Digna was on the verge of tears; she realized her nerves had taken all they could, and she went in search of a few linden flowers to brew herself some calming tea. These last weeks had been a calvary. This strong and long-suffering woman, who without a single complaint had borne such great sorrow and survived poverty, hard work, and the travails of childbirth, felt that in the face of the bewitchment that was consuming her home she had come to the end of her tether. She was sure that she had tried everything that might cure her daughter; she had even taken her to the hospital, breaking her oath never to set foot there again. But it had all been in vain.

As he rang the doorbell, Francisco hoped that it would not be Beatriz Alcántara who answered. He felt diminished in her presence.

"Mother, this is my *compañero* Francisco Leal," Irene had said when she first introduced him several months earlier.

"Colleague, you say?" her mother replied, unable to tolerate the revolutionary implications of the word *compañero.*

Following that meeting, each knew what to expect from the other; they tried, nevertheless, to be amiable, more from habitual good manners than from any desire to please the other. Beatriz quickly found out that Francisco came from a family of impoverished Spanish émigrés who belonged to a caste of salaried intellectuals that lived in middle-class neighborhoods. She suspected that his job as a photographer, his backpack and motorcycle were not indications of bohemianism. The young man seemed to have very definite ideas, and they did not coincide with her own. Her daughter Irene ran around with rather strange people but, since it would be futile, she did not protest; she did, however, oppose Irene's friendship with Francisco in every way she could. She did not like to see their happy camaraderie, the strong bonds of their shared assignments, or, even less, like to imagine the consequences for her daughter's engagement to the Captain. She considered Francisco dangerous, because even she felt attracted by the photographer's dark eyes, slender hands, and serene voice.

For his part, Francisco recognized at first glance Beatriz's class prejudices and ideology. He limited himself to treating her courteously and distantly, lamenting that she was the mother of his best friend.

Once again, seeing the house, he was captivated by the thick wall surrounding the grounds, constructed from round stones from the river and bordered by lilliputian vegetation born of the wet winter. A discreet metal plaque displayed the words RETIREMENT HOME and, beneath them, a name befitting Irene's sense of humor: THE WILL OF GOD MANOR. He always marveled at the contrast between the well-tended garden, where soon dahlias, wisteria, roses, and gladiolas would be blooming in a tumult of perfume and color, and the infirmity of the first-floor occupants of this mansion that had been converted into a residence for the elderly. On the second floor all was harmony and good taste. Here were the Oriental rugs, the exquisite furniture, the works of art Eusebio Beltrán had acquired prior to his disappearance. The house was similar to others in the area but, of necessity, Beatriz had made modifications, keeping the façade intact wherever possible so that from the street the house would look as lordly as its neighbors. In that regard she was extremely circumspect. She did not want to appear to be making her living off old people but, instead, to be playing the role of benefactress: Poor dears, what would become of them if we didn't look after them?

She was equally prudent in references to her husband. She

preferred to accuse him of having left for parts unknown in the company of some low woman rather than to express doubts of a different nature. She suspected, in fact, that his absence was *not* due to an amorous adventure but that the government had carelessly eliminated him or was by mistake detaining him and he was rotting in some prison, as had been rumored in so many cases in recent years. She was not the only one to harbor those black thoughts. At first, her friends observed her with distrust, and whispered behind her back that Eusebio Beltrán had fallen into the hands of the police, in which event he had undoubtedly been concealing some offense: he might be a Communist mingling with decent people, as others had been known to do. Beatriz did not like to remember the threatening and sneering calls, the anonymous messages slipped beneath the door, or the unforgettable night garbage had been dumped on her bed. No one was in the house that night, because Rosa, too, had gone out. When Beatriz and her daughter returned from the theater, everything was in order, although they were surprised that the dog was not barking. Irene went looking for the dog, calling her in every room as Beatriz followed, turning on the lights. Stupefied, they stopped before the mounds of refuse covering the bed, empty tin cans, decomposing peelings, paper smeared with excrement. They found Cleo locked in an armoire, seemingly dead, and there she lay for fifteen hours until she recovered from the soporific. Beatriz sank into a chair, staring at the litter and muck on her bed, unable to comprehend the meaning of such provocation. She could not imagine who would have carried bags of filth to her house, picked the lock of the door, drugged the dog, and defiled everything. This happened before the days of the retirement home on the ground floor, and except for Rosa and the gardener there were no other servants.

"Don't tell anyone about this, darling. It's an insult, we are disgraced," Beatriz wept.

"Don't think about it, Mother. Can't you see it's the work of a maniac? Don't let it worry you."

But Beatriz Alcántara knew that in some way this outrage was connected with her husband, and once again she damned him. She remembered every detail of the evening Eusebio Beltrán had deserted her. In those days he was obsessed with his project of raising sheep for Muslims and with the philanthropic butcher shop that led to his ruin. They had been married for more than twenty years, and Beatriz's patience had run out. She could no longer bear his indifference, his many infidelities, his scandalous manner of squandering money on silver sports planes, racehorses, erotic sculpture, expensive restaurants, gaming tables, and extravagant gifts for other women. As he entered his middle years, her husband had not settled down; on the contrary, his defects became more marked, and his adventurous impulses increased along with the gray hairs at his temple and the wrinkles at the corners of his eyes. He risked his capital in foolish ventures, he disappeared for weeks on exotic voyages—from following a Norwegian ecologist to the ends of the continent to embarking on a solitary ocean-crossing on a raft blown by unpredictable winds. His charm captivated everyone but his wife. In one of their horrendous arguments, she lost all control and assaulted him with a broadside of insults and recriminations. Eusebio Beltrán was a genteel man who despised any form of violence. He held up his hand in sign of a truce and with a smile announced that he was going out for cigarettes. He left the house quietly, and nothing was heard from him again.

"He ran away from his debts," Beatriz speculated, finding unconvincing the argument that he had become infatuated with another woman.

He left no trace. Nor was his body found. In the years that followed, she adapted to her new state, outdoing herself to feign a normal life before her friends. Silent and solitary, she prowled through hospitals, detention centers, and consulates, inquiring about her husband. She approached friends in the upper echelons of the government and initiated secret investigations through a detective agency, but no one could locate him. Finally, weary of wandering through so many offices, she decided to go to the Vicariate. Since any connection with the Vicar's office was frowned on in her social milieu, she did not dare mention it, even to Irene. That branch of the Archbishopric was considered to be a den of Marxist priests and dangerous laymen dedicated to helping enemies of the regime. It was the only organization that openly defied the government, directed by a Cardinal who placed the invincible power of the Church at the service of the persecuted, never stopping to inquire about their political hue. Until the day when she needed help, Beatriz had haughtily proclaimed that the authorities ought to wipe that institution from the face of the earth and jail the Cardinal and his rebel sycophants. Her visit was in vain, however, because not even in the Vicariate could she find news of her missing husband. He seemed to have been swept away on a wind of oblivion.

The uncertainty destroyed Beatriz's nerves. Her friends recommended courses in yoga and Eastern meditation to soothe her constant agitation. While managing, with difficulty, to stand on her head, breathe through her navel, and focus her thoughts on Nirvana, she succeeded in forgetting her problems, but she could not remain in that position all day, and during the moments she did think of herself she was stunned by the irony of her fate. She had become the wife of a *desaparecido*. She had often said that no one disappeared in their country, and that such stories were anti-patriotic lies. When she saw the distraught women marching every Thursday in the plaza with portraits of their relatives pinned to their bosoms, she had said they were in the pay of Moscow. She never imagined she would find herself in the same situation as those wives and mothers searching for their loved ones. Legally, she was not a widow and would not be one for ten years, when the law would issue her a death certificate for her husband. She could not use the funds from Eusebio Beltrán's estate or get her hands on the slippery associates who made the stocks of his business enterprises vanish into thin air. She stayed in her mansion giving herself the airs of a duchess, but with no funds to maintain the lifestyle of a lady of high society. Beleaguered by bills, she was at the point of sprinkling the house with gasoline to burn it to the ground and collect the insurance when Irene cleverly thought of renting the ground floor.

"Now that so many families are leaving the country but can't take their parents and grandparents with them, I think we'd be doing them a favor by looking after them. Besides, it would bring in a little money," Irene suggested.

And that is what they did. The ground floor was partitioned into smaller rooms; new baths were installed, and handrails in the hallways to give support to old age and security to unsteady legs; the steps were covered with a ramp for wheelchairs, and speakers with mood music positioned to assuage displeasure and alleviate depression, overlooking the possibility that it might fall on deaf ears.

Beatriz and her daughter settled into the upper floor with Rosa, who had been in their service from time immemorial. The mother decorated their home with her finest possessions, avoiding any touch of vulgarity, and began to live from the income provided by the patients of The Will of God Manor. If difficulties knocked too insistently at their door, she moved with supreme circumspection to sell a painting, a piece of silver, or one of the many jewels she had acquired in compensation for the gifts her husband bestowed on his lovers.

Irene regretted that her mother was distressed over such pedestrian problems. She was in favor of moving to more modest quarters in order to remodel the entire house and accommodate enough guests to cover all their expenses; but Beatriz would rather work herself to death and perform all manner of juggling acts than reveal her reduced circumstances. To leave the house would be publicly to acknowledge poverty. Mother and daughter differed greatly in their appreciation of life. As they did in their assessment of Eusebio Beltrán. Beatriz considered him to be a villain entirely capable of having committed fraud, bigamy, or whatever felony it was that had forced him to slink off with his tail between his legs, but when she voiced those opinions Irene turned on her like a tiger. She adored her father; she refused to believe he was dead or, even less, to accept that he had defects. His reasons for disappearing from the known world did not matter to her. Her affection for him was unconditional. She treasured the memory of an elegant man with a patrician profile and a formidable character combining admirable sentiments with wild passions that brought him to the brink of questionable dealings. Those aberrations may have horrified Beatriz, but they were what Irene remembered with greatest tenderness.

Eusebio Beltrán was the youngest of a family of wealthy planters, considered by his brothers to be hopelessly incorrigible because of his bent toward extravagance and his unrestrained *joie de vivre*, in contrast to the avarice and melancholy of his family. As soon as their parents died, the brothers divided the inheritance, gave Eusebio his share, and hoped they would never hear from him again. He sold his lands and went abroad, where in a few years he spent his last penny in princely diversions befitting his reputation as a ne'er-do-well. He returned to his native land through the mercy of the Consulate, in itself enough to discredit him forever in the eyes of any marriageable girl, but Beatriz Alcántara fell in love with his aristocratic bearing, his surname, and the aura that surrounded him. She was from a middle-class family, and from the time she was a little girl her one ambition had been to ascend the social ladder. Her capital consisted of her beauty, the artifice of her manners, and a few English and French phrases misused with such assurance that she gave the impression of being fluent in those languages. A veneer of culture served her well in social gatherings, and her skill in dressing and grooming earned her the reputation of being elegant. Eusebio Beltrán was for all practical purposes ruined; he had hit bottom in many aspects of his life but was confident that this was merely temporary, for he had the notion that people from good families always kept their heads above water. Besides, he was a liberal. The ideology of the liberals in those days could be summed up in a few words: help your friends, screw your enemies, and in all other cases be just. His friends did help him, and shortly he was playing golf in the most exclusive club and enjoying a season ticket at the Municipal Theater and a box at the Hippodrome. With the backing of his charm and his air of British nobility, he found associates in a variety of enterprises. He began to live opulently because it seemed to him foolish to live any other way, and he married Beatriz Alcántara because he had a weakness for beautiful women. The second time he invited her out, she asked him, without preamble, what his intentions were, saying she did not want to waste her time. She was twenty-five and did not intend to spend months in a pointless flirtation, since she was interested only in finding a husband. Her frankness greatly amused Eusebio, but when she refused to appear again in his company, he realized that she was serious. It took him one minute to yield to the impulse to propose matrimony, and a lifetime was not long enough to regret it. They had a daughter, Irene, who inherited the angelic bemusement of her paternal grandmother and the constant good humor of her father. While his daughter was growing up, Eusebio Beltrán had undertaken a number of business dealings, some profitable and others openly absurd. He was a man gifted with unlimited imagination, of which the prime example was his coconut-knocking machine. One day he had read in a magazine that picking this fruit by hand greatly increased its price. A native was chosen to climb the palm tree, pick the coconut, and descend. Climbing and descending consumed valuable time, and some pickers fell from the high branches, causing unforeseen expenses. Beltrán was determined to find a solution. He spent three days locked in his office, tormented by the problem of the coconuts, about which, to say the least, he had little firsthand knowledge, since in his travels he had avoided the tropics and in his home exotic foods were not eaten. But he learned. He studied the diameter and weight of the fruit, the climate and terrain suitable for its cultivation, the season for harvesting, the time for maturation, and other details. He devoted hours to drawing plans, and the result of all his sleeplessness was the invention of a machine capable of gathering a surprising number of coconuts per hour. Ignoring the mockery of family and friends, who knew as little as he about coconuts in their natural state, having only seen them adorning the turbans of mambo dancers or shredded over wedding cakes, he went to the Registry and patented a rampant tower outfitted with a retractable arm. Eusebio Beltrán had prophesied that one day his coconut-knocking machine would be useful, and time proved him right.

That was a trying period for Beatriz and her husband. Eusebio wanted to make a clean break and remove himself forever from his nagging wife, who was always harrying him with the same old tune, but she refused, with little reason other than the desire to torment him and to prevent his establishing a new relationship with one of her rivals. She argued that they needed to provide a stable home environment for Irene. Before causing my daughter any pain, she said, you will have to walk over my dead body. Her husband was at the point of doing just that, but tried instead to buy his freedom. On three occasions he offered Beatriz a large sum of money if she would allow him to leave in peace, and three times she accepted but at the last minute, when the lawyers had prepared the papers and all that was missing was the binding signature, she reneged. Their constant battles fortified her hatred. For this, and a thousand sentimental reasons, Irene did not weep for her father. She had no doubt that he had fled to free himself of his attachments, his debts, and his wife.

When Francisco Leal knocked at the door, Irene came to welcome him accompanied by Cleo, who was barking around her feet. She had prepared for the trip with a shawl over her shoulders, a kerchief over her head, and her tape recorder in her hands.

"Do you know where this saint lives?" he asked.

"In Los Riscos, an hour from here."

They left the dog in the house, climbed on the motorcycle, and set out. It was a brilliant, warm, and cloudless morning.

They rode across the entire city, through the shaded streets of the exclusive neighborhoods with their lush trees and lordly mansions, the gray, noisy middle-class zone, and the wide cordons of misery. As they flew along, Francisco Leal thought about Irene, whom he could feel pressed against his back. The first time he had seen her, eleven months before that fateful spring, he thought she had escaped from a tale about pirates and princesses; to him she seemed a marvel that no one else could perceive. At that time he had been looking for work outside his profession. His private consulting room was always empty, producing large expenses and no earnings. He had also been suspended from his appointment at the University when the School of Psychology was closed for being a hotbed of pernicious ideas. He had spent months applying at every school, hospital, and industry, with no result except growing discouragement, until he was convinced that his years of study and his foreign doctorate would be of no use in the new society. It was not that suddenly all human wants had been resolved and the country peopled with happy citizens but, rather, that the rich did not suffer from problems of basic existence and the others, even though they might need him desperately, could not pay for the luxury of psychological therapy. They gritted their teeth and endured in silence.

The life of Francisco Leal, bright with good omens in adolescence, seemed, as he completed his second decade, a failure in the eyes of any impartial observer, and even more in his own. For a while, he drew consolation and strength from his clandestine practice, but soon it became essential for him to contribute to the family income. Stringency in the Leal household was rapidly becoming poverty. He managed to keep his emotions under control until it was clear that all doors were closed to him; then one night his serenity deserted him and he broke down in the kitchen as his mother was preparing dinner. Seeing him in that state, she dried her hands on her apron, removed the stew from the stove, and put her arms around him as she had when he was a boy.

"Psychology isn't the only thing in the world, son. Wipe your nose and look for something else," she said.

Until then it had not occurred to Francisco to change careers, but Hilda's words signaled a new direction. He put his self-pity aside and reviewed his skills, hoping to find something productive but at the same time agreeable. He decided on photography, in which he was minimally skilled. Years before, he had bought a Japanese camera with all the accessories and he thought the moment had come to dust it off and put it to use. He placed a few prints in a portfolio, scoured the telephone book for places to apply, and so found himself at the door of a women's magazine.

The editorial offices occupied the top floor of an old-fashioned building with the name of the founder of the publishing firm chiseled in the portico in gilded letters. During the so-called boom in culture, when there had been an attempt to involve everyone in the fiesta of knowledge and the vice of information and more pages of print were sold than loaves of bread, the owners had decided to redecorate the building to be in tune with the delirious enthusiasm rocking the country. They had begun on the ground floor, carpeting it wall-to-wall, adding exquisite woodwork, replacing the shabby furnishings with glass-and-aluminum desks, removing windows to open up skylights, closing stairwells to provide niches in which to embed safes, locating electronic eyes that opened and closed doors by magic. The diagram of the edifice was turning into a labyrinth when suddenly the rules of the game were changed. The redecorating never reached the fifth floor, which had kept its furnishings of uncertain color, prehistoric typewriters, archival filing cabinets, and disconsolate stains on the ceiling. These modest appointments had little relation to the luxury weekly magazine edited there. From its covers smiled scantily clad beauty queens, and across its slick pages spilled a rainbow of colors and daring feminist articles. Because of the censorship of recent years, however, black patches now covered naked breasts and euphemisms designated forbidden concepts like abortion, ass, and freedom.

Francisco Leal knew the magazine because he had once bought a copy for his mother. The only name he remembered was that of Irene Beltrán, a journalist who wrote with some audacity, a rare commodity in those times. For that reason, when he reached the reception desk he asked to speak with her. He was led into a spacious room lighted by a large window from which one could see in the distance the imposing bulk of the Hill, somber guardian of the city. He saw four desks with as many clacking typewriters and, to the rear, a clothes rack filled with richly colored gowns. A coiffeur dressed in white was combing out a girl's hair while another girl awaited her turn, sitting as motionless as an idol, sunk in the contemplation of her own beauty. They signaled to Irene Beltrán, and the moment he saw her across the room he was attracted by her expression and by the amazing hair falling over her shoulders. She waved him over with a flirtatious smile, the last sign he needed to conclude that this girl would be capable of robbing him even of his thoughts, for he had imagined her, exactly as she was, in his boyhood books and adolescent dreams. As he drew nearer, his confidence evaporated, and he stopped before her, embarrassed, unable to tear his eyes from hers, made even more dramatic by makeup. Finally he found his voice and introduced himself.

"I'm looking for work," he blurted out, placing the portfolio containing his prints on the table.

"Are you on the Blacklist?" she asked candidly, without lowering her voice.

"No."

"Then we can talk. Wait for me outside and when I finish here I'll join you."

Francisco left the room, threading his way among desks and suitcases open on the floor and piled with stoles and fur coats like plunder from a recent safari. He bumped into Mario, the hairstylist, who glided by brushing a wig of pale hair, informing him in passing that this year blondes were very much in vogue. Francisco waited near the reception desk for a time that seemed very brief, entertained by a remarkable parade of girls modeling lingerie, children bringing stories for a children's contest, an inventor determined to publicize his urinometer—a new instrument for measuring the direction and force of a stream of urine—a couple afflicted with amorous problems who were looking for the Advice to the Lovelorn, and a lady with jet-black hair who introduced herself as the composer of horoscopes and predictions. When she saw him she stopped dead, as if she had had a premonition.

"I read it on your forehead—you will experience a great passion!" she exclaimed.

Francisco had broken up with his most recent girlfriend several months before, and had determined to keep himself free of all amorous uncertainties. He sat there like a schoolboy who had been sent to the corner, not knowing what to say and feeling ridiculous. She explored his head with expert fingers, examined his palms, and without affectation pronounced him a Sagittarius, although she suspected an ascendant Scorpio, since he was marked by signs of sex and death. Especially death.

Finally this pythoness disappeared, to the relief of Francisco, who knew nothing about the zodiac and mistrusted chiromancy, divination, and other madness. Shortly afterward, Irene Beltrán appeared and he was able to see her full length. She was just as he had imagined her. She was wearing a long peasant skirt of chambray, a blouse of rough cotton, a multicolored woven sash cinching her waist, and was carrying a leather purse crammed as full as a mailman's pouch. Amid a jangle of brass and silver bracelets, she held out a tiny hand with rings on every short-nailed finger.

"Do you like vegetarian food?" she asked and, without waiting for an answer, took him by the arm and led him down the stairs; like many other things in that publishing house, the elevators were stuck.

As they emerged into the street, the sun blazed down on Irene's hair and Francisco thought he had never seen anything so extraordinary. He could not resist the impulse to reach out and touch it. She smiled, accustomed to producing amazement in a latitude where hair of that color was so rare. When they reached the corner, she stopped, removed a stamped envelope from her purse, and dropped it in the mailbox.

"No one writes to the Colonel," she said enigmatically.

Two blocks down the street they came to a small restaurant, a meeting place for macrobioticists, spiritists, bohemians, students, and gastric-ulcer sufferers. At that hour it was full, but she was a regular customer. The waiter greeted her by name, led them to a corner, and seated them at a wooden table with a checked tablecloth. Without delay he served them lunch, along with fruit juice and a dark bread filled with raisins and nuts. Irene and Francisco savored the food slowly, studying each other. Soon they were exchanging confidences; she told him of her work on the magazine, where she wrote about prodigious hormones shot like bullets into the arm to avoid conception, masks of sea algae for erasing signs of age on the skin, love affairs of princes and princesses of the royal houses of Europe, processions of extraterrestrial or pastoral styles dependent on the caprice of each season in Paris, and other subjects of diverse interest. About herself, she said that she lived with her mother, an aged servant, and her dog, Cleo. She added that four years ago her father had gone out to buy cigarettes, and had disappeared from their lives forever. About her fiancé, Army Captain Gustavo Morante, she said not a word. Francisco would learn of his existence much later.

For dessert, they were served preserved papayas that had been grown in the warm northern regions. She caressed them with eyes and spoon, anticipating her pleasure. Francisco realized that she, like him, respected certain earthly pleasures. Irene did not finish her dessert, but left a bite on the plate.

"That way I can savor it later in my memory," she explained. "And now tell me about yourself. . . ."

In a few words, since by nature and professional training he was more inclined to listen attentively than to talk, he told her that for some time he had not found employment as a psychologist and was looking for any respectable job. Photography had seemed a good possibility, but since he had not wanted to be like those amateurs who end up begging to photograph weddings, baptisms, and birthdays, he had come to the magazine.

"Tomorrow I'm going to interview some prostitutes. Do you want to come along and give it a try?" Irene asked.

Francisco accepted on the spot, brushing aside a shadow

of sadness, thinking how much easier it was to earn a living by clicking a shutter than it was by placing his experience and hard-won knowledge at the service of his fellow man.

When the waiter brought their check, Irene opened her purse to pay, but Francisco's father had given him what he called the strict upbringing of a *caballero*: courtesy, after all, had never stood in the way of revolutionary fervor. To the surprise and displeasure of the young journalist, Francisco reached for the check, ignoring the advances the liberationists had made in their campaigns for equality.

"You're out of work, let me pay," she insisted. In the following months, the check would be one of their few sources of argument.

Soon Francisco Leal had the first indication of the drawbacks of his new occupation. The next day, he accompanied Irene to the red-light district of the city, certain that she had made previous contacts. This was not so. They reached the district at dusk and wandered through the streets with such a lost air that a number of potential clients accosted the reporter, asking her price. After a period of observation, Irene approached a brunette who was firmly ensconced on a street corner beneath the light from multicolor neon signs.

"Excuse me, *señorita*. Are you a whore?"

Francisco prepared to defend Irene in the justifiable eventuality that the brunette should hit Irene over the head with her pocketbook, but nothing like that happened. On the contrary, she further inflated her breasts like two balloons ready to explode from her blouse and smiled, gladdening the night with the gleam of a gold tooth.

"At your service, honey," she replied.

Irene explained why they were there, and the whore offered her collaboration with the good will people feel for the press. This attracted the curiosity of her companions as well as a few passersby. In a few minutes a group had formed, causing a certain urban congestion. Francisco suggested that they clear the way before a patrol car arrived, which happened every time more than three persons congregated without authorization from Police Headquarters. The brunette led them to the Chinese Mandarin, where the amiable conversation continued, now with the madam and other girls of the house, while the clients waited patiently and even offered to participate in the interview on condition that their anonymity be respected.

Francisco was not accustomed to asking intimate questions outside his consulting office or without therapeutic goals in mind, and he had to smile as Irene Beltrán conducted her long interrogation: how many men per night, what was the total pay, the special prices for students and old men, their diseases, sorrows, and abuse, the retirement age, and how much did the percentage increase for pimps and police? From her lips this questioning acquired the pristine air of innocence. By the time she finished her work, she was on excellent terms with the ladies of the night, and Francisco feared that she might decide to move to the Chinese Mandarin. Later he learned that she was always this way, putting heart and soul into anything she did. In the months that followed, he saw her on the verge of adopting a baby after an investigation about orphans, of plummeting from an airplane after some parachutists, and of fainting from fright in a haunted house where they suffered hours of terror.

After that night, he accompanied her on most of her assignments. The photographs contributed to the Leal budget and signaled a change in Francisco's life, which was now enriched with new adventures. Contrasting with the frivolity and ephemeral glitter of the magazine was the harsh reality of the clinic in the working-class neighborhood of his brother José, where three times a week Francisco treated the most desperate patients, always with the sensation of helping very little because there was no consolation for such misery. No one in the publishing house suspected the new photographer. He seemed a tranquil man. Not even Irene knew of his secret life, although occasional hints piqued her curiosity. It would be much later, after they had crossed the frontier of shadows, that she would discover the other face of that gentle friend of few words. In the following months their relationship grew closer. They could not get along without each other; they became accustomed to being together at work and in their free time, inventing pretexts not to be apart. They shared their days, surprised at the number of their meetings. They loved the same music, read the same poets, preferred dry white wine, laughed in unison, were angered by the same injustices, and smiled at the same setbacks. Irene found it strange that at times Francisco disappeared for a day or two, but he eluded explanations and she had to accept the fact without questions. Her feeling was similar to Francisco's during the time she was with her fiancé, but neither of the two knew how to recognize jealousy.

Digna Ranquileo consulted *don* Simón, known in every corner of the region for his medical successes, far more numerous than those of the hospital. Illnesses, he said, are of two kinds: either they cure themselves or they have no remedy. In the first instance, he could alleviate the symptoms and shorten the convalescence, but if he came across an incurable patient he sent him to the doctor in Los Riscos, thus protecting his prestige and, in passing, casting doubt on traditional medicine.

Digna found him resting in a rush chair in the doorway of his house, three blocks from the town plaza. He was scratching his belly contentedly and conversing with a parrot shifting from leg to leg on his shoulder.

"I've brought you my little girl," said Digna, blushing.

"Isn't this the switched Evangelina?" was the healer's brash greeting.

Digna nodded. Slowly the man rose to his feet and invited them inside his dwelling. They entered a large shadowy room lined with flasks, dried branches, herbs hanging from the roof-tree, and printed and framed prayers on the wall; it looked more like the cave of a shipwrecked sailor than the consulting room of a scientist, which was what *don* Simón liked to call himself. He insisted that he had received a medical degree in Brazil, and to anyone who doubted him he displayed a grimy diploma with florid signatures and a border of golden angels. An oilcloth curtain isolated one corner of the room. Eyes rolled back in his head, and lost in concentration, he listened as the mother related the particulars of their misfortune. From the corner of his eye he glanced at Evangelina, detailing the marks of scratches on her skin and the pallor of her face, in spite of cheeks cracked by the cold and violet shadows beneath her eyes. He knew those symptoms, but to be completely sure he asked her to go through the curtain and take off all her clothes.

"I'm going to examine your girl, *señora* Ranquileo," he said, depositing the parrot on the table and following Evangelina.

After examining her in great detail, and making her urinate into a basin in order to study the nature of her bodily fluids, *don* Simón corroborated his suspicions.

"Someone has cast the evil eye on her."

"Is there a cure for that, *don*?" Digna Ranquileo asked, frightened.

"Yes, there's a cure, but we have to find out who did it before we can find the cure, you understand?"

"No."

"Find out who hates the girl and tell me so I can help her get better."

"No one hates Evangelina, *don* Simón. She's an innocent little girl. Who could have anything against her?"

"Some rejected man, or a jealous woman?" the healer suggested, glancing at his patient's minuscule breasts.

Evangelina burst into disconsolate sobs, and her mother quivered with anger; she had watched her daughter closely and was sure she had not strayed, and even less could she imagine anyone who wanted to harm her. Besides, Digna had had less confidence in *don* Simón ever since she learned his wife was deceiving him, believing—rightly so—that he must not be all that wise if he was the only person in the village who did not know he had horns. She doubted his diagnosis but did not wish to be discourteous. With much beating about the bush, she asked for some medicine so as not to leave with empty hands.

"Prescribe some vitamins for her, *don*, to see if she can get over this. Maybe along with the evil eye she has the English disease?"

Don Simón gave her a handful of homemade pills and some leaves that had been ground to dust in a mortar.

"Dissolve this in wine and give it to her twice a day. You also need to put mustard plasters on her and douse her in cold water. And don't forget the sweet chestnut tea. It always helps in these cases."

"And if she takes all this will the attacks go away?"

"The fever in her belly will go away, but as long as she's evil-eyed she won't get any better. If she has another attack, bring her to me and I'll do an *ensalmo*. Maybe she'll need herbs and spells."

Three days later, mother and daughter found themselves back for intensified treatment, because Evangelina was suffering an attack every day, always around noon. This time the healer took energetic measures. He led his patient behind the oilcloth, removed her clothing with his own hands, and washed her from head to foot with a mixture composed of camphor, methylene blue, and holy water, in equal parts, pausing with special attention on the areas most afflicted by the sickness: heels, breasts, back, and navel. Friction, fright, and the healer's strong palms stained the girl's skin a sky blue and made her shiver and shake so hard she nearly swooned. Fortunately, he then administered a calming syrup of agrimony, but that left the girl weakened and trembling. After the *ensalmo*, he gave Digna a long list of recommendations and various medicinal herbs: aspen to combat restlessness and anxiety, chicory for self-pity, gentian to ward off depression, gorse against suicide and weeping fits, holly to prevent hatred and envy, and pine to cure remorse and panic. He told them to fill a pan with spring-water, throw in the leaves and flowers, and let them brew in the sunlight for four hours before bringing them to a boil over a slow fire. He reminded Digna that for love impatience in innocents you must dose their food with alum and avoid letting them share a bed with other family members, because the fever is contagious, like measles. Finally he gave her a flask of small calcium pills and a disinfectant soap for her daily bath.

At the end of a week the girl had grown thin, her gaze was troubled and her hands tremulous, her stomach was constantly churning, but the attacks continued. Conquering her natural resistance, Digna Ranquileo then took Evangelina to Los Riscos Hospital, where a young doctor newly arrived from the capital, who expressed himself in scientific terms and had never heard of the megrims, the cholera morbus, to say nothing of the evil eye, assured Digna that Evangelina was suffering from hysteria. It was his opinion that they should ignore her and hope that when she grew out of adolescence she would also grow out of the attacks. He prescribed a tranquilizer that would fell an ox and warned her that if she kept having her fits she would have to be referred to the Psychiatric Hospital in the capital, where they would restore her good sense with a few electric shocks. Digna wanted to know whether hysteria caused the cups to dance on the shelves, the dogs to howl like lost souls, a noisy rain of invisible stones on the roof, and the furniture to rock back and forth, but the doctor preferred not to venture into such deep waters and limited himself to recommending that they set the dishes in a safe place and tie up the animals on the patio.

When she began taking his medication, Evangelina sank into a deep stupor that resembled death. It was all they could do to get her to open her eyes to be fed. They would put a spoonful between her lips and then splash her face with cold water to remind her to chew and swallow. They had to go with her to the privy, afraid that she would be overcome by sleep and fall in. She stayed fast in bed, and when her parents got her to her feet, she would take a couple of drunken steps and fall to the floor snoring. This dreamlike state was interrupted at midday for her usual trance, the only moment she roused to give any signs of vitality. Before a week had gone by, the pills prescribed at the hospital ceased to have any effect, and she entered a stage of sadness that kept her silent and sleepless both day and night. At that point the mother took the initiative and buried the pills in a deep hole in the garden where they would never be found by any living creature.

Desperate, Digna Ranquileo went to Mamita Encarnación who, after firmly establishing that her specialty was births and pregnancies and never fits provoked by other causes, agreed to examine the girl. She came to the house one morning, witnessed the lunatic trance, and proved with her own eyes that the trembling of the furniture and altered behavior of the animals were not idle talk but the God's truth.

"The girl needs a man," she pronounced.

The Ranquileos were insulted by such a statement. They could not accept that a decent girl they had raised like their own daughter and given special attention to and protected from even the slightest touch by her brothers would act like a bitch in heat. The midwife nodded emphatically, ignoring their arguments, repeating her diagnosis. She recommended giving her enough work to keep her busy at all times, to prevent worse maladies.

"Idleness and chastity make for a sad girl. I tell you, you're going to have to marry that girl off because she won't get free of this whirlwind until she has a man."

Scandalized, the mother did not follow this counsel, but she did keep the girl busy with chores, which restored her happiness and sleep but did not diminish the intensity of the attacks.

Soon the neighbors learned of these odd goings-on and began to snoop around the house. The boldest marauders came early in order to be close enough to observe the phenomenon and try to find some practical application for it. Some suggested that during her trance Evangelina should communicate with souls in Purgatory, predict the future, or slacken the rains. Digna knew that once the matter became public knowledge, people would flock from miles around to tramp down her garden, litter her patio, and make fun of her daughter. Under such conditions Evangelina would never find a man with enough courage to marry her and give her the children she so badly needed. As she could expect no help from science, she visited her evangelical pastor in the blue-painted shed that served as temple to Jehovah's faithful. She was an active member of that small Protestant congregation and the minister received her cordially. Without omitting any details, she told him of the misfortune that was oppressing their home, making it clear that she had seen to it that her daughter was not tainted by any sin, not so much as a look from her brothers or adoptive father.

The Reverend listened to her tale with great attention. He got down on both knees and for long minutes sank into meditation, seeking light from the Lord. Then he opened the Bible at random and read the first verse that met his eyes: "Holophernes took great delight in her, and drank much more wine than he had drunk at any time in one day since he was born" (Judith 12:20). Satisfied, he interpreted God's answer to the problem of His servant Ranquileo.

"Has your husband given up alcohol, Sister?"

"You know that isn't possible."

"How many years have I been preaching abstinence to him?"

"He can't leave it alone, he has wine in his blood."

"Tell him to come to the True Evangelical Church; we can help him. Have you ever seen a drunkard among us?"

Digna listed the reasons she had often repeated to justify her husband's weakness. The problem went back to her stillborn third son. Lacking money to buy an urn, Hipólito had put the little angel in a shoe box, tucked the box beneath his arm, and started out for the cemetery. Along the way he felt the need to drown his sorrow with a few swigs, and lost track of things. Some time later he recovered his senses, laid out in a bog. The box had disappeared, and though he searched for it everywhere, it was never found.

"Imagine his nightmares, Reverend. My poor Hipólito still dreams about it. He wakes up screaming because his little son is calling him from Limbo. Every time he remembers, he takes to the bottle. That's why he gets drunk, not wickedness or meanness."

"The alcoholic always has an excuse on the tip of his tongue. Evangelina is a trumpet of God. Through her infirmity, He is calling your husband to reform before it's too late."

"With all due respect, Reverend, if God left it up to me, I'd rather see Hipólito drunk as a lord than my daughter howling like a dog and speaking in a man's voice."

"The sin of pride, Sister! Who are you to tell Jehovah how to direct our miserable destinies?"

From that day, led by zeal, the pastor, in the company of a few devout members of his congregation, came often to the house of the Ranquileos to help the young girl with the power of communal prayer. But another week went by and Evangelina showed no signs of improvement. One of the interlopers wandering around nervously at the hour of the attack discovered a way to benefit from it. He tripped over a chair and accidentally leaned on the bed where the girl lay in her contortions. The following day, the warts spotting his hand had disappeared. Word of this marvel spread immediately and the number of visitors increased at an alarming rate, certain they would be cured during the trance. Someone dusted off the story of how the Evangelinas had been switched in the hospital, and that added to the prestige of the miracle. At this point the Reverend considered the matter outside the sphere of his knowledge and suggested taking the sick girl to the Catholic priest, whose Church, because it was older, had far more experience with saints and their works.

In the parish church Father Cirilo listened to the story from the lips of the Ranquileos and remembered Evangelina as the only one in her class who had not made her First Communion at school, because her mother belonged to the heretic ranks of Protestantism. She was a lamb from his flock who had been snatched away by the bombast and taradiddle of the evangelicals; he would not, nonetheless, withhold his counsel.

"I shall pray for the child. God's mercy is infinite and He may come to our aid in spite of the fact that you have fallen so far from the Holy Church."

"Thank you, Father, but besides your prayers, can't you exorcise her for me?" Digna asked.

The priest crossed himself in alarm. That idea must have originated with his Protestant rival, for this poor countrywoman could not be versed in such matters. In recent times the Vatican had frowned on these rituals, avoiding even the mention of the Devil, as if it were better to ignore him. He himself had irrefutable proof of the existence of Satan, the devourer of souls, and for that very reason did not feel inclined to confront him in some slapdash ceremony. Beyond that, if such practices should reach the ears of his superior, the mantle of scandal would definitely darken his old age. Nevertheless, common sense told him that the power of suggestion often has inexplicable effects and that maybe a few "Our Fathers" and a sprinkle or two of holy water would calm the sick girl. He told her mother that this would be sufficient, discounting as highly unlikely that she was possessed by the Devil. Exorcism could not be performed in her case. Exorcism meant conquering the Devil himself, and an ailing and lonely parish priest buried in a country village did not constitute a suitable rival for the powers of the Evil One, even supposing that was the cause of Evangelina's suffering. He ordered the Ranquileos to seek reconciliation with the Holy Catholic Church, because such misfortunes tended to happen to those who defied Our Lord with heretical sects. Digna, however, had seen the priest's collusion with the *patrones* in the confessional, all their *mea culpas* and whisperings, spying on the country people and denouncing their petty pilfering, and that was why she mistrusted Catholicism, believing that the Church was the friend of the rich and the foe of the poor, in open rebellion to the mandates of Jesus Christ, who had preached exactly the opposite.

From that day on, Father Cirilo, too, came to the Ranquileo home whenever his many obligations and weary legs permitted. On the first occasion, his firm convictions were shaken before the spectacle of the young girl scourged by that strange malady. The holy water and the sacraments did not alleviate her symptoms, but since they did not aggravate them he naturally deduced that the Devil was somewhere behind the scenes. He joined forces with the Protestant Reverend in a common spiritual undertaking. They were in agreement in treating it as a mental sickness and in no way an expression of the divine, because the crude miracles attributed to the girl were not worthy of the term. Together they combated superstition and, after studying the case, concluded that the disappearance of a few warts, which almost always cure themselves, the improvement in the weather, normal at this time of the year, and the dubious good fortune in games of chance were not enough to justify a halo of saintliness. But the lively arguments of the priest and the pastor did not halt the pilgrimages. Among the visitors who came asking for favors, opinions were divided. While some upheld the mystic origin of the crisis, others attributed it to a simple satanic curse. Hysteria! chorused the Protestant, the priest, the midwife, and the doctor from Los Riscos Hospital, but no one wanted to hear them, enraptured as they were by the carnival of insignificant wonders.

With her arms around Francisco's waist, her face pressed against the rough texture of his jacket, and her hair whipped by the wind, Irene imagined she was flying on a winged dragon. Behind them lay the last houses of the city. The highway advanced between fields bordered by translucent poplars, and on the horizon she could glimpse hills enveloped in the blue mist of distance. Astride the croup of their steed, she was lost in fantasies recovered from her childhood, racing at a full gallop across the dunes of an Arabian fairy tale. She loved the speed, the seismic shuddering between her legs, the tremendous roar penetrating her skin. She thought of the saint they were going to visit, of the title of her article, of the four-page spread with color photographs. Ever since the apparition of El Iluminado, several years before, who had traveled from north to south healing sores and reviving the dead, there had been no talk of miracle workers. The possessed, yes, the spooked, the damned, the loonies, those there were in abundance, like the girl who spit tadpoles, the superannuated earthquake prognosticator, and the deaf-mute who paralyzed machines with his gaze, a fact she herself had corroborated when she interviewed him through sign language and afterward could never get her watch to work. But aside from that luminous personage, no one had bothered much with miracles that benefited mankind. Every day it was more difficult to find appealing stories for the magazine. It seemed that nothing interesting was happening in the country, and when it did occur, it was censored. Irene put her hands beneath Francisco's jacket to warm her stiff fingers. She felt his lean chest, sinew and bones—so different from Gustavo, a compact mass of muscles exercised by fencing, judo, gymnastics, and the fifty push-ups he did every morning with his troops because he would never demand anything from his men that he himself was not capable of doing. "I am like a father for them, a severe father, but just," he always said. When they made love in the semi-darkness of hotel rooms, he always stripped, proud of his physique, and walked naked around the room. She loved that body tanned by salt and wind, toughened by physical exercise, flexible, hard, harmonious. She observed him, contented, and caressed him somewhat absentmindedly, but with admiration. She wondered where he was at that moment. Maybe in the arms of another woman? Although he swore fidelity in his letters, Irene knew his physical needs and could visualize dark mulattoes disporting themselves with him. At the Pole, the situation was different; in the middle of that glacial cold and with no company but the penguins and seven men trained to forget love, celibacy was obligatory. Irene felt sure, however, that in the tropics the Captain lived his life differently. She smiled, knowing how little all that mattered to her, and tried, without success, to remember the last time she had felt jealous of her fiancé.

The roar of the motor brought to mind a song from the Spanish Legion that Gustavo Morante often sang:

> *I'm a man who has known fortune's wrath,*
> *Fended off fate's cruel blows in my manner.*
> *I am the Bridegroom of Death,*
> *I have felt her cold breath,*
> *But I hold her love high as my banner.*

It had been a bad idea to sing that song in Francisco's presence, because ever since he had called Gustavo "the Bridegroom of Death." Irene was not offended. In fact, she seldom thought about love; she never questioned her long relationship, but accepted it as a natural condition inscribed in her fate from the time she was a little girl. She had heard so often that Gustavo Morante was her ideal mate that she had come to believe it, without ever examining her feelings. He was solid, stable, virile, a firmly established fact in her life. She thought of herself as a comet soaring on the wind, but at times, frightened by her own internal rebellion, she yielded to the temptation to dream of someone who might curb her impulses. But such states of mind lasted only briefly. When she pondered her future, she tended to become melancholy, and that was her reason for wanting to live her unfettered life as long as she could.

For Francisco, Irene's relationship with her fiancé was nothing more than the sum of two solitudes and many partings. He said that once Irene and Gustavo had the opportunity to be together for a while, each would realize that the only thing keeping them together was the force of habit. There was no urgency in their love; their meetings were placid and their separations too long. Francisco believed that deep down Irene hoped to prolong the engagement to the end of her days, in order to live in conditional freedom, meeting Morante from time to time and romping around like panther cubs. It was clear that she was frightened by marriage and so invented pretexts to postpone it, as if she could foresee that once wed to that prince destined to become a general, she would have to renounce her swirling skirts, jangling bracelets, and exciting life.

That morning, as the motorcycle swallowed up fields and hills en route to Los Riscos, Francisco calculated the number of days remaining before the return of the Bridegroom of

Death. With his arrival everything would change. The happiness of these last months when he had had Irene to himself would disappear; *adiós* to turbulent dreams, days filled with surprises, waiting with anticipation, laughing at her outlandish projects. He would have to be much more cautious, talk only of trivial things, and avoid any suspicious actions. Until then they had shared a serene complicity. Irene seemed to wander through the world in a state of innocence, oblivious—at least, she had never asked questions—to the small signs of his double life. With her he did not have to take precautions, but the arrival of Gustavo Morante would oblige him to be more circumspect. His relationship with Irene was so precious to him that he wanted to keep it intact. Though he did not want to sow their friendship with omissions and lies, he knew that soon lies would be inevitable. He wished they could prolong this journey to the ends of the earth, where the Captain's long shadow could not touch them, that he could travel the country, the continent, the seas, with Irene's arms around his waist. The trip seemed all too brief. As they turned up a narrow lane, they saw broad wheat fields glistening, in that season, like a fine green down on the land. He sighed with a certain sadness as they reached their destination. They had unerringly hit on the place where the saint lived, but were bewildered by the solitude and silence, since they had expected at the least a handful of gullible souls come to watch the phenomenon.

"Are you sure this is it?"

"Sure."

"Then she must be a pretty shabby saint, because there's no one here."

Before them stood the typical house of poor country folk, whitewashed adobe walls, faded roof tiles, a single window, and a small gallery across the front of the house. There was a large patio bounded by a leafless grape arbor, an arabesque of dry and twisted branches where tiny buds announced the summer shade. They could see a well, a small wooden outbuilding that looked like a privy, and beyond that a simple square room that was obviously the kitchen. Several dogs of various sizes and coats rushed to receive the visitors, barking furiously. Irene, accustomed to animals, walked through the pack speaking to the beasts as if she had known them forever. Francisco, in contrast, found himself reciting the magic verses he had learned as a child to ward off such dangers: "Halt, ferocious beast/trail your tail on the ground/God in His Heaven was born/long before you, vicious hound!" But it was obvious that her system was working better, because although she had calmly walked past them, they had surrounded him and were baring their teeth at him. He was preparing to deliver a few murderous kicks to fiery muzzles when a very young child armed with a stick appeared and yelled at the watchdogs, scaring them away. Following this uproar, other people emerged: a graceless, heavyset woman with an air of resignation, a man with a face as shriveled as a winter chestnut, and children of various ages.

"Is this where Evangelina Ranquileo lives?" Irene inquired.

"Yes, but the miracles are at noon."

Irene explained that they were journalists who had been drawn there by the magnitude of the rumors. The family, overcoming their timidity, invited them inside, in accord with the unvarying tradition of hospitality of the inhabitants of that land.

Soon the first visitors began to arrive and made themselves comfortable on the Ranquileos' patio. In the morning light,

Francisco focused on Irene as she was talking with the family, to capture her unawares because she did not like to pose for the camera. Photographs deceive time, she said, freezing it on a piece of cardboard where the soul is silent. The clean air, and her enthusiasm, lent her the air of a woodland creature. She moved about the Ranquileo property with the freedom and confidence of someone born there, talking, laughing, helping serve the refreshments, threading through the dogs that were thumping their tails docilely. The children followed her, astounded by her strange hair, extravagant clothing, constant laughter, and the charm of her movements.

A group of evangelicals arrived with their guitars, flutes, and bass drums, and began to intone hymns under the direction of the Reverend, who turned out to be a tiny man in a shiny jacket and funereal hat. The plaintive chorus and instruments were never quite in tune, though no one except Irene and Francisco seemed to notice. All the others had been hearing the music for several weeks, and by now their ears were accustomed to the discord.

Father Cirilo also appeared, panting from the enormous exertion of pedaling his bicycle from the church to the Ranquileo home. Seated beneath the grape arbor, lost in melancholy divagations or prayers learned by memory, he moved his lips and swayed his white beard, which from a distance looked like a spray of orange blossoms pinned to his chest. Perhaps he had realized that the rosary of Santa Gemita blessed by the hands of the Pope was as ineffective in this case as the chanting of his Protestant colleague or the many-colored pills of the doctor from Los Riscos. From time to time, he consulted his pocket watch to verify the punctuality of the trance. Other persons, lured by the possibility of miracles, sat silent beneath the eaves of the house, in chairs lined up in the shade. Some discussed with deliberation the next planting, or a long-ago soccer match heard over the radio, never at any moment mentioning what had attracted them there, out of respect for the owners of the house, or because they were shy.

Evangelina and her mother attended the guests, offering cool water with toasted flour and honey. Nothing in the girl's aspect appeared in any way abnormal; she seemed tranquil, with a slightly foolish smile on her red-cheeked apple face. She was happy to be the center of attention in this small gathering.

Hipólito Ranquileo spent a long while rounding up the dogs and tying them to the trees. They were barking too much. Then he explained to Francisco that they had to kill one of the bitches because she had dropped a litter the day before and eaten her own whelps, a crime as grave as a hen crowing like a rooster. Certain vices of nature must be rooted out to avoid infecting other animals. On this subject he was very delicate.

It was at this point that the Reverend planted himself in the center of the patio and began an impassioned discourse delivered at the top of his lungs. All those present listened, not wanting to slight him, although it was evident that everyone except the evangelicals felt uncomfortable. "Rising prices! The high cost of living! This is a well-known problem. There is more than one way to stop it: jail, fines, strikes, among others. What is the heart of the problem? What is its cause? What is this ball of fire that inflames man's greed? Behind it all lies a dangerous tendency toward the sin of avarice, the unrestrained appetite for earthly pleasure. This leads man away from our Holy Lord, it produces human, moral, economic, and spiritual instability, it unleashes the ire of our Lord God Almighty. Our times are like the times of Sodom and Gomorrah, man has fallen into the dark paths of error, and now he is harvesting his measure of punishment for having turned his back on his Creator. Jehovah is sending His warning in order that we may reflect on our ways and repent of our loathsome sins—"

"Excuse me, Reverend, would you like some refreshment?" Evangelina interrupted, cutting the thread of inspiration with flaws still to be enumerated.

One of the Protestant disciples, a squat and cross-eyed woman, went over to Irene to explain her theory about the Ranquileos' daughter: "Beelzebub, prince of devils, has entered her body. Write that in your magazine, *señorita*. He likes to aggravate Christians, but the Salvation Army is stronger than he is, and we will vanquish him. Put that in your magazine—don't forget."

Father Cirilo heard her last words, took Irene by the arm, and led her aside. "Pay no attention to her. These evangelicals are ignorant as sin, my daughter. They are not of the true faith, although they have some good qualities, we can't deny that. Do you know they are abstemious? In that sect even confirmed alcoholics stop drinking. I respect them for that. But the Devil has nothing to do with this. The girl is crazy, pure and simple."

"And the miracles?"

"What miracles are you talking about? Don't believe that humbug!"

Minutes before noon, Evangelina Ranquileo left the patio and went into the house. She unbuttoned her sweater, let down her hair, and seated herself on one of the three beds. Outside, everyone fell silent, moving to the small gallery to watch through the door and the window. Irene and Francisco followed the girl inside, and while he adjusted his camera to the darkness Irene readied the tape recorder.

The Ranquileo home had a dirt floor, so tamped down, dampened, and tamped down again that it had acquired the consistency of cement. The sparse pieces of furniture were of ordinary unfinished wood; there were a few rush chairs and stools, a rough, homemade wooden table, and, as the only decoration, an image of Jesus with a flaming heart. The girls' beds were curtained off from the rest of the room. The boys slept on pallets on the floor in an adjacent room with a separate entrance, thus avoiding promiscuity among brothers and sisters. Everything was scrupulously clean and smelled of mint and thyme; a bunch of red geraniums in a jar brightened the window, and the table was spread with a green linen cloth. Francisco saw in these simple elements a profound aesthetic sense and decided that later he would take a few photographs for his collection. He was never able to do so.

At twelve o'clock noon Evangelina fell back on the bed. Her body trembled and a deep long moan, like a love call, ran through her. She began to shake convulsively; her body arched backward with superhuman force. The girlish expression of a few minutes earlier was erased from her disfigured face and she was suddenly years older. A grimace of ecstasy, pain, or lust marked her features. The bed was rocking, and Irene, terrified, could see that a table a few feet from it was moving with no visible cause. Fear conquered her curiosity and she moved toward Francisco, seeking protection; she took his arm and pressed close to him, mesmerized by the spectacle of madness taking place on the bed, but her friend gently disentangled himself in order to operate the camera. Outside, the dogs howled an interminable lamentation of catastrophe in accompaniment to the sounds of song and prayer. Tin utensils danced in the cupboard, and a strange clatter lashed the roof tiles like a hailstorm of pebbles. A continuous tremor shook a platform in the rafters where the family stored their provisions, seeds, and work tools. From overhead a rain of maize was escaping from the seed sacks, contributing to the sensation of nightmare. On the bed, Evangelina Ranquileo writhed and twisted, the victim of impenetrable hallucinations and mysterious urgencies. The father, dark-skinned, toothless, with his pathetic sad clown's face, watched glumly from the threshold, without moving closer. The mother stood beside the bed, her eyes rolled back in her head, perhaps attempting to hear the silence of God. Inside and outside the house, hope seized the pilgrims. One by one they drew near Evangelina to request their small, humble miracles.

"Cure my carbuncles, *santita.*"

"Don't let them take my Juan off to the Army."

"God save you, Evangelina, full of grace. Heal my poor husband's hemorrhoids."

"Give me a sign—what number should I play in the lottery?"

"Stop the rain, handmaiden of God, before my goddam seeds rot in the ground."

Those who had come motivated by faith, or simply as a desperate measure, filed by in orderly fashion, pausing an instant beside the young girl to offer their plea, and then moved on, transfigured by the confidence that through His intermediary they would be favored by Divine Providence.

No one heard the Army truck pull up.

They heard commands, and before anyone could react, the soldiers invaded in a body, occupying the patio and rushing into the house with weapons in hand. They shoved people aside, scattered the children with their shouts, used their rifle butts to beat anyone who stood in their way, and filled the air with loud orders.

"Face the wall! Hands behind your head!" bawled the bull-necked officer in command.

Everyone obeyed except Evangelina Ranquileo, imperturbable in her trance, and Irene Beltrán, frozen in her tracks, too shocked to be able to move.

"Your documents!" bellowed a sergeant with Indian features.

"I am a journalist and he is a photographer," said Irene in a steady voice, pointing to her friend.

They frisked Francisco, slapping his ribs, armpits, crotch, and shoes.

"Turn around," they commanded.

The officer they would later come to know as Lieutenant Juan de Dios Ramírez stuck the barrel of his machine gun in Francisco's ribs.

"Name!"

"Francisco Leal."

"What the shit do you two think you're doing here?"

"We're doing an article, not shit," Irene interrupted.

"I'm not talking to you!"

"But I'm talking to you, Captain," she smiled, ironically raising his grade.

The officer hesitated, unaccustomed to impertinence from a civilian.

"Ranquileo!" he called.

Immediately, a dark-haired giant, armed with a rifle and with an addled look on his face, stepped forward from the troops and stood at attention before his superior officer.

"Is this your sister?" The lieutenant pointed to Evangelina, who was in another world, lost in tenebrous copulation with the spirits.

"Affirmative, Lieutenant!" the man replied, rigid, heels together, chest expanded, eyes front, face like granite.

At that instant a new and more violent rain of invisible stones lashed the roof. The officer sprawled face-down on the floor, imitated by his men. Stupefied, the others watched them slither on elbows and knees to the patio, where they sprang to their feet and zigzagged to take up positions. From behind the laundry trough, the lieutenant began firing in the direction of the house. It was a prearranged signal. Maddened soldiers, crazed by uncontrollable violence, squeezed their triggers, and in seconds the air was filled with noise, shouts, sobs, barking, crowing, and gusts of gunpowder. The people on the patio threw themselves to the ground; some took shelter in the irrigation ditch or behind trees. The evangelicals attempted to rescue their musical instruments, and Father Cirilo ducked beneath the table, clutching the rosary of Santa Gemita and crying out to heaven for the Lord of All Armies to protect him.

Francisco Leal saw that bullets were striking close to the window; some penetrated the thick adobe walls like a burst of dark omens. He seized Irene by the waist and threw her to the floor, shielding her with his body. He felt her trembling in his arms, not knowing whether she was suffocating from his weight or shivering with fear. The moment the shouting and terror subsided, he got up and ran to the door, sure that he would find a half-dozen corpses; the only cadaver that met his eyes, however, was that of a chicken with its guts shot out. The soldiers were out of breath, possessed with madness, beside themselves with power. Neighbors and curiosity seekers lay on the ground, covered with dust and mud; children were crying; and the dogs were straining at their leashes, frenziedly barking.

Francisco felt Irene pass by his side like an exhalation, and before he could stop her, she was standing in front of the lieutenant with her hands on her hips, shouting in an unrecognizable voice: "Savages! Beasts! Who do you think you are! Don't you know you could kill somebody?"

Francisco ran toward her, certain the lieutenant would place a bullet between her eyes, but was astounded to see that the officer was laughing.

"Don't be so nervous, honey, we were firing in the air."

"Don't call me 'honey'! And what are you doing here in the first place?" Irene scolded, unable to control her nerves.

"Ranquileo here told me about his sister, and I said to him: 'Where priests and doctors have failed, the armed forces will triumph.' That's what I told him, and that's why we're here. We'll see if the kid keeps having her fits once I've taken her prisoner!"

He strode in the direction of the house. Irene and Francisco followed like automatons. What happened then would remain engraved in their memories, and they would remember it as a succession of turbulent and disconnected images.

Lieutenant Juan de Dios Ramírez marched over to Evangelina's bed. The mother made a move to stop him, but he pushed her aside. Don't touch her! the mother managed to scream, but she was too late; the officer had already reached out and grasped the afflicted girl's arm.

Before anyone could have predicted it, Evangelina's fist flashed out and cracked against the officer's ruddy face, striking him in the nose with such force that he tumbled backward to the floor. Like a useless ball, his helmet rolled beneath the table. The girl immediately lost her rigidity, her eyes were no longer wild, she stopped foaming at the mouth. The person who effortlessly seized Lieutenant Ramírez's tunic, lifted him into the air, and carried him out of the house, shaking him like a mop, was a gentle fifteen-year-old girl with fragile bones, who not long before had been serving cool water with toasted flour and honey beneath the grape arbor. Only the prodigious strength betrayed her abnormal state. Irene reacted swiftly. She snatched the camera from Francisco's hands and began to snap pictures, ignoring the aperture, hoping that some shots would come out in spite of the abrupt change in light intensity between the interior shadows and the reverberating light of midday.

Through the lens Irene saw Evangelina haul the lieutenant to the center of the patio and with total indifference throw him to within a few meters of the Protestants who crouched there trembling. The officer tried to struggle to his feet, but she struck a few well-aimed blows to his neck that forced him back to the ground; she kicked him several times without rage, ignoring the soldiers who had surrounded her and aimed their weapons but in their shock did not dare fire. The girl seized the machine gun Ramírez still held clutched to his breast and hurled it aside. It fell in a mudhole where it sank before the impassive snout of a pig that snuffled at it, then watched it disappear, swallowed up in the mire.

At that moment Francisco Leal came to his senses and remembered his training as a psychologist. He approached Evangelina Ranquileo and gently but firmly tapped her on the shoulder, calling her by name. The girl seemed to return from a long somnambulistic journey. She lowered her head, smiled timidly, and went and sat beneath the arbor, while the uniformed soldiers ran to recover the machine gun, clean off the muck, look for the helmet, give aid to their superior officer, help him to his feet, brush off his clothing. Are you all right, Lieutenant? Trembling, the pale officer pushed them aside, clapped the helmet on his head and grabbed his weapon, unable to find in all his vast repertoire of violence any action adequate for this situation.

Motionless, terrorized, everyone waited for some atrocious response, some dark madness, some final calamity that would mean the end of all of them; they expected to be lined up against the wall and shot on the spot, or at least to be kicked into the Army truck and "helped" to disappear in some mountain ravine. After a long moment of hesitation, however, Lieutenant Juan de Dios Ramírez turned and walked toward the truck.

"Retreat, assholes!" he shouted, and his men followed him.

Pradelio Ranquileo, Evangelina's oldest brother, with a stunned, sick expression on his dark face, was the last to obey, reacting only when he heard the roar of the engine. He ran and jumped into the rear of the truck beside his companions. Then the officer remembered the photographs, issued an order, and the sergeant turned and trotted to Irene; he took the camera from her, removed the roll of film and exposed it to the light. Then he tossed the apparatus over his shoulder as if it were an empty beer can.

After the soldiers departed, a total silence reigned in the patio of the Ranquileos. Everyone was frozen in his purpose, as in a bad dream.

Suddenly, Evangelina's voice broke the spell: "May I serve you another refreshment, Reverend?"

And then they could breathe, they could move, recover their belongings, and shamefacedly leave.

"God save us," sighed Father Cirilo, brushing off his dust-covered cassock.

"And keep us," added the Protestant pastor, white as a rabbit.

Irene recovered the camera. She alone was smiling. Once her fright had passed, she remembered only the grotesqueness of what had happened; she was thinking about the title of her article, and wondering whether censorship would permit her to mention the name of the officer who had received the drubbing.

"That was a bad idea my son had, to bring the soldiers," Hipólito Ranquileo offered.

"Very bad," added his wife.

Shortly afterward, Irene and Francisco returned to the city. She was hugging a huge bunch of flowers to her breast, a gift from the Ranquileo children. She was in a good mood, and seemed to have forgotten the incident, as if she had not the slightest idea of the danger they had been in. Apparently the only thing that bothered her was the loss of the film; without it, it would be impossible to publish the information, because no one would ever believe such a story. She consoled herself with the thought that they could return the following Sunday and take new photographs of Evangelina during her trance. The Ranquileos had asked them to come again, since they were planning to slaughter a hog, an annual fiesta that brought together a number of neighbors for a barbaric feast. In contrast, Francisco's indignation mounted throughout the return trip, and by the time he left Irene at her door he could scarcely contain himself.

"Why are you so angry, Francisco? It was only some bullets fired in the air, and a mangled hen," she laughed as she said goodbye.

Until then he had tried to shield her from the unresolvable misery, the injustice and repression that he experienced daily and that were normal topics of conversation in the Leal household. He thought it extraordinary that Irene could sail innocently across the sea of anguish inundating the country, absorbed only in the picturesque and anecdotal. He was amazed to see her floating on air, untouched, buoyed up by her good intentions. Her unjustified optimism, her clean, fresh vitality provided a balm for the torments he suffered knowing he was powerless to change them. That day, nevertheless, he was tempted to take her by the shoulders and shake her until her feet touched the ground and she opened her eyes to the truth. But when he saw her standing by the stone wall of her house, her arms laden with wildflowers for her elderly friends and her hair tangled by the motorcycle ride, he felt that this creature was not made for sordid realities. He kissed her on the cheek, as close as possible to her lips, desiring passionately to remain forever by her side to protect her from the shadows. She smelt of herbs and her skin was cold.

— PART TWO —

Shadows

The warm earth still guards their last secrets.

—Vicente Huidobro

*F*rom the time he started working for the magazine, Francisco had felt as if he were living a life of perpetual surprises. The city was divided by an invisible frontier that he was regularly obliged to cross. The same day that he photographed exquisite dresses of muslin and lace, in his brother José's barrio he treated the little girl who had been raped by her father, then carried the latest list of victims to the airport where, after reciting the password, he delivered it to a messenger he had never seen before. He had one foot in compulsory illusion and the other in secret reality. In each situation, he had to adjust his frame of mind to the demands of the moment, but at the end of the day, in the silence of his room, he would review the day's events and conclude that in facing the daily challenge his best course was not to think much at all, to avoid being immobilized by fear or rage. At that hour the image of Irene would grow in the shadows until it filled the room.

Wednesday night he dreamed of a field of daisies. Normally he did not remember his dreams, but the flowers were so fresh in his mind that he woke up convinced he must have been outdoors. At the office, midway through the morning, he ran into the astrologer, the woman with the coffee-black hair who was determined to tell his fortune.

"I can read it in your eyes, you've come from a night of love," she said the minute she met him on the stairs to the fifth floor.

Francisco invited her to have a beer and, lacking other cosmic signs to aid her in her predictions, told her his dream.

She informed him that daisies are a sign of good luck, and that he could count on something pleasant happening to him within the next few hours.

"That's some consolation, my friend," she added, "because you've been marked by the finger of death." She had told him this so often that the prediction no longer frightened him.

His respect for the astrologer increased, however, when shortly after her prediction was fulfilled: Irene called his house and said she wanted to meet the Leals, and asked him to invite her to dinner. They had scarcely seen each other during the week. The fashion editor had wanted to take a series of photographs in the Military Academy, and Francisco was tied up with the assignment. That season, romantic dresses with bows and flounces were in style, and the editor envisioned contrasting them with heavy artillery and uniformed men. For his part, the Commandant believed that this was an opportunity to present the armed forces in a more favorable light and, after increasing security measures, opened his doors to them. Francisco and the rest of the crew spent several days inside the military compound, at the end of which time he did not know whether he was more repelled by the patriotic hymns and military ceremonies or by the three beauty queens who posed for his camera. Both entering and leaving, they were subjected to a rigorous inspection. Amid a level of confusion akin to an earthquake, the guards turned their cases inside out, pawing through dresses, shoes, and wigs, prodding everything with their electronic equipment in search of any hint of covert activities. The models began the day with expressions of utter boredom, and spent the rest of the day complaining. It was the mission of Mario, the elegant and discreet stylist always dressed in white, to transform the models before each photograph. He was aided by two assistants, recently initiated into the homosexual world, who darted about him like two fire-flies. Francisco, who was responsible for the cameras and film, had to force himself to remain calm if the guards exposed a roll during their inspection and ruined the day's work.

This traveling show, unsettling to anyone not accustomed to such a spectacle, caused some minor breakdowns in Academy discipline. The soldiers who were not excited by the beauty queens were distracted by the assistants, who flirted with them unrelentingly, much to Mario's annoyance. He had no tolerance for bad taste, and years ago had conquered any tendency toward promiscuity. He had come from a miner's family of eleven children. He had been born and raised in a gray town where the dust from the mines coated everything with an impalpable and deadly patina of ugliness and choked the lungs of the inhabitants, turning them into shadows of themselves. He was destined to follow in the footsteps of his father, his grandfather, and his brothers, but he had no taste for crawling into the entrails of the earth to dig at living rock, or for facing the backbreaking labor of a miner. He had delicate hands and a spirit inclined toward fantasy, a quality his father had tried to beat out of him. Drastic measures had not, however, cured his effeminate mannerisms or altered his inclinations. As a child, if the family turned their backs for an instant, he slipped away to entertain himself in solitary pastimes that provoked pitiless ridicule: he gathered stones from the river and polished them for the pleasure of seeing colors shine; he scouted the dismal landscape looking for dry leaves to arrange in artistic compositions; he was moved to tears by a sunset, wanting to capture it forever in a line of poetry or in a painting he could imagine but felt incapable of realizing. Only his mother accepted his peculiarities, seeing them not as signs of perversion but as evidence of a soul that was different. To save him from his father's merciless floggings, she took him to the parish priest to enroll him as an assistant to the sacristan, hoping to disguise his womanly gentleness among the skirts of the mass and offerings of incense. The boy's mind always wandered from his dog Latin, however, diverted by the golden particles floating in the light that streamed through the church windows. The priest overlooked his ramblings and taught him arithmetic, reading, and writing, and some rudiments of culture. At fifteen, Mario knew almost by heart the few books in the sacristy, as well as others lent him by the Turk who ran the general store and whose aim was to lure him into the room behind the store and there reveal to him the mechanisms of pleasure between men. When his father learned of these visits, he led Mario by the ear to the mine whorehouse, accompanied by his two older brothers. There, with a dozen men impatient to spend their Friday wages, they waited their turn. Only Mario noticed the filthy, faded curtains, the stench of urine and Lysol, the infinite desolation of the place. Only he was moved by the melancholy of those women exhausted by wear and the absence of love. Threatened by his brothers, when his turn came he tried to play the macho with the prostitute, but she needed only a glance at the boy to see that he was destined for a life filled with mockery and solitude. She was moved with compassion when she saw him trembling with revulsion at the sight of her naked flesh, and she asked the men to leave them alone so she could do her job in peace. As soon as the others left, she bolted the door, sat on the bed beside Mario, and took his hand.

"This isn't something you can be forced to do," she said to Mario, who was weeping with terror. "Go away, far away, boy, where no one knows you, because if you stay around here they'll end up killing you."

In all his life he had never received better advice. He dried his tears and promised never to spill them again over a manliness that in his heart he did not desire.

"If you don't fall in love, you will go far," the woman told him as she said goodbye. Then she pacified his father, thus sparing Mario another thrashing.

That night Mario talked with his mother and told her what had happened. She reached into the back of her cupboard, pulled out a small roll of wrinkled bills, and put them in her son's hands. With that money, he took the train to the capital and found work sweeping up at a beauty salon in exchange for his food and a place to sleep, a straw mattress in the salon itself. He was dazzled. He had never imagined the existence of such a world: bright colors, delicate perfumes, smiling voices, frivolity, warmth, leisure. He marveled as he watched, in the mirror, the hands of professionals dressing the clients' hair. Seeing the women unveiled, he learned about the feminine soul. At night, alone in the salon, he practiced hairstyles on the wigs, and tried shadows, powders, and pencils on his own face to learn the skills of the art of cosmetics, and so discovered how to improve a face with colors and brushes. Soon he was allowed to work on new clients, and in a few months he was cutting hair better than anyone, and the most demanding ladies were requesting his services. He was able to transform a woman of ordinary appearance, using the frame of a nimbus of hair and the artifice of cosmetics skillfully applied; even more, however, he convinced each one of her attractiveness, because, finally, beauty is merely an attitude. He began to study with dedication, and to practice audaciously what he learned, helped by an infallible instinct that inevitably led him to the best solution. He was sought after by brides, models, actresses, and the wives of foreign ambassadors. Wealthy and influential ladies of the city opened their doors to him, and for the first time the miner's son walked on Oriental rugs, drank tea from translucent porcelain, and admired the glow of wrought silver, polished wood, and delicate crystal. He quickly learned to distinguish objects of real value, and vowed that he would never be satisfied with less, because his spirit suffered when he was faced with any form of vulgarity. Once he was a member of the inner circle of art and culture, he knew he could never go back. He gave free rein to his creativity and his entrepreneurial vision, and within a few years he was the owner of the most prestigious beauty salon in the capital and a small antique shop that served as a front for discreet deals. He became an expert in works of art, fine furniture, and luxury items, and was consulted by people in high positions. He was always busy, always in a hurry, but he never forgot that his first real opportunity had come to him through the magazine where Irene Beltrán worked, and any time they requested him for a style show or an article on fashion and beauty, he set aside whatever he was doing and showed up with the famous kit of wigs that were the tools of his trade. He became so influential that at elegant social affairs ladies wearing his outré maquillage proudly displayed his signature on their left cheek like a Bedouin's tattoo.

When he met Francisco Leal, Mario was a mature man with a narrow, straight nose—the result of plastic surgery— an artificial tan, a slender, trim physique won at the price of diets, exercise, and massage, a man impeccably dressed in the best English and Italian clothes—in sum, he was cultivated, refined, and famous. He moved in exclusive circles and, under the pretext of buying antiques, traveled extensively. He lived like an aristocrat, but he never denied his humble origins; any time the subject of his mining-town past arose, he spoke of it with tact and good humor. His simplicity won the sympathy of people who would not have forgiven his inventing a fictitious family tree. In exclusive circles, those to which one was admitted only by family name or great wealth, Mario was respected for his fine taste and his ease in good company. No important gathering was considered a success without him. He never returned to the house where he was born, nor ever again saw his father or brothers, but every month he sent a check to his mother to provide her with certain comforts and to help his sisters study for a profession, set up a business, or marry with a dowry. His sentimental involvements were discreetly expressed, never strident, like everything else in his life.

When Irene introduced Mario to Francisco Leal, only a slight gleam in his eyes betrayed the impression Francisco made on him. Irene noticed, and later teased her friend, telling him he should guard himself against the hairdresser's advances if he did not want to end up with an earring in his ear and a soprano voice. Two weeks later, they were both in the studio working with the new cosmetics of the season when Captain Gustavo Morante came by to look for Irene. His face changed when he saw Mario. The Captain had a violent antipathy to effeminate men, and it bothered him that his fiancée worked in a place where she brushed elbows with someone he considered a degenerate. Mario was absorbed in stroking golden frost onto the cheeks of a beautiful model, and his instinct failed him; he did not see the Captain's disapproval and, with a smile, held out his hand to him. Gustavo folded his arms across his chest, staring at Mario with unveiled scorn, and said, sorry, he never had anything to do with fairies. A glacial silence fell over the studio. Irene, the assistants, the models, everyone, stood frozen in consternation. Mario paled, and a shadow of pain clouded his eyes. Francisco Leal put down his camera, walked slowly forward, and placed his hand on the stylist's shoulder.

"You know why you don't want to touch him, Captain? Because you're afraid of your own feelings. Maybe all that rough camaraderie at the barracks is just a cover for homosexuality," Francisco said in his usual deliberate and amiable tone.

Before Gustavo Morante could appreciate the gravity of the statement, or react in accordance with his upbringing, Irene stepped in; she seized her fiancé by the arm and dragged him from the room. Mario never forgot the incident. A few days later, he invited Francisco to dinner. Mario lived on the top floor of a fashionable building. His apartment was decorated in black and white, in a tasteful, modern, and original style. Geometric lines of steel and crystal were softened by three or four very old baroque pieces and by Chinese silk tapestries. On one of the soft area rugs purred two Angora cats, and near the hearth where hawthorn logs were blazing dozed a sleek black dog. I adore animals, said Mario as he greeted Francisco. Francisco saw two goblets beside an ice bucket where a bottle of champagne was cooling; he noticed the soft lights, smelled the aroma of the wood fire and incense burning in a bronze censer; he heard the jazz from the hi-fi speakers, and realized he was the only guest. For an instant, he was tempted to turn and walk out, to avoid raising any hope in his host's heart, but his desire not to hurt Mario, to gain his friendship, won out. As he looked in Mario's eyes, Francisco was moved by a mixture of pity and sympathy. He searched among his gentlest emotions for the one most appropriate to give to the man who was timidly offering him his love. He sat down beside Mario on the raw-silk sofa and accepted a glass of champagne, calling on his professional experience to help him steer through uncharted waters without doing something foolish. It was a night they both remembered. Mario told Francisco his life story, and delicately hinted at his growing passion. He anticipated a refusal, but he was too moved not to voice his emotions; no man had ever appealed to him so strongly. Francisco combined virile strength and assurance with the rare quality of gentleness. Mario did not fall in love easily; he distrusted stormy affairs, the cause of much unpleasantness in the past. He was prepared this once, however, to risk everything. Francisco also talked about himself and, without overtly saying so, communicated to Mario the possibility of sharing a solid and deep friendship, but never love. Through that long evening they discovered shared interests, laughed, listened to music, and drank champagne. In a burst of confidence forbidden by the most elementary caution, Mario spoke of his revulsion for the dictatorship and his desire to oppose it. His new friend, able to read the truth in his eyes, offered his secret in return. When they said goodbye, shortly before the hour of curfew, they exchanged a firm handshake, sealing a pact of solidarity.

Following that dinner, Mario and Francisco not only worked together at the magazine, but also in subversive activities. There was never a hint from the stylist of his feelings, of anything that might cloud their friendship. He was a very open person, and Francisco came to doubt that Mario had spoken as he had that memorable night. Irene became the third member of the group, even though they never included her in clandestine activities: by birth and education she belonged to the opposite camp, she had never shown any interest in politics, and, last but not least, she was the fiancée of a military man.

That day at the Military Academy, Mario's patience had worn thin. In addition to the security checks, the heat, and collective bad humor, there was his assistants' constant prancing before the soldiers.

"I'm going to get rid of them, Francisco. These two idiots have no class, and they never will. I should have thrown them into the street the day I found them wrapped in each other's arms in the rest room at the office."

Francisco Leal had also had his fill, primarily because it had been several days since he had seen Irene. Their schedules had not coincided at the office, and by the time she called to announce her wish to come to dinner, he was desperate to see her.

At the Leal home, painstaking preparations to welcome Irene were in progress. Hilda cooked one of her favorite dishes and the Professor bought wine and a bouquet of the first flowers of the season, because he admired the girl and felt that her presence was like a fresh breeze that swept away boredom and worry. They invited their other sons, José and Javier, and his family, because they liked to see them at least once a week.

Francisco had just finished developing a roll of film in the bathroom that served as his darkroom when he heard Irene arrive. He hung up the strips of negatives, dried his hands, locked the door to protect his work from his nephews' curiosity, and hurried to greet Irene. The smells from the kitchen washed over him like a caress. He heard the sound of high childish voices, and supposed that everyone was in the dining room. Then he saw Irene, and felt struck with good fortune; she was wearing a dress printed with daisies, and in her hair, which she had pulled back into a braid, she had tied several of the same flowers. It was the synthesis of his dream and the astrologer's good omens.

Hilda entered the dining room carrying a steaming platter in her hands, and was greeted by a chorus of exclamations.

"Mondongo!" breathed Francisco unhesitatingly, for he would recognize that aroma of tomato and bay leaf at the very bottom of the sea.

"I *hate* mondongo! It tastes like an old towel!" groaned one of the children.

Francisco broke off a piece of bread, dipped it in the flavorful gravy, and took a bite, while his mother, assisted by her daughter-in-law, served the plates. Only Francisco's older brother Javier seemed indifferent to the excitement. He sat silent and removed, toying with a cord. Recently, the only thing that gave him any pleasure was tying knots, knots of all kinds: sailor's, fisherman's, and cowboy's knots; knots for halters, fishing lines, and stirrups; knots to hold hooks, keys, and guy wires; knots he tied and untied with incomprehensible compulsiveness. At first his children had watched with fascination, but subsequently they learned to imitate him, and lost interest in the cord. They were used to seeing their father absorbed in his mania, a peaceable vice that harmed no one. The only dissent came from his wife, who complained of the roughness of his hands calloused by the accursed rope that lay coiled next to their bed every night like a domesticated snake.

"I don't like mondongo!" the child repeated.

"Then have some sardines," his grandmother suggested.

"No! They have eyes!"

The priest struck the table with his fist, rattling the dishes. No one moved.

"That's enough! Eat what you're served," José exclaimed. "Do you know how many people have nothing to eat all day but a cup of tea and a piece of bread? Where I live, children are fainting from hunger in the schoolroom!"

Hilda touched his arm in supplication, implying that if he began talking about the people going hungry in his parish, he risked ruining the family dinner, along with his father's liver. José lowered his head, confused by his own anger. Years of experience had not quelled his fits of rage, or his obsession to see all people treated as equals. Irene broke the tension by toasting the mondongo, and everyone joined in, celebrating the aroma, the texture and taste, and, especially, its proletarian origins.

"What a shame Neruda didn't write an ode to mondongo," observed Francisco.

"But he did write one to conger chowder. Do you want to hear it?" his father offered enthusiastically. He was silenced by a chorus of boos.

Professor Leal was no longer offended by their teasing. His sons had grown up listening to him recite poetry from memory and read the classics aloud, although only the youngest had been infected with his enthusiasm for literature. Francisco was by temperament less exuberant, however, and preferred to indulge his tastes in disciplined reading and in secretly writing poetry, leaving to his father the privilege of declaiming whenever the mood seized him. Sons and grandsons no longer listened. Only Hilda, occasionally in the intimacy of nightfall, asked him to recite. On those occasions, she put aside her knitting and gave him her complete attention; as she pondered the many years of love she had shared with this man, her face was as full of wonder as it had been at their first meeting.

When the Civil War broke out in Spain, they had been young and in love. In spite of Professor Leal's belief that war was obscene, he set off with the Republicans for the battle-front. His wife tied up a bundle of clothing, closed the door of her house without a backward glance, and traveled from village to village, following his movements. They wanted to be together at the hour they were surprised by victory, defeat, or death. Two autumns later, their first son was born in an improvised shelter amid the ruins of a convent. His father did not hold him in his arms until three weeks afterward. In December of the same year, for Christmas, a bomb destroyed the place where Hilda and the baby were temporarily housed. She heard the deafening roar that preceded the catastrophe, and as the roof collapsed, crushing her, she managed to tighten her hold on the baby in her arms and bend over like a closed book; with that act she had saved her baby's life. They rescued the child unharmed, but Hilda suffered a serious skull fracture and a broken arm. For some time Leal lost track of them, but after searching everywhere he found her in a field hospital where she lay without even knowing her name, her memory erased, void of past or future, and with her child suckling at her breast. When the war was over, Professor Leal decided that they must try to reach France. He was refused permission to remove the injured woman from the refuge where she was recuperating, and he had to steal her away by night. He laid her on two large planks mounted on four wheels, placed the baby in her good arm, secured them with a blanket, and dragged them along the roads of sorrow leading to exile. He crossed the frontier with a wife who did not recognize him and whose only sign of reason was singing to her infant. He went without money, he had no friend, he limped because of a bullet wound in his thigh, but he never faltered in his effort to save his loved ones. His only personal belonging was an old slide rule, inherited from his father, that he had used in reconstructing buildings and plotting trenches in the battlefield. On the other side of the border, French police awaited the endless caravan of the defeated. They took the men aside and placed them under arrest. Professor Leal fought like a wild man, trying to explain his predicament; and he had to be dragged forcibly to the detention area.

A French postman found the makeshift wagon on the

road. He approached it suspiciously after hearing a baby's cry; he pulled back the blanket, and saw a young woman with a bandaged head, one arm in a sling, and the other cradling an infant crying from the cold. He took the pair to his house and, with his wife, began the difficult task of caring for them. Through an organization of English Quakers dedicated to charitable works and to helping the refugees, he located Leal on a beach enclosed by high wire fences, where the men passed the day in idleness, eyes scanning the horizon, and where they slept at night buried in the sand, waiting for better times. Leal was nearly mad with anxiety, frantic about Hilda and his son. When he heard from the postman's lips that they were safe, he bowed his head and, for the first time in his adult life, wept and wept. The Frenchman waited, looking out to sea, unable to find a word or gesture to offer in consolation. As he said goodbye to Leal, the postman noticed that he was trembling; he removed his overcoat and, flushing, handed it to Leal. Thus began a friendship that was to last half a century. He helped the Spaniard obtain a passport, resolve his legal situation, and win his release from the refugee camp. Meanwhile his wife tended to Hilda's every need. The Frenchwoman was a practical person, and she combated Hilda's amnesia with a method of her own invention. Since she knew no Spanish, she used a dictionary to identify objects and emotions, going over them one by one. Sitting at Hilda's side for hours, this extraordinary woman patiently worked through the dictionary from A to Z, repeating each word until comprehension gleamed in the sick woman's eyes. Little by little, Hilda recovered her memory. The first face she glimpsed through the mist was that of her husband, then she remembered the name of their son, and finally, in a dizzying torrent, the events of the past came flooding to her mind—beauty, courage, love, laughter. Perhaps in that instant Hilda made up her mind to be selective in her memories, to lighten the ballast in the new journey they were undertaking, knowing intuitively that she must devote all her strength toward building their destiny as emigrants. It was better to erase the pain of nostalgia, homeland, family, and friends left behind, never to speak of them again. She seemed to have forgotten her stone house, and in the years that followed, it was pointless for her husband even to mention it. Hilda gave the impression of having suppressed that memory completely, along with many other recollections. Yet she had never been more lucid in assessing the present and planning the future, and faced her new life with assurance and enthusiasm.

On the day that the Leals set sail for the other side of the globe, the postman and his wife, in their best Sunday clothes, came to the dock to tell them goodbye. Their small figures were the last thing the Leals saw as the ship set out to open sea. Until the coast of Europe vanished in the distance, all the voyagers stood at the rail singing songs of the Spanish Republic in voices hoarse from weeping; all, that is, except Hilda, standing confidently in the bow, the baby in her arms, gazing toward the future.

The Leals wandered the lonely roads of exile; they adjusted to poverty; they looked for work, made friends, and settled into their life on the other side of the world, overcoming the initial paralysis of the uprooted. They found a new strength born of suffering and necessity. To sustain them in their difficulties, they counted on a love that withstood all tests, a love greater than most people possessed. Forty years later, they still maintained their correspondence with the French postman and his wife, because each of the four was blessed with a generous heart and a clear mind.

That night at the table, the Professor was euphoric. The presence of Irene Beltrán stirred his eloquence. The girl listened to his speech on solidarity with the fascination of a child at a puppet show; his exalted orations were light-years away from her world. As he extolled the superior qualities of humankind—ignoring thousands of years of history demonstrating the contrary, and convinced that one generation is all that is necessary to create a superior conscience and a better society if the essential conditions are fulfilled—Irene, entranced, let her food grow cold on her plate. The Professor argued that power is perverse, and that it always falls into the hands of the dregs of humanity, because in the scramble only the most violent and bloodthirsty triumph. It therefore becomes necessary to combat *any* form of government, and to allow men their freedom under an egalitarian system.

"Governments are intrinsically corrupt, and must be eliminated. They guarantee the freedom of the rich, based on property, and they enslave the rest in misery," he pontificated before an astounded Irene.

"For someone who fled one dictatorship and lives in another, hatred of authority can be a serious handicap," mused José, slightly bored after years of having listened to the same flaming oratory.

Over the years, his sons had stopped taking Professor Leal seriously, and worried only about preventing him from committing some truly rash act. In their childhood they had often had to help him, but as soon as they became adults, they had left him to his speeches and had never again run the printing press in the kitchen or set foot in a political meeting. Following the Soviet invasion of Hungary in 1956, even their father abandoned the Party, nearly crushed by disillusion. For days he had suffered from an alarming depression, but soon his confidence in the destiny of humankind rekindled his spirit, helping him overcome his disenchantment and cope with the doubts that were tormenting him. Without renouncing his ideals of justice and equality, he came to the conclusion that man's first right is that of freedom; he removed the portraits of Lenin and Marx from the living room and installed one of Mikhail Bakunin. From today on, he announced, I am an anarchist. None of his sons knew what that meant, and for a while they believed it was a religious sect, or perhaps a group of lunatics. That ideology, out of style and blown away by the winds of the postwar era, left them unconcerned. They accused their father of being the only anarchist in the country, and they may have been right. After the military coup, to protect him from his own excesses, Francisco removed an essential part from the printing press. This was necessary if they were to prevent him from going to any lengths to print his opinions and distribute them throughout the city, as he had always done. Later, José was able to convince his father that it would be best to get rid of the useless relic, and he took the machine to his barrio where, once repaired, cleaned, and oiled, it was used to print assignments for the school during the day and bulletins of solidarity by night. Happily, this precaution saved Professor Leal when the political police raided the neighborhood, house by house. It would have been difficult to explain the presence of a printing press in their kitchen. The sons tried to reason with their father, explaining that his solitary and pointless actions brought more harm than good to the cause of democracy; but with the least relaxation of their attention, he returned to the danger, driven by his burning ideals.

"Be careful, Papa," they begged when they learned of the slogans attacking the military Junta he had thrown from the balconies of the Post Office Building.

"I'm too old to go around with my tail tucked between my legs," the Professor replied impassively.

"If anything happens to you, I will stick my head in the oven and die of asphyxiation," Hilda warned him, without raising her voice or lowering her soup spoon. Her husband suspected she would do exactly as she said, and was motivated to be a little more cautious—but never cautious enough.

As for Hilda, she used a unique method to resist the dictatorship. Her opposition was concentrated specifically against the General, who, according to her, was possessed by Satan and was the very incarnation of evil. She thought it possible to defeat him through systematic prayer and faith in her cause. Toward this goal, she attended mystic evening sessions twice a week. There she met with a constantly growing group of pious souls who were steadfast in their intent to put an end to the tyranny. It was a national movement, a chain of prayer. On the appointed day, at the same hour, the faithful gathered in every city in the land, in isolated towns, in villages bypassed by progress, in prisons, and even on ships on the high seas, to concentrate a tremendous spiritual effort. Energy thus channeled would result in the deafening collapse of the General and his followers. José disagreed with that dangerous and theologically unsound madness, but Francisco did not discount the possibility that this most original system might have positive results; after all, the power of suggestion works marvels, and if the General learned of the formidable weapon directed toward his elimination, he might suffer a heart attack and pass on to a worse life. Francisco compared his mother's activity to the strange events in the house of the Ranquileos, and concluded that in times of repression inventive solutions emerge to combat the toughest problems.

"Forget your prayers, Hilda, and devote yourself to voodoo—it has a more scientific basis," joked Professor Leal.

Her family teased her so unmercifully that Hilda began going to her meetings in tennis shoes and slacks, hiding her prayer book under her sweater. She told them she was going out to jog in the park, and continued serenely in her laborious task of toppling authority with a rosary.

At the Leals' table, Irene clung to her host's every word, fascinated by the sonorous Spanish accent that many years in America had not softened. As she witnessed his passionate gestures, his shining eyes, the fervor of his convictions, she felt she had been transported into the last century, to a dark cellar where anarchists were preparing a rudimentary bomb to place in the way of a royal carriage. Meanwhile, Francisco and José were discussing the case of the raped, mute child, while Hilda and her daughter-in-law occupied themselves with the meal and the children. Javier ate very little, and took no part in the conversation. He had been out of work for more than a year, and those months had changed him; he had become a somber prisoner of his own anguish. The family had become accustomed to his long silences, to the stubble of beard, to his eyes empty of curiosity; they had stopped harrying him with signs of sympathy and concern that he, in turn, rejected. Only Hilda persisted in her solicitude, every so often asking, What are you thinking, son?

Finally, Francisco was able to interrupt his father's monologue to tell the family about the scene at Los Riscos when Evangelina had shaken the officer like a feather duster. Hilda's opinion was that to do something like that you had to have God's protection—or the Devil's, but Professor Leal maintained that the girl was merely the abnormal product of a society gone mad: poverty, the concept of sin, repressed sexual desire, and isolation had provoked her sickness. Irene laughed, convinced that the only one who had correctly diagnosed the case was Mamita Encarnación, and that the most practical solution would be to find a mate for the girl and let them loose in the bushes like rabbits. José agreed, and when the children began to ask about rabbits, Hilda turned everyone's attention to dessert, the first apricots of the season, boasting that no country in the world grew such savory fruit. This was the only form of nationalism the Leals tolerated, and the Professor lost no time in making that fact clear.

"People must live in a united world where all man's races, tongues, customs, and dreams are one. Nationalism is an insult to reason. It doesn't benefit people in any way. It merely serves as an excuse for committing the most outrageous abuses."

"But what does that have to do with these apricots?" asked Irene, completely lost by the direction of the conversation.

Everyone laughed. Any subject could lead to an ideological manifesto, but fortunately the Leals had not lost their ability to laugh at themselves. After dessert, they enjoyed an aromatic coffee Irene had brought. At the end of the meal, she reminded Francisco of the hog-butchering to be held at the Ranquileos' the following day. She told them all goodbye, leaving in her wake a good humor that enveloped everyone except the taciturn Javier, so sunk in his depression and knots that he had not even noticed her existence.

"Marry her, Francisco."

"She already has a fiancé, Mama."

"I'm sure you're much better," Hilda replied, incapable of objective judgments where her sons were concerned.

When he and Captain Gustavo Morante met, Francisco was already so much in love with Irene that he scarcely tried to conceal his dislike. In those days not even he recognized his intense feelings as love, and when he thought of Irene it was in terms of pure friendship. From their first meeting, he and Morante politely detested each other—one feeling the intellectual's scorn for the military, the other the reverse sentiment. The officer acknowledged Francisco with a brief nod, not offering his hand, and Francisco noted the haughty tone that immediately established distance between them but mellowed when he spoke to his fiancée. There was no other woman for the Captain. Long ago, he had marked her for his companion, investing her with every virtue. To his mind, his brief affairs, the adventures of a day—inevitable during the long periods of separation when his profession kept him away from home—had no meaning. No other relationship left a residue in his spirit, or a recollection in his flesh. He had loved Irene forever, even when they were children playing in their grandparents' house, awakening together to the first restiveness of puberty. Francisco Leal trembled when he thought of the games the children had played.

It was Morante's custom to refer to women as ladies, clearly establishing the difference between these ethereal creatures and the rough masculine world. In his social behavior, his manners were rather ceremonious, verging on ostentation, in contrast to his rough-and-ready manner with his comrades-in-arms. He looked every inch the swimming champion that he was. The only time the typewriters in the fifth-floor editorial offices ever fell silent was the day he appeared looking for Irene. Tan, muscular, proud, he embodied the very essence of a warrior. The women reporters, the layout editors, the usually impassive models, Mario's assistants—all looked up from their work and froze as he entered. He strode forward, unsmiling, and with him marched the great soldiers of all times: Alexander, Julius Caesar, Napoleon, along with the celluloid hosts from war films. The air thickened into a deep, concentrated, and melting sigh. That was the first time Francisco had seen him and, in spite of himself, he was impressed by the Captain's compelling presence. Francisco was suddenly filled with a malaise that he attributed to his antipathy for the military, not realizing that what he was experiencing was vulgar jealousy. Normally he would have disguised his feelings, as he was uncomfortable in the presence of petty emotions. He could not, however, resist the temptation to sow the seeds of uneasiness in Irene's mind, and through the succeeding months he often expressed his opinion about the catastrophic state of the nation since the armed forces had come out of their barracks to usurp power. Irene justified the coup, using arguments she had heard from her fiancé. Francisco rebutted them, alleging that the dictatorship had not resolved a single problem; instead, it had aggravated existing problems and created new ones, and government repression was the only reason the truth was not known. A hermetic seal capped reality, and an atrocious brew was fermenting beneath it, building up so much pressure that when the lid blew there would not be enough weapons or soldiers to contain it. Irene listened absentmindedly. Her difficulties with Gustavo were of a different order. She was sure she could never be a model wife for a high-ranking officer, not even if she turned herself inside out like a sock. She suspected that if they had not known each other since childhood, she would never have fallen in love with Gustavo; possibly they would never have met, because the military lived in closed circles, and preferred to marry the daughters of their superior officers or the sisters of their comrades, girls educated to be innocent sweethearts and faithful wives— although things did not always work out that way. It was not for nothing that the men were sworn to warn a comrade if his wife was deceiving him, forcing him to take measures before he was reported to the High Command and his career was ruined by an adulterous wife. Irene thought this was a monstrous custom. At first, Gustavo had argued that it was impossible to measure men and women by the same rule, not only with regard to Army morality, but that of any decent family, because undeniable biological differences do exist, as well as a historical and religious tradition that no women's liberation movement would ever erase. A single standard, he said, could result in great harm to society. But Gustavo prided himself on not being a chauvinist like the majority of his friends. His relationship with Irene, and a year of seclusion at the South Pole refining his ideas and softening some of the harsh edges of his character, had convinced him of the injustice of the double standard. He offered Irene the honest alternative: he would be faithful, for he considered that sexual freedom for both of them was a preposterous idea invented by Scandinavians. As severe with himself as he was with others, adamant once he had given his word, madly in love, and normally exhausted by physical exercise, he fulfilled his part of the bargain under ordinary circumstances. During prolonged separations, calling on his self-control, he struggled against his appetites, captive to a promise. He suffered morally when he yielded to temptation. He was unable to live for long periods in celibacy, but his heart remained untouched, a tribute to his eternal sweetheart.

To Gustavo Morante, the Army was an absorbing vocation. He had chosen it as a career because he was fascinated by the rigorousness of the life and the security of a stable future, and because he had a taste for command as well as a family tradition. His father and grandfather had been generals before him. At twenty-one he had distinguished himself as the best student in his class, and was a fencing and swimming champion.

He chose to enter the artillery, and there fulfilled his desire to command troops and train recruits. When Francisco Leal met Morante, he had just returned from the Antarctic, twelve months of isolation beneath immutable skies—the horizon a leaden dome lighted by a pale sun during six nightless months, followed by a half year of perennial darkness. Once a week, for only fifteen minutes, he was able to communicate with Irene by radio; sick with jealousy and loneliness, he used the time to inquire into every detail of what she was doing. The High Command had selected him from among many candidates for his strength of character and physical conditioning, and he lived in that vast desolate territory with seven other men. He survived storms that raised black waves as high as mountains while defending their most precious treasures: the Eskimo dogs and stores of fuel. At thirty degrees below zero, he moved mechanically to combat the sidereal cold and incurable longing, with his only—his sacred—mission to keep the nation's flag waving above that godforsaken outpost. He tried not to think about Irene, but neither exhaustion, nor ice, nor the corpsman's pills to outwit lust succeeded in erasing her warm memory from his heart. He occupied himself during the summer months by hunting seals to be stored in the snow for winter, and he cheated the hours while verifying meteorological observations: measuring tides and wind velocity, octaves of clouds, temperatures, and humidity; forecasting storms; sending up balloons to divine nature's intentions through trigonometric calculations. He had moments of euphoria and moments of depression, but never fell into the vices of panic and disillusion. Isolation and exposure to that proud icy land tempered his character and his mind, making him more reflective. He devoted himself to books on history, adding a new dimension to his thought. When he was overcome with love, he wrote letters to Irene in a style as diaphanous as the white landscape around him, but he never mailed them since the only means of transport was the ship that would come to pick them up at the end of the year. When finally he returned, he was slimmer, his hands were calloused and his skin burned almost black from the reverberating snow, and he was mad with worry. He brought with him two hundred and ninety sealed envelopes numbered in strict chronological order that he placed in the lap of his fiancée, whom he found inattentive and volatile, more interested in her work than in alleviating her lover's amorous impatience, and not at all inclined to read that pouch of out-of-date correspondence. At any rate, they went away for a few days to a discreet resort where they lived in unbridled passion, and the Captain made up for the time he had lost during so many months of enforced celibacy. The whole purpose of his absence had been to save enough money to marry Irene, because in those inhospitable regions he had earned six times the normal salary for his rank. He was driven by the desire to offer Irene her own house, modern furniture, household appliances, a car, and a comfortable income. It made no difference that she evinced no interest in such things and had suggested that, instead of wedding, they have a trial marriage to see whether the sum of their affinities was greater than that of their differences. Morante had no intention of undertaking an experiment that would prejudice his career. A solid family life was an important qualification for promotion to the rank of major. Furthermore, in the armed forces, after a certain age, a bachelor was looked on with suspicion. In the meanwhile, Beatriz Alcántara, ignoring her daughter's vacillation, was feverishly preparing for the wedding. She searched the shops for hand-painted English china with bird motifs, embroidered Dutch table linens, French silk lingerie, and other luxury items for her only daughter's trousseau and hope chest. Who will iron these things once I'm married, Mama? Irene wailed when she saw the Belgian laces, Japanese silks, Irish linens, Scottish wools, and other ineffable fabrics imported from the four corners of the globe.

At every stage of his career, Gustavo had been stationed in provincial garrisons, but he traveled to the capital to see Irene whenever he could. During those periods, she never communicated with Francisco, even if there was urgent work at the magazine. She disappeared with her fiancé, dancing in dark discothèques, holding hands in theaters and on long walks, dissipating their passions in circumspect hotels where they could satisfy their longing. Irene's absences put Francisco in a black mood. He would lock himself in his room, listening to his favorite symphonies and wallowing in his melancholy. One day, unable to bite his tongue, he committed the folly of asking Irene the extent of her intimacy with the Bridegroom of Death. She laughed until she cried. You surely don't think I'm a virgin at my age! she replied, depriving him even of doubt. Shortly afterward, Gustavo Morante was assigned for several months to a school for officers in Panama. His contact with Irene was limited to passionate letters, long-distance telephone calls, and gifts sent on military aircraft. Thus the all-enveloping ghost of that tenacious lover was responsible for Francisco's spending the night with Irene like a brother. Whenever he remembered it, he clapped his hand to his forehead, amazed at his behavior.

One evening, he and Irene had stayed late at the office to work on an article. They had gathered their information, and needed to organize it for the following day. The hours flew by and they did not notice as the employees left and lights were turned off in the other offices. They went out and bought a bottle of wine and something to eat. Since they enjoyed listening to music as they worked, they put a concerto on the record player and, with the flutes and violins, time went by without regard for the clock. It was very late when they finished, and only then did they become aware of the silence and darkness of the night through the open windows. They saw no sign of life; below them spread a deserted city; it was like science fiction, as if some cataclysm had erased every trace of humanity. Even the air seemed opaque, dead. Curfew, they murmured in unison, realizing they were trapped, for no one was allowed to move through the streets at that hour. Francisco blessed the good fortune that would allow him more time with Irene. She thought how worried her mother and Rosa would be, and ran to the telephone to explain. They drank the rest of the wine, listened twice more to the concerto, and talked of a thousand things; then, since they were both exhausted, Irene suggested they try to get some rest on the sofa.

The fifth-floor lavatory was a large room with multiple functions; it served as a dressing room for the models; as a make-up room, because of an especially well-lighted mirror; and even as a coffee shop, thanks to a hot plate for heating water. It was the only private and intimate spot on the floor. In one corner sat an old divan, a relic of days gone by. It was a huge piece of furniture upholstered in magenta brocade; rusty springs poked through the multiple wounds, in stark contrast to its turn-of-the-century dignity. It was a place to pamper headaches, to cry over love affairs and other, lesser sorrows, or merely to take a break when the pressures of work grew too strong. There a secretary had nearly bled to death after a botched abortion; there Mario's assistants had declared their passion; and there Mario himself had surprised the two of them, trouserless on the stained purplish tapestry. It was on that divan that Irene and Francisco pulled up their coats and lay down to sleep. Irene fell asleep immediately, but Francisco lay awake until morning, tormented by conflicting emotions. He did not wish to become involved in an earthshaking relationship with a woman from the other side of the fence. He felt irresistibly drawn to Irene, however; in her presence all his emotions were heightened and he was unavoidably happy. Irene both amused and fascinated him. Beneath her apparent capriciousness—unwitting, sometimes candid—he found her basically without blemish, like the heart of a fruit waiting to ripen. He also thought about Gustavo Morante and his role in Irene's destiny. Francisco feared that Irene would reject him, and that he would lose even her friendship. Words once spoken cannot be erased. Later, recalling his emotions during that unforgettable night, he reached the conclusion that he had not dared hint of his love because it was obvious that Irene did not share his anxiety. She slept tranquilly in his arms, without a suspicion of how deeply she affected him. To her, theirs was a platonic friendship, without sexual attraction, and he chose not to violate it, hoping that love would softly grow in her, as it had in him. He felt her beside him on the sofa, breathing peacefully in her sleep, her long hair like a dark arabesque covering her face and shoulders. He lay absolutely still, controlling even his breathing to conceal his throbbing and terrible agitation. On the one hand, he wanted to throw himself upon her and ravish her, regretting having accepted that tacit pact of comradeship that had bound him for months. On the other hand, he recognized the need to control an emotion that could divert him from the goals that governed the present stage of his life. Cramped from tension and anguish, but willing to prolong the moment forever, he lay by her side until he heard the first street sounds and saw the light of dawn at the window. Irene wakened with a start, and for a moment could not remember where she was; then she leaped up, splashed cold water on her face, and hurried home, leaving Francisco feeling like an orphan. Ever since that day, Irene had told anyone who wanted to listen that they had slept together, which, Francisco mused, even in the literal sense of the expression was regrettably untrue.

Sunday awoke. The light was oppressive, the air sultry and heavy, like a preview of summer. There is little progress in violence, and the same methods have been used to butcher hogs since the times of the barbarians. Irene thought of this as a picturesque ritual, because she had never seen so much as a hen killed, and barely recognized a pig in its natural state. She went with the purpose of getting an article for her magazine, so enthusiastic about the project that she never mentioned the subject of Evangelina and her boisterous attacks; it was as if she had forgotten them. Francisco felt that they were traveling through unfamiliar territory. Spring had erupted since the previous week; green had taken command of the fields; acacias were in flower—those enchanted trees whose branches from a distance seem to be covered with bees, yellow blossoms that make your head spin with their impossible fragrance as you draw near; hawthorns and mulberries were alive with birds, and the very air vibrated with the humming of insects. When they reached the Ranquileos' house, the job at hand was under way. The Ranquileos themselves, and their visitors, were busy around a bonfire, and children were running around shouting, laughing, and coughing from the smoke; the dogs were happily and impatiently circling the caldrons, sensing the spoils of the feast. The Ranquileos greeted the new arrivals with every sign of courtesy, but Irene noticed a touch of sadness in their faces. Beneath the cordial exterior she perceived distress, but there was no opportunity to inquire about it, or to comment to Francisco, because at that precise moment the hog was being dragged in. It was an enormous animal that had been fattened especially for the family's consumption; all the others were raised to be sold. An expert had selected this pig when it was only a few days old, putting his hand down its throat to verify that it was free of tapeworms, thus guaranteeing the quality of the meat. This pig was fed on grains and vegetables, unlike the other pigs that were given scraps. Isolated, captive, and immobilized, the animal had awaited its fate, adding fat to fat, its hams growing juicy and tender. Today was the first time the beast had traveled the two hundred meters separating its pen from the sacrificial altar, stumbling along on its hopelessly short legs, blinded in the light, deaf with terror. Irene could not imagine how they would be able to kill this mountain of flesh that weighed as much as three husky men.

Beside the bonfire a makeshift table had been fashioned from thick planks set across two barrels. Hipólito Ranquileo was awaiting the hog with an upraised ax; when the animal was before him, he struck a hard blow to its head with the blunt end of the tool, and the hog fell to the ground stunned— not sufficiently stunned, unfortunately, to prevent its screams from echoing through the hills; the dogs' muzzles twitched, and they panted with impatience. Several men bound the hog's feet and with great difficulty lifted it onto the table. This was the moment for the expert. He was a man born with a gift for the kill, a rare skill almost never given to women. He could reach the heart with a single thrust, even with his eyes closed, for he was guided not by anatomical knowledge but an executioner's intuition. He had traveled a long distance, especially invited to sacrifice the animal, because if it was not done skillfully, the pig's dying screams would shatter the nerves of everyone in the neighborhood. The expert took an enormous bone-handled knife with a sharp steel blade, lifted it high with both hands like an Aztec priest, and brought it down in the hog's neck, unhesitatingly plunging it into the center of life. The hog bawled despairingly as a gout of warm blood gushed from the wound, spattering everyone nearby and forming a pool that was immediately lapped up by the dogs. Digna brought a pail to catch the blood, and within seconds it was filled. A sweetish odor of blood and fear floated on the air.

At that moment Francisco realized that Irene was no longer by his side and, turning to look for her, he found her lying motionless on the ground. The others saw her, too, and a roar of laughter celebrated her fainting spell. Francisco bent over her and shook her until she opened her eyes. I want to leave, she begged as soon as she recovered her voice, but Francisco insisted on staying until the end. That's why they had come. He intimated that she should either learn to control her nerves or get a different job. Losing her composure could become a habit, he said, and he reminded her of the haunted house where the mere creaking of a door was enough to cause her to turn pale and collapse in his arms. He kept teasing Irene until the moans from the pig ceased, and when she was sure that it was truly dead, she was able to get to her feet.

The ritual continued. Boiling water was poured over the carcass and the skin was scraped with an iron tool, leaving the pig as shiny, rosy, and clean as a newborn babe; next they split open the belly, cleaned out the viscera, and cut the sides of bacon before the fascinated eyes of the children and the blood-soaked dogs. In the irrigation ditch, the women washed meters and meters of intestines that would later be stuffed to make blood sausage, and to revive Irene they brought her a cup of the broth from the kettle where the entrails were being boiled. She hesitated before accepting that dark-clotted vampires' soup, but took it not to offend her hosts. It turned out to be delicious, and had evident therapeutic properties, because after a few minutes she recovered her good spirits and the color came back to her cheeks. She and Francisco spent the rest of the day taking photographs, eating, and drinking wine from carafes, while the lard was being rendered into great tin drums. Crisped bacon floating in the fat was strained out and served with bread. The liver and heart were also cooked and offered to the invited guests. By dusk everyone was nodding: the men from alcohol, the women from exhaustion, the children from sleep, and the dogs from being gorged for the first time in their lives. It was then that Irene and Francisco remembered they had not seen Evangelina all day.

"Where's Evangelina?" Francisco asked Digna Ranquileo. She looked down without answering.

"And your son who's the soldier—what is his name?" Irene inquired, beginning to realize that something unusual had happened.

"Pradelio del Carmen Ranquileo," the mother replied, and her cup trembled in her hand.

Irene took the woman's arm and led her gently to a quiet corner of the patio that was by now swathed in shadows. Francisco started to come with them, but Irene motioned him to stay behind, certain that if she was alone with Digna they could establish a solid female complicity. They sat down facing one another in two rush chairs. In the dim twilight, Digna Ranquileo saw a pale face devoured by strange eyes outlined in black pencil, hair flying in the breeze, clothes rescued from another era, and armloads of clanking bracelets. Digna knew that in spite of the apparent abyss separating them, she could tell Irene the truth, because in essence they were sisters—as, finally, most women are.

The previous Sunday night, when everyone in the house was asleep, Lieutenant Juan de Dios Ramírez had returned with his subaltern, the one who had exposed Francisco's film.

"The sergeant's name is Faustino Rivera. He's the son of my good friend Manuel Rivera, the one with the harelip," Digna explained to Irene.

Rivera had stood at the threshold holding the dogs at bay while the lieutenant entered their bedroom, weapon in hand, kicking the furniture and hurling threats. He lined up the family, still not completely awake, against the wall, and then dragged Evangelina to his jeep. The last her parents saw of her was the flash of a white petticoat in the darkness as the men forced her into the vehicle. For a while the parents could hear her cries, calling to them. They waited until dawn, their hearts in their mouths, and when they heard the first rooster crow, rode to the Headquarters. After a long wait they were ushered in to see the corporal of the guard, who told them that their daughter had spent the night in a cell, but would be freed early that morning. They asked about Pradelio, and were informed that he had been transferred to a different military command.

"Since that minute, we haven't heard anything about the girl or any news about Pradelio," said Digna.

They had looked for Evangelina in town; one by one they had visited all the farms in the region; they stopped buses on the highway and asked the drivers whether they had seen her; they asked the Protestant pastor, the parish priest, the healer, the midwife, anyone they came across, but no one could give them a clue. They had gone in every direction, from the river to the mountaintops, without finding her; the wind had carried her name down ravines and roads, but after five days of useless searching they understood that she had been swallowed up by violence. Then, dressed in their mourning, they went to the house of the Floreses to tell them the sad news. They went feeling humiliated, because Evangelina had known only misfortune in their home, and it would have been better for her had she been raised by her real mother.

"Don't say that, *comadre*," *Señora* Flores replied. "Don't you know that no one can escape misfortune? Don't you remember that a few years back I lost my husband and my four sons? They took them away—they took them from me just like they did with Evangelina. It was her destiny, *comadre*. It isn't your fault, it's mine—bad luck runs in my blood."

Evangelina Flores, fifteen years old, sturdy, and in robust health, was listening to the two women, standing behind the chair of her adoptive mother. She had Digna Ranquileo's serene face, her square hands and broad hips, but she did not feel as if she were Digna's daughter, because as an infant she had been placed in the other woman's arms and had been nursed at her breast. Nonetheless, for some reason she knew that the girl who had disappeared was more than a sister: that girl was she herself; it was her life the other girl was living, and it would be her death that Evangelina Ranquileo died. It may have been in that instant of lucidity that Evangelina Flores assumed the burden she would later carry through the world in search of justice.

By the time Digna and Irene had finished talking, the last sparks were dying in the bonfire and night had spread across the horizon. It was time for them to leave. Irene Beltrán promised Digna that she would look for Evangelina in the capital, and she gave Digna her address so that she could reach her if there was any news. As they said goodbye, they embraced.

That night Francisco noticed something different in Irene's eyes; he did not find the usual laughter and wonder. Her eyes had become dark and sad, the color of dead eucalyptus leaves. Then he understood that Irene was losing her innocence, and that nothing could prevent her now from beginning to see the truth.

The two friends went to all the usual places, asking about Evangelina Ranquileo with more persistence than hope. They were not the only ones making such inquiries. At detention centers, police lockups, the off-limits section of the Psychiatric Hospital—entered only by straitjacketed torture victims and Security Corps medics—Irene Beltrán and Francisco Leal found themselves in the company of many who knew the route of that calvary better than they, and who guided them along the way. There, as in all places where there is great suffering, human solidarity was the balm that eased shared misery.

"And who are you looking for, *señora*?" Irene asked of a woman standing in line.

"No one, daughter. I spent three years trying to find a trace of my husband, but I know now he is at peace."

"Why have you come, then?"

"To help a friend," she replied, pointing to another woman.

The two had met several years before, and together had searched from place to place, knocking at doors, pleading with office workers, bribing soldiers. One of them had been luckier than the other, and she at least knew that her husband no longer needed her; the other continued her pilgrimage. How could she let her go alone? Besides, she was used to the waiting and the humiliations, she said; her whole life revolved around bureaucratic office hours and forms to be filled out;

she had learned ways to communicate with prisoners and get information.

"Evangelina Ranquileo Sánchez, fifteen—held for questioning in Los Riscos, and never seen again."

"Don't look any longer. I'm sure someone's hand slipped, and they were rougher on her than they intended."

"Go to the Ministry of Defense, there are new lists there."

"Come back next week at this same time."

"The guard changes at five—ask for Antonio, he's a nice man and can give you information."

"It's best to begin at the Morgue. That way you don't waste time."

José Leal was experienced in these inquiries, because a major portion of his energies was spent in such work. He used his contacts as a priest to get Francisco and Irene into places they could never have entered alone. He accompanied them to the Morgue, a timeworn gray building with an air of neglect and foreboding entirely appropriate for the house of the dead. Indigents ended up there, anonymous cadavers from the hospitals, people killed in drunken brawls or murdered by an unknown hand, victims of traffic accidents, and, in recent years, men and women with their fingers amputated at the knuckles, bodies bound with wire, faces burned by blowtorches or beaten beyond recognition, all of whose final resting place would be a nameless grave in Subdivision 29 of the General Cemetery. An authorization from Headquarters was needed to visit the Morgue, but José went there so often that all the employees knew him. In the Vicariate it was his assignment to try to follow the trail of *desaparecidos*. While volunteer lawyers unsuccessfully executed legal maneuvers to protect the missing in case they were still alive, José and other priests carried out the macabre bureaucratic task of sorting through the dead, photographs in hand, trying to identify them. Only rarely did they succeed in rescuing someone who was still alive; but with divine assistance, the priests were confident they could at least deliver the remains to their families to be buried.

Francisco's brother had warned him of what they would see in the Morgue, and Francisco pleaded with Irene to stay outside. But he found her filled with a new determination born of her desire to know the truth; she felt she must cross that threshold. Because of his practice in hospitals and mental asylums, Francisco was a man who thought he was inured to horror, but when he left the Morgue he was numbed, and he continued to feel that way for a very long time. He could imagine, therefore, how Irene must feel. There were too many bodies to be contained in the refrigerated units, and because they could not lay them on the tables, the cadavers were stacked in large storerooms that had formerly been used for other purposes. The air stank of formaldehyde and dankness; shadows filled the large, filthy rooms; the walls were mildewed and stained. Only an occasional bulb lighted the corridors, the shabby offices, the cavernous depositories. An air of hopelessness pervaded the building, and all who worked there were contaminated by indifference, their capacity for compassion drained. The attendants performed their duties handling death like banal merchandise; they lived so close to the dead that they had forgotten life. Irene saw employees eating lunch on the autopsy tables; some were listening to sportscasts on the radio, unconcerned about nearby bodies stiffened in rigor mortis; others played cards in the basement depositories while they guarded the day's cadavers.

Irene and Francisco checked the different sectors one by one, pausing at the bodies of women, which were few, and always naked. Francisco felt his mouth fill with saliva, and

Irene's hand trembled in his. She looked pale and ill as her icy figure glided through room after room as if in an unending nightmare, so dazed she felt as if she were adrift in a pestilent fog. She could not absorb this hellish vision, and not even her wildest imagination could have measured the extent of such horrors.

Francisco had never retreated at the moment of confrontation with violence; he was a link in the long human chain of covert operations, and he knew the inside workings of the dictatorship. No one suspected his connection with political refugees, with money collected from mysterious sources, with names, dates, and information gathered and sent outside the country in case someday someone should decide to write the true story. But he still had barely been touched by repression; he had always managed to slip by, skirting the edge of the abyss. Only once, and then by chance, had he been seized: the time they shaved his head. During the days when he still worked as a psychologist, he was returning home from his consulting office when he ran into a patrol that was stopping all traffic. He thought it was a routine check, and held out his documents, but a machine gun prodded his chest and two hands like grappling hooks yanked him from his motorcycle.

"You, faggot! Get off!"

He was not the only one in this predicament. A pair of school-age boys were on their knees on the ground, and Francisco was forced to kneel beside them. Two soldiers held their weapons on him as a third grabbed him by the hair and shaved his head. Years later, it was still impossible for him to recall that episode without a spasm of impotence and indignation, even though with time he had come to realize how insignificant it was compared with other things that were happening. He had tried to reason with the soldiers, but for his trouble earned a kick in the back and a few cuts on his scalp. He returned home sputtering with rage, more humiliated than he had ever been in his life.

"I warned you they were cutting men's hair, son," his mother wept.

"From this moment you are to wear your hair long, Francisco. We must resist in every possible way," mouthed his irate father, forgetting his own objection to shaggy-haired men. And Francisco had let it grow, sure that he would be sheared again, but a counterorder had been issued that left long-haired men in peace.

Until the day she visited the Morgue, Irene Beltrán had lived in angelic ignorance, not from apathy or stupidity but because ignorance was the norm in her situation. Like her mother and so many others of her social class, she escaped into the orderly, peaceful world of the fashionable neighborhoods, the exclusive beach clubs, the ski slopes, the summers in the country. Irene had been educated to deny any unpleasantness, discounting it as a distortion of the facts. One day, she had seen a car screech to a stop and several men overpower a pedestrian and force him into their vehicle; from a distance she had smelled the smoke of bonfires burning blacklisted books; she had glimpsed the outlines of a human body floating in the dark waters of the canal. She had heard patrol cars and the roar of helicopters shattering the night skies. She had stopped to help someone who had fainted from hunger in the street. Irene had lived surrounded by the gales of hatred, but remained untouched by them behind the high wall that had protected her since childhood. Now, however, her suspicions had been aroused, and making the decision to enter the Morgue was a step that was to affect her entire life. She had never seen a dead body until the day she saw enough to fill her worst nightmares. She stopped before a large refrigerated cellar to look at a light-haired girl hanging on a meat hook in a row of bodies. From a distance the corpse resembled Evangelina Ranquileo, but as she walked closer Irene saw it was not she. Horrified, she stared at the extensive marks of beatings on the body, the burned face, the amputated hands.

"It isn't Evangelina, don't look at her," Francisco begged, leading Irene away, putting his arm around her, rushing her toward the door, as devastated as she.

Even though their journey through the Morgue had lasted only half an hour, when she left Irene Beltrán was no longer the same; something had shattered in her soul. Francisco could see this before she spoke a single word, and anxiously he searched for a way to console her. He helped her onto the motorcycle and they sped off toward the Hill.

They often went there to picnic. An outdoor lunch prevented any argument over who should pay the check, and both of them enjoyed the open air in the splendor of the park. Sometimes they went by Irene's house to pick up her dog, Cleo. Irene liked to let the dog run, for she was afraid that from being around old people all the time and roaming the paths of the retirement home, Cleo would become an idiot and forget all her instincts. The first few times, the poor animal was terrified by the ride, hunched between them on the motorcycle, ears drooping and eyes rolling, but with time she learned to enjoy it and barked wildly at the sound of any motor. Though Cleo's many-colored spots proclaimed her lack of noble pedigree, she was heir to an alertness and cunning bequeathed her by her bastard ancestors. She was bound to her mistress by unwavering loyalty. On the motorcycle, the three of them looked like a circus act: Irene in her fluttering skirts, shawls, and fringe, her long hair flying in the wind; the dog sandwiched between them; and Francisco balancing the picnic basket as he drove.

The enormous natural park in the center of the city was easy to reach, but few people went there and many were not even aware of its existence. Francisco felt as if he owned the place and used it for all his nature shots: soft thirsty hills in summer, golden cinnamon trees and oaks that sheltered squirrels in the autumn, and bared silent branches in the winter. In spring the park awakened pulsing with life, glowing with a thousand different greens, with clusters of insects among the flowers, its slopes gravid, its roots eager, its sap bursting from the hidden veins of nature. Irene and Francisco crossed the bridge over the stream and began to climb the winding road bordered by gardens with exotic plantings. The higher they climbed the more tangled the bushes became; paths began to disappear in the thickening growth of gentle birches showing the first leaves of the year; compact, eternally green pines; slender eucalyptus; red beech.

The heat of midday was evaporating the morning dew, releasing a light mist that lay like a veil over the landscape. When they reached the summit, they had the sensation that they were the only people in that enchanted place. They knew all the secluded nooks, the places where they could sit and observe the city at their feet. Sometimes, when the fog was thick, the base of the hill disappeared in a froth of seafoam, and they could imagine they were on an island surrounded by an ocean of flour. In contrast, on clear days they watched the flow of the endless silver ribbon of traffic and heard its bustle like a distant torrent. In some places the foliage was so dense and the perfume of growing things so intense that it was intoxicating. Francisco and Irene kept their escapes to the park hidden, like a precious secret. Without any spoken agreement, they never mentioned the Hill, keeping it theirs alone.

After they left the Morgue, Francisco felt that only the thick green of the park, the moist earth, and the smell of humus could help Irene forget the silent cries of all those dead. He drove to the summit and looked for a shadowy, secluded spot. Near a stream tumbling downhill between large rocks, they found a willow tree whose strands fell around them, forming a tent of green. Supported by the rough trunk, they sat in silence, without touching, but so united in their feelings they might have been cradled in a single womb. Half-paralyzed with horror, they thought their own thoughts, but each was consoled by the other's nearness. The passage of time, the southern breeze, the murmuring water, the wild canaries, the earth fragrances slowly brought them back to reality.

"We should go back to the office," Irene said finally.

"We should."

Neither moved. Irene chewed on a few sprigs of grass, savoring their sap. She turned to look at Francisco and he felt himself sinking into her hazy eyes. Without thinking, he drew her to him and sought her lips. In truth it was scarcely a kiss, more the suggestion of a long-awaited and inevitable meeting, but one they would always remember. Years later, they would still be able to evoke perfectly the moist, glowing contact of their lips, the aroma of the fresh grass, the storm in their spirits. When Francisco opened his eyes, Irene was standing silhouetted against the sky, her arms crossed over her breast. Both were breathing quickly, afire, suspended in their own space, in their own time. Francisco sat unmoving, shaken by a new and all-enveloping emotion for this woman now bound to him. He heard something like a quiet sob, and understood the struggle that had been unleashed in Irene's heart: love, loyalty, doubt. He was torn between his desire to touch her and his fear of exerting pressure on her. After a long silence, Irene turned and walked slowly to Francisco and knelt by his side. He put his arm around her waist and breathed the perfume of her blouse, the slight, underlying hint of her body.

"Gustavo has waited for me all his life. I am going to marry him."

"I don't believe it," whispered Francisco.

The tension slowly eased. She clasped Francisco's dark head in her hands and looked into his eyes. They smiled, comforted, joyful, trembling, certain that they would never settle for a brief adventure, because they were born to share life in its totality and to undertake together the audacity of loving each other forever.

The afternoon was waning and the green cathedral of the park was somber. It was time to leave. They flew down the Hill like a gust of wind. The shadowy vision of the cadavers would never be erased from their souls, but at that moment they were happy.

The ardor of the kiss stayed with them for days; it filled their nights with delicate ghosts, leaving its memory on their skins like a brand. They found themselves walking on air, laughing for no apparent cause, waking in the midst of a dream. They would touch their lips with their fingertips and trace the shape of the other's mouth. Irene thought about Gustavo in the light of new truths. She suspected that, like any officer, he was involved in the exercise of power, a secret life he had never shared with her. Two different beings existed in the familiar, athletic body. For the first time, she was afraid of him and wished he would never return.

Javier hanged himself on Thursday. That afternoon he had
gone out to look for work as he did every day, but he never
came home. Soon after he left, long before it was time to be
worried, his wife had a presentiment of disaster. By nightfall,
she was sitting in the doorway with her eyes focused on the
street. When the fear of tragedy became unbearable, she went
to the telephone and called her in-laws, everyone she knew, but
learned nothing of her husband's whereabouts. Peering into
the shadows for an eternity, evoking Javier in her thoughts,
she was surprised by the curfew. The darkest hours passed,
and then came Friday's dawn. The children were still asleep
when the police patrol car braked to a stop before the house.
Javier Leal had been found hanging from a tree in the park.
He had never spoken of suicide; he had told no one goodbye;
he left no notes of farewell; nonetheless, she knew beyond the
shadow of a doubt that he had killed himself, and finally she
understood his obsessive toying with the cord.

It was Francisco who collected the body and took charge
of the funeral arrangements. As he completed the laborious
bureaucratic details of death, he carried with him the vision of
Javier lying beneath the ice-cold light of the fluorescent lamps
of the Medical Institute. He tried to analyze the reasons for his
brother's brutal death, and to adjust to the idea that his lifetime companion, the unconditional friend, the protector, was
no longer of this world. He remembered his father's lesson:
work as a source of pride. Idleness was foreign to the family. In
the Leal household, holidays and even vacations were spent in
some worthwhile undertaking. The family had had its difficult
moments, but they had never dreamed of accepting charity,
even from those they had previously helped. When Javier saw
the last door close before him, all that was left was to accept

help from his father and brothers; he chose instead to leave without a word. Francisco thought back in distant memories to the time when his oldest brother had been a youth as just as his father and as sentimental as his mother. The three Leal boys had grown up united, three against the world, three of the same clan, respected in the schoolyard because each was protected by the others and any offense was immediately redressed. José, the second son, was the heaviest and strongest, but Javier was the most feared because of his courage and his skill with his fists. He had spent a stormy adolescence until he fell in love with the first girl to capture his attention. He married her, and was faithful to her until the night he died. He did honor to his name: Leal, loyal—loyal to his wife, to his family, to his friends. He loved his work as a biologist; he had intended to devote himself to a life of teaching, but circumstances had led him to a laboratory job in industry where in a few years' time he had earned a high position; his sense of responsibility was joined to a fertile imagination that placed him in the vanguard of the most daring scientific projects. None of this was of any value, however, when the rolls of persons blacklisted by the military Junta were drawn up. His activities in the union were a stigma, in the eyes of the new authorities. First they watched him, then they hounded him; finally, they fired him. Without a job and without hope of finding another, he began to decline. Pale and wan, he shambled through nights of insomnia and days of humiliation. He had pounded at many doors, suffered long hours in waiting rooms, answered advertisements in newspapers and, at the end of the road, found crushing hopelessness. Without a job, he gradually lost his identity. He would have accepted any offer, however mean the pay, because he desperately needed to feel useful. As a man without employment, he was an outsider, anonymous, ignored by all because he was no longer productive, and that was the measure of a man in the world he lived in. During recent months, he had abandoned his dreams, renounced his goals, considered himself a pariah. His children could not understand his constant bad humor and unremittent melancholy; they looked for jobs washing cars, carrying shopping bags from the market, performing any task to bring home a little money. The day his youngest son put on the kitchen table the few coins he had earned walking rich men's dogs, Javier cringed like a cornered animal. Since that moment, he never looked anyone in the eyes; he sank into total despair. He often lacked the will to dress and spent a large part of the day in bed. His hands trembled after he began to drink secretly, feeling even more guilty for draining much-needed money from his family. On Saturdays he made an effort to be clean and neat when he showed up at his parents' home, in order not to distress his family further, but he couldn't erase the desolation from his face. His relations with his wife disintegrated; in such circumstances love grows weary. He needed consolation but, at the same time, reacted with fury at the slightest gleam of pity. At first, his wife could not believe that there were no jobs available, but later, when she learned of the thousands out of work, she stopped complaining and doubled her hours at work. The fatigue of those months eroded the youth and beauty that she treasured among her remaining possessions, but she had no time to mourn them; she was too busy feeding her children and caring for her husband. She could do nothing to prevent Javier's retreat into solitude. Apathy enveloped him like a cloak, obliterating any notion of the present, sapping his strength, and stripping him of his courage. He moved like a shadow. He ceased to feel he was a man as he watched his home collapsing about him and the light of love dying in his wife's eyes. At some moment that his family was too close to perceive, his will snapped. He lost his desire to live, and decided to seek his death.

The tragedy fell upon the Leals like a thunderbolt. Hilda and the Professor aged overnight, and their house was filled with silence. Even the boisterous birds on the patio seemed to grow still. In spite of the strict condemnation of suicide by the Catholic Church, José officiated at the mass for the peace of his brother's soul. For the second time in his life, the Professor stepped inside a temple; the first time had been for his marriage, and on that occasion he was filled with joy. This was different. He remained standing throughout the ceremony, arms crossed and lips pressed in a thin line, drunk with suffering. His wife surrendered herself to her prayers, accepting the death of her son as one more trial from fate.

Irene, greatly distressed, attended the funeral services, still unable to grasp the cause for such misery. She sat silently beside Francisco, weighed down by the sorrow of this family she had come to love as her own. She had always known them to be jovial, exultant, smiling. She had not realized they were enduring a private sorrow with dignity. Perhaps because of his Spanish ancestry, Professor Leal was able to express every passion except the one that clawed at his soul. Men weep only for love, he often said. In contrast, Hilda's eyes moistened at gentler emotions—tenderness, laughter, nostalgia—but suffering hardened her like steel. She shed few tears at the funeral of her oldest son.

They buried Javier in a small plot of land they acquired at the last minute. The rites were improvised, confused, because until that day they had not given thought to the rituals of death. Like all those who love life, they had felt they were immortal.

"We will not return to Spain, wife," Professor Leal proclaimed when the last shovelfuls of earth fell upon the coffin. For the first time in forty years, he recognized that he belonged to this soil.

The widow of Javier Leal went directly from the funeral to her apartment; she packed her sparse belongings in cardboard boxes, took her children by the hand, and bade the Leals goodbye. She was going back south, back to the province where she had been born; life was gentler there and she could count on her brothers' support. She did not want her children to grow up in the shadow of their absent father. The Leals saw their daughter-in-law and children off; stunned, they accompanied them to the station and watched them climb aboard the train and ride out of sight. They could not believe that in so few days they had also lost the children they had helped to raise. They placed little value on material objects; their hope for the future lay in their family. They had never thought they would grow old so far from their loved ones.

Professor Leal returned from the station and, without removing his jacket or his black tie, sat down in a chair beneath the cherry tree in the patio, his eyes vacant. In his hands he held the slide rule that he had saved from the wreckage of war and brought with him to America. He kept it always beside him on the bedside table, and allowed his children to play with it only as a reward. He had taught the three boys how to slide the pieces and match the correct numbers, and had refused to replace it when it was surpassed by electronic advances. It was a telescoping tube of brass with tiny numbers along the edges, the work of artisans of the last century. Professor Leal sat for many hours beneath the tree, staring at the brick walls he and his sons had built to house Javier and his family. That night Francisco led him almost forcibly to bed, but he could not force him to eat. The next day was the same. On the third day, Hilda dried her tears, gathered strength from the reserves in her innermost being, and prepared to fight once again for her own.

"The trouble with your father is that he doesn't believe in the soul, Francisco. That's why he feels he's lost Javier," she said.

From the kitchen window they could see the Professor sitting in his chair, turning his slide rule over and over. With a sigh, Hilda set his untouched lunch in the icebox; she carried a second chair to the patio and sat down with him beneath the cherry tree, her hands lying idle in her lap—the first time since time immemorial that they were not occupied with knitting or sewing—and remained there for hours without moving. At dusk Francisco begged them to eat something, but received no answer. With difficulty he led them to their bedroom and put them to bed; they lay in silence, eyes wide open, desolate, like two mindless invalids. He kissed their foreheads, turned out the light, and wished with all his heart for a deep sleep to obliterate their anguish. When he got up the next morning, he found them sitting in the same positions beneath the tree, their clothes wrinkled: unwashed, unfed, mute. He had to use all his self-control, remember all his training, not to go out and shake them. Patiently, he sat down to watch them reach the depths of their sorrow.

At midafternoon, Professor Leal raised his eyes and looked at Hilda. "What's the matter with you, woman?" he asked in a voice husky from four days of silence.

"The same thing that's the matter with you."

The Professor understood. He knew Hilda well enough to know that she would sit and waste away at the same rate that he did; loving him without ceasing for so many years, she would not allow him to leave her behind.

"Very well," he said; he rose to his feet with difficulty and held out his hand.

Slowly they walked into the house, each supporting the other. Francisco warmed the soup, and life returned to its routine.

Isolated from the Leals' grief, Irene Beltrán borrowed her mother's automobile and set out alone for Los Riscos, determined to find Evangelina on her own. She had promised Digna that she would help her in her search, and she did not want to give the impression that she had spoken lightly. Her first stop was the Ranquileo home.

"Don't keep looking, *señorita*. The earth has swallowed her up," the mother said, with the resignation of one who has endured many afflictions.

But Irene was prepared, if necessary, to move heaven and earth to find the girl. Later, looking back on those days, she asked herself what had propelled her into the world of shadows. She had suspected from the beginning that she held the end of a long thread in her hands that when tugged would unravel an unending snarl of horrors. Intuitively, she knew that Evangelina, the saint of the dubious miracles, was the borderline between her orderly world and a dark unknown region. Irene concluded that it was not only her natural and professional curiosity that had driven her forward, but something akin to vertigo. She had peered into a bottomless well and had not been able to resist the temptation of the abyss.

Lieutenant Juan de Dios Ramírez received her in his office without delay. He did not seem as burly as he had when she had met him on that fateful Sunday at the Ranquileo home, and she deduced that the size of a man must depend on his attitude. Ramírez was almost amiable. He was wearing his tunic unbelted, he was bareheaded, and he carried no weapons. His hands were puffy, red, streaked with chilblains, the cross of the poor. It was unlikely that he would have forgotten Irene—one glimpse of her, with her wild hair and bizarre clothes, was enough to make anyone remember her; she made no attempt, therefore, to deceive the officer, and without preamble declared her interest in Evangelina Ranquileo.

"She was detained for a brief routine questioning," the officer responded. "She spent the night here and was released early the next morning."

Ramírez dried the sweat from his brow. It was hot in the office.

"Did you put her out in the street without any clothes?"

"Citizen Ranquileo was wearing shoes and a poncho."

"You dragged her from her bed in the middle of the night. She is a minor, why wasn't she returned to her parents?"

"I don't have to discuss police procedures with you," the lieutenant replied curtly.

"Would you rather discuss them with my fiancé, Army Captain Gustavo Morante?"

"What kind of idea is that! I report only to my superior officer."

But Ramírez hesitated. The principle of the brotherhood of the armed services was firmly instilled in his bones: the sacred interests of the nation, and the even more sacred interests of the uniform, rose above petty rivalries among the individual branches. They must all defend themselves against the insidious cancer that was growing and spreading in the very bosom of the public: that was why civilians were never to be trusted—as a precaution, and as strategy for loyally protecting comrades-in-arms. The armed forces must be monolithic;

that had been repeated to him a thousand times over. He was also influenced by the young woman's social class. He was accustomed to respecting the supreme authority of money and power, and she must have plenty of both if she dared question him with such assurance, treating him as if he were her servant. He got out the Duty Log and showed it to her. There was the entry for Evangelina Ranquileo Sánchez, fifteen, held for the purpose of making a statement in regard to an unauthorized gathering on the property of her family, and in regard to a physical assault on the person of officer Juan de Dios Ramírez. At the foot of the page Irene saw an additional entry: Owing to an attack of hysteria, it was decided to cancel the interrogation. Signed, Corporal of the Guard, Ignacio Bravo.

"I'd say she's probably taken off for the capital. She wanted to find a job as a servant, like her older sister," said Ramírez.

"Without money and half naked, Lieutenant? Don't you find that a little strange?"

"The kid was half nuts."

"May I speak with her brother, Pradelio Ranquileo?"

"No. He's been transferred to a different military command."

"Where?"

"That is confidential information. We are in a declared State of Emergency."

Irene realized that she would not learn anything more by following this line of questioning, and as it was still early she drove to the village with the idea of questioning people there. She wanted to find out what they thought of the military in general and of Lieutenant Ramírez in particular. On hearing her questions, however, people turned their heads without answering and scurried away as quickly as possible. Years of authoritarian regime had established discretion as the basis for survival. While a mechanic patched one of the tires of her car, Irene went into an inn near the plaza. Signs of spring were everywhere: in the nuptial flight of the thrushes, the self-satisfied strutting of hens followed by a string of chicks, the quivering of young girls beneath their cotton dresses. A pregnant cat wandered into the inn and, with dignity, curled up beneath Irene's table.

At various times in her life, Irene had experienced strong intuitions. She believed she could read the signs of the future, and imagined that the power of the mind could determine certain events. That is how she explained the appearance of Sergeant Faustino Rivera at the very place she had chosen to eat. When she told this to Francisco later, he expounded a simpler theory: the inn was the only restaurant in Los Riscos and the sergeant was thirsty. Rivera was sweating as Irene watched him enter, walk to the counter, and order a beer; she immediately recognized the Indian features—the high cheekbones, oblique eyes, taut skin, and large, even teeth. He was in uniform, and was carrying his cap in his hand. She remembered what little she'd heard about him from the mouth of Digna Ranquileo, and decided to use it to her advantage.

"Are you Sergeant Rivera?" she asked.

"At your service, ma'am."

"The son of Manuel Rivera, the one with the harelip?"

"The same. What can I do for you?"

From that moment the conversation flowed freely. Irene invited Rivera to drink his beer at her table, and as soon as he was seated with another beer in his hand, he was putty in her hands. By the third glass, it was evident that the soldier did not carry his alcohol well, and Irene directed the conversation to the channels that interested her. She began by flattering him, saying that he had been born to occupy posts of responsibility, anyone could see that; she herself had noticed it in the Ran-quileos' house when he had controlled the situation with the authority and cool head of a true leader; he had been ener-getic, efficient, not at all like that officer Ramírez.

"Is your lieutenant always so reckless? I mean, that shoot-ing! It scared me to death."

"He didn't used to be like that. He isn't a bad man, I swear it," replied the sergeant.

He knew him, he said, like the palm of his hand, because he had served under his command for years. Just out of Of-ficers' School Ramírez had all the virtues of a good military man: he was trim, uncompromising, trustworthy. He knew all the rules and regulations by heart; he had no patience for im-perfection; he demanded a serious attitude on the part of his subordinates; he reviewed the shine on their boots and pulled on their buttons to see that they were firmly attached; and he was obsessive about hygiene. He personally checked the cleaning of the latrines, and each week he lined up his men in the nude to examine them for venereal diseases and lice. He inspected their private parts with a magnifying glass, and any infected men had to undergo drastic remedies and infinite hu-miliation.

"But he didn't do it out of meanness, *señorita*. He wanted to teach us to be decent. I think in those days the lieutenant had a good heart."

Rivera remembered the first execution as clearly as if he were seeing it today. It had happened five years ago, a few days after the military takeover. It was still cold, and it had rained all night; the skies had opened and washed the world, leaving the barracks bright and clean and smelling of moss and moisture.

By dawn, the rain had stopped, but everything was softened in the haze of its memory, and small pools of water glittered among the cobbles like slivers of glass. The firing squad was assembled at the far end of the patio, and two strides before them, deathly pale, stood Lieutenant Ramírez. The prisoner was brought in between two guards, who were holding him up by the arms because he couldn't stand on his own two feet. At first Rivera hadn't realized what bad shape he was in; he'd thought the man was a coward, like others who, after running around out there committing their subversive acts and fucking up the whole country, swooned when the time came to pay for their sins; but then he got a better look and saw that this was the guy whose legs they'd crushed. The guards had to support him between them to keep his feet from bumping over the cobblestones. Faustino Rivera looked at his superior and read his thoughts. During nights of guard duty, they had talked man to man, forgetting differences in rank and analyzing the reasons for the military uprising and its consequences. The country had been divided by anti-patriotic politicians who were weakening the nation and turning it into easy prey for enemies from the outside, Lieutenant Ramírez had said. It is the first duty of a soldier to protect the nation's security; that's why they'd seized power, to make the nation strong again, and, in passing, to do away with their internal enemies. Rivera rejected the idea of torture; he considered it the worst of the dirty war they were all engulfed in; it wasn't a part of his profession; it hadn't been a part of his training; it turned his stomach. It was one thing to rough up some hoodlum a little in the course of a routine interrogation, but it was something else again to torture a prisoner systematically. Why did the bastards clam up? Why didn't they talk in their first interrogation and save themselves all that pointless suffering? In the end they either confessed or they died, like this fellow they were getting ready to execute.

"Detail! Attennnn . . . !"

"Lieutenant," whispered Faustino Rivera, then only a corporal first class.

"Position the prisoner against the wall, Corporal!"

"But, Lieutenant, he can't stand up."

"Then sit him down!"

"Where, Lieutenant?"

"Well, bring a chair, goddammit," and the lieutenant's voice had cracked.

Faustino Rivera turned to the man at his left, repeated the order, and the man departed. Why don't they pitch the prisoner on the ground and shoot him like a dog before it gets light and we can see everybody's face? Why drag it out like this? the corporal thought, uneasy because the patio was getting lighter by the second. The prisoner raised his eyes and looked at each of them with the astounded expression of the dying; he paused when he came to Faustino. He undoubtedly recognized him, because once they'd played soccer on the same field, and there *he* was now standing in the middle of icy pools of water, holding a rifle in his hands that weighed a ton, while the prisoner lay on the ground waiting. At this point the chair arrived and the lieutenant ordered them to tie the prisoner to the chairback because he was swaying like a scarecrow. The corporal stepped toward him with a kerchief.

"I don't want a blindfold, soldier," said the prisoner, and the corporal hung his head, ashamed, wishing the officer would get on with it and give the order to fire, wishing this war would hurry up and get over, wishing that things would get back to normal and he could walk down the street in peace, greeting all his countrymen alike.

"Reaaaaady! Aiii . . . !" commanded the lieutenant.

Finally, thought the corporal. The man who was about to die closed his eyes for an instant but opened them again to look toward the sky. He was no longer afraid. The lieutenant hesitated. He'd been pale as a ghost ever since he'd heard about the execution. An old voice from his childhood had been pounding in his brain, the voice of some teacher or his confessor in the school for priests, perhaps: All men are brothers. But that isn't true; any man who goes around spreading violence is no brother of mine, and the nation comes first, everything else isn't worth shit; and if we don't kill them, they'll kill us. That's what the Colonels say: Kill or be killed, this is war, these things have to be done, pull up your pants and don't tremble, don't think, don't feel, and above all don't look at the man's face, because if you do, you're fucked good and proper.

"Fire!"

The volley jolted the skies and echoed and re-echoed in the icy patio. A startled pigeon flew away. The smell of gunpowder and the noise seemed to linger for an eternity, but slowly the silence returned. The lieutenant opened his eyes: the prisoner was sitting straight and serene in his chair, looking at him. There was fresh blood on the shapeless mass of his pants legs, but he was alive, and his face was ethereal in the dawn light. He was alive, and waiting.

"What's going on here, Corporal?" the officer asked in a low voice.

"They shot at his legs, Lieutenant," replied Faustino Rivera. "All the boys are from around here. They know each other, they're not going to kill a friend."

"So what happens now?"

"Now it's up to you, Lieutenant."

Mute, the officer finally understood. The firing squad

stood watching the dew evaporating off the cobbles. The prisoner, too, was waiting at the far end of the patio, unhurriedly bleeding to death.

"Didn't they tell you, Lieutenant? Everyone knows."

No. No, they had not told him. In Officers' School they had prepared him to fight against neighboring nations, against any son of a bitch who invaded their sovereign territory. They had also trained him to wage war against common criminals, to pursue them mercilessly, hunt them down like dogs, so that decent men, women, and children could walk the streets with a light heart. That was his mission. But no one had told him he would have to beat a bound man to a pulp to make him talk, they had not taught him anything about that; and now the world was spinning backward and he had to walk over and administer the coup de grâce to that poor bastard who was not even complaining. No. No one had told him.

Surreptitiously the corporal nudged the lieutenant's arm, so the squad would not see their leader's vacillation.

"Your revolver, Lieutenant," he whispered.

The lieutenant removed his revolver from its holster and walked across the patio. The dull echo of his boots on the cobblestones rumbled in his men's guts. Now the lieutenant and his prisoner were face to face, looking in each other's eyes. They were the same age. The officer raised his arm, aiming at the temple, holding the revolver with both hands to control his shaking. The bright light of day was the last thing the condemned man saw as the shot penetrated his brain. Blood spurted over his face and chest, splashing on the officer's clean uniform.

The lieutenant's sob hung in the air, reverberating with the gunshot, but only Faustino Rivera heard it.

"Chin up, Lieutenant. They say it's the same in war. It's hard the first time, but then you get used to it."

"Go fuck yourself, Corporal!"

The corporal was right, and as the days and weeks went by it had been much easier to kill for the nation than to die for it.

Sergeant Faustino Rivera stopped talking as he mopped the sweat from his neck. In his drunken haze, he could barely see Irene Beltrán, but he could tell that she was good-looking. He glanced at his watch and sat up straight. He'd been talking with this woman for two hours, and if he wasn't already late for his guard duty, he would tell her a few things more. She knew how to listen, and was interested in his stories—not like a lot of prissy girls who turn up their noses the minute a man gets a few beers under his belt; no sir, a real dish, that's what she was; a good body and some ideas in her head, though maybe a little bit scrawny; he liked a woman with big tits and broad hips, something to grab onto at the moment of truth.

"He wasn't a bad man, the lieutenant, *señorita*. It was later he changed, after he was put in command and didn't have to account to anyone," Rivera concluded, straightening his uniform and rising to his feet.

Irene waited until his back was turned before stopping the tape recorder hidden in the purse she had left lying on a chair. She threw the last pieces of meat to the cat, thinking about Gustavo Morante, wondering whether her fiancé had ever had to cross a patio with a revolver in his hand to give the coup de grâce to a prisoner. Anguished, she forced those thoughts from her mind, trying to recall Gustavo's smooth-shaven face and clear eyes, but all that came to her mind was the profile of Francisco Leal as he bent over the desk beside her: the black eyes shining with understanding; the boyish grin when he smiled; the different mouth, thin-lipped, hard, when he saw evidence of man's cruelty to man.

The Will of God Manor was ablaze with lights; the drapes in the salons were opened wide, and music filled the air; it was visiting day, and relatives and friends of the elderly guests were arriving on their missions of mercy. From a distance the ground floor resembled an ocean liner that had mistakenly dropped anchor in the garden. The hosts and their visitors were strolling around the deck, enjoying the cool evening, or taking their ease in the lounge chairs on the terrace, like tarnished ghosts, spirits from another day, some murmuring to themselves, some making idle chatter, others perhaps recalling years long gone by or searching their memories for the names of their fellow residents or absent children and grandchildren. At that age, reviewing the past is like being deep within a labyrinth: at times the fog makes it impossible to recognize a place, an event, a loved one. The uniformed nurses moved about silently, tucking blankets around feeble legs, distributing nightly pills, serving tea to the residents and cool drinks to their guests. From invisible speakers came the youthful chords of a mazurka by Chopin that did not have the slightest relation to the measured internal rhythms of the inhabitants of the home.

The dog Cleo leaped with joy when Francisco and Irene entered the garden.

"Be careful, don't step on the forget-me-nots," Irene warned her friend as they boarded the ship and she led him toward the voyagers from the past.

Irene's hair was pulled back into a knot that bared the curve of her neck; she was wearing a long, simple cotton dress, and for the first time since Francisco had known her, she had removed her jangling copper and brass bracelets. Something about her puzzled Francisco, although he could not say what it was. He watched her as they circulated among the old people; she was smiling and friendly with them all, especially the ones who were in love with her. Each one lived in a present suffused with nostalgia. Irene pointed out the hemiplegic who dictated his letters to her because he could not hold a pen in his rigid fingers. He wrote to childhood friends, to sweethearts long gone, to relatives dead and buried for decades; Irene never mailed those heartbreaking letters, to prevent his disappointment on receiving the letters returned and marked "Not at this address." She fabricated replies and mailed them to the old man to spare him the pain of knowing he was alone in the world. Irene also introduced Francisco to an addled old fellow who never had visitors. His pockets were stuffed with spicy treasures that he guarded with his life: faded pictures of blooming young girls; sepia-tinted postcards hinting of a thinly veiled bosom; a darling leg exhibiting a garter of ribbon and lace. Then they came to the wheelchair of the wealthiest widow in the land. She was wearing a rumpled dress, a shawl consumed by time and moths, a single white First Communion glove. Dangling from her chair were plastic bags filled with trinkets, and on her knees rested a box of buttons that she counted and recounted to be sure that none was missing. A bemedaled Colonel intervened to tell them in asthmatic whispers that cannon shot had pulverized the lower half of that heroic woman's body. Do you know she has a heavy bag of gold coins she earned fair and square for being nice to her husband? Can you imagine, young man, what a dolt he must have been to pay for what he could have had free? I always counsel my recruits not to squander their pay on whores, because women happily spread their legs at the mere sight of a uniform. I say that from my own experience—I still have more than I can handle. Before Francisco could untangle any of these mysteries, a tall, very thin man with a tragic face approached them and asked about his son, his daughter-in-law, and their baby. Irene spoke to him privately, and then led him to a group engaged in animated conversation, and stood beside him until he seemed calm. Later, she explained that the old man had had two sons. One had left the country to live on the far side of the globe; his only communication with his father was through letters that were increasingly more distant and cool, because absence is as great an enemy as the passing of time. The other son had disappeared, along with his wife and a baby only a few months old. The old grandfather had not been blessed with losing his reason, and the minute they turned their backs he was out on the street looking for his children. Irene wanted to replace his tormenting speculations with the certainty of grief, and she assured him she had proof that his children were no longer alive. He would not, however, give up hope that someday he might find the child, since there were rumors of babies that had been saved through the traffic in orphans. Some already given up for dead had appeared suddenly in faraway countries; some had been adopted by families of other nationalities; others had been located in charitable institutions after so many years they did not even remember having had parents. With compassionate lies, Irene had succeeded in preventing his slipping out every time the garden was left unguarded, but she could not prevent him from wasting his dreams in hopeless torment, or his life in meaningless inquiries and the expectation of visiting the graves of his loved ones. Francisco also met a parchment-and-ivory couple sitting rocking in a wrought-iron love seat; they barely knew their own names but had had the good sense to fall in love in spite of the stubborn opposition of Beatriz Alcántara, who considered it an intolerable breach of decent behavior. Who ever heard of a pair of doddering old fools sneaking around stealing kisses? Irene, in contrast, defended their right to this last happiness, and wished all the guests the same luck; love would save them from loneliness, the cruelest sentence of old age. So leave them alone, Mama. Don't look at the door that she leaves open every night, don't put on that face when you find them together in the morning. Of course they make love, even though the doctor says that at their age it's impossible.

And last, Irene pointed out a woman sipping a cool drink on the terrace: Look carefully, that's Josefina Bianchi, the actress, have you heard of her? Francisco saw a small woman who had doubtless been a real beauty and, in a certain way, still was. She was wearing a dressing gown and satin slippers because she lived her life on Paris time—a difference of several hours and two seasons. Around her shoulders was draped a moth-eaten fox fur piece, with pathetic staring glass eyes and woebegone tails.

"Cleo pounced on her stole one day, and by the time we got it away from her, the foxes looked as if they had been run over by a train," said Irene, restraining the dog.

The actress had trunkfuls of old clothes she had worn in her favorite performances, garments unused for half a century that she frequently brushed off to parade before the bedazzled eyes of her friends in the retirement home. She had lost none of her faculties, including a talent for flirting, and her interest in the world remained undiminished; she read all the newspapers, and from time to time went to the movies. She was Irene's favorite, and the nurses treated her with deference, calling her "ma'am" instead of "dearie." To console her in her

last years, she had her inexhaustible imagination. Entertained
by her own fantasies, she lacked time or will to worry about
the pettiness of life. There was no chaos in her memories; they
were stored in perfect order, and she was happy when hunting through them. In that, she was luckier than other old people from whose minds entire episodes from the past had been
erased, making them fear that they had not lived them. Josefina Bianchi had her full life to sustain her, and her greatest
happiness lay in recalling it with the precision of a statistician.
Her only regret was for opportunities she had missed: the
hand she had not held out; the tears unshed; the mouths left
unkissed. She had had several husbands and many lovers; she
had lived her adventures without assessing the consequences;
she wasted time with great satisfaction, since, she often said,
she would live to be a hundred. She had arranged for her future with a good sense of the practical, choosing the retirement home herself when she realized she could no longer live
alone; and she charged a lawyer with the task of administering
her savings to assure her well-being to the end of her days. She
felt a deep affection for Irene Beltrán; in her youth Josefina Bianchi had been blessed with the same fiery hair, and it amused
her to pretend that the girl was her great-granddaughter, or
was she herself at the height of her splendor. She opened her
treasure-filled trunks, showed Irene her scrapbooks, let her
read letters from lovers who had lost their peace of mind and
all control of their senses over her. She and Irene had made a
secret pact: The day I dirty my drawers, Josefina Bianchi had
pleaded, or can't put on my lipstick, you help me die, daughter.
And of course, Irene had promised.

"Mother's gone away on a trip, so we'll have dinner alone,"
Irene said as she led Francisco up the inside stairway to the
second floor.

The lights from The Will of God Manor—and the music—did not reach the second floor; everything was dark and silent. By the time the visitors had left and the residents had returned to their rooms, the calm of night was settling over the house, casting its peculiar shadows. Rosa, fat and magnificent, met them in the hall with her wide smile. She had a soft spot for the dark young man who always greeted her so warmly, joked with her, and was not above rolling on the floor and wrestling with the dog. She felt much closer and more familiar with him than with Gustavo Morante, although she had no doubt that he was not as good a match for her little girl. In the months she had known Francisco, she had never seen him in anything but the gray corduroy pants and the same rubber-soled shoes. What a pity. Well dressed, always blessed, she thought, but immediately corrected herself with the contrary proverb: Clothes don't make the man.

"Turn on the lights, Irene," she recommended before plunging into the kitchen.

The living room was decorated with Oriental rugs, modern paintings, and a few art books scattered in strategic disorder. The furniture looked comfortable, and a profusion of plants lent their freshness to the room. While Irene uncorked a bottle of rosé wine, Francisco settled onto the sofa, thinking about his parents' house where a record player was the only luxury.

"What are we celebrating?" he asked.

"That we're lucky to be alive," Irene replied, without smiling.

He watched her without speaking, confirming his sense that something about her was different. He watched her pour the wine into the goblets with an unsteady hand, a sad look on her face, tonight innocent of any makeup. To gain a little time and examine his own thoughts, Francisco looked through the records and selected an old tango. He put it on the record player and they heard the unmistakable voice of Gardel coming to them across fifty years of history. They listened in silence, holding hands, until Rosa came to announce that dinner was served in the dining room.

"Wait here, don't move," Irene said, turning off the lights as she left.

She returned in a few minutes carrying a five-branched candelabrum, an apparition from another century in her long white dress, the glimmer of candlelight streaking her hair with metallic highlights. Solemnly she led Francisco along the corridor to the dining room that had been converted from a former bedroom. The furniture was too large for the dimensions of the room, but Beatriz Alcántara, with unfailing good taste, had overcome that obstacle by having the walls painted a Pompeian red, which contrasted dramatically with the glass of the table and the white upholstery of the chairs. The only painting was a still life of the Flemish school: onions, garlic, a shotgun resting in a corner, and three deplorable pheasants hanging by their feet.

"Don't look at it too long or you'll have nightmares," Irene warned.

Francisco silently toasted the absence of Beatriz and the Bridegroom of Death, content to find himself alone with Irene.

"And now, my friend, tell me why you're so sad."

"Because until now I've been living a dream, and I'm afraid to wake up."

Irene Beltrán had been a spoiled child, the only daughter of wealthy parents, protected from any contact with the world and even the restiveness of her own heart. Adulation, pampering, coddling, an English school for young ladies, a Catholic university, careful monitoring of newspapers and television: there's so much evil and violence today, it's better to protect her from those things; she'll suffer enough when she grows up, it's inevitable, but let's give her a happy childhood . . . go to sleep, sweetheart, Mama is watching over you. Pedigreed dogs, gardens, horseback riding at the Club, skiing in winter and the beach all summer long, dancing classes to teach her to move gracefully: she doesn't walk, she bounces, and flops into chairs like a contortionist; leave her alone, Beatriz, don't be at her all the time. We have to, we have to give her guidance: X-ray her spine, keep her face scrubbed, a psychologist because Tuesday she dreamed of quicksand and woke up screaming. It's your fault, Eusebio, you've spoiled her with gifts more suitable for one of your mistresses: French perfumes, lace blouses, jewelry inappropriate for a child of her age. You're the guilty one, Beatriz; because you're so frivolous and lacking in understanding, Irene dresses the way she does to defy you, the analyst himself said so. Well, I say in spite of everything we did for her, look how she turned out: an unconventional girl who mocks everything and gives up painting and music to be a journalist. I never have liked that profession, they're all scoundrels, there's no future in it, and it's dangerous besides! All right, Beatriz, but at least we've made her happy; she laughs easily, and she has a generous heart; with a little luck she'll be happy until she gets married, and then when she has to face the task of living, she'll at least be able to say that her parents gave her a happy childhood. But you went away, Eusebio, damn you, you abandoned us before she finished growing up, and now I'm lost; trouble is seeping in through every crack and crevice, through the leaks in the roof, I'm drowning in it, I can't hold it back any longer; every day it's more difficult to keep Irene from all evil—amen. You see her eyes? They were always a wanderer's eyes, that's why Rosa thinks she won't have a long life, she always seems to be saying goodbye. Look at them, Eusebio, her eyes are different now, they're filled with shadows, as if she were looking into a deep well. Where are you, Eusebio?

Irene had gauged the enormity of her parents' hatred before they themselves suspected it. During the nights of her childhood, she had lain awake, staring at the ceiling, listening to their endless recriminations with an indescribable anxiety in her bones. Her mother's tearful telephone calls, the long, confidential exchanges with her friends, kept Irene awake. She could not hear the words, distorted by closed doors and her own anguish, but her imagination gave them meaning. She knew her mother was talking about her father. Irene never fell asleep until she heard his car drive into the garage and his key in the lock; then her worry evaporated, she breathed a sigh of contentment, closed her eyes, and sank into sleep. By the time he reached her room to kiss her good night, Eusebio Beltrán always found his daughter fast asleep, and he left calmly, thinking she was happy. As soon as the child was able to decipher the many little signs, she knew that one day he would leave—as, finally, he did. Her father was a transient in life, always passing through, shifting from foot to foot, incapable of standing still, his eyes lost in the distance, abruptly changing subjects in the middle of a conversation, asking questions but not listening to the answers. Only when he was with Irene did he seem to acquire any permanence. She was the sole human being he ever truly loved, and she alone held him for more than a few years. He was at her side during the memorable moments of her progress toward womanhood: he bought her her first brassière, her nylons, her high-heeled shoes; he told her where babies come from—an amazing story. Irene could not imagine two persons who hated each other as much as her parents doing that to bring her into the world.

With time she came to realize that the man she adored could be despotic and cruel. He tormented his wife unmercifully, calling attention to each new wrinkle, to the unwanted pounds at her waist. Have you noticed how the chauffeur looks at you, Beatriz? You're cut out for a proletarian taste, darling. Caught between the two, Irene played the referee in their endless squabbles. Why don't you make up, and we'll celebrate with a cake? she implored. Her heart inclined toward her father because her relationship with her mother was colored with rivalry. Beatriz watched as Irene's figure filled out, and felt that with every curve she herself aged a year. Please, God, I don't want her to grow up.

Irene awakened early to the challenge of life. At twelve, she seemed younger, but she was already agitated by an inner turbulence, by a desire for adventure. These stormy emotions fevered her days, and often disturbed her sleep. An avid and indiscriminate reader, in spite of her mother's censoring eye, Irene read any book that came to her hands; the books she did not want Beatriz to see, she read beneath the blankets at night by the light of a flashlight. As a result, she knew more about life than was normal for a child of her environment; what experience had denied, she supplemented with romantic fantasies.

Eusebio Beltrán and his wife were on a trip the day the baby fell through the skylight. That was years ago now, but neither Rosa nor Irene would ever forget it. The chauffeur had picked up Irene at school, and had left her at the garden gate to go do some other chores. It had rained all day; at that hour the winter sky was the color of molten lead and the streetlamps were beginning to come on. Irene was surprised to find her house so dark and silent. She opened the door with her key, but to her amazement Rosa wasn't waiting for her as usual; nor did she hear the six-o'clock serial blaring from the radio. Irene left her books on the entry-hall table and walked down the corridor without turning on the lights. A vague and shadowy presentiment drew her forward. She tiptoed along the hall, hugging the walls, summoning Rosa with all the strength of her thoughts. The living room was empty, and so were the dining room and kitchen. Not daring to go any farther, Irene stood listening to the sound of the drumming in her chest, tempted simply to stand there without moving, without even breathing, until the chauffeur returned. She tried to rationalize, telling herself there was nothing to be afraid of; maybe her Nana had gone out, or maybe she was down in the cellar. Since Irene had never been alone in the house before, her uneasiness prevented her from thinking clearly. As the minutes ticked by, she sank lower and lower against the wall, until finally she was huddled in a little ball. When she noticed that her feet were cold and realized that the heat had not been turned on, she feared something really serious had happened, because Rosa never left her duties undone. Irene somehow found the courage to stand up and go look for her. She moved slowly down the hall, until she heard a moan. Every nerve in her body tensed; then curiosity overcame her fear and guided her steps toward the forbidden territory of the servants' quarters. The hot-water heaters, the laundry and ironing rooms, the wine cellar, and the pantry were here. From Rosa's room, at the far end of the corridor, came the sound of muffled sobbing. Irene walked toward the room, her eyes round, fear pounding at her temples. She saw no light beneath the door, and scenes of horror flashed through her fantasy. Stories from forbidden books rushed to her mind: brigands had invaded the house, and Rosa was lying stretched out on the bed with her throat slit from ear to ear; she was being devoured by carnivorous rats that had swarmed up from the cellar; bound hand and foot, she was being violated by a madman, which had happened in a story the chauffeur had lent her. She could never have imagined what she did find when she went into Rosa's room.

Cautiously, Irene lifted the latch and pushed open the door. She slipped her hand around the doorjamb and felt along the wall until she touched the light switch; she turned on the light. What met her eyes, dazzled by the sudden brilliance, was Rosa, her enormous and beloved Rosa, collapsed on a chair with her dress pulled up around her waist and her heavy, dark legs sheathed in wool stockings up to her blood-stained knees. Her head was thrown back and her face distorted with pain. On the floor between her feet lay a reddish mass encircled by a long, blue, twisted fleshlike cord.

When she saw Irene, Rosa tried to pull down her dress to cover herself, and struggled in vain to get to her feet.

"Rosa! What's the matter with you?"

"Go away, child. Don't come in here."

"What's that?" Irene asked, pointing to the floor.

She ran to her Nana; she put her arms around her and with the tail of her school pinafore she wiped the sweat from Rosa's forehead, and covered her cheeks with kisses.

"Where did that baby come from?" she asked finally.

"From up there—it fell in through the skylight," Rosa replied, pointing to an air vent in the ceiling. "It fell on its head and died. That's why it's covered with blood."

Irene leaned over to observe it; indeed, the infant was not breathing.

It did not seem to be the moment to explain that she knew

a little about such things, and that she could see very clearly that this was a six- or seven-month fetus, approximately three and a half pounds in weight, male, and blue from oxygen deprivation—probably stillborn. The only thing that surprised her was that she had not noticed the pregnancy earlier, but she attributed that to her Nana's abundant flesh. Rosa could easily disguise a swelling belly among her many rolls of flesh.

"What shall we do, Rosa?"

"Ay, child! We mustn't tell anyone. Do you swear you'll never tell?"

"I swear it."

"We'd better throw it in the trash."

"That's a terrible way to end up, Rosa. It isn't the poor little thing's fault it fell through the skylight. Why don't we give it a burial?"

And give it a burial they did. As soon as Rosa could get up, wash herself, and change her clothes, they wrapped the infant in a plastic shopping bag and sealed it with adhesive tape. They hid the plastic coffin until late that night; then, after making sure the chauffeur was asleep, they carried the body to the garden to be buried. They dug a deep hole, placed the package with its sad contents at the bottom, carefully shoveled back the dirt, tamped it down, and said a prayer. Two days later, Irene bought some forget-me-nots and planted them on the place where the baby-that-fell-through-the-skylight lay sleeping. From that time on, Rosa and Irene were united by an affectionate complicity, a secret that neither of them mentioned for many years, until it became so natural to them that the subject began to appear casually in their conversations. No one in the house paid any attention to what they were talking about, and every new gardener was charged by young Irene to tend the forget-me-nots with care. When the tiny flowers bloomed in the spring, she cut some and left them in her Nana's room.

Playing with her cousin Gustavo, Irene discovered shortly afterward that kisses taste like fruit, and that the clumsiest and most inexpert caresses can inflame the senses. They used to hide to exchange kisses, awakening sleeping desires. It was several summers before they experienced the ultimate intimacy, both because they feared the consequences and because they were held in check by the obstinacy of Gustavo, who had been taught that there are two kinds of women: the decent ones that you marry, and the other kind that you take to bed. His cousin belonged to the first group. They knew nothing of how to avoid pregnancy, and it was only later—when Gustavo was initiated into the ways of men by the rough barracks life, and when his morality had become a little more flexible—that they could make love unafraid. During the years that followed, they matured together. Marriage would be a mere formality for these cousins who had already pledged each other their futures.

In spite of Gustavo and the wondrous introduction to love, the center of Irene's universe continued to be her father. She knew his virtues, as well as his many defects. She had surprised him in countless betrayals and lies; she had seen him act with cowardice, and watched him follow women with the eyes of a hound on the scent of a bitch. She had no illusions about him, but she loved him deeply. One evening Irene felt his presence in her room, where she sat reading, and knew before looking up that this was farewell. She saw him standing on the threshold, and had the impression that he was his own ghost, that he was not there, that he had vanished in a puff of smoke, as she had always feared he would.

"I'm going out for a while, sweetheart," said Eusebio, kissing her forehead.

"Goodbye, Papa," the girl replied, certain that he would never return.

And he never did. Four years had passed, but through some subtle compensatory mechanism Irene had not, like everyone else, given him up for dead. She knew he was alive, and that gave her a certain peace of mind; she could imagine he was happy in a new life. Nevertheless, the winds of violence that were currently shaking her world filled her with doubts. She feared for him.

Francisco and Irene had finished eating. Their figures were silhouetted against the walls, tall wavering shadows projected by the tremulous candlelight. They were speaking almost in whispers, in keeping with the intimacy of the moment. Irene was telling Francisco the sad story of the philanthropic butcher shop, and he was thinking that, after this, nothing about Irene's family could ever surprise him.

"It all began when my father met the envoy from Arabia," she said.

The Arab had been appointed by his government to buy sheep. He met Eusebio Beltrán at a reception in the Arabian Embassy, and because each was driven by the same unremitting obsession for beautiful women and lavish parties, they became friends on the spot. After the reception, Irene's father invited his new friend to prolong the festivities at the house of a certain well-known lady, where they continued to celebrate with champagne and beautiful mercenaries until the evening ended in a noisy bacchanal that would have dispatched other, less hardy souls straight to hell. The next morning, the two men awoke with queasy stomachs and blurred memories, but after a shower and a thick, spicy clam chowder, they began to revive. Abstemious, like any good Muslim, the Arab was suffering real torment from his hangover, and for hours Irene's father offered him companionship and consolation with natural remedies such as camphor rubdowns and cold cloths on the forehead. By dusk, they were brothers and had poured out their life secrets to each other. That was when the foreigner suggested to Eusebio that he take charge of the sheep operation, because there were tons of money in it for the man who knew how to take advantage of it.

"Well, I've never seen a ewe on the hoof, but if they're anything like heifers or hens, I shouldn't have any trouble," said Beltrán, with a laugh.

So began the business arrangement that would lead to Beltrán's financial ruin, even to his oblivion, as his wife had prophesied long before she had evidence to support her convictions. Beltrán traveled to the extreme south of the continent where such animals proliferate, and set about constructing a slaughterhouse and refrigeration plant, investing a large portion of his own fortune in the project. When everything was ready, a holy man from the heart of Araby was sent to supervise the ritual killings and thereby insure that everything would be carried out according to the strict laws of the Koran. Kneeling toward Mecca, the holy man was to say a prayer for every slaughtered sheep; further, he was to confirm that the animal was beheaded by a single stroke of the blade and bled in the hygienic manner prescribed by Mohammed. Once they were sanctified, cleaned, and frozen, the carcasses were to be air-expressed to their ultimate destiny. In the first weeks, the proceedings were carried out with appropriate rigor, but the Imam soon lost his initial enthusiasm. He had no incentive. No one around him understood the importance of his duties; no one spoke his language; no one had read the Holy Book. To the contrary, he was surrounded by foreign ruffians who laughed in his face as he chanted his Arabic prayers and constantly taunted him with obscene gestures. Debilitated by the cold southern climate, by nostalgia and culture shock, his spirit was quickly broken. Eusebio Beltrán, always a practical man, suggested that to avoid interruption in the operation, the Imam should record his prayers on a tape recorder. After that, the Imam's decline was apparent to all. His malaise reached alarming proportions; he stopped coming to the slaughterhouse altogether; he capitulated to idleness, gambling, oversleeping, and the vice of liquor—everything his religion forbade—but no one is perfect, as Beltrán consoled him when he found the Arab lamenting his human frailty.

The sheep continued to leave the plant, stiff and cold as lunar rocks, without anyone's being the wiser; no one knew that their impurities had not been bled through the jugular, or that the tape recorder was reeling off *boleros* and *rancheras* instead of the obligatory Muslim prayers. All this would have been of little consequence had his Arab government not sent—without previous warning—a second Imam commissioned to monitor his South American associate. On the same day the new arrival visited the plant and saw how the precepts of the Koran were being subverted, the sheep business was shut down and Eusebio found himself saddled with both a vociferously repentant Muslim mystic, who was nonetheless reluctant to return home immediately, and a mountain of worthless frozen sheep, which Eusebio could not sell because their flesh was not appreciated in his country. Then it was that the magnanimous aspect of Eusebio's personality came into play. He betook himself and his merchandise to the capital, where he drove his truck through the neighborhoods of the poor, giving away meat to the most needy. He was sure that his initiative would be imitated by other wholesalers, whose generosity would be challenged and who would also give a portion of their products to the destitute. He dreamed of a fraternal chain formed by bakers, greengrocers, fishmongers, and storekeepers, by impresarios of pasta, rice, and caramels, by importers of tea, coffee, and chocolate, by processors of preserves, liquors, and cheeses; in a word, Beltrán dreamed that every industrialist and businessman in the land would contribute a part of his earnings to alleviate the evident hunger of the downtrodden, the widows, the orphans, the unemployed—all the afflicted. But none of this came to pass. The butchers termed his grand gesture the work of a clown, and everyone else simply ignored him. But because he enthusiastically continued his crusade in the face of all odds, he was threatened with death for trying to ruin the business and prestige of honorable merchants. When they called him a Communist, it was almost more than Beatriz Alcántara's nerves could stand. She had summoned up sufficient strength to tolerate her husband's extravagances, but she could not bear the brunt of that dangerous accusation. Eusebio Beltrán, personally, continued to hand out legs and shoulders of lamb from a truck plastered with huge posters and equipped with a loudspeaker announcing his program. Soon he was being watched by the police and stalked by hired killers; his competitors had decided to put an end to the whole business. He was harassed with jeers and death threats, and his wife received anonymous letters of unimaginable obscenity. When his truck with its PHILANTHROPIC BUTCHER SHOP sign appeared on television, and the lines of the poor swelled to a throng beyond the control of the guardians of law and order, Beatriz Alcántara lost her last shred of patience, and unleashed all the bile stored up in a lifetime of bitterness. That was when Eusebio had left, never to return.

"I've never worried about my father, Francisco. I was sure that he'd left to get away from Mother and from his creditors, from the damned sheep that had begun to rot when he couldn't get rid of them," said Irene. "But now I'm not sure about anything."

Her nights were filled with fear: in her dreams she saw the ashen bodies in the Morgue; Javier Leal dangling like some grotesque fruit from a tree in the children's park; the endless lines of women inquiring about their *desaparecidos*; Evangelina Ranquileo, barefoot and in her nightgown, calling from the shadows. Among so many alien ghosts she also saw her father, sinking into a quagmire of hatred.

"Maybe he didn't run away. Maybe they killed him. Maybe he's a prisoner—that's what my mother believes," Irene sighed.

"There's no reason why a man of his position would have become a victim of the police."

"Reason has nothing to do with my nightmares, or with the world we're living in."

Just then Rosa entered, announcing that a woman was asking for Irene. Her name was Digna Ranquileo.

Digna carried the weight of the ages on her shoulders, and her eyes had grown pale from so much looking down the road, and waiting. She asked Francisco and Irene to forgive her for coming at such a late hour, and added that it was because she was desperate, she hadn't known whom to turn to. She couldn't leave her children by themselves, so it was impossible for her to travel during the day; but Mamita Encarnación had offered to stay with them tonight. Because of the midwife's kindness, Digna said, she'd been able to catch a bus to the capital. Irene told her she was glad she had come; she led her into the living room, and offered her something to eat, but Digna would accept only a cup of tea. She sat uneasily on the edge of her chair, eyes downcast, hugging her worn black pocketbook to her body. A shawl covered her shoulders and her hose were rolled to her knees, not quite meeting the hem of her narrow wool skirt. Her effort to conquer her shyness was painfully evident.

"Have you learned anything about Evangelina, *señora*?"

Digna shook her head and, after a long pause, she told them that she'd given up hope for Evangelina; everyone knew that searching for someone who'd disappeared was a task that had no end. She hadn't come about Evangelina, but about Pradelio, her oldest son. Her voice faded to an almost inaudible whisper.

"He's hiding," she confessed.

Pradelio had fled from Headquarters. Because the country was in a state of war, he could pay with his life for this act. Once, all you had to do to resign from the police was to go through some red tape, but now they were part of the armed forces and had the same responsibilities as soldiers on the field of battle. Pradelio Ranquileo was in a dangerous position; if they caught up with him, he would be in bad trouble; his mother understood how bad after she'd seen him hunted like an animal. Hipólito, her husband, was the one who made the important decisions in the family, but he'd hooked up with the first circus that set up its tent nearby. All he had to do was hear the boom of the bass drum announcing the spectacle, and he would pull out the suitcase containing the trappings of his trade, join in the hullabaloo, and be off on circuits through villages and towns, and she could never catch up with him. And Digna had not dared tell her problem to anyone else. For several days, she mulled it over, not knowing what to do, until she remembered her conversation with Irene Beltrán and the journalist's interest in the misfortune that had befallen the Ranquileo home. She thought of Irene as the only person she could turn to.

"I have to get Pradelio out of the country," she whispered.

"Why did he desert?"

Digna didn't know. One night he had come to the house, pale and drawn; his uniform was hanging in shreds, and he had the look of a crazy man. He would not tell her anything. He said he was starving, and he wolfed down anything he could find in the kitchen: raw onions, huge chunks of bread, dried meat, fruit, tea. Once he had had his fill, he folded his arms on the table, rested his head on his arms, and slept like a baby. Digna watched him while he slept. For more than an hour she sat by his side, trying to imagine the long journey that had brought him to this point of exhaustion and fear. When he woke up, he said he didn't want to see his brothers and sisters, because they might forget and tell someone he'd been there. It was his plan to flee into the mountains where not even the buzzards could find him. The only purpose for his visit was to say goodbye to his mother, and to tell her they would never see him again, because he had a mission and he intended to carry it out, even if it cost him his life. Later, during the summer, he would cross the border through a pass. Digna Ranquileo asked no questions. She knew her son: he would not share his secret—not with her, not with anyone. She limited herself to reminding him that to cross those endless peaks without a map, even in good weather, was madness; many men had wandered through these mountains until they were overtaken by death. Then the snow fell and covered them, and they disappeared until the next summer when some traveler came across their remains. Digna suggested that he hide until they got tired of looking for him, or head south where the cordillera was not so high and it would be easier to cross.

"Let me be, Mother," Pradelio interrupted. "First I must do what I have to do, and then I'll get away the best I can."

He had gone up into the mountains, led by his younger brother Jacinto, who knew the hills like no one else. High at the summit he had found a hiding place; for food, he ate lizards, rodents, roots, and what little his brother could bring him from time to time. Digna resigned herself to seeing him fulfill his destiny, but when Lieutenant Ramírez had come and searched the area house by house looking for him, threatening anyone who might be concealing him, and offering a reward for his capture, and when Sergeant Faustino Rivera, dressed in civilian clothes, silently turned up one night at her house to warn her in whispers that if she knew where the fugitive was hiding, to tell him that they were going to comb the hills until they found his hideout, his mother had decided not to wait any longer.

"Sergeant Rivera is like one of the family, that's why he felt obliged to warn me," Digna clarified.

For a countrywoman who had lived her entire life in the place where she was born, and who knew only the nearest towns, the idea that a son of hers would end up in another country was as inconceivable as his hiding at the bottom of the sea. She could not imagine the size of the world beyond the peaks outlined against the horizon, but she suspected that the world stretched to regions where they spoke in other tongues and where people of different races lived in unimaginable climes. In those regions it was easy to stray from the straight and narrow and be swallowed up by bad luck, but to go was better than dying. She had heard talk of people going into exile, a frequent topic of conversation in recent years, and she hoped that Irene could help Pradelio escape the same way. Irene tried to explain the insurmountable difficulties of the plan. Anything as audacious as trying to outwit armed police, leaping over an iron fence and safely seeking asylum in an embassy, was out of the question—and no diplomat would give protection to a deserter from the armed forces, particularly one fleeing for reasons unknown. The only solution was to try to find someone connected with the Cardinal.

"I can go to my brother José," Francisco offered finally, very reluctant to jeopardize his organization by letting a military man in on the secret, even if he was a poor guardsman running from his own companions. "The Church has mysterious paths to safe havens, but they will insist on knowing the truth, *señora*. I will have to talk with your son."

Digna explained that he was dug into a hole in the cordillera at a height where it was hard to breathe, and that to get there you had to climb a goat trail, picking your way through rocks and brush. It was not an easy climb; the road would be long and hard for someone not accustomed to mountain trails.

"I will try it," said Francisco.

"If you go, I'm going, too," Irene declared.

That night Digna timidly eased herself into the bed that Irene had improvised for her, and with dazed eyes spent the hours staring at the ceiling. The next day, after Irene had packed a bundle of provisions for Pradelio, the three of them set off for Los Riscos. Francisco suggested that such a huge backpack might hamper their climb, but when Irene looked at him mockingly, he did not insist.

On the way, Digna told them everything she knew about

the ominous disappearance of Evangelina, starting from the instant the lieutenant had dragged her to the jeep that unforgettable Sunday night. Her daughter's cries had floated across the fields, informing every shadow, until a vicious slap had sealed her lips and stilled her kicking. At Headquarters, the corporal of the guard saw them arrive, but had not dared ask any questions about the prisoner, and was reduced to looking the other way. At the very last moment, after Lieutenant Ramírez had hit the girl so hard she could not stand, and was practically carrying her to his office, the sergeant felt so bad he worked up his courage and asked his superior to go easy on her because the girl was sick and she was the sister of a man in the squad. His superior cut him off short, however, and slammed the door, catching a piece of the girl's white petticoat that fluttered there like a wounded dove. For a while he heard sobs; then, silence.

Sergeant Faustino Rivera had thought that night would never end. His heart was so heavy he could not go to bed. He passed some time talking with the corporal of the guard; he made a few rounds to be sure that everything was in order, and then went and sat beneath the eaves of the stables and smoked his strong black cigarettes; he felt the spring breeze carrying the distant perfume of the flowering hawthorns, and smelled the stronger scent of fresh horse manure. It was a still, transparent, starry night. Rivera had no clear idea of what he was waiting for, but he sat there until he could see the earliest signs of dawn, perceptible to those who are born close to nature and accustomed to rising early. At exactly three minutes after four—as he told Digna Ranquileo, and later repeated, defying any threats to seal his lips—he watched as Lieutenant Juan de Dios Ramírez left the building carrying something in his arms. In spite of distance and darkness, Rivera had no doubt that it was Evangelina. Ramirez was stumbling slightly, but not from drunkenness, since he never drank on duty. The girl's hair was almost brushing the ground, and as Ramírez staggered along the path to the parking lot, it actually dragged in the gravel. From where he sat, Sergeant Rivera could hear the officer's ragged breathing, and guessed that it was not from the effort, because the slim body of the prisoner would weigh very little in the arms of a big, muscular man used to heavy exercise. He was puffing like a bellows because he was nervous. Rivera watched the officer lay the girl down on the cement platform used for unloading bales and provisions. The searchlight that circled all night in the tower to warn of possible attacks kept sweeping the scene, illuminating Evangelina's childlike face. Her eyes were closed, but she may have been alive; the sergeant thought he heard her moaning. Lieutenant Ramírez walked to a white truck, climbed into the driver's seat, turned on the motor, and slowly backed toward the platform where he had left the girl. He got out, picked her up, and loaded her into the rear of the vehicle just at the moment the light flashed past. Before Ramírez pulled up the canvas, Faustino Rivera had seen Evangelina, lying on her side, her face covered by her hair and her bare toes protruding through the fringe of a poncho. Then Ramírez had trotted back to the building, disappeared through a kitchen door, and a minute later returned carrying a pick and shovel, which he placed in the back of the truck beside the girl. He climbed back into the truck and drove to the exit gate. The guard on duty recognized his chief, saluted smartly, and opened the heavy gates. The vehicle drove off down the highway, heading north.

Sergeant Faustino Rivera waited, consulting his watch between cigarettes, squatting in the shadow of the stables. Occasionally he stood up to stretch his legs and once, overcome by sleep, he nodded off, leaning against the wall. From his position he could see the guardhouse where Corporal Ignacio Bravo was whiling away his boredom masturbating, unaware of any witness. Just before dawn the temperature dropped and the cold dispelled Rivera's drowsiness. It was six o'clock and dawn was tinting the horizon when the truck returned.

Sergeant Faustino Rivera wrote all that he had observed in the greasy notebook he always carried with him. He had a mania for jotting down everything that happened, whether important or trivial; he could never have imagined that this habit would cost him his life several weeks later. From his hiding place, he watched his superior officer adjust his cartridge belt and holster, get out of the vehicle, and walk to the building. The sergeant ran to the truck and felt the tools, noting the fresh dirt adhering to the blades. He could not swear to what that might mean, or to the officer's activities during his absence; he made that very clear to Digna Ranquileo. But anyone could guess.

The car driven by Francisco Leal stopped before the Ranquileo home. It was not a school day, and all the children came running out to greet their mother and the visitors. Mamita Encarnación, with her pouter-pigeon bosom, dark bun pierced with hairpins, stocky legs marbled with varicose veins, followed close behind, a formidable old woman who had intrepidly sailed through the disasters of life.

"Come in and rest, I'll fix you some tea," she said.

Jacinto took them to Pradelio. He was the only person who knew his brother's hiding place, and he understood that he had to guard that secret, even at the cost of his own life. They saddled the Ranquileos' two horses; Irene and the boy rode the mare, and Francisco rode the other, hard-mouthed and skittish. It had been years since he had been on a horse, and he felt uneasy. Thanks to a childhood friend at whose farm he had learned to ride, Francisco was a good rider, though he had no style. Irene, on the other hand, was a regular Amazon because, during the good years, her parents had given her a pony.

They rode toward the cordillera, up a narrow, lonely path. Normally, no one ever passed that way, and weeds had almost obscured the trail. After they had ridden a way, Jacinto told them they could go no farther with the horses; they would have to climb now, looking for ledges of rock to find a foothold. They tied the horses to some trees and continued the climb on foot, helping one another up the steep slopes. Francisco felt as if he were hauling a cannon in his backpack. He was at the point of asking Irene to carry it for a while, since she had been so stubborn about bringing it, but he took pity when he saw her gasping with fatigue. The palms of her hands were raw from the rocks, her pants were torn at the knee, she was sweating, and every few feet she asked how much farther they had to go. The boy's answer was always the same: Just up there, around that bend. Weary and thirsty, they continued for what seemed hours beneath a pitiless sun, until Irene said she could not go a step farther.

"Going up isn't so bad. Wait till you have to come down," Jacinto observed.

They looked down, and Irene shrieked. They had climbed like goats up a sheer gorge, clinging to any underbrush that had sprouted in the rugged terrain. Far below, they saw the dark splotches of the trees where they had tied the horses.

"I'll never be able to get down. I feel dizzy," whimpered Irene, leaning forward, seduced by the precipice plunging below her.

"You came up—you'll be able to go down," said Francisco, supporting her. "Hang on, *señorita*, it's just up there, around that bend."

Then Irene pictured herself wobbling on a mountaintop, moaning with terror, and her sense of the absurd came to her rescue. She drew a deep breath, took her friend by the hand, and announced that she was ready to go on. Planning to retrieve it later, they discarded the knapsack with the provisions, and Francisco, liberated from the crippling weight, was able to help Irene. Twenty minutes later, they came to a cleft in the cliff where suddenly there were shadows cast by tall brush and the comfort of a miserly stream of water winding down through the rock. They realized that Pradelio had chosen this refuge because of the spring, for he could never have survived in these arid mountains without it. They knelt down and splashed water over their faces, their hair, their clothing. When Francisco looked up, the first thing he saw were cracked boots, then green pants and a sun-reddened, naked torso. Last of all, he saw the dark face of Pradelio del Carmen Ranquileo, who was looming over him, pointing his service revolver at them. He had grown a beard, and his hair, matted from dust and sweat, looked like some sort of exotic seaweed.

"Mama sent them. They've come to help you," said Jacinto.

Ranquileo lowered the revolver and helped Irene to her feet. Through an entrance hidden behind brush and rocks, he led them to a shady, cool cave. There Francisco and Irene stretched out flat on the ground while the boy took his brother to look for the jettisoned backpack. In spite of his extreme youth and frail body, Jacinto seemed as energetic as he had when they started out. For long minutes Irene and Francisco were alone. Irene fell immediately asleep. Her hair was damp and her skin burned. An insect crawled up her neck toward her cheek, but she did not feel it. Francisco moved his hand to brush it away, and touched her face, soft and warm as a summer peach. He admired the harmony of her features, the lights in her hair, her body abandoned to sleep. He wanted to touch her, to bend near her and feel her breath, to cradle her in his arms and protect her from the premonitions that had tormented her since the beginning of this adventure, but he too was overwhelmed with fatigue, and he slept. They did not hear the Ranquileo brothers return, and when one of them touched his shoulder, he waked with a start.

Pradelio was a giant. His enormous frame was inexplicable in a family of short people. Sitting in the cave, reverently opening the knapsack and extracting his treasures, caressing a package of cigarettes in anticipation of the pleasure of the tobacco, he looked out of scale with his surroundings. He had grown thin; his cheeks were sunken and dark circles rimmed his eyes, aging him prematurely. His skin had been cured by the mountain sun; his lips were cracked, his raw shoulders blistered and peeling. Huddled in this small chamber carved from living rock, he looked like a buccaneer who had been blown far off his course. He used his hands carefully, two great paws with gnawed and filthy fingernails, as if he was afraid he would destroy everything he touched. Uncomfortable in his body, he appeared to have shot up suddenly, without time to get used to his own dimensions; incapable of calculating the length and weight of his extremities, he bumped around the world, eternally searching for ways to move and stand. He had lived in this confining lair for many days, eating rabbits and mice he hunted with stones. His only visitor was Jacinto, the link between his solitary confinement and the land of the living. He spent his hours hunting, never using his gun, because the revolver must be saved for emergencies. He had fashioned a sling for hunting birds and rodents, and hunger had refined his marksmanship. A rank smell from one corner of the cave marked the place where he had piled the feathers and skins of his victims, to avoid leaving any traces outside. To ease his boredom, he had only a few cowboy novels his mother had sent him; he made them last as long as possible, for they were his only diversion through the long days. He felt like the survivor of a cataclysm, so lonely and desperate that at times he longed for the walls of his barracks cell.

"You shouldn't have deserted," said Irene, trying to shake off the inertia that had sunk into her soul.

"If they catch me, they'll shoot me. I have to leave the country, *señorita*."

"Turn yourself in, they won't shoot you."

"No, I'm fucked whatever I do."

Francisco explained the difficulty of obtaining asylum. After so many years of dictatorship, now no one left the country by that route. He suggested that Pradelio should hide for a time, while he, Francisco, tried to arrange false documents for him; with new documents he could go to a different province and begin a new life. Irene thought she must have misunderstood; she could not imagine that her friend knew anything about counterfeit papers. Pradelio spread his arms in a gesture of hopelessness, and they realized it would be impossible for a man who stood out like a giant cypress, and whose face was unmistakably that of a fugitive, to escape the notice of the police.

"Tell us why you deserted," Irene insisted.

"Because of Evangelina, my sister."

And then, little by little, searching for words from the still waters of his habitual silence, interrupting their flow with long pauses, he told them his story. What the giant did not say, Irene asked by looking into his eyes, and what his eyes did not tell she could guess from his deep flush, from the gleam of his tears, from the trembling of his huge hands.

When the rumors began to fly about Evangelina and her strange sickness, attracting the nosy and dirtying her good name, putting her in the same class with the *locos* in the insane asylum, Pradelio Ranquileo had lost sleep. Of all the members of his family, Evangelina, from his earliest memory, was the one he loved most, and that love had grown with time. Nothing had ever touched his heart like helping that tiny, frail little thing take her first steps—she, with her blond hair, so different from all the other Ranquileos. When she was born, he was still a boy, too tall and too strong for his age, used to doing a grown man's work and to taking over his absent father's responsibilities. He was a stranger to either pleasure or tenderness. Digna spent her life pregnant or nursing the newest baby, which did not keep her from working the land and doing the household chores, but she needed someone to lean on. She had turned to her oldest son, giving him authority over the other children. In many ways Pradelio was the man of the house. He took on that role while still very young, and even when his father came home, he did not completely relinquish it. Once when his father was drunk and was getting rough with Digna, he had stood up to him—and that was what finally made him a man. The boy had been asleep, but was awakened by the sound of muffled sobs; he leaped out of bed and peered through the curtain that separated the corner where his parents slept. He saw Hipólito with uplifted hand, and his mother huddled on the floor, covering her mouth with her hands to keep from waking the children with her moans. Pradelio had witnessed similar scenes before, and in his heart even believed that a man has the right to keep his wife and children in line, but that night had been more than he could stand and he had gone blind with rage. Without thinking, he rushed at his father, beating him and cursing him until Digna begged him to stop, because a hand raised against your parents will turn to stone. The next day, Hipólito awakened with his body covered with bruises. His son ached from his exertion, but none of his arms or legs were petrified, in spite of what the old proverb said. And that was the last time Hipólito had lifted a hand against any member of his family.

Pradelio del Carmen Ranquileo had always been aware that Evangelina was not his sister. Everyone else treated her as if she were, but to him she had always been different, ever since she was a toddler. Using the excuse of helping his mother, he had bathed her and rocked her and fed her. The little girl adored him, and at every opportunity she put her arms around his neck, or climbed into his bed, or curled up in his arms. She followed him everywhere, like a little puppy, hounding him with her questions; it was his stories she wanted to hear, and she would only go to bed if he rocked her to sleep with his songs. For Pradelio, the games with Evangelina were charged with anxiety. He suffered whipping after whipping for putting his hands on her, in that way repaying his guilt. Guilt for the wet dreams where she called to him, obscene, tempting; guilt for hiding and watching as she squatted in the bushes to pee; guilt for following her to the irrigation ditch when it was time for her bath; guilt for inventing forbidden games where they hid far away from everyone, hugging and petting until they were both on the verge of collapse. Obeying the instinct that all women have, the child kept her brother's secret; she was as sly as he was. She was innocent and shameless, flirtatious and modest, and she used these emotions in turn to drive him crazy, to rub his senses raw, to keep him her prisoner. Their parents' restrictions and vigilance merely fed the fire that boiled in the blood of the adolescent Pradelio, a fire that led him to prostitutes at much too early an age, for he found no consolation in a boy's solitary pleasure. When Evangelina was still playing with dolls, he already dreamed of possessing her, calculating how the thrust of his manhood would go through her like a sword. He sat her on his knees to help her with her lessons, and as he looked for the answer to the problems in her notebook, he felt his bones dissolve, and something warm and sticky flowing through his veins; his strength melted away, he could not think, he felt he would surely die when he smelled the smoke of her hair and the lye soap of her clothes and the sweat of her neck, and felt the weight of her body on his. How could he stand it, unless he howled like a dog after a bitch in heat, unless he grabbed her and gobbled her up, unless he ran to the nearest poplar and hanged himself by the neck till he was dead to pay for the crime of loving his sister with such sinful passion? She could sense what he was feeling, and she wiggled around in his lap, pressing, rubbing, shifting, until she felt him grow tense and moan like a drowning man, pressing his knuckles against the edge of the table as a sharp, sweetish smell enveloped them both. Those games lasted throughout Evangelina's childhood.

At eighteen Pradelio Ranquileo left home to fulfill his military service, and he never went back.

"I left in order not to sully my sister with my hands," he confessed to Irene and Francisco in the mountain cave.

After completing his service, he immediately enlisted with the police. Evangelina had been frustrated, confused; she could not understand why she had been abandoned; she was oppressed by feelings that she could not name but that had been in her heart long before the stirring of sex. This was why Pradelio had fled his destiny as a poor farmer—he had fled from a girl becoming a woman, and from memories of a childhood tainted by incest. In the years that followed, he had grown to his full size and found a certain peace. Change in the political scene had contributed to his maturity and dimmed his obsession for Evangelina; overnight he had ceased to be an insignificant rural guardsman and had found what power was about. He had seen fear in other men's eyes, and he liked that. He felt important, strong—in command. The day before the military coup, he had been told that the enemy intended to wipe out the Army and set up their Soviet tyranny. The enemy must truly have been dangerous and skillful, because to that day no one had ever learned of their bloodthirsty plans except the commanders of the armed forces, who were always vigilant on behalf of the nation's interests. If the military had not made their move, the whole country would have been sunk into civil war, or would have been occupied by the Russians, as Lieutenant Juan de Dios Ramírez had explained to him. The timely and courageous actions of every soldier, Ranquileo among them, had saved the country from a terrible fate. That's why I'm proud to wear the uniform, although some things I don't like. I follow orders without asking questions, because if every soldier started arguing over what his officer told him to do, we'd be in it up to our asses, for sure—the whole country would go straight to hell. I had to arrest a lot of people, I admit that, even men I knew, and friends, like the Floreses. A bad business about the Flores men getting mixed up in the Farmers Union. They seemed like good people, and who would ever have thought they would get it in their heads to attack the barracks? What a crazy idea. How did Antonio Flores and his sons ever get mixed up in something like that?

They were smart enough, they'd been to school. Luckily, Lieutenant Ramírez had been warned by the *patrones* of the neighboring farms and he'd been able to act in time. It was tough for me to arrest the Floreses. I still remember the screams of the other Evangelina as we took off all the men of her family. It hurt me, because she's my true sister, as much a Ranquileo as I am. Yes, there were lots of prisoners in those days. I made a lot of them talk. I took them to the stables and tied them up and beat the hell out of them. We shot some too, and other things I can't tell because it's a military secret. The lieutenant trusted me, he treated me like a son. I respected him and looked up to him. He was a good chief, and he sent me on special missions that he couldn't trust to weaklings and bigmouths like Sergeant Faustino Rivera, who loses his head after one beer and starts blabbing like an old woman. Lieutenant Ramírez told me many times: Ranquileo, you'll go far, because you know how to keep your mouth shut. And you've got courage. Tight-lipped and courageous, those are a soldier's greatest virtues.

Once he had some authority, Pradelio had overcome his horror of his sins, and had escaped the ghost of Evangelina—except during visits home. Then she stirred his blood again with her little-baby hugging and kissing, except she was not a baby now, she was a woman, and she acted like one. The day he had seen her arched backward, turning and twisting and moaning in a grotesque parody of the sexual act, all the torrid, almost forgotten torments came flooding back. He tried desperate measures to get her out of his mind: long ice-cold showers at dawn and chicken skin doused with vinegar, to see whether ice in his bones and fire in his gut would bring him to his senses. But nothing worked. That was when he had told everything to Lieutenant Juan de Dios Ramírez, bound to him by old and strong bonds.

"I'll take care of your problem, Ranquileo," the officer promised after listening to his bizarre story. "I like for my men to tell me their worries. You did right to confide in me."

The very same day of the debacle at the Ranquileo home, Lieutenant Ramírez sentenced Pradelio to solitary confinement. He gave no explanation. Pradelio spent several days on bread and water without knowing the reason for his punishment, although he supposed it had some connection with his sister's indelicate behavior. When he thought about what happened, he couldn't help smiling. He couldn't believe that a skinny little girl who was about as big around as a worm, a kid who didn't even have a woman's breasts yet, just two plums poking out of her rib cage, could have lifted the lieutenant in the air and shaken him like a mop in front of all his men. Ranquileo thought he must have dreamed it; maybe he'd gone a little out of his head from hunger and loneliness and desperation, and that in fact it had never happened. But then he had to ask himself why he was in solitary. It was the first time anything like this had ever happened to him; not even during his military service had he suffered such humiliation. He had been a model recruit, and now for several years he had been a good policeman. Ranquileo, his lieutenant always told him, you were born to wear this uniform. You must always defend it and have faith in your superiors. And he always had. Lieutenant Ramírez had taught him to drive the company vehicles and had even made him his driver. Sometimes they went out together to drink a few beers and visit the whores in Los Riscos, just like good friends. That's why he had dared to tell him about his sister's attacks, about the stones raining on the roof tiles, the dancing cups, and the restless animals. He had told him everything, never dreaming that the lieutenant would take a dozen armed men to raid his parents' house, or that Evangelina would make the lieutenant a laughingstock by dusting him around in the dirt of the patio.

Ranquileo liked his job, he told Francisco and Irene. He was a simple man, and had never liked to make decisions; he would rather keep his mouth shut and follow orders, and was happier when he placed the responsibility for what he did in someone else's hands. He stammered badly as he spoke, and his fingertips were bloody where he had chewed his nails down to the quick.

"I never used to chew them," he apologized.

He was much happier in his rough military life than he had been at home. He didn't want to go back to the country. He had found a life in the armed forces, a destiny, a new family. He had the strength of an ox when it came to standing his shift, or going on wild sprees, or doing nights of guard duty. He was a good comrade, ready to share his rations with a hungrier man, or his poncho with one who was colder. He never took offense at his comrades' clumsy jokes or lost his good nature; he smiled happily when they kidded him about being the size of a Percheron, and hung like one as well. They laughed at his eagerness to do his job, his reverent respect for the sacred military institution, his dream of being a hero and giving his life for the flag. Suddenly all that had collapsed. He had no idea why he was in the cell, or how much time had gone by. His only contact with the outside world were the few words whispered by the man who brought him his food. Once or twice the guard had given him cigarettes, and he'd promised to bring a cowboy novel or some sports magazines, although there wasn't any light to read them by. During those days, he had learned to exist on whispers, on hopes, on little tricks to make the time go by. He tried to sharpen all his senses, to feel he was a part of what was going on outside his cell; even so, there were moments he felt so alone he thought he had died. He listened to the sounds outside; he knew when the guard changed; he counted the vehicles entering and leaving the compound; he tuned his ear to recognize voices and steps distorted by distance. He tried to sleep, to shorten the hours, but inactivity and anxiety robbed him of sleep. A smaller man could have stretched and exercised in that confined space, but for Ranquileo the cell was a straitjacket. Lice from his mattress nested in his hair and rapidly multiplied. He clawed at the nits in his armpits and groin until he was bleeding. He had a bucket for a toilet, and when it was full the stench became his worst torture. He decided that Lieutenant Ramírez was putting him to the test. Maybe he wanted to confirm his endurance and his mettle before he entrusted some special mission to him; that's why Pradelio had not used his right to appeal during the first three days of confinement. He tried to stay calm, not to give in, not to sob or yell as most of the men in solitary did. He wanted to put his best foot forward, to show his physical and moral strength, so his officer would be impressed with him; he wanted to prove that he would not break even under the most extreme conditions. He tried to walk around his cell to stretch his muscles and avoid leg cramps, but it was impossible because his head touched the ceiling and when he opened both arms he touched the walls. In the past they had confined as many as six prisoners in that cell, but only for a few days, never for as long as Pradelio had been there; besides, they weren't ordinary criminals, they were enemies of the nation—Soviet agents and traitors—Lieutenant Ramírez had left no doubt on that point. Pradelio was a man used to exercise and fresh air, and the forced immobility of his body also affected his mind; he got dizzy, he forgot names and places, he saw monsters in the shadows. To keep from going mad, he sang to himself. He liked to sing, although normally he was too shy. Evangelina liked to listen to him sing; she would lie quietly with her eyes closed, as if she were hearing the voices of sirens: Sing me some more . . . sing me some more. . . . While he was a prisoner, he had more than enough time to think about her, to remember everything about her, about the pact of forbidden desire they had shared since they were children. He gave his imagination free rein, and imposed his sister's face on the memory of his wildest sexual excesses. It was Evangelina who opened to him like a ripe red watermelon, juicy and warm; she who sweated that clinging, fishy odor; she who bit him, scratched him, sucked him, moaning with shame and pleasure. It was into her compassionate flesh that he plunged until he stopped breathing and turned into a sponge, a jellyfish, a starfish at the bottom of the sea. For hours he stroked himself, evoking Evangelina's ghost, but there were always too many hours left over. Inside those walls time was frozen in an eternal instant. Sometimes he reached the limits of his endurance and thought that if he banged his head against the wall until his blood trickled under the door and alerted the guard, maybe they would at least transfer him to the infirmary. One evening, when he was at the point of doing just that, Sergeant Faustino Rivera appeared. He opened the slit in the iron door and passed Pradelio cigarettes and matches and chocolate.

"The boys send their greetings. They're going to buy you candles and some magazines to help pass the time. They're worried about you, and want to talk with the lieutenant to see if he won't get you out of here."

"Why *am* I here?"

"I don't know. Maybe because of your sister."

"Everything's all fucked up, Sergeant."

"It looks that way. Your mother came to ask about you, and about Evangelina, too."

"Evangelina? What is the matter with Evangelina?"

"Don't you know?"

"What happened to my sister!" screamed Pradelio, rattling the door like a crazy man.

"I don't know anything. Don't yell like that, because if they find me here I'll pay for it good, Ranquileo. Don't give up hope, now, I'm your kin and I'm going to help you. I'll come back soon," said the sergeant, and hurried away.

Ranquileo dropped to the floor of his cell, and for hours every man who walked through the yard heard a man's wails that he would not soon forget.

Ranquileo's friends organized a committee to go to Lieutenant Ramírez on his behalf, but nothing came of it. The men became restive; there was whispering in the latrines, in the corridors, in the armory, but Lieutenant Juan de Dios Ramírez ignored it. Then Sergeant Rivera, the boldest among them, decided to take things into his own hands. A day or two later, taking advantage of the complicity of darkness and the temporary absence of Lieutenant Ramírez, he approached the solitary confinement cell. The guard on duty saw him coming, instantly guessed his intention, and helped by pretending to be asleep, because he, too, thought Ranquileo's punishment was unjust. Not even troubling to be quiet or avoid being seen, the sergeant took the key hanging from a nail on the wall and walked to the iron door. He freed Ranquileo from his cell, gave him clothes and a service revolver with six bullets, led him to the kitchen, and with his own hands served him a double ration of food. Then he gave Ranquileo a little money his friends had collected, and drove him as far as he dared in the Headquarters jeep. Everyone who saw them looked the other way; they did not want to know any of the details. A man has a right to avenge his sister, they said.

Dragging himself along by night, and lying low in the fields by day, Pradelio Ranquileo was free almost a week before daring to seek help; he could imagine the lieutenant's rage when he discovered the escape, and he knew the guardsmen could not disobey their orders to move heaven and earth to find him. Hulking in the shadows, he waited until impatience and hunger finally drove him home. Sergeant Rivera had been there and had told everything to Digna, so there was no need to talk about that. Vengeance is a man's business. When he said goodbye, Rivera had asked him to go look for his sister, but he really meant, go avenge her. Pradelio was sure of that. As he was sure that she was dead. He had no proof, but he knew his superior officer well enough to imagine.

"I'll pay for doing what I must do, because when I come down from this mountain, I'm a dead man," he told Francisco and Irene.

"Why?"

"Because I know a military secret."

"If you want our help, you'll have to tell us."

"I'll never tell."

Pradelio was highly agitated; he was sweating and gnawing at his fingernails; his eyes were wild, and he was rubbing his face with his hands as if to erase horrible memories. It was obvious that he had left a lot unsaid, but his lips were sealed by loyalty. Once he stammered that it would be better to die and get it over with, because there was no way out for him. Irene tried to calm him: he must not give up hope; they would find some way to help him, they simply needed a little time. Francisco had sensed several omissions in his story, and instinctively mistrusted him, but he kept running through the possibilities in his mind, trying to think of some way to save Ranquileo's life.

"If Lieutenant Ramírez killed my sister, I know where he hid her body," Pradelio blurted at the last moment. "You know that abandoned mine in Los Riscos?"

He stopped abruptly, regretting what he had said; by the expression on his face and the tone of his voice, however, Francisco knew he was not talking of a probability, but of a certainty. He had given them their clue.

It was midafternoon by the time they said goodbye and began their descent, leaving behind a beaten Ranquileo muttering about death. Going down the mountain was as difficult as the climb had been, especially for Irene, who shuddered every time she looked into the ravine, but she did not stop until they reached the place where they had left the horses. There she breathed a sigh of relief, and when she gazed up toward the cordillera, it seemed impossible that they had climbed those sheer cliffs now blending into the color of the sky.

"That's all we can do today. I'll come back later with some tools to see what's in that mine," said Francisco.

"And I'll come with you," said Irene.

They looked at each other and knew that each was committed to follow to the end an adventure that could lead them to death, and beyond.

Beatriz, heels clicking, walked arrogantly across the polished airport floor, following the porter with her blue suitcases. She was wearing a low-cut, tomato-colored linen dress and her thick hair was in a bun at her neck because she had lacked the energy for a more elegant style. A large baroque pearl in each earlobe highlighted her burnt-sugar skin and the gleam of her dark eyes brightened by a new sense of well-being. Several hours of an uncomfortable flight with a Galician nun for a seatmate had not obliterated the happiness of her latest rendezvous with Michel. She felt like a new woman, rejuvenated and sexy. She walked with the insolence of a woman who knows she is beautiful. Men's eyes turned as she passed, and no one could have guessed her true age. She could still wear a low-cut dress without fear of sagging breasts or flabby arms; her legs were trim and the line of her back proud. Sea air had lent happiness to her face, brushing out fine wrinkles around her eyes and mouth. Only her hands, spotted and veined in spite of all her magic creams, betrayed the passing of the years. She was satisfied with her body. She considered it her handiwork, not nature's; it was the end product of enormous willpower, of years of diet, exercise, massage, yoga, and the advances of cosmetology. In her suitcases she carried little bottles of oil for her breasts, collagen for her throat, hormone lotions and creams for her skin, placental extract and mink oil for her hair, capsules of royal jelly and pollen of eternal youth, machines, sponges, and horsehair brushes to tone the elasticity of her skin. It's a losing battle, Mama, age is implacable, and there's nothing you can do but delay it for a little while. Is it worth all that effort? When Beatriz lay on the warm sands of some tropical beach wearing nothing but one tiny triangle of cloth, and compared herself with women twenty years younger, she smiled with pride. Oh, yes, daughter, it's worth it. When she walked into a room and could feel the air charged with envy and desire, she knew then that her efforts had been rewarded. But it was especially in Michel's arms that she was secure in the knowledge that her body was a valuable commodity; it was he who gave her her greatest pleasure.

Michel was her secret luxury, the reaffirmation of her self-esteem, the source of her deepest vanity. He was young enough to be her son: tall, with a *torero*'s broad shoulders and narrow hips, sun-bleached hair, blue eyes, charming accent, and all the necessary knowledge at the hour for love. Leisure, sports, and lack of responsibility kept an eternal smile on his face and gifted him with a playful disposition. He was a vegetarian who neither drank nor smoked; he made no pretense at any intellectual interests but found his delight in outdoor sports and amorous adventures. Gentle, tender, uncomplicated, and always good-humored, he lived in another dimension, like an angel mistakenly fallen to earth. Ingeniously, he arranged his life so that it was an eternal vacation. He and Beatriz had met on a beach beneath swaying palm trees, and when in the darkness of the hotel ballroom he first took her in his arms to dance, they both knew that a greater intimacy was inevitable. That same night Beatriz opened her door to him, feeling like a teenager. She was nervous, fearing that he might discover tiny signs of age that had escaped her stern eye, but Michel gave her little time to worry. He turned on the lights, so he could know her in every detail; he kissed her with expert lips and removed her adornments—baroque pearls, diamond rings, ivory bracelets—leaving her naked and vulnerable. At that moment she sighed with contentment, because in her lover's eyes she found the confirmation of her beauty. She forgot the hurrying years, the wear and tear of the struggle, her boredom with other men. She and Michel shared a happy relationship, and never dreamed of calling it love.

Michel's company was so stimulating that when Beatriz was with him she forgot all her worries. His kisses had the uncanny ability to erase the elderly occupants of The Will of God Manor, her daughter's bizarre behavior, and her financial difficulties. Beside him, there was only the present. She smelled his young animal smell, his clean breath, the sweat of his smooth skin, the salty trace of sea in his hair. She ran her hands over his body, the wiry hair on his chest, the smoothness of his recently shaved cheeks; she felt the strength of his embrace, the renewed thrust of his sex. No one had ever made love to her like this. Her relations with her husband had been clouded with stored-up bitterness and unintentional rejection, and her occasional lovers were older men who made up for lack of vigor with pretense. She tried not to think of their thinning hair, their soft bodies, their pernicious smell of tobacco and liquor, their striving penises, their niggardly gifts, their useless promises. Michel never lied. He never said, I love you; he said, I like you, I feel good when I'm with you, I want to make love to you. He was a marvel in bed, eager to give her pleasure, to satisfy her whims, to arouse new desires.

Michel represented the hidden and, at the same time, the brightest side of her life. She could not possibly share her secret; no one would have understood her passion for a man so much younger than she. She could imagine her friends' comments: Beatriz has lost her head over some boy, a foreigner; of course he will exploit her and take all her money; at her age, she should be ashamed. No one would believe the tenderness and shared laughter, the friendship; he never asked for anything, and would not accept her gifts. They met twice a year, anywhere on the globe, for a few perfect days. She returned with her body gratified and her soul refreshed. Again she took up the reins of her work, resumed her duties, and returned to the elegant relationships with her perennial suitors—widowers, divorced men, unfaithful husbands, endemic seducers who showered her with their attentions without touching her heart.

As she walked through the glass door into the unrestricted area, Beatriz saw Irene waiting for her in the crowd. She was with that photographer who had been accompanying her constantly for months—what was his name? She couldn't hide a grimace of displeasure when she saw how careless Irene was about her appearance. At least when she wore her gypsy garb she showed some originality, but in those wrinkled slacks, and with her hair pulled into a braid, she looked like a country schoolteacher. When she was closer, Beatriz noticed other disturbing signs, although she could not decide exactly what they were. There was a touch of sadness in Irene's eyes, an anxious smile on her lips, but in the commotion of getting the suitcases into the car and beginning the drive home, Beatriz could not pursue her thoughts.

"I bought some beautiful clothes for your trousseau, Irene."

"I may not need them, Mama."

"What do you mean? Did something happen between you and Gustavo?"

Beatriz glanced at Francisco Leal and was about to make an acid comment, but decided to wait until she was alone with Irene. She inhaled and exhaled deeply six times, relaxing her throat, emptying her spirit of all aggression, placing herself in positive syntony, as her yoga instructor had taught her. Relaxing, she began to enjoy the beauty of the city in springtime: the clean streets, the freshly painted walls, the courteous and well-behaved people—you could thank the government for that, everything orderly and neat. She looked at shopwindows filled with exotic merchandise that once had been unknown in this country; high-rent apartments with penthouse swimming pools ringed by dwarf palms; spiral buildings housing luxury boutiques to satisfy the whims of the newly rich; and high walls hiding the slums of the city, where life did not follow the order of time and the laws of God. Since it was impossible to eliminate poverty, it had been forbidden to mention it. The news in the press was soothing; they were living in a fairyland. Rumors of hungry women and children storming bakeries were completely false. Bad news came only from outside the country, where the world struggled over insoluble problems that had no relation to their esteemed homeland. Japanese automobiles so delicate they looked disposable, as well as enormous chrome-trimmed executive motorcycles, crowded the streets. Advertisements offering exclusive apartments for the right people, trips to exotic places—on credit—and the latest advances in electronics were at every corner. Brightly lighted nightclubs had sprung up everywhere, their doors guarded until the hour of curfew. Everyone was talking of opulence, the economic miracle, the streams of foreign capital attracted by the new regime. Anyone who was discontented was considered anti-patriotic; happiness was obligatory. Through an unwritten but universally known law of segregation, two countries were functioning within the same national boundaries: one for a golden and powerful élite, the other for the excluded and silent masses. Young economists of the new school pronounced that this was the social cost, and their words were repeated in the news media.

When their car stopped for a red light, three ragged children rushed out to clean the windshield, sell them religious prints or packets of needles, or, simply, beg. Irene and Francisco exchanged a glance, both with a single thought.

"There are more poor every day," said Irene.

"Are *you* going to sing that tune, too?" complained Beatriz. "There are beggars everywhere. The fact is that people don't want to work. This is a nation of loafers."

"But there aren't enough jobs for everyone, Mama."

"What do you want? For poor people and decent people to be all the same?"

Irene smiled, not daring to look at Francisco, but her mother continued, imperturbable. "This is just a period of transition. Soon we'll be seeing better times. At least we have law and order. And don't you know that democracy leads to chaos? How many times the General has made that clear!"

The trip was completed in silence. When they reached the house, Francisco carried Beatriz's luggage to the second floor, where Rosa was waiting. Grateful for his attention, Beatriz invited Francisco to stay for dinner. It was her first friendly gesture, and he immediately accepted.

"Serve dinner early, Rosa," said Irene. "We have a surprise downstairs."

At Irene's request, Beatriz had bought little gifts for all the residents and employees. Irene had bought cakes and made a fruit punch for a celebration. After dinner they went downstairs, where they found everyone waiting dressed in their best clothes, the nurses arrayed in starched aprons, and large vases overflowing with spring flowers, all to welcome home the *patrona*.

The actress Josefina Bianchi announced that she would entertain them with a scene from a play. Francisco caught Irene's wink, realized that this was the surprise, and immediately tried to think of a way to leave before it was too late, because he suffered when anyone made a fool of himself. Irene, however, gave him no opportunity to find an excuse. She led him to a seat on the terrace beside Rosa and her mother, and disappeared into the house with Josefina. Several minutes passed, extremely uncomfortable minutes for Francisco. Beatriz made banal conversation about the places she had visited on her trip, while the nurses arranged chairs in front of the large dining-room window. The guests made themselves comfortable, wrapped in jackets and blankets to protect them against the chill of advanced age, when not even the warmth of a spring night can warm old bones. The bright lights in the garden were extinguished, the chords of a familiar sonata flooded the air, and the curtains parted. For a moment Francisco wavered between the empathy that impelled him toward flight and the unexpected spell of the spectacle before his eyes. He saw a stage bathed in light, like an aquarium in the darkness, its only furniture a yellow brocade chair beside a floor lamp with a parchment shade; a golden circle of light fell upon a figure transported from the past, a shade from the nineteenth century. At first he thought Josefina Bianchi was Irene; all the havoc of time had been erased from her face. Languorous, seductive—her every move was harmonious. She wore a magnificent dress with accordion-pleated flounces and ivory lace, faded, wrinkled, but still splendid in spite of the ash of years and long travels through wardrobe chests and trunks. Even from that distance he heard the faint rustle of silk. The actress did not so much sit as float on the air like an insect, pale, sensual, eternally feminine. And before Francisco could recover from his surprise, the music from the loudspeakers faded and he heard the ageless voice of the Dame aux Camélias; his hesitation vanished and he surrendered to the magic of the performance, the tragedy of that courtesan, her long, uncomplaining—for that, all the more moving—lament. With one hand she rejected her invisible lover; with the other she summoned him to her, pleaded with him, caressed him. Her elderly audience seemed paralyzed in memories, far away, silent. The nurses felt their hearts constrict, moved by that woman so frail and slight that a breath of air might turn her to dust. No one escaped her spell.

Francisco felt Irene's hand on his shoulder but, seduced by the performance, he did not turn to her. When a paroxysm of coughing—her role or the ravages of age—signaled the end of that immortal lover's words, Francisco's eyes were brimming with tears. Deeply saddened, he did not join in the applause. He got up from his chair and walked to the darkest part of the garden, followed by Cleo, trotting happily at his heels. There from the darkness he watched the slow movements of the old people and their nurses, all drinking punch and opening their gifts with unsure fingers, while Marguerite Gauthier, suddenly aged a hundred years, looked for her Armand Duval with a feather fan in one hand and a cream cake in the other. Ghosts slipping among the chairs and wandering along the honeysuckle-bordered paths, the intense perfume of the jasmine, the yellow radiance of the lamps—all contributed to a dreamlike atmosphere. The night air seemed electric with portents.

Irene saw Francisco and walked toward him, smiling. Then she noticed the expression on his face and guessed his emotions. She rested her forehead upon his chest and her unruly hair brushed his lips.

"What are you thinking?"

He was thinking about his parents. In a few years they would be the age of these old people who, like them, had brought children into the world and worked untiringly to provide for them. They had never dreamed they might end their days cared for by the hands of a paid employee. The Leals had lived together as a family forever, sharing poverty, happiness, suffering, and hope, bound by ties of blood and responsibility. There were still many families like theirs; perhaps the old people who had witnessed Josefina Bianchi's performance were no different from his parents; they were, nevertheless, alone. They were the forgotten victims of a wind that had scattered people in every direction, the residue of the diaspora, those who had been left behind with no place in the new era. They had no grandchildren to look after and watch as they grew up, no children to help them with the task of living; they had no garden of their own, no canary to sing as dusk fell. Their only occupation was to avoid death, but always thinking of it, anticipating it, fearing it. Francisco swore an oath that this would never happen to his parents. He repeated the promise aloud, his lips buried in Irene's hair.

PART THREE

Sweet Land

I carry our nation wherever I go, and the
oh-so-far-away essences of my elongated
homeland live within me.

—Pablo Neruda

*A*fterward, Irene and Francisco would ask themselves at what precise moment the course of their lives had changed, and they would point to the fateful Monday they entered the abandoned Los Riscos mine. But it may have been before that—say, the Sunday they met Evangelina Ranquileo, or the evening they promised Digna they would help in her search for the missing girl; or possibly their roads had been mapped out from the beginning, and they had no choice but to follow them.

They drove to the mine on Francisco's motorcycle—more practical in rugged terrain than a car—carrying a few tools, a thermos of hot coffee, and the photographic equipment. They told no one the purpose of their trip; they were both obsessed with the feeling that what they were about to do was madness. Ever since they had decided to go, at night, to a place they had never been before, and open a mine without permission, they both knew such foolhardiness could cost them their lives.

They studied the map until they knew it by heart and were sure they could reach their destination without asking questions that would raise suspicions. There was no danger in the softly rolling countryside, but once they turned onto the steep mountain roads where shadows lengthen long before sunset, the landscape became wild and lonely, and echoes returned thoughts magnified by the distant cry of eagles. Uneasy, Francisco had debated the prudence of taking Irene along on an adventure whose outcome he could not foresee.

"You're not taking me anywhere. I'm the one who's taking you," she had joked, and perhaps she was right.

A rusty but still legible sign announced that the area was patrolled and entry forbidden. Several threatening rows of barbed wire blocked access to the property, and for a minute Irene and Francisco were tempted to seize the pretext and retreat; immediately, however, they set aside that subterfuge and looked for a break in the network of wire that was large enough for the motorcycle to pass through. The sign and the fence further confirmed their hunch that there was something here to be discovered. Just as they had planned, night was upon them, helping to cloak their movements, by the time they reached the mine. The entrance to the mine drilled in the mountainside looked like a mouth shouting a soundless scream. Sealed with rocks, packed dirt, and masonry, it gave the impression that no one had been near it for years. Loneliness had settled in to stay, obscuring marks of a trail or any memory of life. They hid the motorcycle in some bushes and scouted the area to be sure there were no watchmen on patrol. The search calmed them somewhat since they found no trace of human life but only, some hundred meters from the mine, a miserable hut abandoned to wind and weeds. The wind had blown off half its roof, one wall lay flat on the ground, and vegetation had invaded the interior, covering everything with a carpet of wild grasses. Such a deserted and forgotten place so near Los Riscos and the highway seemed very odd.

"I'm afraid," whispered Irene.

"So am I."

They opened the thermos and drank a long swallow of coffee, a comfort to both body and soul. They joked a little, pretending this was just a game; each tried to make the other believe that nothing bad could happen to them, that they were protected by a guardian angel. It was a clear moonlit night, and their eyes soon grew accustomed to the darkness. They took the pick and flashlight and walked toward the shaft. Neither of them had ever been inside a mine, and they imagined it as a cavern deep beneath the earth. Francisco remembered the tradition that forbade the presence of women in mines because they were thought to bring on underground disasters, but Irene mocked that superstition, determined to continue at any cost.

Francisco attacked the entrance with his pick. He had little skill when it came to physical labor; he scarcely knew how to handle the pick, and soon realized that the job would take longer than they had planned. Irene did not attempt to help him but sat on a rock, her heavy sweater pulled tightly around her, huddled against the wind blowing from the surrounding mountains. She jumped at every sound, afraid that wild animals might be circling around, or, what would be worse, that soldiers were spying on them from the darkness. At first they tried not to make any noise, but they quickly resigned themselves to the inevitable; the ring of steel against rock resounded through gorges and ravines that trapped the echo and repeated it a hundred times. If there was a patrol in the area, as the sign warned, there would be no escape. Before a half hour had passed, Francisco's fingers were stiff and his hands covered with blisters, but his efforts had opened a hole that would allow them to remove loose stones and dirt with their hands. Now Irene helped, and soon they had opened a gap wide enough to slip through.

"Ladies first," joked Francisco, motioning to the hole.

As her answer, Irene handed him the flashlight and stepped back a couple of steps. Francisco thrust head and arms through the opening, shining the light inside. A rush of fetid air assaulted his nostrils. He was tempted to retreat, but he told himself he hadn't come this far to give up before he began. The beam carved a circle of light in the darkness, revealing a small chamber. It was not at all what he had imagined: it was a room excavated from the hard entrails of the mountain, opening onto two narrow tunnels blocked with debris. The wood scaffolding set there to prevent cave-ins when the ore was being mined was still in place, but the timbers had been eaten by time and were so rotten that some were in place only by the grace of a miracle and they looked as if a breath would bring them crashing down. Francisco flashed his light around the room, wanting to see what awaited him before he crawled inside. Suddenly something ran over his arm a few inches from his face. He cried out, more surprised than frightened, and the flashlight fell from his hand. Outside, Irene heard him and, fearing something horrible, grabbed him by the legs and began to pull.

"What was it?" she exclaimed, her heart in her mouth.

"Nothing, only a rat."

"Let's get out of here, I don't like this a bit!"

"Wait, I'll just take a quick look inside."

Francisco wriggled through the opening, carefully avoiding sharp rocks, and disappeared, swallowed by the mouth in the mountain. Irene watched the blackness envelop her friend and felt a pang of anxiety in spite of the fact that her reason told her danger lay outside the mine, not inside. If they were caught, they could expect a bullet in the head and a quick burial on the spot. People had died for far less. She remembered all the ghost stories Rosa had told her when she was a little girl: the Devil lurking in mirrors to frighten the vain; the boogeyman carrying a sack filled with kidnapped children; dogs with crocodile scales on their backs, and cloven hooves;

two-headed men who crouched in the corners to catch little girls who slept with their hands beneath the sheet. Cruel stories that had caused more than one nightmare, but tales so spellbinding she could not stop listening; she would beg Rosa to tell her another, as she trembled with fright, wanting to cover her ears and squeeze her eyes shut so she could not hear them but, at the same time, avid to know every detail. Did the Devil wear clothes or was he naked? Did the boogeyman smell bad? Did pet dogs also turn into ferocious beasts? Could a two-headed man enter a room protected by a picture of the Virgin? That night, waiting at the mine entrance, Irene again experienced the mixture of fright and attraction she had felt in the long-ago days of her Nana's terrifying tales. Finally she decided to follow Francisco and, being both small and agile, she easily crawled through the hole. It took only a few seconds to get used to the darkness. The smell, though, was unbearable, like breathing a deadly poison. She took the kerchief tied around her waist and used it to cover the lower half of her face.

They walked around the cavern and examined the two passageways. The tunnel on the right seemed to be closed only with rubble and loose dirt, while the one on the left was sealed with masonry. They chose the easier and began to move rocks and scratch away the dirt at the mouth of the first tunnel. As they dug, the stench grew stronger, and often they had to go to the entry they had crawled through and lean outside to draw a breath of fresh air, which seemed to them as clean and healthful as a mountain stream.

"What exactly are we looking for?" asked Irene as her raw hands began to burn.

"I don't know," Francisco replied, and continued working in silence, for even the vibration of their voices made the rotted supports quiver.

They were nervous and apprehensive. They stole glances over their shoulders, peering into the blackness behind them, imagining watching eyes, stealthy shadows, whispers from the far side of the room. They heard the old timbers creak and, between their feet, the furtive scurrying of rodents. The air was close and heavy.

Irene tugged at a large rock with all her might. She worked it back and forth, loosened it, and it rolled free at her feet: the light of the flashlight revealed a dark gaping hole. Without thinking, she thrust her hand inside and at that instant felt a terrible scream rising from the pit of her stomach; the sound filled the chamber, ricocheting against the walls as a muffled and alien echo she did not recognize as her own voice. She flung herself against Francisco, who covered her with his body and pushed her against the wall just as a beam crashed from the ceiling. For a moment that seemed eternal, they stood embraced, eyes closed, almost without breathing, and when finally silence returned and the dust raised by the collapse of the beam had settled, they were able to rescue the flashlight and make sure that their exit had not been blocked. Still holding Irene, Francisco pointed the light to the spot where the rock had rolled free, and the first discovery of that cave of horrors leaped toward them. It was a human hand—or, rather, what remained of one.

Francisco pulled Irene outside and, holding her close, forced her to breathe great gulps of the pure night air. When she was able to stand without his help, he brought the thermos and poured her coffee. She was beside herself, speechless, trembling, unable to hold the cup. Francisco held it to her lips, as he would for an invalid; he stroked her hair and tried to calm her, telling her that they had found what they had come to find; surely the body was that of Evangelina Ranquileo, and even though it was gruesome, it couldn't hurt them, it was only a dead body. Although the words had no meaning for her—she was still too shocked to recognize them as her own language—the cadence of his voice lulled her, consoling her slightly. Much later, when she was more herself, Francisco knew he must finish the job they had come to do.

"Wait here for me. I'm going back into the mine for a few minutes. Can you stay here alone?"

Irene nodded wordlessly, and, pulling up her legs like a boy, she buried her head between her knees, trying not to think, not to hear, not to see, not even to breathe, suspended in her unbearable anguish while Francisco, carrying the camera and with the kerchief tied over his face, returned to the tomb.

He pulled away rocks and brushed aside dirt until he had exposed the entire body of Evangelina Ranquileo Sánchez. He recognized her by the color of her hair. She was partially covered by a poncho; she was barefoot, and was dressed in something like petticoats or a nightgown. Her body was in such an advanced state of decomposition—putrefying in a broth in which maggots were feeding, fermenting in her own desolation—that he had to call on every ounce of his strength to control his nausea and get on with his work. He was a man with a great deal of self-control; he had had professional experience with cadavers and he had a strong stomach, but he had never seen anything like this before. The despicable place, the inescapable stench, and his mounting fear—all contributed to his undoing. He could not breathe. Hurriedly, he shot several photographs, not bothering about focus or distance, hastened by the bile that rose in his throat with each flash lighting the scene. He finished as quickly as humanly possible, and fled from that sepulcher.

In the fresh air he dropped the camera and flashlight and fell to the ground on his knees, head sunk to his chest, trying to relax and conquer his retching. The stench clung to his skin like a plague, and etched on his retinas was the image of Evangelina stewing in her last consternation. Irene had to help him to his feet.

"What do we do now?"

"Close the mine, then we'll see," he said as soon as he was able to reclaim his voice from the fiery claws gripping his chest.

They piled up the stones they had removed, and closed the entrance, stunned, nervous, working with frenzy; it was as if in sealing the mine they could erase its contents from their minds and turn time back to the moment before they had known the truth; as if they could again live innocently in a radiant reality, removed from that awful discovery. Francisco took Irene by the hand and led her to the ruined hut, the only visible refuge on the hill.

It was a mild night. In the virginal light, the landscape faded into nothingness, the outlines of the hills and the great shadowy eucalyptus trees disappeared. The shack was barely visible in the soft darkness, rising from the ground like an extension of nature. In comparison with the mine, the interior seemed as welcoming as a nest. They lay down in a corner on the wild grass and stared up at the infinity of the starry sky lighted by a milky moon. Irene put her head on Francisco's shoulder and released her distress in tears. He put his arms around her, and they lay there a long time—hours, perhaps—seeking solace in the quiet and the silence for what they had discovered, and strength for what they would have to bear. They rested together, listening to the faint murmur of leaves stirred by the breeze, the cries of nearby night birds, and the secret movement of rabbits in the meadow grass.

Little by little the weight pressing upon Francisco's spirit began to lighten. He became aware of the beauty of the sky, the gentleness of the earth, the fresh smell of the fields, the feel of Irene against his body. He followed her contours in his mind, and felt the weight of her head on his arm, the curve of her hip against his, her curls caressing his neck, the subtle delicacy of her silk blouse, almost as fine as the texture of her skin. He remembered the day he had met her, how he had been dazzled by her smile. He had loved her from that moment, and the insanity of the events that had led them to this cavern was but an excuse to bring him finally to this precious instant when he had her for himself, close beside him, all her guards lowered, vulnerable. He felt a surge of compelling and overpowering desire. His breath caught in his throat and his heart raced in a frantic gallop. He forgot the tenacious fiancé; Beatriz Alcántara; his own uncertain future—all the obstacles that lay between them. Irene would be his because it had been written from the beginning of time.

Irene sensed the change in Francisco's breathing, and raised her head to look at him. In the faint light of the moon each read the love in the other's eyes. Irene's warm proximity fell over Francisco like a mantle of mercy. He closed his eyes and drew her to him, seeking her lips, opening them in an absolute, promise-charged kiss, the synthesis of all hopes, a long, moist, warm kiss, a defiance of death, caress, fire, sigh, lament, sob of love. He probed her mouth, tasted her saliva, inhaled her breath, hoping to prolong that moment, battered by the hurricane of his emotions, certain that he had lived until then only for this miraculous night when he would plunge forever into the depths of intimacy with this woman. Irene, honey and shadow, Irene, peach, seafoam, the seashell of your ears, the perfume of your throat, the doves of your hands, Irene, feel this love, this passion consuming us in the same fire, dreaming you, awake, desiring you, asleep, my Irene. He did not know how much more he said to her, or what she whispered during the uninterrupted murmuring, the audible mountain stream, the river of moans and sighs of those who make love, loving.

In a flash of intuition Francisco realized that he must not yield to his impulse to hurl himself upon Irene, to tear off her clothes, ripping seams in the urgency of his delirium. He feared that the night, that life itself, would be too brief to quell this gale of passion. Slowly, and with a clumsiness caused by his trembling fingers, he undid, one by one, the buttons of her blouse and discovered the warm hollow beneath her arms, the curve of her shoulders, her small breasts and the hazelnut of her nipples, just as he had imagined them when she had leaned against him on the motorcycle, when she bent beside him over the layout desk, when he held her in his embrace in an unforgettable kiss. Irene's skin, blue in the moonlight, shivered at his touch. He lifted her to her feet and knelt before her, searching out the warmth hidden between her breasts, the fragrance of wood and almond and cinnamon; he untied her sandals and caressed her feet, small as a schoolgirl's, familiar, innocent, and delicate, as he had known them in his dreams. He unzipped her slacks and pulled them down, revealing the smooth path of her belly, the shadow of her navel, the long line of her back, which he explored with feverish fingers, the firm thighs covered with a fine golden down. He looked upon her naked, outlined against infinity, and with his lips traced her roads, dug her tunnels, scaled her hills, wandered her valleys, drawing the indispensable maps of her geography. She knelt, too, and as her head moved, dark strands invisible in the blackness of night danced on his shoulders. When Francisco removed his clothes, they were like the first man and the first woman facing the original secret. There was no room for anything else; the ugliness of the world and the imminence of death were far away; nothing existed but the glow of their encounter.

Irene had not loved like this; she had not known surrender without barriers, fear, or reserve; she did not remember having felt such pleasure, such profound communication, such mutual exchange. Marveling, she discovered the new and surprising form of her lover's body: his heat, his savor, his aroma; she explored him, conquering him inch by inch, covering him with newly invented caresses. Never had she experienced such joy in the fiesta of the senses: take me, possess me, receive me, because in this way I take you, possess you, receive you. She buried her head in Francisco's chest, breathing in the warmth of his skin, but gently he held her away from him to look at her. The black mirror of her eyes returned his image, made beautiful in their love. Step by step they began the stages of an immortal rite. She opened to him, and he abandoned himself, sinking into her most private gardens; each anticipated the other's rhythm, advancing toward the same moment. Francisco smiled in total happiness: he had found the woman he had been pursuing since his adolescent fantasies, had sought in every body through the years: his friend, his sister, his lover, his companion. Slowly, without haste, in the peace of the night, he dwelled in her, pausing at the threshold of each sensation, greeting pleasure, possessing at the same time he surrendered himself. Then, when he felt her body vibrate like a delicate instrument, and a deep sigh issued from her lips to give breath to his own, a formidable dam burst in his groin, and the force of that shuddering torrent swept over Irene, washing her into gentle seas.

They lay closely and tranquilly embraced, letting the fullness of love flow over them, breathing and throbbing in unison until that intimacy renewed desire. She felt him grow within her, and sought his lips. Witnessed only by the sky, scratched by pebbles, coated with the dust and dried leaves that clung to their skin in the riot of love, driven by an unquenchable ardor, an unrestrained passion, they tumbled in play beneath the moon until their souls escaped in their sighs and sweat and they died, finally, in one another's arms, lips touching, dreaming the same dream.

They awakened at the first morning light and chattering of sparrows, giddy from the meeting of their bodies and the complicity of their souls. Then they remembered the corpse in the mine and were catapulted into reality. With the arrogance of mutual love, but still trembling and awestruck, they dressed, climbed on the motorcycle, and set off for the Ranquileo home.

Bent over a wooden trough, a woman stood washing clothes, scrubbing the stubborn spots with a hog-bristle brush. Standing on a plank to protect her broad feet from the mud, she worked energetically, her large hands scrubbing, wringing, then piling the clothes in a pail, to be rinsed later in the running water of the irrigation ditch. At this hour, the children were in school and she was alone. Summer was in the air: ripening fruit, a profusion of flowers, suffocating siestas, and white butterflies fluttering everywhere like handkerchiefs blown on the wind. Flocks of birds had invaded the fields, joining their song to the uninterrupted drone of bees and flies. Digna noticed none of these things; she was up to her elbows in wash water, oblivious to anything not a part of her labor. The roar of the motorcycle and chorus of barking caught her ear, and she looked up. She saw the journalist and her constant companion, the man with the camera, walking toward her through the patio, ignoring the snarling dogs. She dried her hands on her apron and went to meet them, unsmiling, because even before she was close enough to see their eyes, she had guessed their bad news. Irene Beltrán put her arms around Digna in a timid embrace, the only gesture of condolence she could think of. Digna instantly understood. No tears rose to her eyes, so long accustomed to pain. She bit her lips in a grimace, and a hoarse sob escaped her throat before she could contain it. She coughed to hide such weakness and, pushing back a lock of hair from her forehead, she motioned them to follow her into the house. They sat in silence at the table for several moments, until Irene summoned the words to speak.

"I think we found her . . ." she whispered.

And she told Digna what they had seen in the mine, skipping over the gruesome details, and offering the shadow of a hope that the remains might be those of a different person. Digna rejected that possibility, however, because for many days now she had been waiting for proof of her daughter's death. She had known Evangelina was dead by the grief that had weighed on her heart ever since the night they had taken her away; and from the knowledge acquired through long years of living under the dictatorship.

"The ones they take away never come back," she said.

"But this has nothing to do with politics, *señora*. This is a civil crime," Francisco protested.

"It's all the same. Lieutenant Ramírez killed her, and he's the law. What can I do?"

Irene and Francisco, too, suspected the officer. They believed that he had arrested Evangelina to repay to some degree the humiliation he had suffered at her hands in the presence of so many witnesses. He may have intended only to hold her for a day or two, but he had been too rough, not taking into account his prisoner's frailness. And then, when he saw how much damage he had inflicted, he had changed his mind and decided to finish the job and hide her body in the mine; later he had falsified the Duty Log to protect himself in case of an investigation. But these were mere speculations. They had a long way to go before getting to the bottom of the secret. While Irene and Francisco washed up in the ditch, Digna Ranquileo prepared their breakfast. She concealed her sadness in the ritual of stirring the fire, boiling water, and setting out cups and plates. She was always embarrassed by any show of emotion.

When they smelled warm bread, Irene and Francisco realized how hungry they were; they had not tasted food since the previous day. They lingered over their breakfast. They gazed at one another in new recognition; they smiled, recalling their recent fiesta of love; their hands touched in mutual promise. In spite of the tragedy they found themselves involved in, they were suffused with an egotistical peace; it was as if they had fit together the last pieces of the puzzle of their lives, and finally could see their destinies. They felt safe from all evil, sheltered by the enchantment of their new love.

"Shouldn't we tell Pradelio, so he won't keep looking for his sister?" Irene asked.

"I'll go. You wait for me here. That way you can get a little rest, and keep *Señora* Digna company," said Francisco.

After he had eaten, he kissed Irene, and left on his motorcycle. He remembered the road and drove directly to the place they had left the horses when they had come the first time with Jacinto. He parked his motorcycle beneath the trees and continued his climb on foot. He was counting on his sense of direction to lead him to the hideout without too many detours, but soon he realized it was not to be that easy, because the whole look of the country had changed. The first heat of the year had beat down on the mountainside, drying up the vegetation and anticipating the summer's drought. Everything looked bleached and faded. Francisco did not recognize any of the landmarks he had fixed in his memory; he let himself be guided by instinct. Halfway in his climb, he stopped in distress, certain he had lost his way; he seemed to be passing the same place again and again. If it were not for the fact that he was constantly climbing, he would have sworn he was going in circles. He was exhausted from the accumulated tension of the last days and the horror of the night in the mine. Whenever possible, Francisco was a man who avoided putting his nerves to the test by acting on impulse. In his undercover work he had to take risks and was often exposed to danger, but he preferred to make meticulous plans and then try to stick to them. He did not like surprises. Now, however, he could see no point in making plans; his whole life was turning upside down. He was used to the feeling of violence in the air, floating like some insidious gas that a mere spark could ignite into an inextinguishable holocaust; like so many in that situation, however, he never thought about danger. He tried to live a normal life. But in the solitude of this mountain, he knew that he had crossed an invisible frontier and entered a new and terrible dimension.

As noon approached, the heat poured down like lava. There was no merciful shade to offer him shelter. He took advantage of an outcropping of rock, and sat down to rest a moment, hoping to restore the normal rhythm of his heart. Shit, if he was going to fold right here, he might as well turn back. But he wiped the sweat from his face and went on, climbing at a slower and slower pace, taking longer rests. Finally he came to a meager, cloudy stream trickling down between the rocks, and breathed a sigh of relief; he was sure that the trail of water would lead him to the hideout of Pradelio Ranquileo. He wet his neck and face, feeling the sun burning into his skin. He climbed the last yards, found the source of the stream, and looked for the cave in the brush, calling Pradelio at the top of his lungs. No one replied. The earth was dry and cracked; the scrub was covered with a dust that had turned the landscape the color of dried clay. Pushing aside some branches, he found the opening to the cave; he did not need to go in to know it was empty. He examined the surrounding area for traces of the fugitive, and came to the conclusion that Pradelio must have left several days before; there were no vestiges of food, or tracks on the windswept ground. Inside the cave he found empty tin cans and a few cowboy books with yellowed and greasy pages, the only indication that anyone had been there recently. Everything Evangelina's brother had left behind was carefully arranged, as would be expected of a person accustomed to military discipline. Francisco reviewed those pitiful belongings, searching for some sign, some message. There was no evidence of violence, and he decided that Pradelio had not been taken by soldiers; almost certainly, he had managed to leave in time; he may have gone down to the valley and tried to get out of the area; he may have taken his chances crossing the cordillera, in an attempt to reach the border.

Francisco sat down in the cave and leafed through the books. They were cheap paperbacks with rudimentary illustrations, bought in secondhand bookstores or magazine kiosks. He smiled at Pradelio Ranquileo's intellectual nourishment: the Lone Ranger, Hopalong Cassidy, and other heroes of the North American West, mythic defenders of justice; men who protected the helpless against evildoers. He remembered the conversation at their last meeting, how proud Pradelio was of the weapon he wore at his waist. The revolver, the cartridge belt, the boots were those of comic-book heroes, the magical elements that could turn a nobody into a master of life and death, that could give him a place in the world. These things were so important to you, Pradelio, that when they took them from you, only the knowledge of your innocence and your hope of recovering the magic kept you going. They made you believe you had power; they hammered at your brain over the barracks loudspeakers; they commanded you in the name of your country; and they gave you your share of guilt so you could not wash your hands of it but would be forever bound by ties of blood. Poor Ranquileo.

Sitting in the cave, Francisco Leal remembered his own emotions the only time he had ever held a firearm in his hands. He had passed his adolescence without major emotional disturbances, more interested in reading than in political militancy—a reaction against his father's clandestine printing press and inflamed libertarian speeches. Nevertheless, after he graduated from high school, he had been recruited by an extremist group that attracted him with their dream of revolution. Often he had searched his memory to discover why violence held such fascination, what the vertiginous attraction of war and death could be. He was sixteen when he went south with some novice guerrillas to train for an unlikely rebellion and a Great March somewhere. Seven or eight boys who needed a nursemaid more than a rifle had formed that ragged little band commanded by an officer three years older than they, the only one who knew the rules of the game. Francisco was not motivated by their goal of implanting Maoist theories in Latin America—he had not even troubled to read them—but by a simple and pedestrian longing for adventure. He wanted to escape his parents' tutelage. Eager to prove that he was a man, he left home one night without saying goodbye and with nothing in his knapsack but an explorer's knife, a pair of wool socks, and a notebook for his poetry. His family looked everywhere for him; they even went to the police, and when finally they traced his steps, they were inconsolable, feeling they had been betrayed. Professor Leal sank into silence and melancholy, wounded to the quick by the ingratitude of a son who would leave without so much as a word of explanation. Francisco's mother donned the habit of a nun of the Order of Lourdes, appealing to heaven for the return of her favorite son. For Hilda, who was always careful about her appearance—following the styles in raising or lowering the hems of her skirts, in adding a tuck here or removing a pleat there—this was an enormous sacrifice. Her husband, who at first had been prepared to put his pedagogical experience into play and calmly await his son's voluntary return, lost his composure completely when he saw his wife in the white tunic and blue girdle of Lourdes. Absolutely beside himself, he tore off her robes, vehemently denouncing all such forms of barbarism, and threatened to march out of the house, out of the country, out of America itself, if he ever saw her in that ridiculous garb again. Then he overcame his misgivings, called upon his better nature, and set out in search of his missing son. For days, he wandered the burro trails, investigating every shadow that lay in his path, and while he walked from village to village, from hill to hill, his anger steadily mounted, and he made plans to give the boy the only real thrashing of his lifetime. Finally someone told him that down in the woods they sometimes heard rifle shots, and that filthy young boys emerged once in a while to beg for food and steal hens; in truth, no one thought they were witnessing the first sketchy outlines of a revolutionary plan for the entire continent but, instead, the followers of some heathen sect inspired in India, like others seen before in these parts. That was all the information Professor Leal needed to find the guerrilla encampment. When he saw them in their rags, filthy and uncombed, eating canned beans and stale sardines, drilling with a rifle left over from the First World War, stung by wasps and all the insects of the forest, his rage evaporated in a flash to be replaced by his perennial compassion. A disciplined political militancy had persuaded him to consider violence and terrorism as strategic errors, especially in a country where social change could be effected through other means. He was convinced that such tiny armed bands did not have the ghost of a chance for success. All they would achieve was to be massacred by the regular Army. Revolution, he always said, must come from an awakened people who become aware of their rights and their strengths, and then march forward demanding liberty—but never from seven bourgeois boys playing at war.

Francisco was kneeling beside a small bonfire, heating water, when he saw an unrecognizable figure approaching through the trees. It was an old man with a three days' growth of beard and unruly hair, dressed in a dark suit and tie, covered with dust and thistles, carrying a small black suitcase in one hand and a large stick for support in the other. Francisco rose to his feet, amazed, and his companions imitated him. Then he realized who the man was. He had always thought of his father as a large, sturdy man with flashing eyes and an orator's booming voice, never as this melancholy, shabby, stooped creature limping toward them in mud-covered shoes.

"Papa!" he managed to say before he choked on a sob.

Professor Leal, dropping the crude staff and small suitcase, opened his arms. His son leaped over the bonfire, ran between his friends, and hugged his father, proving in the act that he was too old now to find shelter in those arms, because he was not only stronger but half a head taller.

"Your mother is expecting you."

"I'm coming."

While the boy ran to collect his belongings, the Professor used the occasion to deliver a brief speech to the other boys, arguing that if they wanted a revolution they would do better to proceed by following standard methods, not by improvising.

"We don't improvise, we're Maoists," said one.

"Then you're mad. What works for the Chinese won't work here," the Professor stated categorically.

Much later, those same youths would spread through forest, mountain, and jungle distributing bullets and Chinese slogans in villages forgotten by American history. But this the Professor could not suspect when he took his son from their camp. The boys watched them leave arm in arm, and shrugged their shoulders.

During the train ride home, the father sat in silence, observing Francisco. When they reached the station, he put into a few words everything that was in his heart.

"I trust this won't happen again. In the future I will give you a stropping for every tear your mother sheds. Does that seem fair?"

"Yes, Papa."

In his heart, Francisco was content to be home again. Shortly afterward, cured forever of the temptation to become a guerrilla, he submerged himself in psychology textbooks, fascinated by the game of illusions, of ideas contained within other ideas, and they, in turn, within others, in a never-ending challenge. He also lost himself in literature; seduced by the work of Latin-American writers, he realized he lived in a country in miniature, a spot on the map, buried in a vast and marvelous continent where progress arrives several centuries late: a land of hurricanes, earthquakes, rivers broad as the sea, jungles where sunlight never penetrates, where mythological animals creep and crawl over eternal humus alongside human beings unchanged since the beginning of time; an irrational geography where you can be born with a star on your forehead, a sign of the marvelous; an enchanted realm of towering cordilleras where the air is as thin as a veil, of absolute deserts, dark, shaded forests, and serene valleys. Here all races are mixed in the crucible of violence: feathered Indians; voyagers from faraway lands; itinerant blacks; Chinese stowed like contraband in apple crates; bewildered Turks; girls like flames; priests, prophets, and tyrants—all elbow to elbow, the living as well as the ghosts of those who through the centuries trod this earth blessed by seething passions. These American men and women are everywhere, suffering in the cane fields; shivering with fever in the tin and silver mines; lost beneath the water, diving for pearls; surviving, against all odds, in prisons.

Hungry for new experiences, when Francisco completed his training, he decided to perfect his knowledge by studying abroad; this disconcerted his parents somewhat, although they agreed to help finance him, and were sufficiently restrained not to utter dire warnings about the perversions awaiting young men traveling alone. Francisco spent several years outside the country, at the end of which he had gained a doctorate and an acceptable command of English. To keep body and soul together, he washed dishes in a restaurant, and from time to time photographed the revels of lesser celebrities in the barrios.

Meanwhile, his country was in full political ferment, and the year he returned a Socialist candidate was elected to the Presidency. In spite of pessimistic prophecies and failed conspiracies—and to the stupefaction of the North American Embassy—this candidate was sworn into office. Francisco had never seen his father so happy.

"You see, son. We didn't need your rifle."

"But you're an anarchist, *viejo*. Your party isn't represented in the government," Francisco teased.

"Details, details. The important thing is that the people have the power, and now it can never be taken from them."

As always, his head was in the clouds. The day of the military coup, he thought the takeover was the work of a few reactionaries whom those in the armed forces loyal to the constitution and the republic would rapidly subdue. Now, several years later, he continued to hope for this. He fought the dictatorship in outlandish ways. At the height of the repression, when stadiums and schools were being pressed into service to confine thousands of political prisoners, Professor Leal printed one of his broadsides on his kitchen printing press, climbed to the top floor of the Post Office Building, and scattered them into the street. A favorable wind was blowing and his mission was unexpectedly successful: a few copies landed on the Ministry of Defense. The text contained certain opinions that to Professor Leal seemed appropriate to the moment in history.

The education of the military, from the boot soldier to the highest-ranking officer, inescapably transforms them into enemies of civilian society and of the people. The uniform itself, with all the ridiculous embellishments that distinguish the regiments and ranks, all the infantile nonsense that occupies a large part of military life and would make all soldiers seem like clowns if it were not that they are always a threat—all this separates the military from society. The garb they wear and the thousand puerile ceremonies in which they waste their lives, with no object other than training to kill and destroy, would be humiliating for men who had not lost the last shred of human dignity. These men would die of shame had they not, through a systematic perversion of ideas, converted those symbols into a source of vanity. Passive obedience is their greatest virtue. Subject to despotic discipline, they end by feeling horror toward anyone who acts with freedom. They wish to impose by brutal discipline the stupid order of which they themselves are victims.

One cannot love the military without detesting the people.

—Bakunin

If he had given it a second thought, or consulted a more expert opinion, Professor Leal would have realized that this text was too long to be launched from the air, because before anyone could read it through, he would be arrested. But his admiration for the father of anarchism was so great that he had said nothing about his plan. His wife and children found out twenty-four hours later when the press, radio, and television published a military proclamation, and the Professor cut it out to paste in his scrapbook.

Military Proclamation Number 19

1. The citizenry is hereby informed that the Armed Forces will not tolerate public demonstrations of any kind.

2. Citizen Bakunin, the author of a slanderous pamphlet attacking the sacred honor of the Armed Forces, must present himself voluntarily at the Ministry of Defense before 4:30 p.m. today.

3. Failure to report will signify that this Bakunin has chosen to ignore the directive of the Junta of the Commanders-in-Chief, with readily foreseeable consequences.

That day, the three Leal brothers removed the printing press from the kitchen, hoping to prevent their father from falling into the trap of his impassioned idealism. From then on, they tried to give him few causes to be uneasy. None of the three told him of their activities in the opposition, but when José, along with various priests and nuns of the Vicariate, was arrested, they had not been able to prevent Professor Leal from sitting in the Plaza de Armas holding a placard that read: AT THIS VERY MOMENT, MY SON IS BEING TORTURED. If Javier and Francisco had not arrived in time to pick him up bodily and carry him away, he would have doused himself with gasoline like a bonze, and set fire to himself before the eyes of any who had gathered in sympathy.

Francisco became a part of a group organized to help fugitives escape across one border and to slip members of the opposition into the country across another. He collected funds to help survivors in hiding, and to buy food and medicines; he compiled reports to send outside the country, hidden in the soles of priests' shoes and in dolls' wigs. He carried out several almost impossible missions: he photographed parts of the confidential files of the Political Police, and recorded on microfilm the identity cards of torturers, believing that one day the material would help to see justice done. He shared this secret only with José, who did not want to know names, places, or other details, because he had already had a taste of how difficult it is not to talk in the face of certain pressures.

There, in Pradelio Ranquileo's grotto, feeling the bond of their complicity in the opposition, Francisco thought about José. He regretted not having asked earlier for his brother's help. If Pradelio had disappeared into the silence of the mountains, they would never pick up his trail; and if he had gone down to the valley seeking his revenge, and was arrested, there would be nothing they could do to save him.

Francisco shook off his weariness, splashed water on his clothing to cool off, and began his descent with the heat of early afternoon weighing on his head like a physical burden; at times he was blinded as brightly colored dots danced before his eyes. When finally he reached the grove of trees where he had left the motorcycle, he found Irene waiting for him. Worried, she ran to Francisco's arms. She had been too impatient to stay at the Ranquileo home, and had flagged down the first farmer who passed and asked for a ride in his wagon. She led Francisco to the welcoming shade of the trees, where she had removed the rocks and made the ground smooth. She helped him lie down, and while he rested, wishing he could control the jerking of his legs, she wiped the sweat from his face with her handkerchief. She split open a melon Digna had given her, and fed it to him, biting off pieces and then transferring them to his mouth with a kiss. The fruit was warm, and too sweet, but it seemed to Francisco that each mouthful was a miraculous restorative, capable of nullifying his fatigue and fending off his dejection. When there was nothing left of the melon but the tooth-marked rind, Irene wet the handkerchief in a puddle and cleaned their faces and hands. Beneath the merciless three-o'clock sun they renewed the promises they had whispered the night before, kissing and caressing with new awareness.

In spite of the exhilaration of their burgeoning love, Irene could not forget the vision of the mine.

"How did Pradelio know where his sister's body was?" she kept asking.

Actually, Francisco had not thought about that, nor did this seem the moment to do so. He was completely drained, and all he wanted in the world was to sleep a few minutes and get over his dizziness, but Irene did not let him rest. Sitting with legs crossed like an Indian fakir, she spoke rapidly, leaping from idea to idea, as she always did. If they knew the answer to *how* Pradelio knew, she said, they would have the key to some very fundamental mysteries. While Francisco's strength slowly returned, and he tried to clear his head to think rationally, Irene steered her way through the problem, raising questions and looking for answers, until she concluded emphatically that Pradelio Ranquileo knew about the Los Riscos mine because he had been there with Lieutenant Juan de Dios Ramírez. They must have used the mine to hide something. Pradelio knew it was safe, and had conjectured that his superior officer would go there if he needed such a place again.

"I don't understand," said Francisco, with the face of an awakened sleepwalker.

"It's very simple. We'll go to the mine and dig into the other tunnel. We may be surprised at what we find."

Later, Francisco would smile when he remembered that moment, because even as the circle of terror closed in around them, his overwhelming desire had been to take Irene in his arms. Forgetting the dead who were beginning to spring out of the ground like weeds, and his fear that he and Irene would either be arrested or murdered, he could think of only one thing: his eagerness to make love. More important than charting the morass they were groping their way through, he wanted to find a comfortable place where they could take their pleasure; more powerful than his fatigue, the heat, and his thirst was his urgent need to hold Irene in his arms, to engulf her, breathe her, feel her under his skin—possess her right there beneath the trees by the roadside, in full view of anyone happening by. Irene, however, had more sensible ideas. You must have a fever, she said as he tried to get her to lie down beside him. She tugged at his sleeve and pulled him to his feet, led him to the motorcycle, and prevailed on him to leave; she climbed on behind him and, hugging his waist, breathed peremptory commands and loving words into his ear, until the jolting of the machine and the white light of the sun overhead calmed her lover's impetuous passion and restored his habitual calm. And once again they were on their way to the Los Riscos mine.

It was night by the time Irene and Francisco reached the house of the Leals. Hilda was just taking a potato omelet from the stove, and the strong aroma of freshly brewed coffee filled the kitchen. After the printing press had been removed, the true proportions of the room became apparent for the first time, and everyone could appreciate its charm: the marble-topped wooden furniture, the old-fashioned icebox and, in the middle of the room, the table of a thousand uses, the place where the family gathered. In winter it was warm and cozy; light and heat from the kerosene stove, the oven, and the iron reflected off the sewing machine, the radio, and the television. It was

Francisco's favorite place in the world. His happiest childhood memories were centered on this room where he had played, studied, talked for hours over the telephone with some sweetheart with schoolgirl curls, while his mother, still young and very beautiful, went about her chores humming a tune from her faraway Spain. The fragrance of the fresh herbs and spices she used for seasoning stews and fried potato cakes always lingered on the air, the mouthwatering harmony of sprigs of rosemary, bay leaves, garlic cloves, and onions melding with the more subtle fragrance of cinnamon, clove, vanilla, anise, and chocolate used in baking breads and cakes.

That night Hilda had brewed several cups of real coffee, a gift from Irene Beltrán. This was an occasion that called for the small porcelain cups from the collection in the cupboard, all different and each as delicate as a sigh. The aroma from the coffeepot was the first thing that greeted Irene and Francisco as they opened the door, and it led them to the center of the house.

Francisco once again felt wrapped in that warm ambience, as he had when he was a thin, sickly child, the victim of the rough games of cruel and stronger boys. When he was only a few months old, he had been operated on for a congenital leg malformation. His mother had been the pillar of those early years: he lived in the shadow of her skirts; she nursed him longer than was usual; she carried him on her back, or in her arms, straddling him on her hip like an appendage of her body, until his bones healed completely and he could stand on his own feet. He came home from school every day dragging his heavy book bag and anticipating the calm, welcoming smile of his mother, waiting for him in the kitchen with a snack. That memory had left its indelible mark, and throughout his life, whenever he needed to recapture the security he had known as a boy, he reconstructed in his mind, in precise detail, the room that was the symbol of maternal love. That night, when he saw his mother turning the omelet in the frying pan and quietly humming, Francisco felt the same sensation. His father was sitting beneath the ceiling light, bent over his notebooks, correcting examinations.

The Leals were startled by the appearance of Irene and their son, the wrinkled and dirty clothing, their drawn faces, and their indefinable expressions.

"What has happened?" the Professor exclaimed.

"We found a clandestine grave. There are a *lot* of bodies," Francisco replied.

"The fuck . . . !" his father burst out, the first time he had ever cursed in his wife's presence.

Hilda, completely ignoring her husband's vulgarity, clapped the kitchen towel to her mouth, her blue eyes wide with fright. She could only stammer, "Blessed Virgin, Mother of God!"

"We think they're victims of the police," said Irene.

"*Desaparecidos?*"

"Could be," said Francisco, shaking a few rolls of film onto the table from his backpack. "I have photographs. . . ."

Hilda crossed herself automatically. Irene, at the very limits of her strength, sank into a chair as Professor Leal strode about the room, unable in all his extensive and exalted vocabulary to find words to fit the occasion. Although he was given to grandiloquence, this news had left him speechless.

Irene and Francisco told them what had happened. They had reached the Los Riscos mine in midafternoon, tired and hungry, but prepared to investigate it thoroughly, clinging to the hope that once they had resolved the matter, they would be free to return to their normal lives and to love one another in peace. In the full light of day there was nothing sinister about the site, but the memory of Evangelina caused them to approach the mine with reluctance. Francisco wanted to go in alone, but Irene was determined to overcome her revulsion and help him open up the second passage; she wanted to get it over with and be out of there as quickly as possible. They easily removed the rubble and stones at the mine entrance; they ripped Irene's kerchief into two pieces, tying the halves over their faces to protect them against the overpowering stench, and crawled into the main chamber. It was not necessary to turn on the flashlight. The sun poured through the opening, illuminating in its diffuse rays the body of Evangelina Ranquileo. Francisco arranged the poncho over the body to spare Irene that horror.

Irene had to lean against the wall to keep her equilibrium; her legs seemed to be made of rubber. She tried to put her mind on her garden at home when the forget-me-nots were blooming over the grave of the baby-that-fell-through-the-skylight, or on baskets of fresh ripe fruit on market day. Francisco pleaded with her to go outside, but she succeeded in overcoming her nausea and, picking up a piece of iron from the ground, attacked the thin layer of cement that sealed the tunnel. Francisco joined her with his pick. The mortar must have been mixed by an inexpert hand, because with every blow it crumbled into fine particles. In addition to the stench, the air was fouled by a dense cloud of dust and cement, but they did not retreat; each stroke of the tools made them increasingly certain something was waiting for them behind that barrier, a truth hidden for a very long time. Ten minutes later, they unearthed a few shreds of cloth and some bones. It was a man's ribcage, still clothed in a light-colored shirt and heavy blue sweater. While they waited for the dust to settle, they turned on the flashlight and examined the bones to determine beyond any doubt that they were human in origin. They had to dig only a little farther to find a skull; it rolled to their feet with a clump of hair still rooted in the forehead. Irene could not stomach any more, and she stumbled from the mine while Francisco kept digging mindlessly, like a silent machine. As new remains continued to emerge, he realized that they had discovered a tomb filled with corpses, and, judging from the state of the remains, they had probably been buried for some time. Parts of bodies erupted from the earth, along with tatters of clothing stained with a dark, oily substance. Before he left the tunnel, Francisco took his photographs with complete calm and precision, moving as if he were in a dream; he had passed the bounds of amazement. The extraordinary had come to seem natural, and he even found a certain logic in the situation; it was as if the violence had been there forever, waiting for him. Those dead bodies bursting from the earth, with fleshless hands and bullet holes in their skulls, had waited a long time, ceaselessly calling to him, but it was only now he had ears to hear. He found himself talking aloud, apologizing for his delay, feeling that he had failed in the rendezvous. Irene's voice calling from outside the mine brought him back to reality. He left part of his soul behind.

Between them, they closed the entrance, leaving it just as it had looked when they found it. For some minutes they gulped the pure, fresh air, gripping each other's hands and listening to the racing of their hearts. Their agitated breathing and trembling bodies informed them that they were at least alive. The sun was sinking behind the hills, and as they climbed on the motorcycle and rode off toward the city, the sky was turning the color of crude oil.

"And now what do we do?" was Professor Leal's question when they had completed their story.

For a long time they debated the best method to deal with the problem, obviously rejecting the idea of seeking help from the law, which would have been tantamount to placing their necks in a noose. They conjectured that Pradelio Ranquileo had known his sister was in the mine because he had used it to hide other crimes. If they advised the authorities, that would assure Irene and Francisco's disappearance within a matter of hours, and the Los Riscos mine would be covered with a few new shovelfuls of earth. "Justice" was an almost forgotten term, no longer mentioned because, like the word "liberty," it had subversive overtones. Though the military enjoyed impunity in all its activities, at times it created inconveniences for the government itself, since each branch of the armed forces had its own security system, and the Political Police, which was the highest power in the State, was independent of any controls. The professional zeal of these various agencies often produced lamentable errors and gross inefficiency. Not infrequently, two or more groups squabbled over who had the right to interrogate the same prisoner, for different reasons, or agents who had infiltrated an agency failed to recognize one another and ended up killing each other.

"Oh, dear God! Whatever made you go into that mine?" Hilda sighed.

"You did the correct thing. Now we must find a way to get you out of this," the Professor replied.

"The only idea that occurs to me is to report it in the press," Irene suggested, referring to the few opposition newspapers still being published.

"I'll go to them tomorrow with the photographs," Francisco said decisively.

"You won't get very far. They will kill you at the first street corner," Professor Leal assured him.

Nonetheless, they all agreed that Irene's was not such a far-fetched idea. The best solution was to shout the news from the rooftops, to send it echoing around the world, awakening consciences and shaking the very foundations of the nation. Then Hilda, drawing on her incontestable common sense, reminded them that the Church was the only entity left standing; every other organization had been broken up and swept away by governmental repression. If they had the backing of the Church, there was a chance they might accomplish the impossible: unseal the mine without losing their lives in the process. They decided to place their secret in the Cardinal's hands.

Francisco ordered a taxi to take Irene to her house before curfew; she did not have enough strength to ride behind him on the motorcycle. Francisco, who had to develop the film, was much later getting to bed. He slept badly, tossing and turning in anguish, seeing in the shadows the face of Evangelina framed by yellowed bones clacking like castanets. He cried out in his dreams and awakened to see Hilda standing by his bedside.

"I made you some linden tea, son. Drink it."

"I think I need something stronger. . . ."

"Just be quiet and do what I tell you, that's what a mother is for," she ordered, smiling.

Francisco sat up in bed, blowing on the tea to cool it, and began to sip it slowly while his mother observed him through narrowed eyes.

"Why are you staring at me like that, Mama?"

"You didn't tell me everything that happened yesterday. You and Irene made love, didn't you?"

"Dammit, Mama. Do you have to know everything?"

"I have a right to know."

"I'm too old to tell you everything I do," Francisco said, laughing.

"Look. I want to warn you that Irene is a decent young woman. Your intentions had better be honorable or you'll have to answer to me. Is that clear? And now drink your tea, and if you have a clear conscience, you'll sleep like a baby," Hilda concluded, pulling up his covers.

Francisco watched his mother leave the room, setting the door ajar so she could hear him if he called her; he felt the same tenderness he had known as a child when she sat on his bed and patted him gently until he fell asleep. Many years had gone by since then, but she still treated him with the same impertinent solicitude, ignoring the fact he was a grown man who often had to shave twice a day, who had a doctorate in psychology, and who could have lifted her off the ground with one hand. He teased her, but did nothing to change the habit of that uninhibited affection. He felt he was especially privileged, and he intended to enjoy it as long as he could. Their relationship, begun in the womb and strengthened by recognition of their mutual defects and virtues, was a precious gift they both hoped would last beyond life itself. The rest of the night Francisco slept soundly, and when he awoke he did not remember his dreams. He took a long, hot shower, ate his breakfast, draining the last of the imported coffee, and, with the photographs in his backpack, left for his brother's neighborhood.

José Leal, when not working as a plumber with blowtorch or monkey wrench, was kept busy with countless activities in the poor community where he had chosen to live in accordance with his incurable passion for serving his fellow man. He lived in a large, densely populated neighborhood that was invisible from the road, hidden behind walls and a row of poplar trees with naked branches stretching toward the sky—a place where not even vegetation thrived. Behind that discreet screen lay dirt streets and torrid heat in summer; mud and rain in winter; shacks constructed from discarded materials; garbage; clotheslines; dogfights. Idle men passed their hours in little groups on street corners, while children played with bits of junk and women struggled to prevent bad from deteriorating into worse. It was a world of deprivation and penury in which the only consolation was solidarity. Here no one dies of hunger, José said, in explanation of the communal stewpots, because before that last desperate step is taken, someone holds out a helping hand. Neighbors formed groups and contributed whatever each could scavenge for the soup shared by all. Distant relatives moved in with those who at least had a roof over their heads. In the soup kitchens the Church had set up for the children, a daily ration of food was apportioned to the youngest. Even after many years, the priest's heart still melted when he saw the freshly bathed and combed children standing in line for their turn to enter the shed where rows of aluminum plates of food waited on huge tables, while their brothers and sisters, too old now to be fed by charity, loitered around, hoping for scraps. Two or three women cooked the food the priests obtained by means of pleas and spiritual threats. Besides serving the food, the women watched to see that the children ate all their portions, because many hid food and bread to take home to a family that had nothing to put in the cooking pot but a few vegetables picked up on the rubbish heap behind the market and a bone that more than once had been boiled to lend a hint of flavor to the broth.

José lived in a wooden shack similar to many others, although his was larger because it also served as an office to minister to the temporal and spiritual needs of his disconsolate flock. Francisco, along with a lawyer and a doctor, took his turn treating the inhabitants in their disputes, illnesses, and depressions; all of them frequently felt totally useless, knowing there were no solutions to the mass of tragic problems confronting their patients.

Francisco found his brother ready to go out, dressed in his workman's overalls and carrying the heavy bag containing his plumber's tools. After making sure that they were alone, Francisco opened his pack. While the priest, turning paler and paler, looked at the photographs, Francisco told him the story, beginning with Evangelina Ranquileo and her attacks of saintliness—José had known something of this when he helped them look for her in the Morgue—and ending at the moment when the remains in the photographs lay at their feet in the mine. Francisco omitted nothing but the name of Irene Beltrán, in order to keep her safe from any possible consequences.

José Leal listened to the end, then sat in an attitude of silent meditation, staring at the floor. His brother guessed that he was struggling to gain control of his emotions. When he was young, any form of abuse, injustice, or evil had sent a searing electric current through him, blinding him with rage. His years in the priesthood and a gradual mellowing of his character had given him the strength to control these fits of anger and—with the methodical discipline of humility—to accept the world as an imperfect work where God puts souls to the test. Finally he looked up. His face was once again serene and his voice sounded calm.

"I will speak with the Cardinal," he said.

"May God watch over us in the battle we are about to undertake," said the Cardinal.

"Amen," seconded José Leal.

Once more the prelate reviewed the photographs, holding them gingerly with his fingertips, studying the stained and ragged clothing, the empty eye sockets, the rigid hands. To anyone who did not know him, the Cardinal was always a surprise. At a distance performing his public duties, on the television screen, or officiating at mass in the Cathedral in his gold-and-silver-embroidered vestments and surrounded by his court of acolytes, the Cardinal looked slim and elegant. In fact, he was a short, muscular man with a farmer's large hands, who spoke very little, and almost always in a brusque tone—more from shyness than discourtesy. Although he was notoriously taciturn in the presence of women and at social gatherings, he displayed little reticence while performing his responsibilities. He had few close friends, for experience had taught him that to one in his position, reserve is an indispensable virtue. Those few persons who had penetrated his inner circle testified that he had the affable nature typical of country people. Indeed, he had come from a large provincial family. Of his parents' home, he treasured the memory of splendid noon meals, of the enormous table where he sat with a dozen brothers and sisters, of the wines bottled in their patio and stored for years in wine cellars. He had never lost his taste for succulent vegetable soups, corn cakes, chicken stews, highly spiced seafood chowder, and, above all, homemade desserts. The nuns responsible for maintaining the Cardinal's residence took great pains to copy his mother's recipes and send to his dining table the dishes he had enjoyed as a boy. Although José Leal did not claim to be the Cardinal's friend, he knew him through his work in the Vicariate, where often they worked side by side, united in their compassionate desire to bring human solidarity where divine love seemed to be lacking. In the Cardinal's presence, José always relived the faint bewilderment he had felt at their first meeting, for in his mind he carried the image of a man of distinguished bearing quite different from this stocky old man who looked more like a villager than a Prince of the Church. José felt a deep admiration for the prelate but he was careful not to show it, because his superior would not tolerate any form of flattery. Long before the rest of the country was aware of the true dimensions of the man, José Leal had seen proof of the courage, good will, and astuteness that the Cardinal would later demonstrate in dealing with the dictatorship. Neither the campaign of hostilities, nor priests and nuns in prison, nor warnings from Rome could deflect him from his purpose. This leader of the Church took upon his own shoulders the burden of defending the victims of the new order, placing his formidable organization at the service of the persecuted. If the situation became dangerous, he changed his strategy, backed by two thousand years of prudence and acquaintance with power. He avoided open confrontation between the representatives of the Church and those of the General. On occasion he gave the impression of retreat, but soon it was apparent that this was merely an emergency tactical maneuver. He did not deviate one iota from his task of sheltering widows and orphans, ministering to prisoners, keeping count of the dead, and substituting charity for justice if that became necessary. For these and many other reasons, José considered him to be their only hope in unearthing the secret of Los Riscos.

But now they were in the Cardinal's office. The photographs on the massive antique desk were starkly lighted by the sun streaming through the windowpanes. From his chair, the visitor could see the clear blue sky of spring and the tops of the century-old trees in the street outside. The room was simply furnished with dark furniture and book-lined shelves. The walls were bare except for a cross of barbed wire, a gift from prisoners in a concentration camp. A teacart held large white china cups and quantities of pastry and marmalade provided by the Carmelite nuns. José Leal drank his last sip of tea and picked up the photographs, returning them to his plumber's bag. The Cardinal pressed a bell and his secretary answered immediately.

"Please, I want to see the people on this list . . . today!" he directed, handing the secretary a list of names he had written in his perfect script. The secretary left the room and the Cardinal turned toward José. "How did you learn of this story, Father Leal?"

"I told you, Your Eminence. It's a secret of the confessional," José said, smiling and indicating that he did not want to talk about it.

"If the police decide to interrogate you, they will not accept that answer."

"I'll take that risk."

"I hope it will not be necessary. I understand you have already been arrested—twice, is it not?"

"Yes, Your Eminence."

"You should not call attention to yourself. I would prefer that for the present, at least, you not go to that mine."

"But I have a strong interest in this matter and, with your permission, I would like to see it through to the end," José replied, flushing.

The prelate looked at José inquisitively, pondering his deepest motives. He had worked with José for years and considered him to be a bulwark of the Vicariate, which required strong, brave men of generous heart like this man dressed in workingman's clothes and holding on his knees a plumber's bag containing evidence of unspeakable evil. The priest's honest gaze convinced the Cardinal that he was not acting from curiosity or pride, but from a desire to learn the truth.

"Be cautious, Father Leal, not only for your sake but for the sake of the Church. We want no war with the government, you understand?"

"Perfectly, Your Eminence."

"Come this evening to the meeting I called. If God wills it, tomorrow you will open that mine."

The Cardinal rose from his chair and accompanied his visitor to the door, walking slowly, with one hand on the muscular arm of this man who, like himself, had elected the difficult challenge of loving his neighbor more than himself.

"Go with God" was the elderly Cardinal's farewell, accompanied by a firm handshake that cut short José's move to bow and kiss his ring.

At dusk a group of carefully chosen individuals gathered in the office of the Cardinal. The event did not go unnoticed by the Political Police and the State Security Corps, both of which reported to the General personally but had not dared to interfere because of specific orders to avoid confrontation with the Church: Bloody hell! Those damned priests stick their noses in where no one asks them—why don't they attend to the soul and leave the governing to us? But don't interfere with them. We don't want to get into another fracas there, said the General, fuming; but find out what the hell they're plotting so we can put a cork in it before the genie gets loose, before those bastards begin shooting off their mouths from the pulpit, fucking up the whole country, and leave us no choice but to teach them a lesson—though I would certainly not take any great pleasure from that, being an apostolic, Roman, practicing Catholic. I'm not planning any fight with God.

They did not learn what was spoken that night, however, in spite of sensitive listening devices purchased in Biblical lands, instruments that could capture the sighing and panting of lovers in a hotel three blocks away; in spite of all the telephones tapped in an effort to hear every intent whispered throughout the vast prison of the nation; in spite of agents who had infiltrated the residence of the Cardinal himself, dressed as exterminators, deliverymen, gardeners, even the lame, blind, and epileptic who had stationed themselves at the door asking for alms and benedictions from the passing cassocks. The Security Corps used every tactic at their command but could ascertain only: for a number of hours the persons on this list remained behind closed doors, General, sir, and then went from the office to the dining room, where they were served a seafood bisque, roast beef with parsley potatoes, and, for dessert, a— Get down to brass tacks, Colonel, I don't want menus, I want to know what they said! No idea, General, sir, but if you want we can interrogate the secretary. Don't be an ass, Colonel!

At midnight the invited guests said good night at the door of the Cardinal's residence before the vigilant eyes of the police openly stationed in the street outside. Everyone knew that from that moment their lives were in danger, but none hesitated: they had grown accustomed to walking on the edge of an abyss. They had worked for the Church for many years. Except for José Leal, all were laypersons and some were unbelievers who had had no contact at all with religion until the military coup, after which they had banded together in an inevitable pledge to resist in the shadows. Once he was alone, the Cardinal turned out the lights and went to his room. He had dismissed his secretary early, and all his staff, because they did not approve of his late hours. As he grew older, he needed less sleep and he liked spending his wakeful hours working in his office. He walked through the house, making sure the doors were locked and the shutters closed; after the latest bomb explosion in his garden he had taken simple precautions. He had flatly rejected the General's offer to provide him with a team of bodyguards, and had refused a similar offer from a group of young Catholic volunteers who wanted to protect him. He was convinced that he would live until his appointed hour, not a second more or a second less. Besides, he said, representatives of the Church cannot go around in bulletproof cars and anti-flak jackets like politicians, mafiosi, and tyrants. If any of the attempts against his person should be successful, within a very short time another priest would take his place to carry on his work. That knowledge gave him enormous peace of mind.

He went into his bedchamber, closed the thick wooden door, removed his clothing, and pulled on his nightshirt. Only then did he feel his weariness and the weight of his new responsibility, but he did not allow himself to doubt. He knelt at his prie-dieu, buried his head in his hands, and spoke with God, as he had done all his life with the deep certainty of being heard and of finding a response to his questions. At times the voice of his Creator was slow in making itself heard, or was manifest in tortuous ways, but always there was an answer. The Cardinal knelt immersed in prayer until he became aware of his icy feet and the crushing burden of his years. He remembered that he could no longer make such demands of his old bones, and he climbed into bed with a sigh of satisfaction, because the Lord had blessed his decisions.

Wednesday dawned as sunny as a midsummer day. The commission arrived in Los Riscos in three automobiles, headed by the Auxiliary Bishop and directed by José Leal, who, instructed by his brother, had marked the route on a map. Journalists, representatives of international organizations, and a number of attorneys were observed from a distance by the General's agents, who had kept them under surveillance since the evening before.

Irene wanted to be a part of the team from her magazine, but Francisco would not allow it. Journalists had no guarantee of safety, unlike the other members of the commission, whose positions afforded them a measure of security. If Irene and Francisco were ever connected with the discovery of the bodies, they could not hope to escape with their lives; and there was a good possibility they would be, since both had been present when Evangelina tossed Lieutenant Ramírez around, were known to have made inquiries about the missing girl, and had maintained contact with the Ranquileo family.

The cars halted a short distance from the mine. José Leal was the first to attack the rubble at the entrance, using to advantage his bearlike strength and his familiarity with hard labor. The others followed his lead, and within a few minutes they had made an opening. From their position, the Security Corps communicated by radio to inform the General that the suspects were trespassing, and opening a sealed mine in spite of posted warnings: We await instructions, General, sir; over and out. Limit yourself to observation, as I ordered you, and make no move to intervene. No matter what happens, do not get into a confrontation with those people; over and out.

The Auxiliary Bishop had decided to take the initiative, and he was the first to enter the mine. He was not an agile man, but he managed to get his legs through the opening and then, twisting like a mongoose, slipped the rest of his body inside. The stench struck him like a club, but it was not until his eyes became adjusted to the darkness and he saw the cadaver of Evangelina Ranquileo that he uttered a cry that brought the others running. He was assisted back through the entrance, helped to his feet, and led to the shade of the trees to recover his breath. Meanwhile, José Leal improvised torches from rolled newspapers, suggested that everyone cover his face with a handkerchief and led the members of the commission, one by one, inside the sepulcher, where, half kneeling, each saw the decomposing body of the girl and the Vesuvius of piled-up bones, hair, and tattered cloth. Every stone they removed revealed new human remains. Once outside, no one was capable of speech; trembling and pale, the observers stared at one another, struggling to comprehend the enormity of what they had seen. José Leal was the only one who had the heart to close the entrance again; he was thinking of dogs that might nose among the bones, or of the possibility that the authors of those crimes, warned by the gaping hole, might spirit away the evidence—a futile precaution, since some two hundred yards away sat a parked police van equipped with European telescopes and North American infrared-ray machines that informed the Colonel of the contents of the mine almost at the same moment the Auxiliary Bishop saw them for himself. But the General's instructions were very clear: Don't interfere with the priests, wait until they take the next step to see what the shit they have in mind. After all, there's nothing there but a few unidentified bodies.

It was still early when the commission returned to the city; after swearing not to comment, they went their separate ways, planning to meet that evening to give an account of their activities to the Cardinal.

That night the lights in the Archiepiscopal Residence remained on until dawn, to the discomfiture of the spies stationed in the treetops with apparatus acquired in the Far East that enabled them to see through walls in the dark. But we still don't know what they're planning, General, sir. It's past curfew now and they're still talking and drinking coffee. If you give us the word, we'll break in, search the place, and arrest everyone there. What did you say? Idiots! Try not to be such assholes!

At dawn the visitors left and the prelate bade them good-bye at the door. Only he seemed serene, for his soul was at peace and he was a stranger to fear. He went to bed for a while, and after breakfast he called the Chief Justice of the Supreme Court to ask him to receive as expeditiously as possible three of his envoys, the bearers of a letter of great importance. One hour later the envelope was in the hands of the Justice, who wished he were on the other side of the world, anywhere far away from this ticking time bomb that must inevitably explode.

To the Honorable Chief Justice,
The Supreme Court
Sr. Chief Justice:

Some days ago a person communicated to a priest, in the secrecy of the confessional, that he had knowledge and proof of the existence of a number of cadavers which were to be found in a place whose location he supplied to the priest. The priest, authorized by the informant, called the aforementioned information to the attention of ecclesiastical authorities.

With the purpose of establishing the veracity of the information, yesterday, in the early hours of the morning, a commission composed of the signers of this letter, the directors of the newsmagazines *Acontecer* and *Semana*, respectively, along with officials from the Office for

Human Rights, went to the location described by the
informant. The site is a mine, at present abandoned,
located among the foothills in the vicinity of Los Riscos.

Once at the site, and after removing the loose matter
that blocked the mouth of the mine, the aforementioned
individuals corroborated the existence of remains corre-
sponding to an undetermined number of human beings.
Following this verification, we cut short our inspection
of the site, as our only objective was to confirm the
gravity of the report received; we were not authorized to
proceed further in a matter more appropriate for judicial
investigation.

Nevertheless, it is our opinion that the appearance
of the locale and the disposition of the remains whose
existence we have established substantiate the eventual
discovery of a large number of victims.

The public outcry that the aforementioned information
may evoke has caused us to bring the matter directly to
the attention of the highest judicial power in the land,
so that the Supreme Tribunal may adopt the necessary
measures for a rapid and exhaustive investigation.

With regards to Your Honor,

    we, the undersigned, remain,

Very sincerely yours,

Alvaro Urbaneja (Auxiliary Bishop)

Jesús Valdovinos (Vicar General)

Eulogio García de la Rosa (Attorney)

The Chief Justice knew the Cardinal. He recognized that
this was not a skirmish and that the Cardinal was prepared to
wage all-out war. He must have all the aces up his sleeve, because he was too astute to lay that pile of bones in *his* hands

and challenge him to bring the forces of law to bear unless he was very sure. It required no great experience to conclude that the perpetrators of those crimes had acted with the approval of the government, and so, having no confidence in the authorities, the Church had intervened. He dried the sweat from his forehead and neck and reached for a pill for his high blood pressure and another for his heart, fearing that his moment of truth had arrived after years of juggling justice in accord with the General's instructions; after years of "losing" files and tying up the Vicariate's lawyers in bureaucratic red tape; after years of fabricating laws to fit, retroactively, recently invented crimes. Oh, why didn't I retire in time, why didn't I take my pension while it was still possible to do so with dignity, go cultivate my roses in peace and pass into history free of this burden of guilt and shame that won't let me sleep by night and that haunts me by day if I relax for so much as an instant; it's not as if I did it from personal ambition; I only meant to serve the nation, as the General himself asked me to do a few days after he assumed command; ah, but it's too late now, that damned mine is yawning at my feet like my own grave, and since the Cardinal decided to intervene, these dead cannot be silenced as so many have been; I should have retired on the day of the military coup, the day they bombed the Presidential Palace, jailed the Ministers, dissolved the Congress, when the eyes of the world were focused on us, waiting for someone to stand up and defend the constitution; that is the day I should have gone home, claiming that I was old, that I was ill; that is what I should have done instead of placing myself at the service of the Junta, instead of undertaking the purge of my own courts of law.

The first impulse of the Chief Justice of the Supreme Court was to call the Cardinal and make him a proposition, but even as the thought occurred to him, he realized that this matter was beyond his capacity as a negotiator. He picked up the telephone, dialed the secret number, and spoke directly with the General.

A circle of iron, helmets, and boots was drawn around Los Riscos mine, but nothing had been able to prevent the rumor from spreading like a firestorm, from mouth to mouth, house to house, valley to valley, until it was known everywhere and a deep shudder had run along the spine of the nation. The soldiers held the curious at bay but did not dare block the passage of the Cardinal and his commission as they had blocked journalists and the observers from foreign countries drawn there by the atrocity of the massacre. At eight o'clock on Friday morning, personnel from the Department of Criminal Investigation, wearing masks and rubber gloves, began removal of the terrible evidence under instructions from the Supreme Court, which had in turn received its instructions from the General: Open the damned mine, get those bones out of there, and assure the people that the guilty will not go unpunished. Then we'll see—the public has a short memory. The investigators arrived in a small truck loaded with yellow plastic bags and a crew of masons to dislodge the rubble. They made orderly and accurate notations of every item: one human body, female, in an advanced state of decomposition, covered with a dark blanket; one shoe; strands of hair; bones of an inferior extremity; one scapula; one humerus; various vertebrae; a trunk with both superior extremities attached; one pair of pants; two skulls, one complete, the other lacking the mandible; a section of jawbone with metal-filled teeth; more vertebrae; pieces of ribs; a trunk with shreds of clothing; shirts and socks of various colors; a pelvic bone; and various additional bones . . . all of which filled thirty-eight bags duly sealed, numbered, and carried to the truck. It took several trips to transport the bags to the Medical Institute. The Deputy Minister counted fourteen cadavers, based on the number of heads found, but he was not unmindful of the gruesome possibility that, had they done their job more carefully, other bodies would have appeared beneath successive layers of time and earth. Someone made the macabre joke that if they dug a little deeper they would find skeletons of conquistadors, Incan mummies, and fossils of Cro-Magnon man, but no one laughed; the horror had depressed them all.

Since early that morning, people had begun to gather, coming as near as possible before being stopped by the line of rifles, then standing directly behind the soldiers. First to arrive were the widows and orphans of the area, each wearing a black strip of cloth on the left arm as a sign of mourning. Later came others, almost all the country people from around Los Riscos. About noon, busloads from the outlying barrios of the capital arrived. Affliction hung in the air like the forewarning of a storm, immobilizing the very birds in their flight. For many hours, the people stood beneath a pale sun that washed out the outlines and colors of the world, while bag after bag was filled. From afar they strained to recognize a shoe, a shirt, a lock of hair. Those who had the best view passed information to the others: There's another skull, this one has gray hair. It might be our friend Flores, do you remember him? Now they're closing another bag, but they're not through—they're bringing out more. They say they're going to take the remains to the Morgue and that we can go there to get a closer look. And how much will that cost? I don't know, we'll have to pay something. Pay to identify your own dead? No, sir, that's something ought to be free.

All afternoon people kept coming, until they covered the hillside, listening to the sound of the shovels and picks moving the dirt, the coming and going of the truck, the traffic of police, officials, and legal advisers, the near riot of newspapermen who had been denied permission to go any closer. As the sun set, a chorus of voices was raised in a burial prayer. One person set up a tent improvised from blankets, prepared to stay for an indefinite time, but the guardsmen beat him with their rifle butts and ran him off before others prepared to stay, too. That was shortly before the appearance of the Cardinal in the archdiocesan automobile; he drove through the line of soldiers, ignoring their signals to stop, descended from the vehicle, and strode purposefully to the truck, where he stood and implacably counted the bags while the Deputy Minister hastily invented explanations. When the last load of yellow plastic bags had been driven away and the police had ordered the area cleared, night had fallen and people began to walk home in the darkness, exchanging stories of their own dramas, proving that all misery has a common thread.

The next day, people from all parts of the country crowded into the offices of the Medical Institute hoping to identify their loved ones, but they were forbidden to view them by a new order: the General had said that it was one thing to disinter cadavers but quite a different matter to put them on exhibit so anyone who wanted could come take a look. What do those damn fools think this is, a sideshow? I want this matter squelched, Colonel, before I lose patience.

"And what shall we do about public opinion, the diplomats, and the press, General, sir?"

"What we always do, Colonel. You don't change your strategy in mid-battle. Take a lesson from the Roman emperors."

Hundreds of people held a sit-in in the street in front of

the Vicariate, displaying photographs of their missing loved ones, whispering, Where are they? Where are they? Meanwhile, a group of working priests and nuns in slacks fasted in the Cathedral, adding to the total uproar. Sunday the Cardinal's pastoral letter was read from every pulpit, and for the first time in so long and dark a time people dared to turn to their neighbors and weep together. People called one another to talk about cases that multiplied until it was impossible to keep count. A procession was organized to pray for the victims, and before the authorities realized what was happening, an unmanageable crowd was marching through the streets carrying banners and placards demanding liberty, bread, and justice. The march began as little trickles of people from the outlying poor barrios. Gradually the trickles flowed together, the ranks swelled and finally grew into a compact mass that surged forward chanting in unison the religious hymns and political slogans stilled for so many years that people believed they had been forgotten forever. The crowds overflowed the churches and cemeteries, the only places that until then the police had not entered with their instruments of war.

"What shall we do with this mob, General, sir?"

"What we always do, Colonel" was the reply from the depths of the bunker.

Meanwhile, television continued its usual programming of popular music, contests, lottery drawings, and light comedy and romantic films. Newspapers gave the results of the football games, and front pages showed the Commander-in-Chief cutting the ribbon at a bank opening. But within a few days word of the discovery in the mine and photographs of the cadavers had traveled around the world by teletype. The news services sent the story out over their wires, back to the country where it had originated and where it was impossible to contain the news of the atrocity any longer, in spite of censorship and in spite of imaginative explanations by the authorities. People saw on their screens a fatuous announcer reading the official version: the bodies were those of terrorists executed by their own henchmen; but everyone knew they were murdered political prisoners. The atrocity was discussed amid fruits and vegetables in the market, among students and teachers in the schools, among workers in the factories, and even in the closed living rooms of the bourgeoisie, where for some it was a surprise to discover that everything was not going well in the country. The timid murmur that for so many years had been hidden behind doors and closed shutters now, for the first time, came out in the street to be shouted aloud, and that lament, augmented by the countless new cases that had come to light, touched everyone. Only the most apathetic could ignore the signs and remain impervious to the truth. Beatriz Alcántara was one of those.

Monday at breakfast, Beatriz found her daughter in the kitchen reading the newspaper, and noticed that her arms were covered with welts.

"What *is* that on your arms!"

"It's just some allergy, Mama."

"How do you know?"

"Francisco told me."

"So now photographers are doctors! What will be next?"

Irene did not respond, and her mother examined the welts closely, satisfying herself that in fact they did not seem contagious and possibly the young man was right, it was just an allergy of some kind. Placated, she picked up a section of the newspaper to glance at the news, and the first thing that met her eyes was the banner headline on the front page: "DESAPARECIDOS! HA! HA! HA!" She sipped her orange juice, slightly taken aback, because even for someone like her this seemed a little extreme. Still, she was sick of hearing nothing but talk about Los Riscos, and she seized the moment to give her daughter and Rosa her thoughts on the subject. Episodes like this were bound to happen in the kind of war the heroic military had been forced to wage in eradicating the cancer of Marxism; there were casualties in every battle; the best thing was to forget the past and look to the future, erase the slate and make a clean start; why keep talking about people who had disappeared? Why not give them up for dead, settle the legal problems, and get on with it?

"Why don't you do that with Papa?" Irene asked, scratching madly.

Beatriz ignored the sarcasm. She was reading aloud: " 'What is important is to continue our march on the road of progress, striving to heal our wounds and overcome animosities; dwelling upon cadavers merely hinders that endeavor. We owe to the Armed Forces the fact that we have reached the present stage in our programs. The period of emergency so happily surmounted was characterized by the exercise of the broad powers of established authority, which acted with all necessary strength to impose order and restore civic pride.' "

Beatriz added, "I completely agree. What is the point of identifying the bodies in the mine and looking for the guilty parties? It happened years ago. Those bodies belong to the past."

Finally things were going well; they could buy whatever suited their fancy; it was not the way it used to be when they had to stand in line to buy a miserable chicken. Now it was easy to get domestic servants, and the Socialist agitation that had caused so much trouble had all fizzled out. People should work a little more and talk a little less about politics. It was as Colonel Espinoza had so brilliantly stated, and she had memorized: "Let us meet the challenge together for the sake of this magnificent nation, blessed with its magnificent sun, its magnificent commodities, and its magnificent freedom."

At the sink, Rosa shrugged her shoulders, and Irene's itching became unbearable.

"Stop scratching, you'll get those things infected and look like a leper by the time Gustavo gets home."

"Gustavo got back last night, Mama."

"Oh! Why didn't you tell me? When's the wedding?"

"Never," Irene replied.

Beatriz's cup froze midway between the saucer and her lips. She knew her daughter well enough to know when her decisions were irrevocable. The look in her eyes and the tone of her voice told her that Irene's allergy had not been caused by romantic problems, but something else. She thought back over the last few days and deduced that something truly abnormal was happening in Irene's life. She had not been keeping her regular hours; she disappeared all day and came home totally exhausted and with the car covered in dust; she had abandoned her gypsy skirts and fortune-teller's necklaces to dress like a boy; she was eating hardly anything and woke up crying at night. Beatriz had no inkling, however, that those signs were connected with the Los Riscos mine. She wanted to ask her daughter more questions, but Irene was on her feet finishing her coffee and saying she had to rush, that she was working on a story out of town and wouldn't be back until after dark.

"That photographer's to blame, I know that much!" Beatriz exclaimed after her daughter left.

"When the heart leads the way, the foot will obey" was Rosa's reply.

"I bought that girl an expensive trousseau, and now she tells me this. She's been Gustavo's sweetheart too long to ruin things at the last minute."

"All's well that ends well, *señora*."

"I won't take any more from you, Rosa!" and the door slammed behind Beatriz.

Rosa said nothing about what she had seen the night before when the Captain had returned after so many months' absence and her little girl Irene had greeted him like a stranger. I only had to take one look at her face to know that I might as well forget the bridal gown and my dreams of a brood of blue-eyed children to look after in my old age. Man proposes and God disposes. When a woman offers her cheek to her sweetheart so he can't kiss her on the mouth, even a blind man can see that she doesn't love him; if she takes him into the living room, sits as far away as possible, staring at him without a word, it's because she's planning to tell him right there, straight out, just like the Captain had to hear it: I'm sorry, but I can't marry you because I love someone else. That's how she said it, and him not a word, poor thing, it breaks my heart, he turned as red as a beet and his chin trembled like a child about to cry, and me watching it all through the crack in the door, not from curiosity, God save me, but because I have a right to know what's troubling my little girl—how can I help her if I don't know? I didn't look after her all these years and love her more than her own mother for nothing. I felt heartsick when I saw that boy perched on the edge of the sofa with all his packages wrapped in pretty paper and his fresh haircut, not knowing what to do with the love he's been storing up all these years for Irene; he's a good man, I've always thought, tall and handsome as a prince, always so well dressed and holding himself as straight as a broomstick, a real gentleman, but little good his looks do him, because my baby doesn't take any notice of such things, and even less now that she's fallen in love with the photographer; while the cat's away, the mice will play! Gustavo shouldn't have gone off and left her alone for so many months. I don't understand these modern couples; in my time there wasn't all this running around, and everything worked out the way it was supposed to, a woman's place is in the home. Girls who were engaged stayed home and embroidered sheets and didn't go gallivanting around straddling some other man's motorcycle. The Captain should have seen what was coming, instead of going off calm as you please. I saw it from the beginning, and I said to myself: Out of sight, out of mind, but no one pays any attention to Rosa, they look down on me as if I was an old fool, but I'm dumb like a fox—the Devil wouldn't be so smart if he hadn't been around so long. I think Gustavo knew his goose was cooked and that there was nothing he could do, their love was dead and buried. His hands were sweating when he put the packages on the coffee table, asked if that was her final word, listened to her answer, and marched out without looking back, without even asking his rival's name, as if in his heart he knew it couldn't be anyone but Francisco Leal. I love someone else, was all Irene said, but it was enough to smash to smithereens a love that had lasted I can't remember how many years. I love someone else, my little girl said, and her eyes shone with a light I'd never seen before.

By the end of a week, the news about Los Riscos had been replaced by other stories, eclipsed by the public's insatiable hunger for new tragedies. Just as the General had predicted it would, memory of the atrocity was beginning to fade. It was no longer front-page news, and was being carried only in a few opposition magazines of limited circulation. Faced with this reality, Irene decided to go after more information about the case to keep interest alive, hoping that the public's outrage would be stronger than their fear. Finding the murderers and identifying the bodies became her obsession. She knew that one false step or a change in her luck could cost her her life, but she was determined that the crimes should not sink into oblivion because of censorship and the judges' complicity. In spite of her promise to Francisco to stay in the background, she was helplessly caught up in her own compulsion.

When Irene called Sergeant Faustino Rivera to invite him to lunch, using the pretext that she was doing an article on highway accidents, she knew the risk she was running, and for that reason left without telling anyone. The sergeant's long pause before replying made it clear that he suspected the article was only an excuse to discuss other matters, but for him, too, the bodies in the mine had become a nightmare, one he wanted to share.

They agreed to meet two blocks from the town plaza, at the inn where they had met before. The smell of charcoal and grilled meat spilled into the adjoining streets. The sergeant, in civilian clothes, was waiting in the doorway beneath the protecting red tile eaves. Irene had some difficulty recognizing him, but he remembered her perfectly and made the first gesture of greeting. Rivera took pride in being an observant man; he was accustomed to remembering the smallest details, an indispensable virtue in his profession as an officer of the law. He noticed the change in the girl's appearance, and wondered what had become of the clanking bracelets, the flying skirts, and the dramatic eye makeup that had impressed him so favorably at their first meeting. The woman who stood before him with her hair tied back, with her gabardine slacks and a voluminous shoulder bag, bore almost no resemblance to the woman he remembered. They chose a discreet table in the thick shade of a magnolia at the back of the courtyard.

While he was eating the soup, which Irene Beltrán did not even taste, the sergeant reeled off various statistics about traffic victims in his district, keeping a close watch on his hostess out of the corner of his eye. He recognized her impatience, but he was not going to give her an opportunity to turn the conversation in the direction she desired until he was satisfied about her intentions. The appearance of a golden, crisp suckling pig resting on a bed of fried potatoes, with a carrot in its mouth and sprigs of parsley in its ears, reminded Irene of the hog-slaughtering at the Ranquileos', and she felt the bile rise in her throat. Her stomach had been queasy ever since she and Francisco had entered the mine. Almost as soon as a bite of food touched her lips, she thought of the decomposing body, smelled the unforgettable stench, and shivered with fear as real as the fear she had felt then. She was grateful for the moment of silence that accompanied the pig, and tried to tear her eyes from her guest's large teeth and greasy mustache.

"I suppose you are informed about the bodies in the Los Riscos mine," she said finally, seeking a direct approach to the subject.

"Affirmative, *señorita.*"

"They say that one of the bodies is Evangelina Ranquileo."

The sergeant poured himself another glass of wine and devoured another slab of pig. Irene sensed that the situation was under control, because if Faustino Rivera had not wanted to talk, he would have refused the interview. The fact that he was there was proof enough of his readiness to cooperate. She gave him time to wolf down a few more mouthfuls, then began to use her tricks as an interviewer and her wiles as a woman to loosen his tongue.

"Anyone who stirs up trouble is asking to get it right in the fucking ass, begging your pardon, *señorita*. That's our mission, and we're proud to carry it out. Civilians get out of hand at the slightest excuse. You can't trust them for a minute, and when you deal with them you have to come down with a heavy hand, as Lieutenant Ramírez always says. On the other hand, the killing should be legal—otherwise, it's nothing less than slaughter."

"And wasn't it just that, Sergeant?"

No, he didn't agree; that's what traitors to the nation were calling it; those were Soviet lies to discredit the General's government. The worst thing you could do was pay attention to those rumors; a few bodies in some mine doesn't mean that every man who wears a uniform is a murderer. He couldn't deny that there were fanatics around, but it wasn't fair to put the blame on everyone, and besides it's better to have a little abuse than to push the armed forces back in their barracks and leave the country in the hands of the politicians.

"Do you know what would happen the minute the General fell from power, God forbid? The Marxists would rise up and slit the throats of every soldier, along with their wives and children. We're marked men. They would kill us all. That's the thanks we get for doing our duty."

Irene listened without interrupting, but after a moment her patience ran out and she decided to challenge him, once and for all.

"Listen, Sergeant, stop beating about the bush. Why not tell me what's really on your mind?"

Then, as if he had been waiting for that signal, the dam

burst and the sergeant told Irene everything he had told Pradelio Ranquileo earlier concerning the fate of his sister, and he
told her his suspicions, which he had never formulated aloud.
He went back to that fateful early morning when Lieutenant
Juan de Dios Ramírez had returned to the compound after
driving away with the prisoner. A bullet was missing from his
revolver that day. You had to inform the corporal of the guard
when service weapons were fired; they kept a record in a special armaments log. For the first months following the military
coup, the sergeant explained, the registers were all fouled up,
because no one could keep track of the numbers of munitions
fired by rifles, carbines, and revolvers issued at Headquarters,
but once things had got back to normal, they returned to the
old system. That's why when the lieutenant had to give an explanation, he said he had killed a rabid dog. He had also entered in the Duty Log that the girl was released at seven in the
morning, leaving under her own will.

"But that isn't true, *señorita*, and I have it all written down
in my notebook," the sergeant added through a mouthful of
food, handing her a small notebook with filthy, tattered covers. "Look, it's all there. I wrote down we would be meeting
today, and I wrote about our conversation a couple of weeks
ago, you remember? I don't forget anything—it's all spelled
out there."

Irene had an impression of great weight as she took the
notebook. She stared at it, horrified, feeling a strong sense of
foreboding. She wanted to ask Rivera to destroy the book, but
she put the idea out of her mind, forcing herself to act rationally. Frequently during the last few days, she had had inexplicable impulses that made her doubt her sanity.

The sergeant told her that Lieutenant Ramírez had signed
his statement and had ordered Corporal Ignacio Bravo to do the

same. Nothing was said about the lieutenant's having carted off Evangelina Ranquileo during the night, nor had his men asked him about it; they knew his foul disposition all too well, and didn't want to end up in solitary confinement like Pradelio.

"He was a good man, Ranquileo," said the sergeant.

"Was?"

"They say he's dead."

Irene Beltrán swallowed a gasp of dismay. That was a real setback to her plans. Her next move had been to find Pradelio Ranquileo and convince him to appear in court. Because his desire to avenge his sister outweighed his fear of the consequences, he might be the only witness to what had happened at Los Riscos who was prepared to accuse the lieutenant and describe the murders. The sergeant repeated a rumor he had heard that Pradelio had fallen into a ravine in the mountains, although the truth was, he wasn't sure; no one had seen the body. By the time he began the second bottle of wine, Rivera had cast discretion to the winds and had begun to string together his suspicions: The good of the nation comes first, but that isn't threatened here and justice should be done, I say, even though they threaten me and ruin my career and I end up plowing dirt like my brothers. I've decided to see it through to the end, I'll go to the court, I'll swear on the flag and the Bible, I'll tell the truth to the newspapers. That's why I wrote everything down in my notebook: the day, the hour, all the details. I always carry it beneath my undershirt, I like to feel it next to my heart. I even sleep with it, because once someone tried to steal it. Those notes are worth their weight in gold, *señorita.* They're evidence that other people want to sweep under the rug, but like I told you, I forget nothing. I'll show my book to the judge, if I have to, because Pradelio and Evangelina deserve justice. They were my kin.

The sergeant says he can imagine what happened the night of Evangelina's disappearance as clear as if he was seeing it in a movie: Lieutenant Ramírez is driving down the highway, whistling—he always whistles when he's nervous; he would be thinking about the road, although he knows the area well and knows that at this hour he won't be meeting any other vehicles. He's a careful driver. He figures that four or five minutes after leaving the gate and flicking a salute to Corporal Ignacio Bravo standing guard at the gate, he will reach the main highway and turn north. A few miles farther along he will turn off toward the mine on a terrible dirt road filled with potholes; that's why when he got back the truck was filthy and the wheels were caked with mud. Rivera imagines his lieutenant choosing a place as close as possible to the mine to stop. He doesn't turn off the headlights because he needs both hands free and the flashlight will be a nuisance. He goes around to the back, removes the canvas, and sees the girl lying there. He must have smiled that twisted grin his men all know and fear. He lifts Evangelina's hair from her face and gazes approvingly at her profile, her neck, her shoulders, her schoolgirl breasts. In spite of the bruises and blood, she looks beautiful to him, like any young girl beneath the stars. He feels a familiar warmth between his legs and starts to breathe heavy; he laughs slyly. What a brute I am, he mutters.

"You'll forgive my frankness, *señorita*," Faustino Rivera interrupts himself, sucking the bones of his feast.

Lieutenant Juan de Dios Ramírez touches the girl's breast and perhaps finds she is still breathing. So much the better for him, and so much the worse for her. The sergeant seems to be seeing with his own eyes as his superior, damn him to hell, removes his revolver and lays it on the toolbox beside the flashlight, unbuckles his belt and opens his trousers and throws himself on the girl with unnecessary violence, because he meets no resistance. He enters her in haste, squeezing her against the metal floor of the truck, pressing, scratching, biting the girl crushed beneath the weight of his hundred and eighty pounds, his military belt, his heavy boots, recovering the macho pride she snatched from him that day on the patio of her house. Sergeant Rivera can't stand to think of this scene, because he has a daughter just Evangelina's age. When the lieutenant is through with his prisoner, he must have lain on her until he notices she isn't moving at all, that she isn't moaning, that her eyes are staring at the sky in amazement at her own death. Then he must have adjusted his clothes, taken her by the feet, and dragged her out on the ground. He looks for the flashlight and his revolver; in the circle of light, he holds the barrel of the revolver to her head, and after releasing the safety, fires at point-blank range, remembering that long-ago morning when with a similar gesture he administered the coup de grâce to his first victim. With the shovel and pick he opens the entrance to the mine, brings the poncho-wrapped body, forces it through the opening any which way, drags it into the tunnel on the right, which he blocks with rubble and stones, and then crawls out the opening. Before he leaves, he closes the mine entrance, and with his foot he rakes dirt over the dark stains and bits of soft matter spattered on the ground at the site of the shooting; next he carefully searches the area until he finds the cartridge casing, which he puts in his shirt pocket for the accounting to the munitions records, all according to regulations. That must have been the moment he invented the story of the mad dog. He folds the canvas, tosses it in the rear of the truck, picks up the tools, returns his revolver to the holster, and gives a last look around to be sure he hasn't left any trace of his activities. He climbs into the vehicle and drives back to Headquarters. He is whistling.

"Like I told you, *señorita*, he always whistles when he's nervous," Sergeant Rivera concluded. "I admit I don't have any proof of what I've told you, but I swear on the memory of my sainted mother, may she rest in peace, that that's more or less the way things happened."

"Whose are the other bodies in the mine? Who killed them?"

"I don't know. Ask the farmers around here. Many have disappeared. Go see the Flores family. . . ."

"Are you sure you will have the nerve to repeat in a court of law everything you told me today?"

"Yes. I'm sure. The ballistics expert and the autopsy on Evangelina will prove I'm right."

Irene paid the bill, surreptitiously tucked the tape recorder into her shoulder bag, and bade her guest goodbye. As she shook his hand, she felt the same irrational fear she had felt holding his notebook. She could not look him in the eye.

Sergeant Faustino Rivera did not ever give his statement to the judge, because that same night he was run over by a white truck that immediately sped away from the scene. The sergeant was killed instantly. The only eyewitness, Corporal Ignacio Bravo, testified that everything had happened so quickly he did not have time to get a look at the license plate or the driver. The notebook was never found.

Irene went to look for the Floreses' house. It was made of wood and sheets of zinc, like all the others around it. The property was part of a cooperative of poor farmers who had been given a few acres of land during the reform; later the few acres had been taken from them, leaving them once more with their small family plots. The long road that crossed through the valley joining the pieces of land had been laid out by the farmers using the labor of the entire community—even old people and children, who had contributed by carrying rocks. That was the road the military vehicles used when they had come to search the houses, one by one. They had lined up the men in an endless row, selected one from every five at random, and shot them as a warning; they also shot the cattle and set fire to the pastures, leaving behind a trail of blood and destruction. There were few small children now because many homes had been without a man for years. The occasional births were celebrated with emotion, and the children were given the names of the dead, so that no one would ever forget them.

When she found the house, it was so desolate and dismal that Irene thought it was abandoned. She called for a few moments without hearing even the barking of a dog. She was about to turn and leave when among some trees she saw a gray woman, barely visible against the landscape, who told her that *Señora* Flores and her daughter were at the market, where they sold vegetables.

A few steps from the plaza in Los Riscos rose the market in an explosion of noise and color. Irene searched among the pyramids of fruit—peaches, melons, watermelons—and wandered through labyrinths of fresh vegetables, mountains of potatoes and young corn, counters of spurs, stirrups, harness, and straw hats, rows of red and black pottery, cages of hens and rabbits—all amid an uproar of hawking and haggling. Deeper inside the market were other stalls: cold meats, fish, seafood, cheeses—an unleashing of smells and tastes. She walked slowly back and forth, absorbing everything with her eyes, sniffing the fragrances of earth and sea, stopping to taste one of the first grapes, a ripe strawberry, a fresh clam lying in its mother-of-pearl shell, a smooth pastry baked by the same hands that sold it. Fascinated, Irene thought that nothing terrible could befall a world where such abundance flowered. But then she came upon Evangelina Flores, and remembered why she was there.

The girl's resemblance to Digna Ranquileo was so strong that Irene immediately felt at ease with her, as if she had known her before, and respected her. Like her mother and her brothers and sisters, she had glossy dark hair, light skin, and large, very dark eyes. Short-legged, robust, energetic, and healthy, she moved with vitality and spoke with assurance and simplicity, accentuating her words with expansive gestures of her hands. She was unlike her real mother in her jovial nature and the poise that allowed her to express opinions without fear. She seemed older, much more mature and developed than the other Evangelina, the one who had mistakenly assumed her fate, and died in her place. Far from burdening her with resignation, the accumulated suffering of her fifteen years had given her vigor. When she smiled, her coarse features were transformed and her face shone. She was gentle and affectionate with her adoptive mother, whom she treated with a protective air, as if she wanted to shield her from new sorrows. Together they looked after the tiny stall where they sold their produce.

Sitting on a wicker stool, Evangelina told Irene their story. Her family had been punished more than others, because shortly after the first raid, the law had come back and descended on them again. In the years following, the surviving children had found out how useless it was to search for the ones who had been taken away, how dangerous it was even to talk about them. But the girl was indomitable. When she heard of the discovery of the bodies in Los Riscos mine, she had hoped to hear some news of her missing father and brothers; that is why she was willing to talk with a journalist who was a complete stranger to her. Her mother, in contrast, was withdrawn and silent, observing Irene with distrust.

"The Floreses aren't my own parents, but they brought me up. I love them as if they were my own," the girl explained.

She could tell Irene the very day their misfortunes began. It was a day in October, five years ago, when a jeep from Headquarters drove down the road of the cooperative and stopped in front of their house. They had come to arrest Antonio Flores. Pradelio Ranquileo had been assigned to carry out the order. He beat on the door, flushing with shame because he was bound to that family by bonds of destiny that were as strong as blood ties. Respectfully, he explained that this was a routine questioning; he allowed the prisoner to put on a jacket and walk to the vehicle on his own. *Señora* Flores and her children could see the owner of Los Aromos Vineyard sitting beside the driver's seat, and were surprised; they had never had any problems with him, not even during the stormy days of the Agrarian Reform, and they could not imagine the reason for his denunciation. After Antonio Flores had been taken away, neighbors came to console the family, and the house swelled with people. There were plenty of witnesses, then, when a half hour later a truck filled with armed guardsmen braked to a halt. Men jumped out, yelling as if they were in combat, and arrested the four oldest brothers. Beaten, half-dazed, they were pushed and dragged to the vehicle, and the last the others saw of them was a cloud of dust disappearing down the road. Everyone who had watched what happened stood stunned by the show of brutality, because none of the brothers had ever been involved in politics and their only sin was to have joined the Farmers Union. One of them did not even live at home; he was a construction worker in the city, and happened to be visiting his parents that day. Their friends decided it was all a mistake and sat down to wait for the young men to be brought home. They could identify the guardsmen; they knew them by name, since they had been born in the region and all attended the same school. Pradelio Ranquileo was not part of the second group and they speculated that he had been left at Headquarters to guard Antonio Flores. They went to him later when he was off duty but found out nothing; they could not get a word out of the Ranquileos' oldest son.

"Our life had been peaceful up to then. We were hard-working people and had everything we needed. My father had a good horse, and was saving to buy a tractor. But then the law came down on us and everything changed," said Evangelina Flores.

"Bad luck runs in the blood," murmured *Señora* Flores, thinking of the accursed mine where maybe six of her family lay rotting.

They looked for them. For months they made the obligatory pilgrimage of anyone following the trail of *desaparecidos*. They went from place to place, asking futile questions, and received nothing but the advice to consider the men dead and sign the legal papers; that way they would be entitled to an orphan's and a widow's pension. You can find another husband, *señora*, you're still good-looking, they told her. The legal formalities were long and drawn out, vexing, and expensive. The process ate up all their savings and put them into debt. Papers were lost in offices in the capital, and with the passing of time they saw their hopes fading like the lines of an old drawing. The children who were still alive had to quit school and look for work on neighboring farms; they were not hired, though, because they were marked. Each of them had tied up his bundle of miserable belongings and set off looking for a place where no one knew his misfortune. The family was scattered to the winds, and as the years went by, only the switched daughter still lived with *Señora* Flores. Evangelina had been ten when her adoptive father and brothers were arrested. Every time she closed her eyes, she saw them being dragged away, bleeding. Her hair fell out, she grew thin, she walked in her sleep, and when she was awake she seemed to drift in an idiot haze that earned her the gibes of other schoolchildren. Thinking it would be best to get her away from that house of bad memories, *Señora* Flores had sent Evangelina to another town to live with an uncle, a prosperous dealer in firewood and charcoal, who could offer her a better life. The child, though, missed her mother's love, and only grew worse, so they brought her back home. For a long time nothing could console her, but when she had her first menstruation, at twelve, she suddenly threw off her melancholy and woke up one morning transformed into a woman. It had been her idea to sell the horse and put up a vegetable stall in the Los Riscos market; and hers, too, the decision not to go on sending food, clothing, and money through the military to their missing relatives, for in all those years there was not a single bit of evidence that they were still alive. The girl worked ten hours a day selling and transporting vegetables and fruit; in the remaining six, before falling into bed exhausted, she studied the notebooks her teacher had prepared as a special favor. She had not wept again, and she began to speak of her father and brothers in the past tense, to accustom her mother little by little to the idea of never seeing them again.

When they opened the mine, she was right behind the soldiers, lost in the crowd, wearing her black armband. From a distance she saw the large yellow bags, and squinted her eyes, hoping to see some clue. Someone told her it would be impossible to identify the remains without a study of dental records and every scrap of bone and clothing that had been found, but she was sure that if she could see them up close, her heart would tell her whether they were theirs.

"Can you take me where they have them now?" she asked Irene Beltrán.

"I'll do everything I can, but it won't be easy."

"Why don't they give them to us? All we want is a grave where they can lie in peace, where we can bring them flowers and pray for them, and visit them on the day of the dead."

"Do you know who arrested your father and brothers?" Irene asked.

"Lieutenant Juan de Dios Ramírez and nine men from his command," Evangelina Flores replied without hesitation.

Thirty hours after the death of Sergeant Faustino Rivera, Irene was shot down at the entrance to the publishing house. She was leaving work, rather late, when an automobile parked across the street started up, accelerated, and swept by her like an ominous wind, loosing a burst from an automatic weapon before disappearing into the traffic. Irene felt a powerful blow in the center of her being, but did not know what had happened. She fell to the sidewalk without a cry. All the breath rushed from her soul, and she was consumed with pain. She had an instant of lucidity in which she reached out to touch the blood forming around her in a spreading pool, then immediately sank into sleep.

The doorman and other witnesses were also unaware of what had happened. They heard the shots but did not identify them as such, thinking they came from a car backfiring or an airplane overhead, but when they saw Irene fall, they ran to

her aid. Ten minutes later, she was in an ambulance with sirens screaming and lights whirling. Her life was spurting from
countless bullet wounds in her abdomen.

Francisco Leal learned of the shooting by chance an hour
or two later, when he called her house to ask her to dinner; it
had been some days since he had seen her alone, and he was
drowning with love. Weeping into the telephone, Rosa told
him the bad news. That was the longest night of Francisco's
life. He spent it sitting beside Beatriz in the hospital corridor
on a bench opposite the intensive-care unit where his beloved
was roaming aimlessly through the shadows of the valley of
death. After several hours on the operating table, no one had
any hope that she would live. Connected to a half-dozen tubes
and cables, she lay awaiting her death.

The surgeons had opened her up and attempted to repair
the damage, discovering for every stitch they took another
opening to close. Quarts of blood and plasma were poured
into her body, she was flooded with antibiotics, and, finally,
crucified on a bed, suffering the enduring torture of cathe-
ters, she was sedated in a mist of unconsciousness to allow
her to bear her martyrdom. With the complicity of the phy-
sician on call, who commiserated with such obvious grief,
Francisco was permitted to see Irene for a few minutes. She
was naked, transparent, afloat in the glaring white light of the
operating room; a respirator was connected to a tube in her
trachea, cables joined her to a cardiac monitor on which a
scarcely perceptible signal kept hope alive, and her veins were
pierced with numerous needles; she was as pale as the sheet,
dark shadows purpled her eyes, and a compact mass of bandages covered her stomach, from which erupted the tentacles
of rubber drains. A mute sob gripped Francisco's chest, and
lingered there for an interminable time.

Beatriz assaulted him the minute she saw him: "It's your fault! From the instant you came into my daughter's life, we have had nothing but trouble!"

She was grief-stricken, beside herself. Francisco actually felt sorry for her; for the first time, he saw her free of artifice: nerves rubbed raw, human, suffering, approachable. She collapsed onto the bench and wept until she had no tears to shed. She could not understand what had happened. She wanted to believe that this was the work of an ordinary felon, as the police had assured her it was; she could not bear the idea that her daughter had been pursued for political reasons. She had not a hint of Irene's role in discovering the bodies in the mine, and could not imagine her involved in murky activities directed against the government. Francisco went to buy a cup of tea for each of them, and they sat side by side drinking it in silence, united by an identical feeling of catastrophe.

Like so many others during the previous administration, Beatriz Alcántara had gone into the streets banging pots and pans to protest the food shortages. She had backed the military coup because it seemed infinitely more desirable than a Socialist regime, and when the time-honored Presidential Palace had been bombed from the air, she uncorked a bottle of champagne in celebration. She burned with patriotic fervor, although her enthusiasm had not been so great as to cause her to donate her jewels to the fund for rebuilding the nation; she feared she would see her jewels adorning some colonel's wife, as wagging tongues had rumored. She adjusted to the new system as if she had been born to it, and learned never to speak of what it was best not to know. Ignorance was indispensable to peace of mind. That horrible night in the hospital, Francisco was at the point of telling her about Evangelina Ranquileo, about the dead of Los Riscos, about the thousands of victims—about her own daughter—but he took pity on her. He did not want to use this moment when she was convulsed with grief to destroy the illusions that had until that moment sustained her. So he confined himself to asking questions about Irene, about the years of her childhood and adolescence, taking pleasure from each anecdote, begging for the tiniest detail, with the curiosity every lover has for everything connected with his beloved. They talked about the past and, between confidences and tears, the hours went by.

Twice during that night of torment, Irene was near death, so near that returning her to the world of the living was a phenomenal feat. While the doctors clustered around her, battling to revive her with electric shocks, Francisco Leal felt he was losing his grip on reason, regressing to the days of prehistory—to the cave, to darkness, to ignorance, to terror. Despairing, he sat and waited as evil forces dragged Irene toward the shadows, believing that only magic, chance, or divine intervention could save her from dying. He wanted to pray, but could not utter the words that as a child he had learned from his mother's lips. Distraught, through the strength of his passion he tried to bring Irene back. He exorcised the darkness with the memory of their pleasure, setting against the shadows of hovering death the light of their coming together. He longed for a miracle, for his own health, his blood, his soul to pass to her and give her life. He repeated her name a thousand times, beseeching her not to give up, to go on fighting; from the bench in the corridor he called to her in secret; he wept openly, felt crushed beneath the weight of centuries, waiting for her, seeking her, desiring her, loving her. He remembered her freckles, her innocent feet, her smoky pupils, the aroma of her clothing, the silk of her skin, the line of her waist, the crystal of her laughter, the peaceful abandon with which she lay in his arms after making love. He sat there, muttering to himself like a madman and suffering insufferably, until the new day dawned and the hospital awakened; he heard doors opening and closing, elevators, footsteps, instruments clanking on metal trays, and the sound of his own racing heart. Then he felt Beatriz Alcántara's hand in his, and remembered her presence. Drained, they looked at each other. They had lived through those hours in similar pain. Bare of makeup, Beatriz's face was ravaged, the fine scars of her plastic surgery revealed; her eyes were puffy, her hair limp with sweat, her blouse wrinkled.

"Do you love her?" she asked.

"Very much," replied Francisco Leal.

Then they embraced. At last they had discovered a common language.

For three days Irene Beltrán wandered along the frontiers of death, at the end of which she drifted into consciousness, pleading with her eyes to be allowed to fight using her own resources, or to die with dignity. They took the respirator away, and little by little her breathing stabilized, as did the rhythm of the blood in her veins. Then they transferred her to a room where Francisco Leal could stay by her side. She was submerged in the stupor of drugs, lost in the fog of nightmare, but she felt Francisco's presence, and when he left she called for him in a voice as weak and helpless as a baby's.

That evening Gustavo Morante came to the hospital. He had read about Irene in the police reports in the newspaper; the item had been published, much delayed, along with a list of other bloody offenses attributed to common criminals. Only Beatriz Alcántara, however, clung to the official version of events, just as she believed that the search of her house was some strange mistake on the part of the police. The Captain, however, had no illusions. He requested permission to travel from his garrison to visit his former fiancée. He was dressed in civilian clothes, following the recommendation of the High Command: No uniforms in the street, we don't want to give the impression that this is an occupied nation. Morante knocked at the door of Irene's room and Francisco opened it, surprised to see him there. They took one another's measure, each probing the other's intentions, until a sigh from the patient drew them both precipitously to her side. Irene lay motionless on the high hospital bed, like a white marble maiden sculpted on her own sarcophagus. Only the living foliage of her hair emitted light. Her arms bore the marks of needles and tubes; she was breathing shallowly, her eyes tightly closed, the lids dark smudges. When Gustavo Morante gazed upon the woman he had loved for her vitality, reduced now to a poor lacerated body that looked as if it might evaporate into the surreal air of the sickroom, a shock of horror ran through him that left him weak and trembling.

"Is she going to live?" he whispered.

Francisco Leal had watched over her for several days and nights, and had become expert in reading the slightest sign of improvement; he counted her sighs, weighed her dreams, observed her fleeting expressions. He was euphoric because she was breathing without the aid of a machine and could move the tips of her fingers, but he realized that for the Captain—who had not been present when she was truly dying—the sight of her was a cruel blow. He forgot that his rival was an Army officer and saw him only as a man suffering for the woman he, too, loved.

"I want to know what happened," Morante asked, dumbstruck, his head bowed with grief.

And Francisco Leal told him, not omitting their participation in the discovery of the bodies, hoping that Morante's love for Irene would supersede his loyalty to the uniform. The same day of the attempt on Irene's life, armed men had burst into her house and turned everything upside down, from mattresses, which they ripped open with knives, to jars of cosmetics and kitchen canisters they emptied onto the floor. They took with them her tape recorder, her agenda, her notebook, and her address book. Before they finished, they shot Cleo for good measure, leaving the dog in a pool of blood. Beatriz was not at home; at that very moment she was sitting in a hospital corridor outside the room where her daughter lay dying. Rosa had tried to stop the men, but received a rifle butt in her chest that had left her speechless and gasping for air; after they were gone, she gathered up the dog in her apron and cradled her so she would not die alone. The men took a quick look through The Will of God Manor, terrifying the residents and nurses, but did nothing when they realized that the frightened old people lived on the fringes of life and had nothing to do with politics. The following morning, the magazine offices were searched and everything in Irene Beltrán's desk was requisitioned, including the ribbon from her ancient typewriter and her discarded carbon paper. Francisco also told the Captain about Evangelina Ranquileo, the untimely death of Sergeant Rivera, the disappearance of Pradelio Ranquileo and most of the Flores family, the massacred farmers; he told him about Lieutenant Juan de Dios Ramírez, and everything else that came to his mind, shedding the discretion that for years he had worn almost like a second skin. He poured out the rage that had been dammed up so long by silence; he painted a different picture of the government—a picture Morante had not seen because he was not inside the barbed wire circle—not omitting the tortured, the dead, the wretched poor, the rich who were profiting from the nation as if it were just another business. The Captain, pale and silent, listened to words that at any other time he would not have allowed to be spoken in his presence.

Francisco's words exploded in Morante's head, along with others he had learned in military training. For the first time, he found himself on the side of the victims of the regime, not among those exercising absolute power, and he was hurt where he was most vulnerable: through his Irene, motionless between the sheets; seeing her so wan, his soul shivered like a bell tolling for the dead. He could not remember a moment in his life when he had not wanted her, and he had never loved her more than now that she was lost to him. He thought of their years growing up together, his plan to marry her and make her happy. Silently, he spoke to her, telling her all the things he had not had an opportunity to say. He reproached her for her lack of confidence; why hadn't she told *him*? He would have helped her; he would have opened the damned tomb with his own hands, not only to be beside her, but for the honor of the armed forces as well. Such crimes could not go unpunished or their society would go to the devil, and it would make no sense for them to have taken up arms against the previous government, accusing it of illegal acts, if they themselves were acting outside the law and common morality. There are only a few guilty of such misconduct, and they must be punished. The honor of the institution, though, is intact, Irene; in our ranks there are many men like me, men ready to fight for the truth, ready to dig through the rubble until all the filth is removed, even if they lose their lives doing it. You betrayed me, my dearest. Perhaps you never loved me as much as I loved you; maybe that's why you turned away from me without giving me a chance to prove that I am not a party to such barbarism. My hands are clean, I have always acted in good faith—you know me. I was at the South Pole during the coup. My work is computers, blackboards, confidential files, strategy; I have never fired a regulation weapon except in target practice. I thought the nation needed a respite from the politicians, and that we needed order and discipline if we were to eradicate poverty. How could I dream that the people would despise us? How many times have I told you, Irene, that the process itself is painful but the crisis will be surmounted? Although now I am not so sure. It may be that it is time for us to return to the barracks and to reinstate a democracy. Where was I that I did not see that? Why did you not tell me in time? You didn't have to be riddled with bullets to open my eyes— you didn't have to turn away, leave me with more love than I can bear, with my whole life ahead of me without you. Ever since you were a little girl you have wanted the truth. That's one reason I adore you so, and it's also why you are lying there now. So still. Dying.

Francisco had no idea how long the Captain stood watching Irene. The light faded from the window and the room sank softly into shadow, blurring the objects in the room and transforming Irene into a pale blotch on the bed. Morante was saying goodbye to her, convinced that he would never again love anyone as he did her, and gathering strength for the task ahead. He bent to kiss her parched lips, pausing in his caress, recording in his memory her tormented face, breathing the odor of medications on her skin, imagining the delicate form of her body, stroking her rebellious hair. The Bridegroom of Death left with dry eyes, a determined expression, and a resolute heart. He would love Irene the rest of his life, and he would never see her again.

"Do not leave her for a moment, or they will come and finish the job. I can do nothing to protect her. You must get her out of here and hide her" were his only words.

"All right," Francisco replied.

Their handshake was prolonged and firm.

Irene's progress was extremely slow; it seemed at times she might never recover, and she suffered excruciating pain. Francisco assumed responsibility for all her bodily needs, as devoted in easing her pain as he had been in giving her pleasure. He never left her side during the day, and at night he lay on a sofa beside her bed. Normally he slept calmly, and deeply, but during that period his ear was as sharp as that of a night stalker. He was immediately awake if he noticed a change in her breathing, heard her stir or moan.

That week they removed the intravenous feeding tubes and she drank a cup of broth. Francisco fed it to her, spoonful by spoonful, his heart in his mouth. When she saw his anxiety, Irene smiled as she had not done in a long time, the flirtatious smile that had captivated him the moment he met her. Crazed with joy, he leaped through the hospital corridors, rushed outside, zigzagged through the streams of traffic, and flung himself onto the grass in the park. All the emotions he had held back for days erupted, and he laughed and wept unashamedly before the astonished eyes of the nannies and old men strolling in the warm sun. That was where his mother came and found him, to share his joy. Hilda had spent many hours knitting silently by Irene's bedside, gradually adjusting to the idea that her youngest son, too, would be going away; life could never again be the same for him, or for the woman he loved. For his part, Professor Leal brought his classical records to fill

Irene's room with music and restore her joy in living. He visited her every day, and sat and told her happy stories, never mentioning the Spanish Civil War, his experiences in the concentration camp, the severity of exile, or other painful subjects. His affection for her stretched so far that he could even tolerate Beatriz Alcántara without losing his good humor.

Soon Irene was walking a few steps, supported by Francisco. Her paleness was a measure of her pain, but she had requested that they lower the dosage of painkillers because she needed to think clearly and recover her interest in the world around her.

Francisco came to know Irene as well as he knew himself. Through sleepless nights they told each other the stories of their lives. There was no memory from the past, no dream of the present, no plan for the future that they did not share. They surrendered all their secrets; going beyond the physical, they abandoned their souls to one another. He sponged her, rubbed her with cologne, brushed the tangles from her unruly curls, moved her to change her sheets, fed her, anticipated her every need. He welcomed every small act, every gesture, every glance that made her his. Never did he perceive even a flicker of prudishness; without reservation, she gave to him her tormented, afflicted body. She needed him as she needed air and light; she claimed him; it seemed normal to her that he was by her side day and night. When he left her room, she lay staring at the door, waiting for his return. When she was racked with pain, she reached for his hand and whispered his name, seeking his comfort. She yielded her entire being, creating an indissoluble bond that helped them endure the fear that hovered over their lives like an evil presence.

As soon as Irene was allowed to receive visitors, all her friends at the magazine came to see her. The astrologer, swathed in a theatrical tunic, her black locks sweeping her shoulders, came carrying as a gift a mysterious flask.

"Rub her from head to foot with this balm. It is an infallible remedy for weakness," she recommended.

It was useless to argue that Irene's prostration had been caused by bullets, not debility. The astrologer insisted on blaming the zodiac: Scorpio attracts death. It was similarly pointless to remind her that Scorpio was not Irene's sign.

Journalists, editors, artists, and beauty queens came to visit the patient; the cleaning lady came, bearing a few teabags and a packet of sugar. She had never been in a private hospital and had thought it proper to help by bringing some kind of food, believing that the patients were hungry, as they were in the hospitals for the poor.

"Oh, this is the way to die, *Señorita* Irene," she exclaimed, dazzled by the bright, sunny room, the flowers, and the television.

All the ambulatory residents of The Will of God Manor, accompanied by their nurses, took turns coming to see Irene. In her absence, they felt as if a light had gone out of their lives, and they languished, waiting for their treats, their letters, their jokes. Everyone had heard of her misfortune but some immediately forgot, because their ephemeral memories could not contain bad news. Josefina Bianchi was the only one who understood precisely what had happened. She insisted on coming often to the hospital, always bringing some small gift for Irene: a flower from the garden, an ancient shawl from her trunks, a poem written in her elegant English hand. She would appear in a cloud of pale chiffon, or in old lace, diaphanous as a ghost from another era, leaving the scent of roses on the air. Surprised, doctors and nurses would interrupt their duties to watch her pass by.

The day after Irene was shot, before the news was published in the papers, the word reached Mario's ears through secret channels. He promptly appeared to offer his assistance. He was the first to notice that the hospital was being watched. Day and night an automobile with dark window glass was parked across the street, and secret-police agents were loitering around the entrances, unmistakable in their new disguises of blue jeans, sport shirts, and imitation-leather jackets that could not conceal the bulge of their pistols. In spite of the presence of these agents, Francisco attributed the attempt to a paramilitary group, or even to Lieutenant Ramírez himself, because if the order to eliminate Irene had been official, the agents would simply have stormed in and kicked down the doors to the operating room itself to finish her off. This surreptitious surveillance, however, indicated that they could not really afford the luxury of raising a commotion but felt it prudent to wait for an opportune moment to finish the job. Mario had acquired experience in such matters during the course of his clandestine activities, and he was busy working out an escape plan for Irene to be undertaken as soon as she could get around on her own.

Meanwhile, Beatriz Alcántara swore that the machinegun fire that had come so close to ending her daughter's life was meant for someone else.

"This has something to do with the underworld," she said. "They intended to kill some thug, but their bullets hit Irene."

She spent days telephoning her friends to tell them her version of events. She did not want anyone to have the wrong impression about her daughter. In passing, she also told them the news of her husband, who, after years of searching, and great personal torment for her, had been located by detectives on a remote island. When Eusebio Beltrán, bored with the enormous mansion, his wife's nagging, the unnegotiable sheep, and his creditors' pressures, had walked away that evening, he had wandered for only a brief while before he realized that he had a number of good years before him and it was not too late to begin again. Following the impulses of his adventurous spirit, he arrived in the Caribbean with very little money in his pocket, a new, flashy pseudonym, and his head swimming with wonderful ideas. For a while he had lived like a beachcomber, at times fearing he would be consumed by the fever of oblivion. Nevertheless, his keen nose for detecting a fortune had made him a wealthy man, thanks to his machine for harvesting coconuts. That harebrained apparatus, designed with so little scientific knowledge, had captured the attention of a local millionaire. Shortly thereafter, those tropical lands were filled with coconut-knockers shaking palm trees with their articulated tentacles, and Beltrán could again give himself over to the disturbing luxuries that he was addicted to and that only money could buy. He was happy. He was living with a girl thirty years younger than himself, dark-skinned and fat-bottomed and always ready for pleasure and laughter.

"Legally, that scoundrel is still my husband and I'm going to take him for every cent he's got—that's what good lawyers are for," Beatriz vowed to her friends. She was more concerned about getting her claws into her elusive enemy than she was about her daughter's health. She was particularly satisfied that she had proved Eusebio Beltrán to be a shameless rogue and not a leftist at all, as some slanderous friends had insisted.

Since Beatriz read only agreeable news, she had no idea of what was happening to the country. She did not know that the remains in Los Riscos mine had, through dental records and other characteristic marks, been identified as those of the local farmers who had been arrested by Lieutenant Ramírez shortly after the military coup, and of one Evangelina Ranquileo, who had been said to work minor miracles. Beatriz was oblivious to the public outcry that, in spite of censorship, swept the nation and traveled around the globe, once again making front-page news of the *desaparecidos* under Latin-American dictatorships. And she was the only person who, when she again heard pots and pans clanging, thought it was in support of the military leaders, as it had been during the previous government. She could not understand that this form of protest was being directed against the very ones who had invented it. When she heard that a group of jurists were backing the families of the dead in a complaint against Lieutenant Ramírez and his men for the crimes of unlawful search, kidnapping, coercion, and proven homicide, she pointed to the Cardinal as the person responsible for such monstrous accusations and declared that the Pope ought to defrock him, because the Church should confine its activities to spiritual matters, and not concern itself with the sordid affairs of this world.

"They're accusing that poor lieutenant of the murders, Rosa, but no one stops to remember that he helped liberate us from Communism," Beatriz had commented that morning in the kitchen.

"Sooner or later, the chickens will come home to roost," replied Rosa, imperturbable, gazing through the window at the flowering forget-me-nots.

Lieutenant Juan de Dios Ramírez was brought before the bench along with several men from his command. The atrocity at Los Riscos was again on the front pages, because for the first time since the military coup, members of the armed forces had been summoned to appear in court. A sigh of relief ran the length and breadth of the nation; people imagined a crack in the monolithic power structure, and dreamed of an end to the dictatorship. Meanwhile, the General, unconcerned, laid the cornerstone for a monument to the Saviors of the Nation, and no glimpse of his intentions penetrated the black lenses of his glasses. He did not reply to the cautious questions posed by reporters, and made a contemptuous gesture if the subject was broached in his presence. Fifteen bodies in a mine did not merit such an uproar, and when other accusations began to surface and new horrors were discovered—common graves in cemeteries, in ditches along the roads, bodies in bags washed up on the coast, ashes, skeletons, human remains, even bodies of infants with a bullet between their eyes, guilty of having suckled at their mothers' breast exotic doctrines harmful to national sovereignty and to the supreme values of family, property, and tradition—he shrugged his shoulders calmly, because the Nation comes first, and let History be my judge.

"And what shall we do about the storm that's brewing, General, sir?"

"What we always do, Colonel," he replied from his sauna three floors belowground.

Lieutenant Ramírez's statement at the trial was published under banner headlines, and had an invigorating effect on Irene Beltrán's will to live and fight.

The commanding officer of Los Riscos Headquarters swore before the court that shortly after the coup the owner of Los Aromos had accused the Flores family of constituting a threat to national security because of their affiliation with a leftist group. They were activists who were planning an attack against Headquarters. For this reason, Your Excellency, I proceeded to arrest them. I incarcerated five members of that family, and nine additional persons, for crimes ranging from

possession of firearms to use of marijuana. I was guided in
making the arrests by a list I found in the possession of Antonio Flores. I had also found a map of Headquarters, evidence
of their plot. We questioned these men in accordance with
our usual procedures, and obtained their confessions: they
had received terrorist training from foreign agents who had
infiltrated the nation by sea, but they could not provide any
details of that training and their statements were filled with
contradictions—you know how these people are, Your Excellency. It was after midnight by the time we finished with them,
and I ordered them sent to a stadium in the capital, which in
those days was still being used as a detention camp. At the
last minute, one of the prisoners asked to speak with me, and
that was how I found out that the suspects had committed the
treasonous act of hiding arms in an abandoned mine. I loaded
the suspects into a truck and drove to the place he had described. When the road became impassable, we all got out of
the truck and continued on foot. We had the activists mana-
cled and under close guard. As we advanced through the darkness, we were suddenly attacked from different directions by
gunfire. I had no alternative but to order my men to defend
themselves. I cannot give you many details about the attackers because of the darkness. I can only report that there was a
heavy exchange of fire lasting for several minutes, at the end
of which the rain of bullets ceased and I was able to reorganize
my troops. We began the search for the prisoners, expecting
to find they had escaped, but we found them scattered around
the area, all dead. It is impossible to determine whether they
died as the result of our bullets or those of our attackers. After
due consideration, I decided on a cautious course of action,
hoping to avoid retaliation against my men and their families.
We hid the bodies in the mine, and sealed the entrance with

rubble, stones, and dirt. We did not use mortar, and I cannot comment on that point. Once the entrance was closed, we all swore we would not repeat what had occurred. I accept my responsibility as the leader of the patrol, and I want to make clear that there were no wounded among the personnel under my charge, except for minor scratches obtained in moving through the rough terrain. I ordered the surrounding area to be searched for the attackers, but we found no trace of them, or of their spent cartridges. I admit having obscured the truth when I wrote in my report that the prisoners had been sent to the capital, but I repeat that I did it to protect my men from future retaliation. Fourteen persons died that night. I have been surprised to learn that there has also been mention of a female citizen allegedly named Evangelina Ranquileo Sánchez. She was detained at Los Riscos Headquarters for some hours, but she was released, as recorded in the Duty Log. This is all the light I can shed on the matter, Your Honor.

This version of the events produced the same incredulity in the court as in public opinion. Considering that it was impossible to accept the story without making himself look ridiculous, the judge disqualified himself and the case was transferred to a military court. From her convalescent bed, Irene Beltrán saw her hopes slowly fading that the guilty would be punished, and she asked Francisco to go immediately to The Will of God Manor.

"Take this note to Josefina Bianchi," she instructed him. "She is holding something important for me, and if it wasn't taken in the search, she will give it to you."

Francisco had no intention of leaving Irene alone, and when she pressed him, he told her that they were under surveillance. He had kept it from her in order not to frighten her, but now he realized that she already knew, because she showed no sign of surprise. In her heart, Irene had accepted death as a real possibility as well as the fact that they would be fortunate to escape with their lives. Only when Hilda and Professor Leal came to replace him at Irene's bedside did Francisco leave to call on the elderly actress.

Rosa greeted him, moving gingerly because of her three broken ribs. She looked thinner, and tired. She led Francisco through the garden where, in passing, she pointed to the fresh earth that marked the place she had buried Cleo, beside the grave of the baby-that-fell-through-the-skylight.

Josefina Bianchi, dressed in a morning gown with full, lace-edged sleeves, was reclining in her room amid a nest of cushions. An exquisite mantilla was thrown around her shoulders, and a ribbon pulled her white hair into a chignon. Within arm's reach lay a baroque silver mirror and a crowded tray: bottles and jars, face powders, sable makeup brushes, creams of every seraphic hue, swan's-down blusher brushes, bone and tortoiseshell hairpins. Josefina was applying her makeup, a delicate task she had undertaken daily for over sixty years, without missing a single day. In the bright early-morning light, her face stood out like a Japanese mask on which a trembling hand had stamped the purple line of her lips. Her eyelids quivered, blue, green, silver over the pearly-white powdered base. For a brief moment, absorbed in her dream, perhaps standing in the wings on opening night and waiting for the curtain to rise, the actress did not recognize Francisco. Eyes lost in the past flickered, and slowly she returned to the present. She smiled, and her face was rejuvenated by two perfect rows of false teeth.

During the months since he had met Irene, Francisco had learned a great deal about the peculiarities of the aged, and had discovered that affection is the only key to communicating with them, because reason is a labyrinth in which they too easily lose their way. He sat on the edge of the bed, and patted Josefina Bianchi's hand, adjusting himself to her own personal rhythm. It was useless to hurry her. She recalled the days of her great success, when the loges were filled with her admirers and baskets of flowers overflowed her dressing room, when she had traveled the continent in tumultuous tours, and five porters had been needed to carry her luggage to various ships and trains.

"What has happened, my child? Where are the wine, the kisses, the laughter? Where are all the men who loved me? The crowds who applauded me?"

"They're all right here, Josefina, in your memory."

"I may be old, but I'm not an idiot. I know I am alone."

She noticed Francisco's camera case and wanted to pose for him, to leave a souvenir behind after she died. She adorned herself with rhinestone necklaces, velvet bows, mauve veils, her feather fan, and a smile from a past century. She held the pose for some minutes, but tired quickly, closed her eyes, and lay back, breathing with difficulty.

"When is Irene coming back?"

"I don't know. She sent you this note. She says you are keeping something for her."

The octogenarian took the paper in lace-sheathed fingers and clasped it to her breast without reading it.

"Are you Irene's husband?"

"No, I am her lover," Francisco replied.

"All the better! Then I can tell you. Irene is like a bird, she has no sense of permanence."

"I have enough for two," Francisco said, laughing.

Then she agreed to give him three cassettes she had hidden in a beaded evening bag. Irene was never able to say why she had entrusted the tapes to the actress. She had acted on a generous impulse. She had no way of knowing that there would be an attempt against her life, or that her house and office would be searched for the tapes, but she suspected their value as evidence. She had given them to the actress to make her an accomplice in something that was not yet a mystery, and to give some meaning to her life. It was a spontaneous gesture, like so many of the things she had done for the residents of the home, the equivalent of celebrating nonexistent birthdays, organizing games, inventing theater performances, giving presents, and writing letters from imaginary family members. One night she had visited Josefina Bianchi and found her melancholy, murmuring that she would rather be dead, since no one loved her or needed her. Her health had deteriorated during the winter months and, seeing herself frail and worn, she fell into frequent depressions, although her good sense and memory had never failed. Irene wanted to do something to divert her from her loneliness and to pique her interest in other things; she had given her the tapes, emphasizing their importance, and asked her to hide them. The elderly actress was enchanted with her mission. She had dried her tears and promised to stay alive and healthy in order to help Irene. She thought she was guarding an amorous secret. Thus, what had begun as a game had ended by fulfilling a purpose, and the tapes were protected not only from the curiosity of Beatriz Alcántara, but from seizure by the police.

"Tell Irene to come. She promised she would help me when it was my time to die," said Josefina Bianchi.

"It isn't time yet. You can live a long time, you're strong and healthy."

"My dear boy, I have lived like a lady, and I want to die like one. I feel a little tired. I need Irene."

"She can't come now."

"What I hate about old age is that no one respects us.

They treat us as if we were spoiled children. I lived my life as I wanted. I had everything. Why would you deprive me of a dignified death?"

Francisco kissed Josefina's hands with affection and respect. As he left, he saw the residents in the garden, attended by their nurses, feeble, lonely in their wheelchairs, with their wool shawls and their mean little possessions, deaf, almost blind, mummified, barely alive, remote from the present, from reality. He walked closer to say goodbye. The Colonel, tinfoil medals pinned to his chest, was, as always, saluting the nation's flag that waved for his eyes alone. The poorest widow in the land was clutching to her bosom a tin box that contained some miserable treasure. The hemiplegic, from force of habit, was still watching for the mail, although in his heart he had from the beginning suspected that Irene was inventing answers to make his life happy, while he, in turn, pretended to believe her compassionate lies in order not to disappoint her. Without Irene, he had no dreams left to dream.

A melancholy old man stopped Francisco at the door. "Tell me, now that they're opening up graves, do you think we might hear something of my son or his wife or their baby?"

Francisco Leal did not know how to answer him, and he fled that world of pathetic ancients.

The tapes recorded by Irene Beltrán contained her conversations with Digna and Pradelio Ranquileo, Sergeant Faustino Rivera, and Evangelina Flores.

"Take them to the Cardinal to use at the trial against the guardsmen," she said to Francisco.

"Your voice is on them, Irene. If they identify you, it will be your death sentence."

"They're going to kill me, anyway, if they can. You *must* give them the tapes."

"First we have to get you somewhere safe."

"Then call Mario, because I'm leaving here this very evening."

At nightfall the cosmetician appeared carrying his famous case; he locked himself in the hospital room with Irene and Francisco, where he proceeded to cut and change the color of their hair, modify the arch of their eyebrows, try different makeups, eyeglasses, mustaches—all the artifices of his profession—until he had converted them into different people. Irene and Francisco looked at each other: strangers, amazed, not recognizing themselves or one another beneath their masks. They smiled, incredulous, thinking that with these new faces they would have to learn to love each other all over again.

"Can you walk, Irene?" Mario asked.

"I don't know."

"You will have to walk without help. Come, darling, on your feet . . ."

Slowly, Irene got out of bed without any assistance from the two men. Mario removed her nightgown, choking back a gasp when he saw her bandage-swathed stomach and the red antiseptic stains on her breast and thighs. From his miraculous suitcase he extracted a roll of plastic foam shaped to simulate a pregnancy and secured it over her shoulders and between her legs, because she could not have borne the pain of having it tied around her waist. Then he dressed her in a pink maternity dress, placed low-heeled sandals on her feet, and, with a kiss for good luck, departed.

Irene and Francisco walked from the clinic without so much as a glance from any of the staff that had attended them during her illness. They crossed the street in front of the parked vehicle with the dark window glass, walked in leisurely fashion to the corner, and there climbed into Mario's car.

"You will hide in my house until you can travel," Mario instructed.

He drove them to his apartment, opened the brass-and-beveled-glass door, shooed away the Angora cats, ordered the dog to lie in a corner, and turned to greet them with a graceful bow, but before he could complete the gesture, Irene slipped to the rug without a sound. Francisco picked her up in his arms and followed their host to the room he had chosen, where a large bed with fine linen sheets welcomed the prostrate girl.

"You're risking your life for us," said Francisco.

"I'll fix some coffee—we all need it," Mario replied as he left the room.

Irene spent several days recovering her strength in the calm atmosphere of the apartment, while Mario and Francisco took turns caring for her. Mario tried to distract her with light reading, card games, and an interminable store of anecdotes: stories of the beauty salon, his love affairs, his travels, his suffering in the days when he was a nobody, the rejected son of a miner. When he saw that Irene liked the animals, he installed the huge black dog and the cats in her room, and changed the subject any time she spoke of Cleo, because he did not want her to know of Cleo's sad death. He cooked special dishes for the convalescent, watched her while she slept, and helped Francisco change her dressings. He shut the apartment windows, closed the heavy drapes, removed the newspapers, and turned off the television, so she would not be perturbed by the disorder of the external world. When police sirens howled, helicopters zoomed overhead like prehistoric birds, saucepans clanged in the distance, or machine guns rattled, he turned up the volume of the music so she would not hear. He dissolved barbiturates in her soup, to assure her rest, and avoided mentioning in her presence the events that were convulsing the comic-opera peace of the dictatorship.

It was Mario who took Beatriz Alcántara the news that her daughter was no longer in the hospital. He had planned to explain to her that Irene had to leave the country if she was to stay alive, but with his first words he could see that Beatriz was incapable of dealing with the truth: Irene's mother lived in an unreal world where any difficulty was annulled by decree. He decided to tell her that Irene and Francisco had left on a brief vacation—an unlikely story, given the state of the girl's health—and the mother accepted this fiction because she was grasping at straws. Mario observed her unsympathetically, repelled by this egotistical, unfeeling woman who found refuge in the elegance of ritual and formalities, in the hermetically sealed living room where no whisper of discontent was allowed to enter. He imagined her on a raft with the feeble and forgotten old people in her care, adrift on a motionless sea. Like them, Beatriz lived divorced from reality; she had lost her place in the world. Her fragile security could collapse at any instant, buffeted by the wild hurricane of the new era. To him, this silk-and-suède-clad vision was distorted like a reflection in a fun-house mirror. He left without saying goodbye.

Faithful to her custom, Rosa had been standing outside the door listening. She signaled him to follow her to the kitchen.

"What's happened to my little girl? Where is she?"

"She's in danger. We must help her get away."

"Out of the country?"

"Yes."

"May God keep her and protect her! Will I ever see her again?"

"When the dictatorship falls, Irene will return."

"Give her this from me," Rosa begged, handing him a small packet. "This is soil from her garden, to go with her wherever she goes. And please tell her that the forget-me-nots are in bloom. . . ."

José Leal went with Evangelina Flores to identify the remains of her father and brothers. Irene had told José about the girl, and asked him to help, because she was sure Evangelina would need his aid. As she did. In the courtyard of the Department of Criminal Investigation, on two long tables of rough wood, had been spread the contents of the yellow plastic bags: rotted clothing, bits and pieces of bones, clumps of hair, a rusted key, a comb . . . Evangelina Flores walked slowly past this terrible array, pointing in silence to every recognizable item: that blue sweater, that cracked shoe, that skull with the missing teeth. Three times she walked the length of the tables, painstakingly examining the contents, until she had found some trace of each of her family members, and was sure that all five were there and none was missing. Only the sweat moistening her blouse betrayed the effort every step cost. Beside her walked the priest, not daring to touch her, and two officials of the court, taking notes. Finally the girl read their statement, signed it with a firm hand, and strode from the courtyard with her head held high. Once in the street, and with the gate closed behind her, she was again, for an instant, a simple country girl. José Leal put his arms about her.

"Go ahead, child, cry—it will do you good," he said to her.

"I will cry later, Father. But now I have things to do," she replied and, rubbing away the tears with the back of her hand, she hurried off.

Two days later, she was summoned before the Military Tribunal to testify against the accused murderers. She was dressed in her work clothes and wearing a black armband, the one she had worn the day they opened Los Riscos mine and her intuition had told her the time had come to wear mourning. The trial was being held in a closed courtroom. No one— not her mother, José Leal, or the lawyer from the Vicariate assigned by the Cardinal—was allowed to accompany her. A soldier led the girl, alone, down a wide corridor, the sound of her footsteps echoing like a bell, to the chamber where the court was in session. The room was enormous and brightly lighted, with no adornment except a flag and an oil painting of the General displaying the Presidential sash across his chest.

Evangelina walked forward, without any sign of fear, until she stood before the dais where the officers of the court sat. She looked them directly in the eyes, one by one; then, unintimidated, in a clear voice and without changing a single detail, she repeated the story she had told Irene Beltrán. Unhesitatingly, she pointed to Lieutenant Juan de Dios Ramírez, and to each of the men who had participated in her family's arrests, because through the years she had carried their likenesses engraved in fire on her memory.

"You may retire, citizen Flores. You shall remain at the disposition of this Tribunal, and you may not leave the city," the Colonel instructed.

The same soldier who had led her in escorted Evangelina to the exit. José Leal was waiting outside, and together they started down the street. The priest realized that an automobile was following them and, as he had been prepared for this eventuality, he seized Evangelina by the arm and began to run, pushing and dragging her until they were lost in the crowd.

They took refuge in the nearest church, and from there communicated with the Cardinal.

Evangelina Flores escaped the clutches of government repression and left the country under cover of the shadows of night. She had a mission to fulfill. In years to come, she left behind the peaceful fields where she had been born, and traveled throughout the world, denouncing the tragedy that had befallen her nation. She appeared before an assembly of the United Nations, in press conferences, on television, at congresses, universities—everywhere—speaking about the *desaparecidos*, to insure that the men, women, and children swallowed up by that violence would never be forgotten.

After the bodies of Los Riscos had been identified, their families asked to be allowed to claim them in order to provide them with a decent burial; their requests were refused for fear of public disturbances. The government had had enough upheaval. Then the relatives of those victims, and of the victims unearthed from other clandestine graves, crowded into the Cathedral, settled themselves before the main altar, and announced their intention to hold a hunger strike beginning that moment and lasting until their pleas were heard. They were no longer afraid and had no hesitation about placing their lives in jeopardy, though life was all they had left; everything else had been taken from them.

"What is all this damned uproar, Colonel?"

"They keep asking about their *desaparecidos*, General, sir."

"Tell them we don't know whether they're alive or dead."

"And what shall we do about the hunger strikers, General, sir?"

"What we always do, Colonel—don't bother me with all that horseshit."

The police were prepared to drive the hunger strikers from the church with water cannon and tear gas, but the Cardinal, along with a number of persons who in a gesture of solidarity were also fasting, planted himself in the doorway while observers from the Red Cross, the Commission on Human Rights, and the international press photographed the scene. After three days the pressure became intolerable and the clamor from the streets penetrated the walls of the Presidential bunker. Much against his will, the General ordered the remains to be returned to their families. At the last moment, however, as the families were waiting with funeral wreaths and lighted candles, the hearses, acting on orders from above, changed their route and secretly drove in the rear gate of the cemetery, where the contents of the bags were dumped into a common grave. Only the body of Evangelina Ranquileo Sánchez, still undergoing autopsy in the Morgue, was recovered by her parents. She was taken to Father Cirilo's parish, where she was given a modest burial. She at least had a grave, and never wanted for fresh flowers, because the local populace still had faith in her small miracles.

Los Riscos mine became a shrine. A seemingly endless chain of the faithful, José Leal at their head, made a pilgrimage there. They went on foot, chanting hymns and revolutionary slogans, carrying crosses, torches, and photographs of their dead. The next day the Army closed off the site with a high barbed-wire fence and an iron gate, but neither the fence nor the soldiers posted in nests of machine guns could stop the processions. Then they used dynamite charges to blast the mine from the face of the earth, hoping also to eliminate its memory from history.

Francisco and José Leal turned Irene's tapes over to the Cardinal. They knew that Irene would be identified and arrested as soon as the tapes reached the hands of the Military Tribunal. They had to get her to safety as quickly as possible.

"How many days do you need to get away?" the prelate asked.

"It will be a week before she can walk unassisted."

So they made their agreement. The Cardinal had the tapes copied, and exactly one week later he distributed the copies to members of the press and delivered the originals to the prosecutor. By the time the government attempted to destroy the evidence, it was already too late; the interviews had been published in the newspapers and had spread around the world, giving rise to a wave of unanimous repudiation. Abroad, the General's name was ridiculed and his ambassadors were pelted with tomatoes and rotten eggs whenever they appeared in public. Intimidated by this outcry, the military court declared Lieutenant Juan de Dios Ramírez and the men of his command who had participated in the slaughter guilty of murder, based on their contradictory testimony, on laboratory evidence of the manner in which the deaths had occurred, and on Irene Beltrán's tapes. Irene was summoned repeatedly to testify as the Political Police carried out sweeping, though unsuccessful, searches for her.

Satisfaction over the sentences lasted only a few hours, until the guilty were set free, delivered by a decree of amnesty improvised at the last possible moment. Popular fury was translated into street demonstrations so riotous that not even the police shock troops and Army heavy equipment could control the people who poured into the streets. At the construction site of the monument to the Saviors of the Nation an enormous pig was released, costumed in cockades, a Presidential sash, a dress uniform cape, and a general's cap. The beast ran squealing through the throng, who spit on it, kicked it, and hurled insults at it before the eyes of irate soldiers who used every trick to intercept it in order to rescue the trampled sacred emblems; finally, amid screams, sticks, and howling sirens, they shot the beast. Nothing remained but the enormous humiliated carcass lying in a pool of black blood on which floated the insignia, the kepi, and the tyrant's cape.

Lieutenant Ramírez was promoted to the rank of captain. He went about with great self-satisfaction and with an unruffled conscience until the day he heard that in the south a ravenous, ragged, wild-eyed giant was seen from time to time who was rumored to be looking for his sister's murderer. No one there paid any attention to him; they considered him to be a madman. But the officer lost sleep thinking of the vengeance hanging over his head. There would be no peace for him as long as Pradelio Ranquileo drew a breath of life.

In a provincial garrison far removed from the capital, Gustavo Morante was closely following developments, gathering information, and laying his plans. When he had sufficient evidence of the illegal acts of the regime, he held secret conclaves with a number of his comrades-in-arms. He had lost his illusions, convinced now that the dictatorship was not a temporary stage on the road to progress but, rather, a final stage on the road to injustice. He could not bear any longer the repressive machinations he had served so loyally, believing them always to be in the best interests of the nation. Terror, far from securing order, as he had been taught in officers' training, had sown a hatred whose harvest would inevitably be greater violence. His years as a career officer had given him an intimate knowledge of the institution, and he decided to use that knowledge to overthrow the General. It was his opinion that this was a task appropriate for younger officers. And he believed that because of the failure of the economy, the increasing inequality among social classes, and the brutality of the system and corruption of high officials, other military men must harbor the same doubts as he—others, like himself, who wanted to cleanse the image of the armed forces and rescue it from the depths to which it had sunk. A less audacious and impassioned man could perhaps have achieved his objective, but Morante had such a compelling urgency to obey the dictates of his heart that he committed the error of underestimating the Intelligence Service, whose tentacles reached everywhere. He was arrested, and he survived seventy-two hours. Not even the experts could force him to divulge the names of others involved in the planned rebellion; he was stripped of his rank and at dawn his corpse was symbolically shot in the back as a lesson to others. In spite of every precaution, the story leaked out. When Francisco Leal learned what had happened, he felt respect for the Bridegroom of Death. With men like that in the ranks, there was still hope, he said to his father. Rebellion cannot be controlled forever. It will grow and spread through the barracks until there are not enough bullets to crush it. On that day, the soldiers will join the people in the street, and from shared grief and vanquished violence a new nation will emerge.

"You're daydreaming, son!" was Professor Leal's reply. "Even if there are military men like that Morante, the essence of the armed forces will never change. Militarism has already caused too much harm to humanity. It should be abolished!"

At last Irene Beltrán was well enough to move about. José Leal obtained false passports for her and for Francisco, to which they affixed photographs of their new faces. They were unrecognizable: Irene's hair was short, and dyed, and contact lenses had changed the color of her eyes; Francisco was wearing a heavy mustache and eyeglasses. After their initial difficulty in recognizing each other, they became used to their disguises and forgot the faces they had fallen in love with. Francisco was surprised to find himself trying to remember the color of Irene's hair, which had so fascinated him. And now the moment had come for them to leave behind their familiar world to become a part of the enormous wave of nomads that characterized their age: expatriates, émigrés, exiles, refugees.

On the eve of their departure, the three Leals came to tell the fugitives goodbye. Mario closed himself in his kitchen for hours, and would not allow anyone to help with the dinner preparations. He put his best tablecloth on the table and arranged flowers and fruit in an attempt to mitigate slightly the tragedy in which they were so inextricably enmeshed. He selected discreet music, lighted candles, set wine to cool, feigning a euphoria he was far from feeling. But it was impossible to avoid the subject of the imminent parting, and of the dangers that awaited the couple the moment they stepped outside this haven.

"After you get across the border, children, I think you should go to our house in Teruel," Hilda Leal said suddenly, to everyone's surprise, for it had been thought that the house was one of the memories erased by her amnesia.

She had forgotten nothing. She described the enormous shadow of the massif of Albarracín outlined against the evening sky, not unlike the mountains that stretched the length of her adopted country; the naked vineyards, sad and twisted in winter but storing up sap for the explosion of grapes in the summer; the dry, precipitous landscape ringed by mountains; the house that one day she had left forever to follow her man to war: the noble, rough dwelling of stone, wood, and red roof tiles, the small wrought-iron-covered windows, the high mantelpiece over which Mudéjar plates were set into the wall, like eyes observing down through the years. She remembered with precision the smell of woodsmoke when the fire was lighted in the evening, the fragrance of the jasmine and mint beneath the window, the coolness of the well water, the large linen chest, the woolen blankets on the beds. A long silence followed her recollections, as if she had been transported in spirit to her former hearth.

"The house still belongs to us, and it is waiting for you," she said finally, with those words erasing time and distance.

Francisco reflected on the capricious fate that had obliged his parents to abandon their home and go into exile—only for him, many years later and for the same reasons, to reclaim it. He imagined himself unlocking the door with the same turn of the wrist his mother had used to lock it almost half a century before, and he felt as if during that time his family had wandered in a great circle. His father guessed what he was thinking, and spoke of what it had meant to them to leave their own land and seek new horizons: the courage that was needed to confront suffering; how they had fallen, and gathered strength, and risen again, time after time, while learning to adapt and survive among strangers. Everyplace they had stopped, they had made a home with vigor and determination, even if only for a week or a month, because nothing wears down inner strength as quickly as living from day to day.

"All you will have is the present. Waste no energy crying over yesterday or dreaming of tomorrow. Nostalgia is fatiguing and destructive, it is the vice of the expatriate. You must put down roots as if they were forever, you *must* have a sense of permanence," concluded Professor Leal, and his son remembered that the elderly actress had said the same.

The Professor drew Francisco aside. His eyes were grief-stricken and he was trembling as he embraced his son. He took a small object from his pocket and shyly handed it to Francisco: it was his slide rule, his only treasure, a symbol of the impotence and desolation he felt at this separation.

"It is just a keepsake, son. It won't help you to make calculations about life," he said hoarsely.

And, in truth, that was how he felt. Reaching the end of his life, he knew the futility of calculations. He could never have imagined that one day he would find himself, weary and sad, with one son in the grave, another in exile, his grandchildren lost to him in some remote village, and José, his only remaining son, in constant jeopardy from the Political Police. Francisco thought of the residents of The Will of God Manor and bent to kiss his father's forehead, wishing with every ounce of his being that he could twist the designs of fate so his parents would not have to be alone when they died.

Seeing his guests so disheartened, Mario decided to serve dinner. They stood around the table, eyes moist, hands shaking, and lifted their glasses in a toast.

"I offer a toast to Irene and Francisco. May good fortune go with you, my children," said Professor Leal.

"And my toast is that your love will grow with every passing day," Hilda added, unable to look at them without revealing her anguish.

For a while everyone made an effort to be festive; they praised the delicious food and expressed their gratitude for the many kindnesses of their noble friend, but soon despondency spread like a shadow that covered them all. In the dining room there was no sound but the clinking of silverware and glass.

Hilda, sitting beside her most beloved son, could not take her eyes from him, imprinting his features forever in her memory: his gaze, the fine wrinkles at the corners of his eyes, the slim, long-fingered hands. Although her knife and fork were in her hands, her food remained untouched. Stern when it came to her own grief, she held back her tears, but could not hide her suffering. Francisco put his arm around his mother's shoulders, and kissed her temple, as shaken as she.

"If anything should happen to you, son, I couldn't bear it," Hilda whispered into his ear.

"Nothing is going to happen, Mama. Don't worry."

"When will we see you again?"

"Soon, I'm sure. And until then we will be together in spirit, as we always have been. . . ."

Dinner ended in silence. Then they sat in the living room, staring at one another, smiling without joy, until the approaching curfew forced the moment of farewell. Francisco led his parents to the door. At that hour the street was empty, quiet, shuttered; there was no light in neighboring windows, and their voices and footsteps resounded dully in the desolate air like an ominous omen. They would have to hurry if they were to reach home in time. Tense, beyond words, they embraced for one last time. Father and son clasped each other for a long moment filled with unspoken promises and guidance. Then Francisco felt his mother in his arms, tiny and fragile, her adored face unseen against his chest, her tears at last overflowing, her slender hands convulsively stroking the cloth of his jacket, clinging like a desperate child. It was José who gently forced them apart, made his mother turn and walk away without looking back. Francisco watched the figures of his parents, hesitant, vulnerable, bowed, grow smaller in the distance. In contrast to his parents, his brother seemed solid and resolute, a man who recognized his risks and accepted his destiny. When they turned the corner, a harsh sob of farewell escaped Francisco's breast, and the tears he had held back during that terrible evening rushed to his eyes. He sank to the threshold, his face buried in his hands, crushed by ineffable sadness. There Irene found him and sat by his side in silence.

Over the years Francisco Leal had never bothered to count the numbers of desperate people he had helped. In the beginning he had acted alone, but gradually a group of totally committed friends formed around him, united by the goal of aiding those in trouble, hiding them whenever possible or using various routes to help them escape across the border. At first these activities were simply humanitarian and, in a way, unavoidable labor, but with time that labor had become a passion. Francisco threaded his way through danger with mixed emotions, a combination of rage and fierce joy. He knew the gambler's vertigo, that constant tempting of fate, but not even in moments of greatest daring did he abandon caution, because he knew that he would pay for any rash act with his life. Every move was planned down to the last detail, and he always tried to insure that an operation would be carried out without any surprises. This had allowed him to survive on the edge of the abyss longer than others who played the same game. The Political Police had no inkling that his small organization even existed. His brother José and Mario often worked with him. The priest had been detained on several occasions, although he had been questioned only in regard to his activities on behalf of the Vicariate and the working-class neighborhood in which he lived, where his cries for justice and courage in confronting authority were notorious. Mario, for his part, had the perfect cover. The Colonels' wives flocked to his beauty salon, and frequently a bulletproof limousine came for him and drove him to the underground palace where the First Lady waited in the glitter and ostentation of her chambers. Mario advised her in the choice of her wardrobe and her jewels; he created new hairstyles to accentuate the hauteur of power; he offered his advice on the Italian raffia, Pharaonic marble, and cut-glass chandeliers imported to ornament the mansion. All the most important people attended Mario's receptions, and behind the coromandel screens in his antique shop, negotiations were carried out with youths blessed with gifts for forbidden pleasures. The Political Police followed their orders not to interfere in his smuggling, his trafficking, his pipelines for discreet vices, never imagining how the distinguished stylist was pulling the wool over their eyes.

Francisco had supervised his group in difficult assignments, but not until recently had he anticipated that one day he would use their talents to save his life and Irene's.

It was eight o'clock in the morning when a truck stopped before Mario's apartment building, loaded with exotic plants and dwarf trees for his terraces. Three servicemen, dressed in overalls, plastic helmets, and fumigation masks, unloaded tropical philodendrons, flowering camellias, and miniature orange trees; they connected hoses to the insecticide tanks and proceeded to spray the bushes, their faces covered by their masks. Then, while one man stood guard in the hallway, the other two, at a sign from Mario, slipped out of their uniforms. Irene and Francisco quickly donned the overalls and masks, then unhurriedly joined the driver, and all three drove off without a second glance from anyone. Irene and Francisco spent some time circling the city, leaving the truck and twice changing taxis; finally they were met on a street corner by a grandmother with an angelically innocent face, who handed them the keys and documents to a small automobile.

"So far, so good. How do you feel?" Francisco asked, getting in behind the wheel.

"Fine," replied Irene, so pale she looked as if she might dissolve into mist.

They drove south, out of the city. Their plan was to reach a certain mountain pass and cross the border before the police net closed around them. The name and description of Irene Beltrán was in the hands of authorities from one end of the country to the other; their difficulty was compounded by the fact that they would not be safe even in neighboring dictatorships, because those governments exchanged information, prisoners, and corpses. In such transactions, there were at times too many dead on one side and too many identity cards on the other, causing considerable confusion when it was time to identify the victims. Thus people were arrested in one country, only to turn up dead in another under a different name, and families who wanted to bury their dead had been known to receive a stranger's body. Although Francisco had contacts on the other side of the border, he knew that they must make their way as quickly as possible either to a democratic country on their own continent or to their final destination—the mother country, as those who fled Latin-American countries grew to think of Spain.

They made the journey in two stages, because Irene was still very weak and nauseated and could not bear many hours in the car, in pain and without resting. My poor darling, you have grown so thin during the last weeks; you have lost your freckles and golden skin but you are as beautiful as ever, even without your long, queenly hair. I don't know how to help you; I wish I could take your suffering and your uncertainties onto myself. Damn the fate that has brought us to this, swaying along in this car with terror gripping our guts. Irene, how I wish we could go back to the carefree days when we used to walk Cleo in the park on the Hill; when we sat side by side beneath the trees and gazed at the city spread out below our feet; when we drank wine, feeling we were sitting on top of the world, free and immortal. I never imagined that I would be driving you down this interminable, nightmarish road with every nerve on edge, jumping at the slightest sound, constantly on my guard, suspicious of everything and everyone. Since that terrible moment when the hail of bullets almost cut you in two, I have had no rest, either waking or sleeping, Irene. I must be strong, larger than life, invincible, so that nothing can harm you, so that I can protect you from pain and violence. When I see you like this, lying back against your seat, eyes closed, limp and half dead with fatigue, tortured by every lurch of the car, my chest tightens with terrible anxiety, with the yearning to take care of you, the fear I may lose you, the desire to stay by your side forever and keep you from all harm, to watch over your sleep, to make your days happy. . . .

As it grew dark, they stopped at a small provincial hotel. Irene's weakness, her faltering step, and the somnambulistic air that had sunk into her bones stirred the compassion of the innkeeper, who accompanied them to their room and insisted on serving them food. Francisco removed Irene's clothing and checked the light bandages she wore as protection; then he helped her into bed. A waiter brought soup and a glass of warm wine with sugar and cinnamon, but she was so exhausted she could not even look at them. Francisco lay down by her side; she put her arm around his waist, rested her head on his shoulder, sighed, and was immediately asleep. He lay completely still, smiling in the darkness, happy as always when they were together. The intimacy they had shared these last weeks still seemed a miracle. He knew this woman's most subtle secrets; the smoky eyes that could turn savage with pleasure, or gratefully moist as they carried out the inventory of their love, held no mysteries for him; he knew her body so intimately that he could trace it from memory, and he was sure that as long as he lived he would be able to recall her smooth, firm geography; even so, each time he held her in his arms he was overcome by the same suffocating emotions he had felt the first time they made love.

The next morning, Irene awakened feeling as cheerful as if she were waking from a night of love, but her good spirits could not disguise the waxen pallor of her skin and the dark, unhealthy circles under her eyes. Francisco brought her a large breakfast, hoping she might regain a little strength, but she barely tasted it. She lay staring out the windows, absorbing the fact that spring had passed. Having lain so long in the lap of death, her life had taken on new meaning. The world seemed miraculous to her and she was thankful for its most inconsequential detail.

Early, because they had hours still to travel, they climbed into the car and continued on their way. They drove through the inebriating light of a small village, passing carts of fresh vegetables and vendors with trays of trinkets, and bicycles and broken-down buses filled to bursting. Church bells were ringing, and two ancient women dressed in black tottered along, all mourning veils and widows' prayer books. They drove past a line of schoolchildren being led toward the plaza by their teacher, singing, Little white pony, on this fair morn, carry me back to where I was born. On the air came the fragrance of freshly baked bread and the song of cicadas and thrushes. Everything looked clean, orderly, tranquil; people were calmly and peacefully going about their daily business. For a moment Irene and Francisco doubted their sanity. Were they delirious, the victims of a horrible fantasy? Could it be true that no danger threatened them? Was it possible they were fleeing from their own shadows? But then they felt the false documents burning a hole in their pockets, they looked at their transformed faces, and they remembered the turmoil of the mine. No, they had not lost their senses. It was the world that was insane.

They drove for so many hours along those eternal roads that they lost the ability to focus on the landscape, and by the end of the day one mile faded into another. They felt as if they were marooned on earth from another planet. Only the police checkpoints at the toll booths interrupted their journey. Every time they surrendered their papers, they felt an electric charge of fear that left them sweaty and limp. The guards glanced casually at the photographs and waved them on. But at one post they were ordered out of the car and held ten minutes answering peremptory questions; the car was thoroughly searched, and just when Irene was ready to scream, certain that they had been apprehended, the sergeant gave them permission to continue.

"But be careful, there are terrorists in this area," he warned them.

It was several minutes before they could speak. They had never felt danger so near, so tangible.

"Panic is stronger than love or hatred," a subdued Irene admitted.

From that moment on they ridiculed their fear, making jokes to save themselves useless worry. Francisco sensed that he had discovered Irene's only secret. Any form of shyness or embarrassment was foreign to her; she gave herself to her emotions freely, holding nothing back. But somewhere, deep inside her, there was something she was ashamed of. She blushed at weaknesses she considered to be intolerable in others, and unacceptable in herself. And the terror she had discovered in herself was a source of shame that she tried to hide from Francisco. This fear was profound and consuming and had absolutely no resemblance to the fright she had occasionally experienced, the kind of scare against which laughter had been her defense. She had never feigned bravery in the face of simple fears like the slaughtering of the pig, or a creaking door in a haunted house; she was, however, shamed by this new emotion that clung to every pore, invading her entire being, making her cry out in her sleep and tremble when she was awake. At times, the impression of nightmare was so strong that she was not sure whether she was alive dreaming, or dreaming she was alive. Those fleeting instants when he peered into the depths of her shame, her fear, were when Francisco loved her most.

Finally they turned off the main route and followed a road that wound up into the mountains to a spa that had once been famous for its miraculous waters, but, with the advent of modern pharmacopoeia, had sunk into relative oblivion. The building still retained the memory of its resplendent past when, at the turn of the century, it had welcomed the most distinguished families, and foreign guests had come from afar in search of a cure. Neglect had not destroyed the charm of the large salons with their balustrades and wainscoting, period furniture, brass lamps, and fringe- and pompom-trimmed draperies. The room Francisco and Irene were assigned was furnished with an enormous bed, an armoire, a table, and two straight-backed chairs. The electricity was cut off at a fixed hour, and after that any moving about meant carrying a candle. Once the sun went down, the temperature dropped abruptly, as always at such altitudes, and then aromatic thorn logs were set ablaze in the fireplaces. The sharp, pungent odor of dry leaves and manure being burned in the courtyard drifted in through their windows. Aside from themselves and the administrative personnel, the guests were all patients afflicted with various illnesses, or the elderly seeking relief from pain. Everything was slow and gentle, from the guests' footsteps shuffling along the corridors to the rhythmic sound of engines pumping water and curative clay to the great marble and iron baths. During the day, a line of the hopeful crept along the lip of the precipice to the fumaroles, leaning on their canes, wrapped in pale sheets, looking like distant ghosts. Higher up on the slopes of the volcano bubbled hot springs where patients, lost in the amber fog, went to sit in the thick sulfurous vapor. At dusk a bell sounded in the hotel, and its reverberating summons rumbled across the mountainside into ravines and hidden places. It was the signal to return for the rheumatic, the arthritic, the ulcerous, the hypochondriacal, the allergic, and the incurably old. Meals were served on precise schedules in a vast dining room where air currents sang and kitchen odors danced.

"I only wish we were here on our honeymoon," mused Irene, who was enchanted with the place and hoped the contact who was to lead them to the border would not come too soon.

Weary from the long ride, they held each other close in the elemental bed that was their fate, and immediately lost all notion of time. They were awakened by the first light of a radiant morning. Francisco was relieved to see that Irene looked much improved; she even proclaimed that she had a truck driver's appetite. They dressed, after making love with joyous restraint, and went outside to breathe the air off the cordillera. The continuous stream of guests on their way to the thermal baths began very early. While others were concentrating on their cures, Irene and Francisco used their available hours to cherish each other with stolen kisses and eternal promises. They cherished each other strolling the rugged paths on the volcano, they cherished each other sitting on the fragrant humus of the deep forest, they cherished each other whispering amid the foggy yellow spirals of the fumaroles, until at midday a mountain guide wearing rough leather boots, a black poncho, and a wide-brimmed hat arrived, bringing with him three mounts and bad news.

"They've picked up your trail. We must leave right now."

"Who was it they caught?" asked Francisco, fearing for his brother, or Mario, or some other friend.

"No one. The manager of the hotel where you stayed the night before last was suspicious, and reported you."

"Can you ride, Irene?"

"Yes," she said, smiling.

Francisco bound Irene's waist firmly with a broad sash so she could more easily bear the swaying of the ride ahead. They lashed their few belongings behind the saddles, and set out, riding Indian file along a barely visible path formerly used by smugglers that would lead them to a forgotten pass between two border checkpoints. When the trail disappeared completely, swallowed up by an indomitable nature, the guide took his bearings from marks carved on tree trunks. It was not the first time—nor would it be the last—that this tortuous trail had been used to save people fleeing for their lives. Larches, oaks, and manius watched over the travelers; in some places their foliage met overhead, forming an impenetrable green dome. They rode on for hours, without stopping, and without meeting a single human being. They were alone in a damp, cold solitude like a tunnel, a green labyrinth in which they were the only adventurers. Soon they were riding past large patches of snow still unmelted from the winter. They rode into low-hanging clouds, and for a while were enveloped in ethereal foam that blotted out the world. When they emerged, there suddenly lay before them the majestic spectacle of the cordillera snaking toward infinity: purple peaks, white-crowned volcanoes, ravines and gorges whose sheer, icy walls would melt in summertime. From time to time, they glimpsed a cross marking the site where some traveler had given up the ghost, dwarfed by desolation; at those places the guide crossed himself, reverently, to appease that spirit.

The guide rode first, then Irene, and Francisco brought up the rear, never taking his eyes from his beloved, alert for any sign of fatigue or pain, but she showed no weariness. She had given herself to the slow rhythm of the mule, her eyes drinking in the wondrous landscape around them, but weeping inside. She was leaving her home. Next to her heart, beneath her clothing, she carried the small packet of soil from her garden that Rosa had sent so she could plant forget-me-nots on the other side of the sea. She thought of the magnitude of her loss. She would never again walk the streets of her childhood, or hear her language spoken as she loved it; she would not see the outline of her sweet land's mountains at dusk; she would not be lulled by the song of its rivers; gone would be the aroma of sweet basil in her kitchen, of rain evaporating from her roof tiles. She was not only losing Rosa, her mother, her friends, her work, and her past. She was losing her homeland.

"My country . . . oh, my country," she said, sobbing. Francisco spurred his horse and, catching up to her, took her hand.

When the light began to fade, they decided to make camp

for the night, because it was impossible in darkness to go any farther through that maze of steep grades, sheer slopes, high precipices, and bottomless ravines. They did not dare light a campfire, fearing that this close to the border there might be patrols. The guide shared the contents of his saddlebags: beef jerky, hardtack, and liquor. They huddled together beneath their heavy ponchos, and curled up within the circle of their animals, embraced like three brothers; nothing, though, could protect them from the cold penetrating their bones and hearts. All night they shivered beneath a sky as somber as mourning, as ashes, as black ice, surrounded by the sighs, the soft whistlings, the infinite voices of the forest.

Finally dawn came. Light spread like a flower of fire and slowly the darkness receded. The sky cleared and the blinding beauty of the landscape materialized before their eyes like the birth of a new world. They roused themselves, shook the frost from their blankets, stretched their stiff arms and legs, and drank the remaining liquor to restore their circulation.

"The border is over there," said the guide, pointing to a spot in the distance.

"Then this is where we part," Francisco said. "Friends will be waiting on the other side."

"You should go on foot. Follow the markings on the trees and you can't get lost. The trail is clear. Good luck, *compañeros*."

They said goodbye with an embrace. The guide turned back, leading his animals, and Irene and Francisco started walking toward the invisible line dividing this vast chain of mountains and volcanoes. They felt dwarfed, alone, vulnerable, two desolate sailors adrift on a sea of mountain peaks and clouds amid a lunar silence, but they also felt that their love had taken on a new and awe-inspiring dimension, and that it would be the source of their strength in exile.

In the golden light of dawn they stopped to look for the last time at their native soil.

"Will we be back?" whispered Irene.

"We will return," Francisco replied.

And in the years that followed, those words would point the way to their destinies: we will return, we will return. . . .

In the Midst of Winter
Isabel Allende

'Allende has an unflashy wisdom, a maturity that
illuminates her storytelling'
Financial Times

Amid the biggest Brooklyn snowstorm in living memory,
an unexpected friendship blossoms between three people
thrown together by circumstance. Richard Bowmaster, a
lonely university professor in his sixties, hits the car driven
by Evelyn Ortega, a young, undocumented migrant from
Guatemala. But what at first seems an inconvenience takes
an unforeseen and darker turn when Evelyn comes to him
and his neighbour Lucia Maraz, desperately seeking help.

Sweeping from present-day Brooklyn to Guatemala to
turbulent 1970s Chile and Brazil, and woven with Isabel
Allende's trademark humanity, passion and storytelling
verve, *In the Midst of Winter* is a mesmerizing and
unforgettable tale.

SCRIBNER

The Japanese Lover
Isabel Allende

'A gripping and tender tribute to the human heart'
Mail on Sunday, **Books of the Year**

In 1939, as the world goes to war, young Alma Belasco's parents send her to live in safety in her aunt's opulent San Francisco mansion. There she meets Ichimei Fukuda, the son of the family's Japanese gardener, and between them a tender love blossoms – but theirs is a love they are forever forced to hide.

Decades later, Alma is nearing the end of her long and eventful life. Irina, a care worker, meets the older woman and her grandson, Seth, at Lark House nursing home. As they forge a friendship, Irina and Seth become intrigued by the mysterious gifts and letters Alma receives, and learn about Ichimei and the secret passion that has endured for almost seventy years.

SCRIBNER

The Stories of Eva Luna
Isabel Allende

'Vital and compelling' *The Times*

Eva Luna is a young woman whose powers as a storyteller bring her friendship and love. Lying in bed with her lover, European refugee and journalist Rolf Carlé, Eva answers his request for a story 'you have never told anyone before' with these twenty-three samples of her vibrant artistry.

Interweaving the real and the magical, she explores love, vengeance, compassion and female power, depicting worlds that are at once poignantly familiar and intriguingly new.

Rendered in her sumptuously imagined, uniquely lyrical style, *The Stories of Eva Luna* is a cornerstone of Isabel Allende's work, and in her character Eva Luna she creates a modern-day Scheherazade.

SCRIBNER